the FEAR ARTIST

ALSO BY TIMOTHY HALLINAN

The Queen of Patpong
Breathing Water
The Fourth Watcher
A Nail Through the Heart
The Bone Polisher
The Man with No Time
Incinerator
Skin Deep
Everything but the Squeal
The Four Last Things

the
FEAR
ARTIST

Timothy Hallinan

**SOHO
CRIME**

Published by
Soho Press, Inc.
853 Broadway
New York, NY 10003

"A Few Words in Defense of Our Country" lyrics used with permission from Alfred
Publishing Co. Inc. Words and music by Randy Newman © 2006 RANDY
NEWMAN MUSIC. All rights outside the U.S. and Canada administered by WB
MUSIC CORP. All rights reserved.

Library of Congress Cataloging-in-Publication Data

Hallinan, Tim.
The fear artist / Tim Hallinan.
p. cm.

ISBN 978-1-61695-112-2 (hardback)
eISBN 978-1-61695-113-9
1. Bangkok (Thailand)—Fiction. I. Title.
PS3558.A3923F43 2012
813'.54—dc23
2012009728

Interior design by Janine Agro, Soho Press, Inc.

Printed in the United States of America

10 9 8 7 6 5 4 3 2 1

To
Munyin Choy
for making me possible
on a daily basis.

A President once said,
"The only thing we have to fear is fear itself"
Now it seems like we're *supposed* to be afraid
It's patriotic in fact and color-coded
And what are we supposed to be afraid of?
Why, of being afraid
That's what terror means, doesn't it?
That's what it used to mean

—Randy Newman,
"A Few Words in Defense of Our Country"

Part One
IN THE DARK

The Rules by Which I Live

TWO TWO-GALLON CANS of paint weigh about five times as much as he'd thought they would.

Feeling as burdened as a prospector's donkey, the wire handles of the cans cutting into his palms, he manages to pull open the door of the shop unaided. The door immediately swings shut on his chest, so he pushes it with his knee and edges through it sideways, left side first. One hundred percent of his attention is focused on not letting the door close on the can in his right hand.

Which means that when Poke Rafferty steps onto the wet sidewalk with his back to the road, he's too preoccupied to hear the people running. So he's unprepared when the crowd suddenly floods past, going at top speed, and the very large man strikes him from behind.

Rafferty pitches forward at a diagonal and bounces off a couple of running men on the way down. He instinctively throws his hands in front of him to break his fall, then tries to yank them back again when he registers the dangling paint cans. He fails on all counts, landing on his elbows with bone-chipping force and allowing the cans to hit the pavement hard enough to burst open in two eruptions of color, Apricot Cream (Rose's choice) and a sort of rotted eggplant called Urban Decay, which Miaow picked for her room.

The man who ran into him has come down on top of him, all the way to the pavement. Rafferty is trying to struggle out from under, his hands slipping on the apricot concrete, when he hears three sounds, like the crack of a bat in a stadium, and the man shudders as though he's been shocked, then shudders again and rolls off Rafferty and into the paint, on his side.

His blue eyes, wide with surprise, look at Rafferty as though Rafferty is the most important question he's ever been asked and he doesn't know the answer.

Rafferty pulls his head back for a better look, and the man opens his mouth, but all that comes out is a ragged tatter of air.

He's a once-tough, sixty-five or so, the planes of his face softened by the passage of years, wearing a T-shirt and a photographer's vest over cargo shorts, both soaked from the rain. The chunky garments emphasize the thirty or thirty-five extra pounds that suggest he might be American or German. His fair, wet hair, vaguely military and brush-cut, all of an inch long, is in retreat from a high, balding forehead. For some reason what draws Rafferty's attention, as people continue to run past, is that the skin on the top of the man's head is crimson from sunburn. It's been raining for days, but the man is sunburned.

Rafferty glances up the sloping road, sees that the running crowd is thinning, and says to the staring man, "I've got to get up. Are you okay?"

As he pulls himself to a sitting position, the wide eyes follow him and the mouth opens and closes noiselessly again. Then the man reaches up with his right hand and it lands heavily on the pocket of Rafferty's T-shirt, tearing it slightly before the hand rises again and comes down on Rafferty's left shoulder. The weight of it tugs Rafferty down a few inches, and the gesture opens the man's vest. Up close, Rafferty sees the blackish red, like a third paint pigment, saturating the white T-shirt beneath.

"Hold it," Rafferty says to no one. "You're . . ."

The bat cracks again, and it looks as if the man has been yanked by an invisible cord, jerked three or four inches, headfirst, over the slick, colorful pavement. His head slowly turns to the right, with so much effort that Rafferty wouldn't be surprised to hear it creak, and he stares disbelievingly in the direction the running crowd came from.

The red fluid pools into the apricot under the man's chest.

"Let me get you up," Rafferty says. All he can think is that the bleeding might slow if the man is upright instead of facing down-hill. Rafferty slips an arm under the bleeding man's shoulders and slowly, carefully, pulls him to a sitting position. The man's head wobbles and then lolls left and drops forward, his chin hitting his chest so hard that Rafferty can hear his teeth snap together.

Rafferty is looking wildly for help when the man suddenly raises his head and says something, almost a whisper.

"What?" Rafferty says. "What did you say?"

The man's mouth works two or three times, like someone get-ting ready to pronounce an unfamiliar sound, and he coughs a thick, dark, oyster-size gout of blood down over his chin. The muscles in his face stiffen into a mask, rigid with will. He peels his upper lip free of his teeth and says, in a voice that's almost all air, "Helen." With a tiny nod, he brings his head back up. "Eckersley." Another cough, more blood. "Cheyenne," he says, and he slumps to his left.

Rafferty bends over him, looking for a breath, feeling for a pulse, and the gray day is shoved aside by a burst of light. He looks up to see a television crew—a cameraman with a shoulder-mounted rig, a lighting man with a blinding sun gun, and a third guy, probably the producer, pushing the other two into position. Rafferty's shouting, "Get a doctor!" but the crew comes in closer, closer, the cameraman going into a gradual crouch to catch the dying man's face, and Rafferty reaches behind him with his free hand, snags the wire handle of one of the mostly-empty cans of paint, and slings it at the camera.

The can clatters on the camera's grip, sending its remaining paint in an airborne arc of Urban Decay, and the cameraman rocks onto his seat, yanking the camera back and throwing out a hand to catch himself. The producer advances on Rafferty, shouting, but then three brown-uniformed police materialize between them. One of them slams his chest into the producer, backing him off, and the other two come over to Rafferty.

"Are you all right?" one of the cops asks. His English is heavily accented.

"Yes, sure," Rafferty says in Thai, "but this man—"

Before Rafferty can finish the sentence, though, a new man, wearing an elegant raincoat over street clothes, steps in between him and the man lying flat on the pavement. "We'll take care of him," the man in the raincoat says in English. "You just go with the officers."

"But he's—"

"I've got him," the man says, leaning close and holding Rafferty's gaze. He's tall for a Thai, sleek and handsome, if a little puffy beneath the eyes, and his English is as accent-free as California. "Either go with the officers willingly or they'll drag you." He kneels in front of the man wearing the photographer's vest, blocking Rafferty's view.

One of the uniforms bends down and extends a hand. The other has his hip cocked and his hand resting on the butt of his pistol.

Rafferty gets up, avoiding the outstretched hand. The patrolman closer to him wraps his fingers around Rafferty's bicep and tugs him away. And then there are three more cops coming down the street, eyeing the TV crew. The producer helps his cameraman up, whispers something to him, and hauls the lighting man toward the cops. Instantly the cameraman is sprinting down the hill, his feet splashing in the gutter, as the producer and the lighting guy dance interference in front of the oncoming police. By the time one of the cops shakes free and takes off in pursuit, the cameraman has rounded the corner at the bottom of the hill.

The uniforms manhandle Rafferty downhill and position him in a doorway, out of the rain, so the fallen man and the other police are behind him. The street is empty now, except for the knot of men in front of the paint shop. Rafferty tries to turn to look behind him, but the cop pulls him back into position and says, "Papers."

"That man's been shot," Rafferty says, the realization dawning on him at last. "He needs a doctor."

"Nobody got shot." The cops exchange a fast glance, and the one who's not holding Rafferty lets his eyes flick up the hill. "He'll be fine," his partner says.

"I heard the gun," Rafferty says. "He was bleeding like—"

"He wasn't shot," the cop says. "There wasn't any gun." He gives Rafferty's arm a token shake. "Let me see your papers."

Rafferty says, "Oh, for Christ's sake," but he digs in the rear pockets of his jeans and pries his wallet out. As he begins to open it, he sees the smear of blood on his hand. "Look," he says, holding it under the nose of the nearer cop. "He was bleeding. Don't tell me he wasn't—"

"Nosebleed," the cop says. "Papers, *now*."

Rafferty wipes the blood on the thigh of his jeans and fishes through the wallet until he comes up with two tissue-soft sheets of paper, almost transparent with wear. He opens one and then the other. "Passport. Current visa."

"Where are the originals?" the nearer cop says. He's meaningfully lean, the kind of thin that rarely signals an easy nature, and his lips are as sharp as a parrot's beak. His partner, younger and fleshier, seems to be fixated on what's happening up the hill, his mouth half open.

"At my apartment."

"Philip Rafferty," the cop reads aloud, mangling both names. "You're a resident of Thailand?"

"That's what the visa says."

The cop gives him small, tight eyes, as though he's already sighting a weapon. "I ask you questions," he says in English. "You answer, you understand?"

"Yeah, I think I can follow that."

"Why don't you carry originals?"

"Because someone might take them, some cop or someone, and I'd have to get new ones."

The cop says, "Puh," just barely not a spit. He holds out the copies and, as Rafferty reaches for them, drops them. They flutter to the wet pavement.

For a few seconds, Rafferty looks into the cop's eyes. What he sees there makes him nod and bend down to pick up the papers.

The cop puts his foot on them.

"Fine," Rafferty says, straightening. He can hear the blood in his ears. "Fuck them, I can make new ones."

The cop moves his foot. The papers are translucent with water and smeared with mud. "Pick up," he says. "If you not, if you walk away, I stop you and say I want papers, then arrest you because you don't have."

Rafferty leans against the wall, feeling the pulse thrum at the side of his neck. "Back up," he says. "Until you back up, I'll stand here and we'll look at each other."

The soft-faced cop tells his partner, in Thai, to stop fooling around. After a moment the lean cop backs away and then makes a gesture, palm up, in the direction of the documents.

Rafferty bends and peels the papers free of the sidewalk, but as he straightens, the lean cop steps closer again, and his fingers dart into the pocket of Rafferty's T-shirt. When they come out, they're holding a yellow slip of paper, tightly folded. He opens it to reveal a small diamond shape, cut into the center by someone who's folded it into quarters and then snipped off the tip of the central fold. "What's this?"

"That's my yellow piece of paper," Rafferty says. He's never seen it before.

"What does it say?"

"The rules by which I live," Rafferty says. "The Diamond Sutra."

The other cop looks over his partner's shoulder and laughs. "It's your laundry ticket," he says.

Rafferty says, "It's in code."

The plump cop laughs again, and even the lean one relaxes a little. He hands the ticket back, saying, "You going to need the clean clothes. You all dirty."

"Thanks. I hadn't noticed."

The lean cop backs away. "You go now. Go home."

"I need to buy some more paint."

"Home. Cannot go in store now."

Rafferty turns to look uphill again, and the plump cop stands in his way, although Rafferty gets a quick glimpse of a tight knot of uniforms and plainclothes around the fallen *farang*.

"Go," the plump cop says. "Go now or we arrest you."

"I've got an apartment to paint," Rafferty says, pocketing the yellow ticket.

"Have too much paint in Bangkok," says the plump cop. "Can buy anywhere. You go."

"I go," Rafferty says, sidestepping the lean cop and plodding downhill. A siren emits a short, throat-clearing whoop behind him, and he turns to see an ambulance glide into position in front of the paint store. The lean cop waves him on: *Keep going.*

At the foot of the mild little hill is a good-size four-lane boulevard, and Rafferty is surprised to see the wet pavement shining in a flat, uninterrupted slab, as empty as outer space. A block to his right, he sees a barrier: white sawhorses set up on the far side of the turn that leads up to the hill with the paint shop on it. Half a dozen policemen wearing yellow slickers have assumed poses of varying vigilance, facing the oncoming traffic.

Turning around, Rafferty sees a mirror version of the blockade two blocks in the other direction. Since there's no traffic on the street he's just hiked down, it's not a difficult guess that it's been barricaded, too, a few blocks away in both directions.

It feels strange to him; Bangkok is many things, but it's never empty. As he walks, he sees the wide blue eyes and feels again the sudden jerk of the body atop his when the first bullet struck it. Feels retroactively an unbidden thrill at having been missed. Whoever was shooting was either very good or completely indifferent. Or both.

The man's odd haircut, the haircut of someone who might not have been able to let go of being military. When Rafferty was growing up in the desert outside Lancaster, California, he had met men like that, friends of his father, men who had gone into service at eighteen, probably leaving behind a teenager they no longer wanted to be, and then spent three or four decades having everything decided for them. Men who, at the age of fifty, had never given a thought to how they should comb their hair.

But if one of those men had been killed, he thinks as he makes his way down the center of the wet, deserted boulevard, there might have been a cop or two, maybe an ambulance. Not half a dozen policemen, barricades, plainclothes guys, multiple ambulances, and—he remembers the handsome one with the puffy eyes—spooks.

Definitely spooks.

Despite the rain, his clothes are stiffening with the paint, his entire front and left side a patchwork of apricot with artistic mottlings of Urban Decay. Looking down at it now, in the even gray light, he decides the apricot is too strong for the living room. It needs more white.

Spooks.

H E   K N O W S   W H A T   the apartment will look like, since he's responsible for its looking that way, but his spirits still plummet as he comes through the door. Everything—couch, glass table, white leather hassock, his weensy cheap desk—has been shoved uselessly into the middle of the room, like mismatched dancers coming together for the fancy steps. The carpet, which he's wanted to replace for years, is covered by a funereal black drop cloth giving off a sour reek of mold.

There is literally nowhere to sit.

Okay, why didn't he turn the couch around so he could sit on it? What was he thinking?

He stinks of paint. He's soaked, even dripping. His elbows are swollen where they hit the pavement. The underside of his left forearm is scraped. One of his favorite T-shirts is ruined.

He eases out of his wet shoes and leaves them by the door. The noise the door makes when it closes resonates, as though the room were a hollow vault.

"I'm alone," he says aloud, listening to the echo chamber. "Deserted. Abandoned. Bleeding." His voice sounds lower than usual, bouncing off the barren walls.

His scraped arm sends off a spiteful little telegram of sting, and he shakes his head, blows out a breath he doesn't remember having drawn, and checks out the scrape, which looks like it's been disinfected with apricot puree. "Medication," he says aloud. "And solace."

The refrigerator surprises him by opening easily, extending, it seems to him, the first cooperation of the day. Five tall brown Singha soldiers stand at frosty attention, their caps just waiting to be popped. He hefts one and rolls its chill smoothness over his cheeks and forehead, then opens the drawer, pulls out the opener, and flips it into the air, closing his eyes and extending his hand in the precise spot the opener will come down. This trick used to delight Miaow, back when she used to be easily delighted. When he hears it hit the floor, he bends to pick it up, seeing for an instant the implacable eyes of the lean cop. His spirits droop, but the hiss of the beer lifts them a bit.

He knocks back about a third of the bottle in one icy, heart-slowing pull. With an operatic burp, he underhands the opener into the drawer from five feet away—nothing but net—and goes around the counter to sink onto one of the stools where the members of the family—although rarely at the same time these days—eat breakfast.

The running crowd, he thinks. He hasn't seen one of those since the Red Shirts took to the streets to protest the coup that deposed the prime minister they'd voted in by the millions. Now that prime minister's sister has been elected, the Red Shirts have faded, but Rafferty, like everyone, has heard rumors of isolated, apparently spontaneous crowd incidents since, protesting this or that inequality. The Thai media, which can accurately be characterized as cautious, hasn't run the stories. He wonders whether the TV crew's footage will ever make it onto the screen.

He tilts the beer again and swallows, looking idly through the sliding glass door at the darkening sky above Bangkok. The apartment is eight floors up, and their previously panoramic view has been divided vertically by two new condominium towers, both still skeletal at the upper floors. The sky is still there, although it's been broken up into rectangles by girders like black fold lines, and he scans it for the halting, zigzag flight of bats. Bats in the city delight him—the preservation of wildness they suggest. Sees a lot of them, random tatters of black against a lowering gray sky.

To the north the sky grows even darker and the world disappears, as it has for weeks, in a shroud of rain: the worst monsoon season in sixty years, a huge blunt-force weapon a quarter of a country wide, striking wherever it pleases, filling and overfilling dams, swelling rivers, flooding entire towns, heedless of human life, human dreams, human prayers. As random, murderous, and unmalicious as a bolt of lightning.

And feeding billions of gallons of water into the Chao Phraya River, threatening Bangkok with the worst flood since the 1940s. Rafferty can't see the river, but, like everyone in the city, he can feel the water level rising, and he's seen the trucks, loaded with sandbags, splashing toward the city's low-lying neighborhoods.

King Taksin established Bangkok in 1767 at the site of a trading center on the floodplain of the Chao Phraya, the River of Kings. The city sprawls across an expanse of ground as flat as the palm of a hand, its low points and high points separated by a matter of a few meters. Its buildings sprout from saturated soil, soil that doesn't accept much water. The city has always had its feet-dry areas and its feet-wet areas, but the difference in elevation between them is precariously small. Over the centuries Bangkok's builders formalized some of the river's small tributaries as canals and dug other canals from scratch to spread the water's flow over a larger area, trying to avoid the inundation that a significant rise in the river's level would guarantee. Most years the strategy is successful, although in 1942 the city almost drowned.

This year looks like it could be worse than 1942. A city of 12 to 14 million, depending on the time of day, is following the daily rainfall reports with a degree of attention usually reserved for the World Cup.

Mentally Poke follows the surging water upstream, over an imaginary map, back to the rainy northeast, where his wife and daughter have been for two days now, visiting Rose's family. He misses them even more than he'd thought he would.

And once again he thinks about the death, on a wet, apricot-colored sidewalk, of a former soldier.

2

The Color of Spring Gone Wrong

FOUR HOURS LATER the knot of furniture in the living room has been untangled and the big pieces are back in their original places, but two feet from the walls. Rafferty has showered and scrubbed where he got scraped on the pavement, and he's done a little self-barbering to snip some apricot patches out of his hair. He's cut his hair shorter on one side than the other, so markedly that it makes him want to tilt his head to compensate. Studying it in the mirror, he thinks Miaow, whose own hair changes on a moment-by-moment basis, would probably approve.

Except that she'd never notice. She's developed a selective vision impairment. No one who's much more than five feet tall is visible to her.

When someone knocks on the front door, Rafferty's already on his way toward it, wearing jeans and a Japlish T-shirt he's liberated from Miaow's room that says LET'S TOGETHER!! With the paint-splattered clothes rolled up under one arm and one of Rose's umbrellas in his free hand, he stops, surprised by the twinge of uneasiness the sound causes.

He confronts the uneasiness head-on by peeking boldly through the peephole in the door. He sees no one, which does not reassure him. With a deep breath, he tosses the bundle of spattered clothes onto the couch and opens the door.

What he sees is a scrawny Vietnamese kid of twelve or so with a slender neck and a head so big it looks like a golf ball on a tee. He's too short to have been visible through the peephole. The kid is carefully disreputable in his after-school clothes: a T-shirt that hangs almost to his knees, a pair of jeans about three inches too long for him that have accordioned around his big, clunky running shoes, and a pair of round, crooked, black-rimmed spectacles. His hair, Rafferty realizes with a start, has been dyed precisely the same shade as Miaow's. He glances up at Rafferty, and his mouth tightens and travels a really remarkable distance toward his left ear, a semaphore of disappointment.

"Hello, Mr. Rafferty," Andrew Nguyen says dubiously. He peers around Poke into the room as though he half believes that Rafferty is intentionally concealing something. "Is Miaow home?"

Rafferty says, "You know she's not, Andrew."

"Oh," Andrew says. He blinks a couple of times and uses his index fingers to push the big black frames up his almost-nonexistent nose. Since he and Miaow met in a school production of *The Tempest*, they've been inseparable. The incipient romance delights Rose, but Rafferty is conflicted about it, which is a fancy way of saying it makes him crazy.

Andrew is pretty much occupied with looking at the finger he used to adjust his glasses, so Rafferty says, "Was that it, Andrew? Just 'Oh'?"

"Well, no," Andrew says, wiping the fingertip on his jeans. "She hasn't . . . umm, she hasn't phoned me."

"She's only been gone two—"

"And when I phone her, I get her voice mail." Andrew blinks again and pushes at the glasses, even though they haven't moved a fraction of an inch, and in the gesture Rafferty recognizes loneliness.

"She doesn't have her phone," he says, a bit more gently.

"Whoa," Andrew says, tilting back. "That's kind of raw."

"It's not a punishment, Andrew. She's in a two-buffalo town in the middle of nowhere, and the phone would probably be useless." He doesn't add that Rose had insisted on it, saying she wasn't going to spend the entire visit apologizing to her mother because all Miaow does is text.

"Huh?" Andrew screws up his eyes. "I thought Mrs. Rafferty's family had a big estate, with . . . you know, farms and everything."

Rafferty feels like someone watching a movie in a foreign language at the moment the subtitles disappear. "Right," he says, his mind on full spin, trying to reconcile the "estate" Miaow has conjured up with the one-room thatched hut in which Rose grew up. "Um, rice paddies and huts for the farmers and a little river." At least he's not lying. That's pretty much everything there is in Rose's village.

"But no cellular," Andrew says.

"They're . . . they're *older*," Rafferty improvises, wondering why he's elaborating on what is clearly a whopper of a lie. "You know, they can't even work the remote."

"They've got a TV but no cell service?"

"One thing you're not, Andrew—you're not dumb." Rafferty looks over Andrew's head at the elevator, wishing he could cross the hall and get into it. "That's a really good point, and the answer is yes. They have TV but no cell service. That's exactly what they've got. And listen,there's nothing I'd rather do than stand around at my front door and chat with you, but I have places to go, and—"

"Where?"

"A *bar*, Andrew. I intend to go to a bar. Why? Would you like to come?"

"I'm too young," Andrew says with perfect seriousness.

"By golly, you are. And I was looking forward to taking you with me. How are you getting home?"

Andrew blinks, so perhaps the question wasn't as diplomatic as Rafferty hoped it was. "My father's driver. He's waiting."

"Your father's—"

"Driver."

"Well," Rafferty says as the reasons behind Miaow's lie become apparent. "How nice. Listen, she'll be back in four or five days, and if Rose calls me—I mean, if she finds a cellular signal somewhere and calls me—I'll tell her to ask Miaow to call you. Okay?"

"Yeah," Andrew says. He shuffles his feet from side to side, and Rafferty has a sudden urge to hug him. "That'd be cool." He takes a step back, although he seems to have chosen the direction at random. He's clearly lost. "I kind of miss her," he says.

"Me, too," Rafferty says. "I miss her a lot."

"Even though she's sort of . . . you know."

Rafferty says, "Do I ever."

"She's got a shirt just like that one."

"No, she doesn't," Rafferty says. "*I've* got a shirt like this one, and she steals it."

"Ahh," Andrew says, and this time he turns around. "Okay, thanks, Mr. Rafferty. Maybe she'll call me."

"I'm sure she will. Bye, Andrew."

He watches the kid cross the hall, the cuffs of the jeans flapping around and threatening to trip him with every step, and in the big head and the narrow shoulders he sees what Miaow may like, or even love, about him.

Andrew needs her.

Rafferty waits until the elevator arrives and the doors have closed behind Andrew before he says, "Well, I need her, too."

FIVE MINUTES LATER he jams the damp wad of paint-stiff clothes down the trash chute to the basement and pushes the button for the elevator.

As he hits the street and opens Rose's umbrella, he feels a bit of the old tingle, the little carbonated fizz of anticipation he'd felt all those years ago, when he first arrived, when Bangkok was just one jaw-dropper after another. When he spoke none of the language, when he might as well have been blind for all the sense the signs made to him. When he felt that the odds were fifty-fifty, each time he went down a new street, that it would be dedicated to holiness—temple carvers, amulet makers, gold-leaf hammerers—or hedonism—bars, restaurants, flamboyant neon signifying the fall-off edge of his middle-class map of life. Whether the people on the sidewalks would be housewives toting plastic bags full of groceries or children playing tag or transsexual hookers gossiping as they waited for dark. When it felt like the whole city changed every time he went out, as though they knocked it down behind him and built it up in front of him.

Before he met Rose.

It's only a couple of extremely wet blocks from their apartment to the point at which Patpong 1 empties into Silom and the usual snarl of traffic, slowed by the line of taxis and *tuk-tuks* waiting for the sweltering hordes and their compensated companions for the evening. Patpong had its best days, if the adjective is applicable, decades ago, but it retains a kind of overstimulated, faintly gangrenous energy, and the street between the bars is jammed, despite the weather, with sex tourists, gawkers of both sexes, and the ever-present 10 percent of hypocrites who pretend they came to browse the junk on sale in the night market that stretches down the center of the street and are shocked—*shocked*, do you hear?—to discover all these bars full of rowdy, half-naked women who seem unusually friendly. There's no way, the hypocrites' body language announces, that they'd have come here if they'd known what a *sewer* it was.

They're usually the ones who stay forever.

It's kind of melancholy, Rafferty thinks as he picks a path between the drunk and distracted and tries to avoid the chill little waterfalls off the plastic sheeting over the stands, that he has so few friends at this point that the best thing he can think to do, on his second evening alone, is to spend time with a bunch of aging sexpats. The *family*, this totally unexpected and all-consuming planetary cluster of Rose, Miaow, and Poke, has absorbed him so completely that he has almost no relationships outside it.

With a guilty pang, he sees the face of his best friend, Arthit, but Arthit is out of contention these days if what Rafferty wants is some light, meaningless male bonding. Since the death of Arthit's wife, Noi, his friend's spirit seems to have dimmed like a candle under a glass. Rafferty worries about him, even though Arthit has apparently put the heavy grief drinking behind him, but, to be brutally honest, a couple of hours tiptoeing around Arthit's heartbreak isn't what Poke has in mind tonight, after . . . after the day he's had. He'll see Arthit, he tells himself, tomorrow.

If he were being honest with himself, he thinks, he's actually afraid to be alone after what happened on that painted sidewalk. A murder in plain daylight, denied—by a cop—before the body cools.

What he needs now is dumb stuff. Guys arguing with complete

conviction over things they don't care about. A few beers to befriend the two he drank at the apartment.

The Expat Bar.

A holdover from the 1970s, when Patpong was full of small bars that actually made most of their money by selling alcohol' as opposed to skin, the Expat Bar is jammed between a coffee shop and a big, forever-cursed space that seems to be a disco this week and will probably be empty again next week. The bar staked its narrow claim fifty-plus years ago, and some of its patrons have been sitting at it ever since.

"Zo," Leon Hofstedler says in Wagnerian English even before Rafferty lets go of the door, "Poke comes. Look, people, look who finds ze key to his cage tonight."

"Can I use it to get in?" Bob Campeau asks. Campeau has been a bit edgy with Rafferty ever since he took Rose off the market, as Campeau puts it, although Rose says she never met him.

"You could," Rafferty says. "But you wouldn't get out alive. Anyway, the birds have flown."

Campeau returns to his depressive survey of the bar's battered surface, every square millimeter of which he could probably draw , blindfolded.

Hofstedler, who's been a regular for so long that his name is engraved on a brass plate on the back of his stool, swivels to face Poke. "Would it be rude to ask—"

"Yes, it would," Rafferty says. "Hi, Toots."

The bartender, a cheery, ageless Thai woman whose real name has been lost since before clocks began to run, gives him a smile bright enough to make him blink. "Beer Singha," she says with the certainty of someone who pulls out a plum every time she puts in her thumb. "Big one."

"Zo," Hofstedler says as Poke climbs onto the only empty stool at the bar. He tilts his stool back so he can swivel into position again without knocking the bar over with his belly. "Ze lovely Rose and ze little one, her name will come to me, zey haff gone"— he puts his fingertips to his temples and closes his eyes—"up north," he says in a tone of profound mystery. "Yes?"

"You're amazing, Leon." Rafferty takes the bottle, served

without a glass, as he used to order it all those years ago, and makes the sign of the cross over Toots. "May your children have children," he says.

"Have already," Toots says. "Many, many."

"Why, you're a child yourself," Rafferty says.

"She's taken," Campeau says sourly. He's as gaunt as Hofstedler is fat, the kind of thin that announces he's never tasted anything he liked.

Toots wiggles her eyebrows. "Not every night."

"I don't know what you've got," Campeau says to Rafferty, "but I wish you'd lose it."

"*Miaow,*" Hofstedler says triumphantly. His conversational principle is that no discussion actually exists unless he's a part of it, which makes it impossible for him to interrupt anyone. "I am right, yes?"

"Flown north," Rafferty says, "as you so cannily deduced. So what's the news?"

"King's Group bars," Campeau says immediately. He lifts a hand and lets it land flat on the bar with a thwack. "Raised the bar fine. Six hundred baht, can you believe it. Just to get the girl out the door. I remember when all night long didn't—"

"Two dollars," Hofstedler says. "Toots?" Toots bends down beneath the bar and comes up with a big brandy snifter half full of loose one-dollar bills. "Zis is a new rule," Hofstedler continues for Poke's benefit. "Two dollars every time somebody says 'I remember when.'"

Campeau drops a thousand-baht bill into the snifter and makes change, very decidedly in his favor.

"And the principle is?" Rafferty says.

"To keep us from haffing ze same conversation we've been haffing zince Nixon was president—"

"That crook," says the Growing Younger Man, sitting in his usual spot at the far end of the bar. He looks up at everyone, his eyebrows yanked higher than Lucille Ball's by his most recent face lift. "Just saying," he adds apologetically.

"But why?" Rafferty asks. "It was a perfectly good conversation. I had it many times."

"They want six hundred baht," Campeau repeats in a tone sharp enough to etch glass. "And me on a fixed income."

"That's awful," Rafferty says, putting a little extra on it.

"Easy for you to say," Campeau snarls, "considering what you've got at home."

Rafferty smiles. "Careful, Bob."

"Toots," Hofstedler says soothingly, "top Bob up, would you? Put it on my tab."

"So." Rafferty is already tiring of his night out. "What does anybody hear about the Red Shirts? Or riots in general?"

Toots gets very busy polishing beer mugs.

"Red Shirts are mostly lying low, since the new prime minister was elected, hoping she's the miracle that will solve everything," the Growing Younger Man says. "I was with a girl three or four days ago, says her village has a couple of Red Shirt biggies in it, organizers, and they're just staying in the house. Playing cards, she says. Nobody wants to put the new prime minister on the spot. Not yet anyway."

"Girl from where?" Campeau asks, drawn from his sulk by the only topic that interests him.

"Rainbow 2, over at Nana."

"You're shitting me. That place is *ruined*, all those Japanese guys, paying two thousand, three thousand—"

"Where's the village?" Rafferty asks, mostly to shut Campeau up.

"Isaan." The Growing Younger Man tears the top off a small packet and empties a fine green powder into his glass. He clinks his ring against it, and Toots puts down a very well-polished mug and hurries to take the glass. "Practically in Laos," he says, his eyes on Toots as though he's on the lookout for knockout drops. He raises a hand to tell them all that he'll be back after the commercial and leans forward to watch her pour two fingers of bourbon into his glass and top it off with steaming water from a heat pump. She wraps a napkin around it and carries it to him. It's a green that Rafferty doesn't really want to look at, the color of spring gone wrong. "Probably *was* in Laos fifty years ago," the Growing Younger Man continues, studying the glass. "Uttaradit, up where that bird's-beak piece of Laos pokes into Thai territory."

"I know where it is. Heard about anything, any demonstrations in Bangkok?"

"You will not," Hofstedler says. "Never. If two hundred people were rioting upstairs in ze King's Castle right now—across ze *street*—we would never hear of it. There would be zecret people, people without uniforms, everywhere. Every tourist with a camera would haff to give it up. Now we haff ze zecret cops."

"It's not the Red Shirts anymore," the Growing Younger Man says. "These days when there's a crowd of people throwing things, it's either Buddhists from down south screaming for people to control the Muslims or it's Muslims screaming that they're the victims of prejudice. Either side, they come up to Bangkok and shout for attention. Get a bunch of people tramping the streets now, that's probably what it's going to be about."

Rafferty says, "Really."

"And it's not all Thais either. There's a lot of outside players." The Growing Younger Man stirs the drink, studying it for something, perhaps a chemical reaction. "Every country that's ever had a bomb go off. And then there's all the international business interests. Multinationals, American, German, even Chinese. Lot of big money depends on Thai people turning up for work and their factories not getting blown up or burned down. So no, not just the Red Shirts anymore."

"Do you know what he is drinking?" Hofstedler says, leaning in confidentially.

Rafferty wants the Growing Younger Man to keep talking, but there's no sidestepping Leon. "I'm not sure I want to."

"Tell him." Hofstedler doesn't call the Growing Younger Man by name because he can't remember it. Neither can Rafferty; he's just the Growing Younger Man, the plastic surgeons' retirement plan, twenty-five years of trying to look young for bar girls who don't care about anything except the weight of his wallet.

"It's nothing, just a drink." The Growing Younger Man looks as embarrassed as Botox will let him look. He fingers his newest set of hair plugs, wistful little tufts of aspiration.

"*Nein, nein,*" Hofstedler says. "Tell him."

"It's an invention of mine. I call it a Hot Whiskey Boom-Boom."

"What's in it?"

He spreads his fingers and ticks them off as he goes. "Whiskey, hot water, Lipo-C—that's a liquid vitamin C with very small molecules, plus human growth hormone and spirulina."

"Spirulina," Campeau says. "Pond scum. Yum, yum."

"The Aztecs ate it. All the time." The Growing Younger Man slaps his bicep. "Aztec guys were up for it day and night."

Campeau looks over at him. "Yeah?"

"It's like natural Viagra," the Growing Younger Man says. He sips his drink and produces a minor grimace. "Better, because it doesn't affect your blood pressure. Have you read all the warnings on a package of Viagra?"

"The one I like," Campeau says, "is 'Call your doctor if an erection persists more than four hours.' I'd call a lot of people, but my doctor wouldn't be one of them."

"Four hours," Rafferty says, "you could hang your umbrella on it. Be handy in this weather."

"I've been drinking it for two years," the Growing Younger Man says, "and I've never had old Buster fail to show up since."

Hofstedler says, "Buster?"

Campeau says, "Not once?"

Rafferty says, "How's it taste?"

The Growing Younger Man says, "Awful. Look at it, for Chrissakes. Green as the meat at Foodland."

"But you drink it," Campeau says.

"Buster," says the Growing Younger Man with a decisive nod. "He's *always there*."

There is a moment of religious silence as everyone, except probably Toots, contemplates the fickleness of Buster. This is, after all, why these otherwise-intelligent men packed up their lives and moved here from less carnal climes. Only to be double-crossed by Buster.

"I'll try one," Campeau says. "Gimme."

"Do you know how much this stuff costs?" The Growing Younger Man pulls his glass closer to his chest.

"Are you kidding me? Twenty years you been sitting next to me, knocking back one throat-closer after another, and I been sitting here, really nice about it, no matter what it looked like. And I listened to you whine about Jah for two years—"

"I did not whine about Jah—"

"In a city with twenty-nine million available women in it, I nodded and said 'poor you' a thousand times while you droned on, Jah this, Jah that—"

"Buy your own," The Growing Younger Man says. "Jah was nothing—"

"She sure wasn't," Campeau said. "Barely competent."

The Growing Younger Man says, attempting to narrow his eyes, "Excuse me?"

"Me, too," Hofstedler says to him. "If you haff anger for Bob, you haff anger for all of us. You talked about her zo much that we all—"

"Leave me out of it," Rafferty says. "I wouldn't know Jah if she walked through the door wearing a neon hat."

"Like *you* need—" Campeau says, and breaks off.

Rafferty leans forward. "Yes, Bob?"

"Nothing," Campeau says. "Jesus, everybody's so fucking touchy. I remember when you could—"

"Two dollah," Toots says, slapping the snifter on the bar again. "And this time I make change."

The tips of Campeau's ears turn a deep red. For a moment, Rafferty thinks, things could get ugly, and then he realizes he's just forgotten what it's like. He says, "This is great, you know?"

Hofstedler says, "What is?"

"This. Just guys. Everybody bullshitting, not even expecting anyone to believe anything. Nobody's talking about *feelings*, nobody will remember in ten minutes what anyone else said. We can all get wound up and then let it blow away. You know, the way things should be."

"You should come more often," the Growing Younger Man says. "It's like this every night."

"I'll pay Campeau's fine," Rafferty says. "Just because I'm happy to see him." The beer announces its alcohol content with a welcome glow. Like pink lampshades in a dim restaurant, it makes everybody look better. "I remember when people weren't so touchy, too. So there, that's four bucks I owe, and I'll buy a round for everybody."

"I don't really want to drink that shit anyway," Campeau says almost affably to the Growing Younger Man.

"I actually did Jah, too," Rafferty says to the Growing Younger Man. "A couple of times." He raises both hands. "Just kidding. Honest."

3

You'd Still Be Wearing That Shirt

THE APARTMENT HOUSE is right where he left it. He approaches it at a diagonal, following an invisible ley line that he can't sense when he's completely sober. Or half sober. He's been out three hours, he's had three more king-size beers on top of the two at the apartment, and the last thing he ate was a small helping of stir-fried chicken with basil and chilies about noon, before he went to the paint store. The beer has the whole hotel to itself.

"Eighth floor," he says to the elevator, accompanying the words with a lordly wave of the hand. Once inside, he says, "Here. Allow me," and pushes the button. As it rises, he bends his knees in a little plié that made Miaow laugh back when he invented it to help her with her fear of elevators. When he adopted her off the sidewalk, she'd never been in an elevator, and they did their plié together for months. With the dissonant emotional chords alcohol usually sounds in him, he immediately sinks into a kind of depressive nostalgia for the days when Miaow and he were closer, when she looked up to him. When she still thought he knew something.

She's always been spiky and strong-willed, but when he summons up the picture of her with her hair parted strictly down the middle and pasted down with water, the way she'd worn it for years, looking up at him with a mixture of hope, faith, and potential disappointment—the emotional attitude created by a childhood of betrayal and homelessness—he can't help missing the little girl she was then. And how essential she made him feel.

This is an issue Rose laughs off, as she does Miaow's relation-ship, whatever it is, with Andrew. The last time he talked about it, Rose said, "If you didn't want her to change, you should have bought a table instead."

"A table," he says aloud as the elevator doors open and the two men in uniform peer in at him.

Bruisers, both of them, wearing uniforms he doesn't recognize. One's smiling, one's not.

"Wrong floor," he says, pushing the CLOSE DOORS button, but the one who's smiling sticks his foot in front of the door. In a moment of alcohol-fueled misjudgment, Rafferty aims a kick at the foot, misses, and staggers backward.

The smiling one laughs. He says, "We thought you'd never get home, Mr. Rafferty."

The one who isn't smiling takes Rafferty's T-shirt in both fists and pulls him out of the elevator as though he's an autumn leaf. The smiling one pushes the button that holds the elevator.

"There," he says in more-than-serviceable English. "Now we don't have to think about the elevator, do we? It'll be here when we want it."

"Who are you guys?" Rafferty slaps at the hands of the man holding his shirt, and the man raises them in mock surrender and takes a step back.

"We've come to take you with us," Smiley says.

"Really." Rafferty says, heading for his door, "shame you went so far out of your—" He's almost yanked off his feet by the neck of his T-shirt, which has stopped moving so suddenly it feels like he snagged it on a building.

"Yes," Smiley says, stepping into the elevator as his friend hoists Rafferty under his arm and carries him back across the hall. "With us."

THE ROOM, WINDOWLESS and badly lit, is about half the size of Miaow's bedroom. Which, Poke thinks—working on staying calm—he should be painting right now.

He's been given some time to worry about why he's here, in this piss-colored room with the splintered table, the requisite mirror along one wall, the ghost fragrance of sweat and tobacco, and the mysterious and deeply unsettling stains on the floor.

It's cold in here, but he's sweating and he can smell himself. On the other hand, at least some of his drunkenness is abandoning him, probably looking for a more lighthearted environment.

The only furniture in the room is the battered table with two chairs across it. Smiley had put him into the chair facing the door. After five or ten uncomfortable minutes spent in cheerless speculation about the stains on the floor, Rafferty realized that the two front legs on his chair had been sawed down by half an inch, so that he was continually sliding forward. With a cheery wave at the mirror, he got up and swapped chairs. Then he sat there for another twelve minutes, breathing as evenly as possible, at which point he got up and tried the door, which was locked.

"Okay," he said to the microphone high in the corner. "It's nine forty-one. At nine-fifty I'm throwing the chair through the mirror." He went to the mirror and held his wrist to the glass. "Synchronize watches."

At 9:49 the door opens and the slender, handsome Thai with the pouches beneath his eyes—the one who'd moved him away from the fallen *farang*—comes in. He's no longer in street clothes. Instead he wears a tightly creased uniform like the ones worn by the men who brought Rafferty here. He closes the door behind him, giving it a little tug to make sure the latch is engaged, and extends a long-fingered hand to drop a manila envelope onto the table.

Rafferty takes a closer look. The man's hair is slicked back to reveal a sharp widow's peak, the point of which is echoed by the tip of his long chin. In a gene pool that mostly dictates rounded features, he's all acute angles, almost fox-faced. His shoulders are broad and his hips narrow, and his uniform fits in a way that says *expensive tailor* with a mild French accent.

He smiles, and his teeth are breathtaking. "Sorry to have kept you waiting," he says in that same pure, American English. "It's a bad time in Bangkok, and not just because of the rain. Although after what you went through today, I'm sure that's no news to you."

He pushes back the chair on his side, the one with the

sawed-off legs, and his smile broadens. He slips out of his shoes, puts one chair leg inside each of them to even it, and sits. "Old trick, the sloping chair," he says. "Not meant for you, of course. They should have brought you a different one."

Rafferty says nothing, just watches the man squeeze out the charm.

The slender man nods appreciation of Rafferty's lack of response. He picks up the envelope and tilts it. Five color photos slide onto the table. He fans them out, one-handed: Rafferty up on his elbow on the sidewalk, the bleeding white man clinging to him. Talking to him.

"Who is he?" the slender man says.

"Who are you?" Rafferty says.

"Oh, good heavens," he says with a good-natured chuckle. He resists, Rafferty thinks, slapping his forehead. "I'm Major Shen. And you're Philip Rafferty, American travel writer, born in California in the United States, now a Bangkok resident, married to a Thai national and the adoptive father of a Thai child."

"Ah, the power of intelligence," Rafferty says. "Or maybe just information. Major in what?"

"I'm sorry?" The man looks down at himself and tugs his sharply creased sleeve. "Oh, the uniform. Well, yes, we haven't put much effort into public relations. But the question on the table, so to speak, is who is *he?*"

"Quid pro quo," Rafferty says, half expecting two guys to burst into the room toting rubber hoses.

"Really?" Major Shen purses his lips. "If you must. In America you'd probably say we're affiliated with Homeland Security."

Rafferty says, with a sinking feeling, "Mmmmm."

"But don't let that bother you. We'll talk for a few minutes and then you'll be on your way and you can forget all about me." The smile gets switched on and off. "Who is he?"

"I have no idea. He's someone who got shot and bumped into me and then got shot again."

Major Shen looks down at the table. "I see. You're shortchanging me."

Rafferty's vision dims and flickers with sudden rage. "Well, what do you think happened? You think he got mixed up in a running crowd and steered it through the streets of Bangkok until he found the one person he was looking for? Maybe he knew someone was going to shoot at him and he wanted to die in my arms? So he could give me the password that opens the cave or something?" He sits back, reminding himself he's been drinking and his judgment may not be at its sharpest.

Major Shen shrugs. It's a completely remote shrug, and suddenly it's easy for Rafferty to see him, immaculate, standing far enough away not to get anything on his clothes as he directs the activities of two men using pliers on a third. Making stains on the floor. "Perhaps he knew you would be there. Perhaps you had made an appointment to meet him."

Rafferty turns the pictures around and breathes twice to calm himself. "Have you looked at these? See all the spilled paint? See the open cans? See the store I was coming out of? It's a paint store."

Major Shen taps a slender, unimpeachably manicured finger against the surface of one of the photos. "He's talking to you." He has cloves on his breath and, beneath that, the reek of cigarettes.

"A couple of words."

"The film says otherwise. The film says he spoke to you for ten seconds or so."

"The film?"

"The TV crew. You gave them their best footage of the day."

"Did I make the seven-o'clock? Am I famous?"

"I'm afraid not." He shifts his weight, and the chair wobbles. "It's remarkable how uncomfortable this chair is, even with my shoes under it. We should really treat our guests better."

"Why wasn't it on television?"

The smile peeks out and goes away again. "As I said, it shows he spoke to you for ten seconds or thereabouts."

"Mostly not. Mostly he was working up to talking. He had blood in his throat, and he made a bunch of noises before he could actually say anything." Major Shen's eyes have drifted with apparent disinterest until he's looking over Rafferty's shoulder. "You say you saw the film. You must have seen all the blood he coughed up."

Major Shen's eyes come back. "But *then* he spoke."

"Yes." The alcohol chimes in again, bringing anger with it. "And even though I resent the hell out of being dragged down here like this and I *really* resent your bringing my wife and daughter into the conversation, I'll tell you what he said. He said a name—a woman's name, I think—and then the name the name of a city."

"A city?" Shen smooths an eyebrow with the tip of his index finger. "What city?"

What city had it been? Rafferty draws a blank, and then the name appears before him, and he grabs at it. "Helena."

Major Shen closes his eyes and furrows his brow for a moment, as though he thinks he might have seen Helena at some point and is trying to picture it. When he opens them, he's looking over Rafferty's shoulder again. "In Montana?"

"If that's where Helena is. Montana, Wyoming—sure, Montana. I guess."

The pouchy eyes, which Rafferty's altered perspective suddenly recognizes as the aftermath of alcohol, return to Rafferty's face. "You remember 'the name of a town in Montana' but not the name."

"I've been to Montana. I went there once, when I was a kid. The woman's name was just a name, and I was a little rattled."

"Rattled."

"Yeah, you know. American slang? Rattled? Having a guy die on me and all that. People running. Shots being fired. Shots you denied, by the way. Not the ideal spot for concentration."

"You're not used to having people die on you."

"Not especially."

Major Shen sits back and crosses his legs, a man with all the time in the world. "And yet people die *around* you with some regularity."

The room suddenly feels not so much cool as frigid. Rafferty tries to keep his face blank as he ransacks his mind for anything that could connect him directly to any of the people who actually *have* died around him since he came to Bangkok. "You must know something about my life I don't."

Shen lowers his head and looks at Rafferty from under his eyebrows. "A Chinese gangster. An American defense contractor who apparently had some sort of relationship with your wife." He checks his perfect nails female–style, extending his arm, fingers straight, and looking at the back of his hand. "To name just two." He lifts his head and turns the smile on again, the picture of someone whose memory has just kicked in. "Oh, and that billionaire Pan, so that's three. That we know of. Not exactly a bookish life, is it?"

Rafferty doesn't reply. But there's only one person in Bangkok who might conceivably have told Shen about both Howard Horner, the defense contractor, and Chu, the Chinese triad leader. Under his breath he says, "Fucker."

"Excuse me?"

"I said 'Fucker,'" Rafferty says to the mirror. "But it wasn't aimed at you."

"Well, I'm sure that whoever it is, he's shaking in his boots. Anyway, to get back to our business. We're concerned with this man and what he might have said. You're the person he said it to, and I have to observe that you're leading an interesting life here. In times of crisis, we tend to clump interesting people together, at least to the point of asking them polite questions, but—"

"You know what's *really* interesting?"

"—but sometimes mistakes are made," Shen finishes.

"Meaning sometimes you're not so polite to people who haven't done anything."

The remote shrug again. "I'd be lying if I said it never happened."

"I'll remember that for when the press talks to me."

Major Shen smiles. "The press will not talk to you."

Rafferty listens to the statement several times in memory. It has the effect of sobering him up. He nods.

"The woman's name," Shen says.

Rafferty sits back. "I don't remember it."

"Why 'Helena'?"

"I have no idea. It's probably where she lives, whoever she is."

Tented fingertips. "So your hypothesis is that he was asking you to contact this woman?"

"I don't have a hypothesis. For all I know, Helena, or Montana, is his Rosebud."

Shen leans forward a quarter of an inch, and for such a small move it's immensely unfriendly. "But it isn't his Rosebud. It's a city. He gives you a name and a city. A who and a where, so to speak."

"I suppose so."

"But you don't remember the name."

Rafferty raises a hand to stop him and shuts his eyes. Pictures the fallen man, feels the chill of rain on the back of his neck, sees again the jolting, out-of-focus chaos in the background and the brilliance of the TV crew's light. Forces himself to concentrate on the man's lips, thinking of the close-up in *Citizen Kane* when Kane says "Rosebud." But the man's lips barely move at all.

He opens his eyes. "No, I don't."

Major Shen sighs and then says, "So what you're *willing* to tell us is that he said three words: a name you can't remember and a city in Montana." He nods as though something has been confirmed. "You *have* been to Montana, haven't you? You've been all over. You spent quite a bit of time in Manila, for example, and Jakarta. Denpasar. I could name some more if I looked at my notes."

Rafferty knows where this is going, and it makes him very uneasy. "That's not exactly a secret. I wrote books about both the Philippines and Indonesia."

"You have to admit, you've got an unusual profile."

"I don't have to admit shit."

"This is not a constructive atti—"

"What happened today had nothing to do with me. Your crowd was chasing his crowd, or the crowd he got caught up in. He got shot, he had to grab onto someone, and I was there. Are you suggesting that I went to Indonesia and the Philippines because I'm involved with Muslim separatists or terrorists of some kind? Because if you are, I want my embassy here now."

"My, my," Major Shen says.

"My, my yourself." Poke looks back at the mirrored window with its unspoken threat. Whatever else this is, it's bullying, and he learned long ago that giving in to bullies just signals weakness. "I'm finished talking. Arrest me or something."

"Please, Mr. Rafferty." Shen does that glance over Rafferty's shoulder again, as though there were a teleprompter back there. "You grew up in California, isn't that right?"

"You know it is."

"And so did I. Orange County, whereas you were in . . ." He seems either to be searching for the name or giving Rafferty a chance to supply it, but Rafferty doesn't. "Lancaster," he says.

"Just a couple of California boys," Rafferty says. "Under other circumstances we'd probably go surfing."

"This is a different world," Major Shen says. "It's no longer necessary to arrest people."

"It never really was," Rafferty says. "Bullies in uniforms have always found shortcuts."

"This . . . posturing is not helpful, not to either of us."

"Possibly not. Let me go back to my earlier question. You want to know what's really interesting?"

Shen rubs his eyes with both hands, his first admission that he's tired. "Not particularly, no."

"That you're asking me who he was and what he said, but not who shot him."

Rafferty is rewarded with a blink. "That's not a question that—"

"I mean, if I had arranged the . . . whatever you want to call it—meeting, collision, whatever—then I should be a suspect, shouldn't I? Accomplice at least. I brought him within range of the rifle, right?"

Major Shen purses his lips and turns his head away from Rafferty, putting himself in profile to whoever is behind the window. It's almost the same as saying, *Wouldn't it have been nice if someone had anticipated this question?*

"You *know* who shot him," Rafferty says. "Don't you? And you know who *he* was, too."

Shen doesn't seem to have heard a word. "Give me the woman's name."

"Arrest me or I'm leaving, and then you'll *have* to hold me."

Major Shen pushes both hands down on the tabletop as though

to rise and opens his mouth, but there's a *clack* that Rafferty identifies as a coin, or some other object made of metal, being rapped against the other side of the mirror. The major sits back in his seat, closes his eyes slowly, and opens them again, and he's once more looking over Rafferty's shoulder. "Of course we're not going to hold you," he says, and he produces a smile a lot less polished than the one Rafferty's been seeing, the smile of someone who's not very good at masking rage. "This is just a discussion."

Rafferty gets up, unsure of what's happening. The rap of the coin changed everything. He says to Shen, "Don't forget your shoes."

"And you, Mr. Rafferty." Although Rafferty is now standing beside him, Shen does not turn his head but continues to address the chair Rafferty vacated. "If you think of the name, you'll call me."

"Absolutely."

"That's good, then. Well," Major Shen says to the chair, "we'll meet again."

"I'll look forward to it." Rafferty goes to the door and opens it, almost surprised to find it unlocked. "I'll find my own way out."

"Wait—" Major Shen is pushing himself to his feet like he's coming out of a trance, but he's too slow to keep Rafferty from opening the door and going through it, into the short hallway beyond. There's a door to Rafferty's right, and he turns the knob and then kicks it open. It bangs against the wall, and two men leap to their feet in front of the trick mirror.

The nearer man is thin all the way: thin body, thin lips, thin rimless spectacles clinging to a thin nose. He's all verticals, just bones in a black suit. "Richard," Rafferty says to him, "just to complete the thought, fuck you."

"You're way too confident for your own good, Poke," Richard Elson says. He sounds almost frightened.

"What happened? Secret Service lend you to the Ghostbusters? Kind of a demotion, isn't it?"

"*Hey*," says the other man in the room, a ball of fat topped by a thatch of unruly reddish-gray hair that's been slapped any old way on top of a fat red face. He's much shorter than Elson, thirty years older, and maybe eighty pounds heavier. The loud, ragged Hawaiian silk shirt he wears above his worn-looking jeans is buttoned for dear life over a paunch the size of an elephant's rump.

"And you are?" Rafferty's so angry his voice feels thick in his throat.

The redheaded man shoulders Elson aside. Protruding from each nostril is a tuft of red hair so substantial that Rafferty imagines himself grabbing them in his fists and chinning himself on them. "Somebody who could squash you by snapping my fingers." He's got a voice like gravel in a glass.

"Yeah, but what good would it do you? You'd still be wearing that shirt."

The redheaded man's face goes a deep, cardiac scarlet, and Elson says, "Poke."

Rafferty feels a hand on his arm, and then it becomes a grip, and he's pulled from behind, out the door, which slams closed.

"Very foolish," Major Shen says. His forehead is wet. "Very foolish indeed."

Rafferty says, "Let go of me."

"You've been in Thailand long enough to know the value of keeping a cool heart," Shen says without loosening his grip. He seems actually shaken. "It's a shame you haven't adopted it as a policy." He propels Rafferty down the hall, away from the interrogation room, and through a pair of swinging doors that open onto a broader corridor. Seated there on metal folding chairs are the two heavyweights who'd met Poke in his elevator. The one he thinks of as Smiley leaps to his feet when he sees Shen.

Shen shoves Rafferty hard, so hard he stumbles halfway across the corridor. Only the opposite wall keeps him from going down "My men will take you home," Major Shen says, smoothing his hair. "Bangkok is very dangerous right now."

THE PLACE LOOKS wrong.

He sees it the moment he comes in. Even with all the furniture out of place for painting, it's obvious that someone has been here, but it takes him a moment to spot what it is that caught his eye. The black drop cloth, which he had painstakingly aligned with the baseboards, isn't tucked in as neatly as he'd left it. He feels a clamping around his heart, and he goes double-time to the bedroom.

But the safe in the headboard above the bed is closed and locked, and the sliding panel that hides it is still on its latch. Rafferty tugs the panel open anyway, in a gingerly fashion, half expecting it to explode, but all it does is catch slightly at the point where it always catches. He tugs the safe door, and it reassuringly refuses to swing open. He sits on the side of the bed he shares with Rose, thinking about the men who invaded this room, pawing at their things, and the image sends him to the closet, where he sees that some of her clothes, which she hangs at precise intervals, with about an inch between hangers, have been moved. For a moment he sees little bright objects, like crinkles of aluminum foil, floating in front of his eyes. They recede, leaving him with his pulse trying to hammer its way out at his temples.

Just to be sure, he goes back to the bed and opens the safe. The oilcloth wrapped around the Glock is right where it should be. He prods it with his index finger, and its weight reassures him.

But the ten one-thousand-baht bills are gone. Just, he thinks, by way of a snicker.

Rafferty pushes sharply at the upper-right corner of the safe's back wall, and it pops open a quarter of an inch or so. He gets his fingertips into the gap and slides the wall to the left.

The rubber-banded packet of thousand-baht bills, fifty of them, is still there. He regards it for a moment and then pulls it out, secures the wall again, and closes the safe. He folds the thousands once and shoves them into his pocket. Cash seems like a good idea. Sits on the bed, not really thinking about anything, just trying to get a sense of how cold the water really is.

It feels pretty cold.

It's almost midnight. He knows he won't sleep, so he leaves the apartment and goes down to Silom in the rain, crosses over to Patpong, and reenters the Expat Bar. He's greeted by the same crew as though they haven't seen him for years. Toots produces his beer, sans glass. He holds up a finger for another. It's a two-at-a-time night.

At two o'clock he wobbles into the street, drunker than he's been in years. The bars are closing, their lights blinking out, and shirtless country boys are tearing down the night market. Their skin is gleaming wet as they wheel up and down through the drizzle on forklifts, hissing cigarettes clenched in their teeth, just barely missing as many tourists as possible. Ignoring the come-ons of a couple of dodgy ladyboys in a darkened shop doorway, Rafferty takes a zigzag path back home. Without even turning off the bedroom light, he collapses in his wet clothes on the bed and immediately passes out, only to wake up moments later thinking, *The trash.*

He hauls himself to his feet and takes the elevator, barefoot, to the basement. For the first time all day, he's in luck; the wad of clothes he dropped down the chute is on top of the pile. When he rifles through it, almost the first thing he sees is the yellow stub of paper with the little diamond cut from its center. Feeling obscurely victorious at recovering the one thing Shen's men hadn't spotted on the videotape, he tucks the stub into his hip pocket, puts the clothes back on the pile, and drops a couple of full trash bags on top of it for verisimilitude. He rides the elevator back up, keeping his eyes open because the world spins when he closes them.

With the precision of the very drunk, he gets a roll of masking tape from the pile of paint supplies, goes back into the hall, and folds the stub into a narrow strip, which he tapes on top of the lintel above the door to the stairs, at the far end of the hall. He presses it flat, so it's invisible from beneath. Then he wobbles his way back inside and crawls on his hands and knees onto the bed.

When he wakes up the next morning, the lamp on the table is burning cheerlessly in the shaft of sunlight falling through the window, he feels as if a small airplane is being assembled inside his head, and he's still wearing his damp jeans and the shirt that says LET'S TOGETHER!! But the woman's name has arrived while he was sleeping: *Helen,* not Helena, Eckersley. And not Montana but the other one, the one he always confuses with Montana—Wyoming. *Cheyenne,* Wyoming.

A Climate of Highly Evolved Uncertainty

THE LITTLE BOUQUET of rain-beaded flowers beside Arthit's breakfast plate is an unwelcome surprise.

Standing beside his chair, he looks down at it as he might a millipede. This is the work of Pim, the eighteen-year-old former aspiring tart whom Rafferty and Rose grabbed off the street and foisted upon him as a combination maid and spy, charged with letting them know if he started drinking again.

He has watched with some uneasiness as the gardens created by his late wife, Noi, have come back to life beneath Pim's fingers. It had caused him actual physical pain to see the gardens go to seed as Noi's condition worsened. After she died, he stopped seeing them altogether, literally keeping his eyes averted as he walked to and from the house. And here they are, reborn. He supposes he should be happy about it, but those were *Noi's* flowers. No one else's to tend, no one else's to nurse back to health.

Noi had started digging the beds the day after they moved into the house, back when her illness was an occasional inconvenience rather than a constant torment. Even as her condition worsened, she had delighted in filling the house with sunbursts in glass jars and a potpourri of fragrances: jasmine, lavender, tuberose, gardenias, old roses—Bourbons and damasks, varieties that had been popular a hundred years ago, before all the scent had been bred out.

And here they are again.

He hears Pim in the kitchen, rattling pans and singing a pop song with a tune she can't carry, and his heart grows even heavier. The situation has to be confronted. Even if he's wrong about what's happening, it has to be confronted. He can't have Pim thinking their relationship is anything other than what it is.

He's been telling himself he was imagining it. But he's been ignoring signals for months. He's not a garden, and he can't be tended by another.

But she's taken such good care of him. And she's so vulnerable. He closes his eyes and draws a calming breath, then takes the first difficult step.

"Pim," he says.

The doorbell rings.

"Yes?" she calls. There's water running; she hasn't heard the doorbell.

"Is the coffee ready?" he asks, grasping the opportunity to dodge. "Someone's at the door."

She bustles through the door, drying her hands, chubby and frizzy-haired, with an adult face that's just beginning to shape itself out of the child's. "I'll get it," she says.

"No, no." He waves her back toward the kitchen. "You can't do everything. I can still walk."

"Coffee," she says. Her eyes go to the flowers and then up to his, but he's turning to avoid her gaze, heading for the door.

As he goes, he checks the heavy steel watch on its too-loose band—8:45. Early for anyone he knows to come ringing the bell.

And it isn't anyone he knows.

The woman who stands with no umbrella beneath the sheltering overhang of the roof is in her late thirties or early forties. She's fit, but not in that grim, zero-carb, no-pain-no-gain way Arthit sees a lot of these days, in the minor wives of rich men, in the secretaries and receptionists who want to *become* the minor wives of rich men. She's . . . she's *sleek*. It's easy to see her emerging from the sea, with a little ornamental glisten going on, and climbing up onto a rock to let the sun dry her. Water, he thinks, a bit wildly, would bead on her skin. And in fact it has, on the side of her neck.

A movement of her hands stops the avalanche of impressions, and Arthit feels his face heat up. There's a glint in her own eyes that suggests she has some idea where his mind was. Arthit forces a smile through his blush and waits for her to say something.

She tilts her head to one side, very slightly, and gives a tiny shrug. Then she looks down at her black alligator purse, and Arthit takes advantage of the moment to look again at her long, slender neck. There's a smooth little layer of fat just beneath the skin, softening the contours of her throat. A faint crease runs the base of her neck, between the short crop of black hair and the collar of her blouse, as though the skin had been folded once, very carefully. The crease is so shallow he doubts he could feel it even with the most sensitive part of the tip of his finger.

Neither of them has spoken a word.

Arthit clears his throat to say something, but as he does so, she takes a business card out of the purse and presents it to him politely, both hands extended. Now there's a shadow of regret in her face, somehow formal.

DR. ANCHALI "ANNA" CHAIBANCHA, it says, PROJECT SUPERVISOR, WITTAYALAI SCHOOL FOR THE DEAF.

She's looking at him expectantly, and two shoes drop simultaneously: He knows why she hasn't spoken, and he knows who she is.

"Anna," he says, and there's a sudden tangle of emotions that threatens to clamp his throat shut. "I'm sorry," he continues, aware of her eyes on his lips. "I didn't recognize you."

She holds her right hand up, vertically, making a small side-to-side gesture, erasing the mistake. Then she startles him by reaching down and grasping his wrist, looking directly into his eyes.

"I'm better," he says, understanding. "Every day is a little easier."

Anna pulls in the corners of her lips a bit.

He shakes his head and abandons the lie. "No, it's not. Every day feels just exactly like the day before. But I'm not as bad as I was, so every day must be somewhat better, even if I'm not conscious of it. Please," he says, suddenly seeing the rain, suddenly remembering his manners. "Won't you come in?" And he turns, her fingers still around his wrist, and sees Pim standing in the hallway, her hands dangling forgotten at her sides. In one is a saucer, and hanging from the other, her finger looped through the handle, is one of Noi's everyday coffee cups. All the spirit has fled from her face.

"Pim," he says, hearing a ghastly heartiness in his voice, "this is Anna—Dr. Chaibancha, a friend of my . . . my wife's. I haven't seen her since . . . since the cremation."

THEY'RE AT THE dining-room table, the breakfast plates still empty, the bowl of Pim's bright flowers between them. Coffee cools in their cups, strong, with a dark brown fragrance.

Pim has learned to make it exactly as he likes it.

Arthit looks at the fine porcelain cups, which he hasn't seen since Noi died, and then at Anna, and he gives Pim credit. She can spot a lady when she sees one.

"It wasn't good for me to live alone," Arthit says, although nothing Anna has done seems to be a request for an explanation. She watches his lips in a way that's somehow both personal and not. "A *farang* friend of mine forced himself in here one day and found me drunk at ten in the morning, and the next thing I knew, Pim was here." He's suddenly certain that Pim is listening on the other side of the door. "She's been wonderful," he says.

Anna has a thin gold ballpoint and a pad bound in pale blue leather. She writes and turns it toward him. It says, *She's in love with you.*

"That's possible," he says, a bit stiffly. He tilts his head toward the door. "It's something I'm thinking about."

Poor man, Anna writes. She shakes her head, but there's a hint of humor in it, too. Watching him across the table, she must be seeing a tired-looking man in his middle forties with a heavy, downturned mouth, permanently flared nostrils, slightly receding hair, and the eyes of an orphaned five-year-old. He's not very well shaved, and his shirt is badly ironed. He needs a haircut. She reaches over to pat his hand, but he speaks before she can do it.

"This is the kind of thing," he says, "that I could use some help with." He picks up the coffee and drinks it in self-defense.

She gives him a smile that lifts his heart in a way it hasn't been lifted in some time and sips her own coffee.

"You're . . . ahhh, teaching," he says. Her silence hovers between them, seeming to need to be filled. "How long have you been . . . ?" He abandons the question. "It's very nice to see you. Noi and I were such hermits," he says, not wanting to bring up the illness that had kept her home. "We let a lot of old friends slip away. She talked about you, though."

It was true. Noi and Anna had been children together, back in what Arthit always thought of as Noi's golden childhood, spent in the lap of the family that had been extremely displeased at her marriage so far below her social status—to a lowly policeman, the son of another policeman. Anna has the same gloss to her, a kind of natural polish buffed by privilege that rough wear hasn't scratched.

She's writing now, and he watches with pleasure. She's left-handed, her fingers long and cream-colored, with varnished, untinted nails. The pen appears weightless in her hand, and Arthit enjoys the play of delicate muscles beneath smooth skin.

She tears off the page and slides it over to him, then goes back to writing.

I've wanted to come for months, it says. *But I didn't want to intrude. And I was afraid a little, too. You were so devastated at the temple. I didn't know how you'd be and whether I could do anything . . .*

The next piece of paper skims the table.

. . . no matter how you were. And I felt terrible about it, because I knew that Noi would have wanted me to make sure you were all right. But I'm a coward.

She's stopped writing and is watching him read. When he's finished, Arthit says, "But you've come now, and—"

Anna is shaking her head, denying herself any credit. She reaches down and brings up the purse again.

When her hand comes back into view, it's holding a four-by-five photograph, in color. She places the very tips of her fingers on its edge, as though she's hesitant to touch it, and pushes it across the table. There's something apologetic in the way she pulls her hands back.

A big man lying in the rain on an oddly colored sidewalk, his torso in the lap of another man, who's clearly calling for help.

Arthit looks at the sitting man's face.

• • •

FORTY MINUTES LATER Rafferty says, "I hope this is interesting. I was sitting at home, just sort of wishing for a merciful death."

Arthit, heading through the dining room toward the kitchen, says, "It's interesting. Sit down and you'll find out."

Rafferty chooses the armchair he's chosen for years and sits carefully, trying to keep his head from rolling off his neck. His throat is dry, and his tongue feels like it has a seat cover on it. The morning light, even through the thick clouds, is bright enough to make noise.

He has to stand again almost immediately as Arthit comes back with Pim in tow. She's carrying a fancy coffee cup, thin enough to let him see the coffee through the porcelain. She hands it to him without meeting his eyes or saying hello and trudges away, shuffling her feet like someone who's polishing the floor with her socks. Arthit returns Poke's questioning glance with a man-to-man combination of wide eyes and shrugged shoulders that means, *I'd scream and break things if I could, but I can't, and I'll tell you about it when there are no women around.*

Rafferty starts to sit again, but no such luck. Into the room comes a very trim and, he thinks, quite beautiful woman about Arthit's age.

She's wearing a dark blue blouse, possibly silk, with loose half sleeves that bare elegant forearms and an exquisite pair of hands. The blouse hangs over white linen slacks, only slightly wrinkled despite the damp of the day. She has a short chop of thick, willful hair, brushed back to reveal a porcelain forehead and large, rounded eyes, a brown that goes golden in the sunlight streaming through the windows.

"This is Anna," Arthit says, and Rafferty hears a note in his friend's voice that he hasn't heard in months and months.

He greets Anna in Thai, and she makes a fluid, practiced gesture, first almost touching her fingertips to her lips and then to her ear and ending with her upraised palm facing him. Arthit says, "Anna doesn't hear or speak. But she can read your lips."

Rafferty says, "In English?" and at the last moment diverts the question to her instead of Arthit.

Anna gives him a broad smile, and Arthit says, "In Serbo-Croatian, probably."

Still smiling, Anna sits on the couch and tucks her legs under her.

Arthit takes the other end of the couch and clears his throat. "It's because Anna reads lips that we're all here."

Rafferty hears a floorboard creak in the dining room. Since Arthit is still looking at him, he makes a small movement with his head toward the noise.

"Poke," Arthit says, a bit stagily. "Why don't you go into the kitchen and get Pim? She lives here, too, and she ought to hear this."

"Let me have a gulp of coffee first," Rafferty says. He takes a long sip, replaces the cup on the saucer with a clatter, and yawns loudly to give Pim the chance to duck back into the kitchen. He glimpses the look that passes between Arthit and the woman—Anna, her nickname is Anna—as he leaves the living room. The look was shared amusement, and it's a look that, Rafferty thinks, usually takes a while to develop.

"Hey, Pim," he says. She's sitting at the kitchen table with an empty cup—a chipped mug, not one of the good ones—in front of her. He goes to the coffeemaker and hoists the carafe. "Want some more?"

She shakes her head.

He carries it over anyway, glances down at the cup, and says, "Well, you can't have more if you haven't had any." He pours her half a cup. "It's good. Come on, it'll get your heart beating."

He's been speaking English, and he knows she understands only bits of it. From the look on her face, she's not even trying.

"Can I have more?" He holds up his empty cup.

"Can have what you want," she says.

She's such a puffy, hapless little thing, short, plump-faced, uncertain. When he'd first met her, she was trying to work the sidewalk on Sukhumwit Soi 7, and he'd dragged her home to meet Rose. He and Rose had thought they were doing a favor for both her and Arthit when they suggested she come to help him with the house, but looking at her now, he's not sure he was right.

"Why don't you come into the living room for a minute?"

"I'm not really a servant," she says in Thai. "I can stay here if I want."

"It's not an order. I think Arthit just wants to make sure you know what's happening."

She blows out a gallon of air in a way that reminds him she isn't really that much older than Miaow and gets up, mug in hand.

"Wait," he says. He turns to the cupboards, which he had helped Arthit clean and organize in the aftermath of Noi's death, and pulls out one of the porcelain cups, with saucer. It takes him only a few seconds to fill it with fresh coffee and hold out his hand for the mug. She hesitates for a moment, and then they swap, and Rafferty follows her into the living room.

Arthit gets up as they enter and ushers her to the second armchair. Anna's eyes follow Pim as she crosses the room. When they're all seated and Anna's gaze has dropped to her lap, Rafferty leans back and sees, for an instant, the same tableau but with different people: Rose and himself in the armchairs, Arthit and Noi on the couch. Seeing Anna in Noi's place, he feels a sharp, almost-physical twinge of loss, an emotional cramp.

Since someone has to say something, he toasts Pim with his cup and says, "This is great coffee."

"You've met Anna before, I think," Arthit said. "At the temple. For Noi's . . ."

"I remember," Rafferty says, just to break in on Arthit's pause.

"She and Noi grew up together," Arthit says. "Now, once in a while, she reads lips for the police when there's video evidence that doesn't have sound or where the voices aren't audible."

"Ahh," Rafferty says. "The footage that didn't make the news."

"You already know about this?" Arthit asks. "That there's official interest, I mean?" Anna watches Arthit's lips and then turns to Rafferty for his answer.

"They hauled me in last night, about nine o'clock."

"Who?"

"A Major Shen."

"Not *a* Major Shen," Arthit says astringently. "The one and only Major Shen."

"Who is he?"

"I don't know him personally, but my impression is that he's the worst possible news."

"I've got worse," Rafferty says. "He grilled me in a crappy little room with one of those mirrors in it, and on the other side of the mirror were a couple of guys from my own country—you know, the land of the free. One of them was our pal Elson."

Anna nods and holds up her free hand. With the other she's writing on a small pad. She tears off a sheet and hands it to Arthit.

"She says that makes sense. Shen works with the Americans."

"On what?" Rafferty asks Anna, who's writing again.

"The situation in the south," Arthit reads from her pad.

"Sure," Rafferty says. "He was all over me about Indonesia and the Philippines, like I was some sort of courier for militant Islam."

Arthit is nodding before Rafferty finishes speaking. "It's just a matter of time before one of the big jihadists is caught here, either down south or in Bangkok," Arthit says. "We've got a big Arab population in Bangkok and a lot of native Muslim discontent down there."

"Who's Shen with? I didn't recognize the uniform."

"It hasn't been worn in public much. It's a little operatic if you ask me. Listen, I know him for only one reason, and that's because he was given permission to take pretty much anyone he wanted from any department he wanted. And he chose knuckle-draggers, the kind of guys you'd take into the street if you thought you might have to fire into a crowd."

Anna is writing again, but this time she holds the pad up for everyone to see. It says, in English, *Who was the other one?*

Rafferty says, "You mean, with—"

"With Elson," Arthit says. Anna nods and pulls from the pad the page she'd begun to write on. She folds it neatly in precise halves and puts it on the coffee table.

"Never saw him before," Rafferty says. "Short, fat, redheaded, red-faced. High blood pressure and a short fuse, great combination. Maybe sixty-five, maybe seventy. Had what would have been a handlebar mustache if it had been on his upper lip instead of coming out of his nose. Dressed like a budget tourist."

Arthit shakes his head. "No idea."

Anna is writing again, and they all wait. Even Pim is watching her with half-concealed curiosity. When Anna holds the pad up, it says, *They wanted to know what the man in the street said to you?*

"Yes. Could you see what it was?"

She shakes her head. *No plosives*, she writes. *No fricatives. No rounded vowels. He was in profile.*

"A plosive is like a *b* or a *p*," Arthit says, with the air of someone parading new knowledge. "A fricative is an *f* or a *v*. They're easy to see."

"And a rounded vowel," Rafferty says, "is a rounded vowel." He thinks for a moment. "No *m*'s either. How about that?"

Impossible to read in profile, Anna writes.

"Major Shen was . . . upset with her," Arthit says. "He swore at her, accused her of lying." Rafferty is surprised at the anger behind those words, and Pim listens with her mouth open. Anna puts a hand on Arthit's wrist as though to stop him, but he's too steamed to slow down. "Even though he knows her, she said he treated her like a . . . like trash off the street."

Anna is writing. She holds up the pad, and it reads *Very bad man.*

"What do you mean, he knows you?"

"When they were kids," Arthit says. "They're both from respectable families without much money, people who all pretty much know each other. Old families, but not powerful." Anna nods. "It's a relatively small circle, all living in Bangkok, all going to the same schools. She knew him when they were ten or eleven. Hell, Noi probably knew him."

Anna has been writing, and they wait until she finishes. She holds up the pad. *Bad even then. He hurt weak kids. He stole things.*

"He's lived in America," Rafferty says, and waits as she writes.

Military school, Anna's upraised pad says.

"He lived there long enough to get dual citizenship," Arthit says. "That's part of his legend, the only Thai cop with dual citizenship." He shakes imaginary water from his fingers as though to say, *Big deal.* "People say he got recruited by the American spooks, and then a couple of years ago he was back here again, sent by the U.S. to help us deal with the problems in the south, although we all know what that really means. It means they want a listening post and an errand boy in the department."

"He did go all glimmery about my potential Muslim connections."

"Sure he did," Arthit says. "For Shen's department 'Muslims' is the answer to every question. Probably looks for an imam under his bed every night."

"Well," Rafferty says, "*Somebody* killed about five thousand people down south."

"I'm not saying the problem isn't real. What I'm saying is that we're using bad people to fight bad people, and you do *not* want to be in the middle of that."

"Yeah, well, that's where I think I am."

Anna is pointing at her pad again. It says, *What did you tell them?*

He hesitates for a moment and sees that she registers the hesitation. "I told them he said 'Helena.'" He remouths it when he sees Anna squinting at him. "As in the city in Montana. And I said couldn't remember the other thing he said to me, which was a woman's name."

"Not smart," Arthit says.

Rafferty allows his irritation to show. "Well, I *couldn't* remember it. But when I woke up this morning, I had it loud and clear. So I guess the question is whether I should call Major Shen and tell him what it is."

"American name?"

"Yes."

"Let's think about it," Arthit says. "About your calling Major Shen. While we try to figure out what's going on."

"Why? Why not just tell him?"

Arthit holds up three fingers, Thai style, beginning with the middle finger and ending with the pinkie. "Three reasons. First, Shen is paranoid enough to believe that you were lying last night—that you actually knew it all along and stalled so you could warn people or clean things up or some other nonsense. Second, you have no idea why the man on the street told you that name—and no, I don't want to know what the name is, and I certainly don't want Anna to know. For all *you* know, it leads to a massive booby trap." He stops and stares at the floor as though he's just heard what he said.

"And third?"

"Third, Shen's people have a lot on their plate right now. They haven't got time for irrelevancies. Maybe if you stay off their radar, just live a normal life, they'll forget about you. Maybe."

"But you don't think they will, do you?"

"No," Arthit says. "I don't."

Pim surprises all of them by saying, "Why am I here? Why did you want me to hear this?"

"Because you live here," Arthit says. "Because it could affect you."

Pim says, "That means you're going to do something? To help Poke?"

"Well," Arthit says, "of course I am."

Pim smiles for the first time since Rafferty arrived and gets up. "I'm going to make more coffee," she says. And she leaves.

"MORE COFFEE" TURNS into an impromptu meal, since no one but Anna has eaten breakfast. Anna has gone into the kitchen to help Pim clean up, leaving Poke feeling guilty that he's not in there, too, rather than sitting with Arthit, who's been waited on by women all his life. Arthit is using Anna's absence to talk about things he's not comfortable sharing with her.

"We've got to look at how Shen's people reacted," he says. "They were there, on the scene, almost before the American bumped into you. It's impossible that they showed up so quickly. He drew them, or someone else in that crowd drew them. And they get a few seconds of film of the dead man's face and share it, and people snap to attention—both here and in America, if Elson and the other guy are any indication. Everybody desperately needs to know what he said."

"A climate of highly evolved uncertainty."

"Okay," Arthit says. "One: They know who the man is, or there wouldn't be all this hand-wringing. Two: It's important enough to keep the footage off TV, and I'll bet there won't be anything in the papers. Three: They're crazy to know what he said. What does that suggest to you?"

"One of two things," Rafferty says. "Either he's someone who wasn't supposed to be here at all, and they have no idea what he was up to and what he was doing here. Or he's somebody they lost."

Arthit says, "Lost," but Rafferty can't tell whether it's a question, a confirmation, or just a repetition.

"Yeah. Like he's a piece that disappeared from the board, and when he suddenly turns up, it catches everybody off guard and they all scurry. Why did he disappear? Where's he been? Why is he back? Who is he working for? And whatever they think he told me, it's important, so even if they're ninety percent sure he just accidentally bumped into me, the ten percent is probably enough to keep them interested."

"There's another issue, too," Arthit says. "Who shot him? If it was Shen's guys, then they were killing someone with information they needed, and apparently they needed it pretty badly. Doesn't make a lot of sense."

"Maybe they didn't need it," Rafferty says. "Maybe what they needed was to make absolutely certain he didn't pass it to anyone else."

There's a silence as they both consider the implications. Pim laughs in the kitchen.

"I'll call in a few favors," Arthit says. "See whether I can learn anything. In the meantime you keep a low profile and don't do anything stupid."

Rafferty says, "You know about hawks?"

"I know a few things about hawks," Arthit says patiently. "What did you have in mind?"

"Hawks have amazing eyesight, but they can only see something when it's moving. As long as I don't move around, just—as you say—live a normal life, stand still . . . well, maybe they won't look at me."

Arthit's expression is not encouraging.

"Works for rabbits," Rafferty says.

"Sooner or later," Arthit says, "most rabbits get eaten."

CLOSING THE DOOR after Poke, Arthit turns to see Anna standing a few feet behind him. She holds up her pad, and he reads: *Will he be careful?*

"It depends," Arthit says.

She shrugs the question.

"On whether he gets mad. He's a good guy, but he gets a little crazy when he's mad. Fortunately, he seems to have miraculous karma, because otherwise he'd have been dead years ago."

She nods. She seems to be waiting for something.

Arthit says, "Well," and can't think of anything to follow it with.

She watches for a moment to make sure he's not going to continue and then starts to write. She lifts the pencil and swivels the pad toward him. It says, *Lunch?*

The word opens an unexpected door in Arthit's day. He hasn't gone anywhere with a woman since Noi's death. He feels his mouth open and close a couple of times, realizes that's exactly the wrong reaction since his mouth is mostly what she looks at. He says, "We just ate breakfast. And I have to work." As she begins to put the pad into her purse, he lays a hand on her arm. "What about dinner?"

5

Hand Puppets

"DON'T MOVE AROUND," Rafferty quickly finds, means don't do anything even remotely interesting.

It means no going across town to check out the laundry that the yellow ticket came from. It means no phoning Cheyenne, Wyoming, and trying to get a listing for Helen Eckersley. It means, if he's going to be really careful, not even trying to find her online. It means don't call Floyd Preece at the *Bangkok Sun*—who got his job because Rafferty gave him the biggest scoop of his career—to find out whether pressure was brought on the paper not to cover the shooting death of a *farang* in Bangkok and, if so, by whom it was brought.

Because, for all Rafferty knows—and Arthit drove the possibility home with some force—he's under surveillance. His cell phone might as well be a radio station.

"Don't move around" even means not going anywhere near the no-name bar where all the obsolete spooks hang out, to see whether anyone can match an identity to his description of Mr. Nose-Hair.

What it *does* mean is, paint the apartment.

So he goes back to the paint store, trying not to check for watchers, trying not to look like a bad actor who knows he's on camera. The cabbie, like every other driver in Bangkok, has the radio tuned to the news, which is monitoring centimeter by centimeter the rise of the water level in the Chao Phraya and the flooding—rapidly spreading some say—in the ancient capital city of Ayutthaya, about forty miles upstream. The rain, the cresting waters, seem real to him in a way that Shen and the redheaded spook don't. By the time he's in the paint store, all he's thinking about is buying, for the second time, the Apricot Cream that Rose picked for the living room—he adds some white this time—and the Urban Decay that Miaow will probably love for all of three weeks before it's replaced in her affections by Advanced-Rot Brown or Swollen-Lip Fuchsia or Infected-Piercing Scarlet. He comes back out into the drizzle, toting the familiar weight of the paint, focusing on the task at hand, and finds himself standing dead center in the splash he'd made when the first cans burst open. It's dappled now by a confused pattern of footprints, a diagram of some impossible dance step. Surrounded by a wash of Apricot Cream, he thinks, *The man died in my arms.* Then he thinks, *And there's nothing I can do about it.* He goes home.

The paint rolls on smoothly, and for a while Rafferty is able to submerge his simmer of uneasiness in the well-being that comes only with mindless work where progress is obvious: *A larger area is Apricot Cream now, and a smaller area is white.* More of life, he tries to convince himself, should be like this.

In between stretches of precariously maintained well-being, he misses Rose and Miaow. He goes back to worrying about Major Shen and worrying more sharply about the Americans. He feels—like an old bruise he can't do anything about except wait for it to fade—a sense of unfulfilled responsibility toward the man who died.

He had used his last breath to tell Rafferty something and his last burst of energy to give him something. What was Rafferty supposed to do about that?

Paint these fucking walls?

WITH PART OF the longest wall in the living room done and the apartment's air gelatinous with the smell of paint, he begins to feel twinges of a new anxiety, a tiny and unpleasant electrical charge fizzling its way up his spinal column. What will he do with himself when he runs out of walls? The hallway immediately presents itself as a solution. It's white, and there's no reason for it *not* to be white, but he hasn't got any white paint. He grabs his wallet and Rose's umbrella and locks the door behind him.

White paint is simple—no mixing needed, so he can buy it anywhere. Also, he can use the errand as a way to take the situation's temperature. Maybe's he's got delusions of grandeur, maybe he's not on anyone's watch-and-report list. He walks a couple of blocks toward a hardware store, doing his best not to look like he's checking reflections in shop windows, scoping the sidewalk, stealing glances at slow-moving cars, which on this stretch of Silom, especially in this weather, is all of them.

A few years earlier—doing research for a book—he'd taken lessons in tailing people and in spotting people who might be tailing him. His instructor had been a possibly-retired, possibly-not-retired CIA guy named Arnold Prettyman. Prettyman had *claimed* he was retired, but the likelihood of any statement's being true declined the moment Arnold said it was. Rafferty always figured Prettyman was on some sort of string, like so many of Bangkok's substantial population of old spooks. Arnold, unfortunately, has gone into Permanent Deep Cover, but his lessons still ring true. Arnold didn't eat it because he failed to pick up a tail.

So Rafferty does as he was taught. He's got an advantage because people aren't out wandering in the rain unless they have to be, so the sidewalks, usually thronged, are thinly populated. He goes into a few stores he doesn't need anything from and buys something cheap and plausible. Once or twice he turns around, the image of a man who should make lists but doesn't, and goes back to a store he passed a minute or two before, looking for scrambling, for stalling, for people suddenly turning to study the traffic. Twice he comes out of a store and does Bangkok's distinctive dodge-the-traffic dance to cross the boulevard and go into a shop on the other side, looking through the new store's window to see whether anyone goes into the shop he just vacated.

The second time someone does. It's a young, short-haired woman wearing reflective aviator shades on a rainy day. He'd seen her when he first hit Silom. She's inside just long enough, he figures, to present some identification, ask a couple of questions, and get a look at the shopkeeper's copy of the receipt. Then she's out again, raising the lapel on her stylish raincoat and talking on a cell phone. She smiles at it, as Thai women often do, but it seems unlikely anyone is being amusing on the other end of the line.

He buys two pairs of athletic socks he actually needs and accepts the cashier's apology for giving him half a pound of change. This is the second shop to give him coins, and his pants are sagging. Wondering whether it's some sort of plot to make it impossible for him to run away, he goes two more shops down to buy a can of eggshell-white flat enamel.

Probably four people, he decides as he treks back home, tugging his pants up every few steps. Maybe five. Pretty expensive. And who has that kind of money? Old Uncle Sam, that's who.

He wants to hold his wife, he wants to see his daughter, he wishes all of this would go away, and he's certain to the soles of his shoes that it won't.

When he opens the apartment door, the smell of the paint rolls out at him with an almost liquid impact. He stands there looking at his handiwork and sees where the coat is uneven, where the join with the ceiling is jagged, where he laid it on thick enough to carve graffiti into the paint.

He discovers that he hates apricot.

Breathing the fumes shallowly, he puts the can of white on the floor in the hallway and goes into his bedroom to drain his pockets of change before his jeans fall off.

All year long he puts his coins into a couple of sixteen-ounce cans that originally held tomato sauce. He has no idea why he ever bought tomato sauce, but the cans work as piggy banks. The arrangement is that he empties all his loose change into the cans every night, and on Miaow's birthday—which they celebrate on Rose's, since no one knows what Miaow's birthday actually is—he and she count it together, and the next day he totes it to the bank and gets the equivalent in paper currency and gives it to her.

She hadn't been particularly eager to count with him on her most recent birthday, but she'd still wanted the bills. He more or less coerced her to join him on the floor, sliding the coins around on the glass-topped table and making countable piles until he announced that she had four hundred thirty baht coming.

Now he dumps handfuls of change on top of the dresser, and as he does it, the anxiety and frustration he feels about his present situation blends into his unhappiness about his relationship with Miaow, and it all becomes a single dark wind blowing on the back of his neck.

Too many of the things he and Miaow used to share with joy are disappearing, being replaced by a kind of weary tolerance on her side and a baffled and apparently useless love on his. More and more it seems to him that she's on the other side of a thick membrane, permeable to her, allowing her to come through for brief visits, but solid as glass to him. It even—it *especially*—repels his feelings.

His pockets empty at last, he looks down at the mountain of coins. It's a sad pile. He opens the drawer and stands there, stupefied.

The tomato cans are empty.

He's almost meditatively thought-free for a long moment, just registering what he sees. One of the cans had been full and the other about one-third full. Now there are ten or fifteen coins in each can. He picks up the nearer can and rattles it, as though that will prove something.

He turns slowly and surveys the room, as if he expects to see an untidy heap of coins glistening in the center of the bed or on the carpet. Or a path of dropped coins leading to the door.

And then he has a truly terrible notion.

He goes to the bed, slides aside the door in the headboard, and opens the safe. There it is, the oilcloth with the Glock wrapped in it. On the previous evening, he'd jabbed it with his finger, checking its weight.

The moment he wraps his hand around it, his heart plummets.

He pulls it out, takes a corner, lets it fall open, and looks down at the big, doubled Ziploc bag that's been jammed full of coins and rubber-banded into a semblance of solidity. His gun is gone.

THINKING IS PREFERABLE to panicking, but harder to do.

It's early for a beer, only about four-thirty. Given the thorniness of the mental list he's making, though, he decides to pretend that his watch and the sun are both slow. He sits at the counter with a Singha sweating in front of him, and he draws a crude map, a diagram of his situation. He writes so much that he knows he can accidentally mislead himself with narrative, working instinctively to create plausibility. But he lacks spatial imagination, so diagrams force him to stick to the facts.

In the first rough draft, he puts himself in the center of the horizontal page, with a line leading to the fallen *farang*. From the *farang* other lines lead, like spokes, to Major Shen, Richard Elson, the red-haired man, Cheyenne, Helen Eckersley. Whoever or whatever Helen Eckersley might actually be.

He looks at it and pushes it aside. The beer waves at him, so he pays it a little attention.

The second draft puts the *farang* in the center and transforms Rafferty into one of a planetary system of satellites that include Shen, the red-haired man, Elson, Cheyenne, and a little black circle for Helen Eckersley. Even as he adds the dry-cleaning shop to the little solar system, he realizes that the image is wildly unbalanced in favor of nations other than Thailand. That reminds him of the Growing Younger Man saying that one of the factors in the current political situation is the pressure that comes from other countries—to contain the Muslim situation, to maintain a profitable peace.

He studies his diagram for a moment, assigning countries of origins to its components. Then he crumples it up and takes another sheet of paper.

America, America, America, America: The third diagram presents a situation in which Thailand is almost marginal, represented by Shen and his grand-opera thugs, whom Rafferty suddenly visualizes as hand puppets. Outnumbering them, overwhelming them, possibly providing the hands that animate them, are the fallen *farang*, Elson, American multinational companies and their governmental and diplomatic shills, Cheyenne, Helen Eckersley, and the kind of organization that mounts a four- or five-person tail. Even Shen has a connecting line to America: years spent there before his return to the kingdom as a sort of semi-indigenous American spook. A hand puppet.

It's a very American diagram.

And in the center of the third diagram—the diagram he thinks is closest to the truth—he places a malicious caricature, all big belly and flaring, tufted nostrils: the red-haired man.

6

Hiding Behind a Woman

MRS. PONGSIRI IS partly made up for her night's work in the bar she either runs or owns; her hair is pulled back and her face powdered ghost white, awaiting the application of a foundation of some kind. There's a snowy little sifting of powder on the tip of her nose and on her red T-shirt, and a new scar, a fine reddish line, on the side of her slender neck. A little less than a year ago, she'd been hurt quite badly when she tried to prevent two knife-wielding men, each of whom was probably double her weight, from breaking up Rafferty and Rose's apartment. Rafferty's been waiting ever since for a change in attitude, a telltale wince that says she's become wary of him, and he's never caught a glimpse of it.

Working in a bar for a few decades is a toughening experience.

Of *course* Rafferty can use her phone, she says, she says, sorry to come to the door looking like a monster in the movies; you know where the phone is, please excuse me while I turn myself into someone not so scary. Have you heard any more about the flooding?

And would he like a glass of water?

Rafferty declines the water and waits until she's gone back into the bathroom. Her apartment is pretty much a duplicate of his, although he has no idea what she's done with the second bedroom—used it as a closet, probably, since she owns an enormous amount of evening wear. The decor is surprisingly unfrilly, open and coolly austere, not too many pieces of furniture to jam up the room. A couple of very good carpets, antique from the look of them, take the curse off the building's generic wall-to-wall. A robed monk of gilded wood sits, hands raised palms together in worship, knees drawn up beside him, all alone on a table in the corner.

The sliding glass door to her balcony is ajar; she's on the down-wind side of the building, and rain has gathered in little pools on the balcony floor, but it's not slanting sharply enough to get into the apartment. She's got the rising river on her side, a thick gray-brown snake a mile or two away, but he can't see anything out of the ordinary, not that he'd recognize anything short of the city's being full of water.

"It's your husband," he says into the phone in Thai when Rose answers.

"I know," she says. She's also speaking Thai. "Who else would call me in the autumn of my life?"

"You wouldn't say that if you'd heard the way they talked about you at the Expat Bar last night."

"Them," she says. "They remember a much younger woman. No, you've frightened off all my admirers."

"You bet I have."

"And a good thing, too. Motherhood being what it is." She sniffles. "I thought I was supposed to call you tomorrow."

"That's right. You were."

"That's so sweet. You couldn't wait to hear my—"

"Actually, there's a problem."

"On your end, too? Good. It doesn't seem fair that I've got Miaow all to myself."

"Well, you're going to have her longer." She doesn't reply, so he says, "What is it this time?"

"She's become a vegan."

"You mean, no meat?"

"Oh, it's not *that* easy," Rose says. "Nothing that's ever *heard* of meat. Nothing that's ever been in the room when the word 'meat' was spoken. Nothing that came in a package made of anything that moves faster than a tree. Did you know that shrimp raised in captivity don't have enough swimming space?"

"Is she serious about it?"

"Loudly serious. My mother starts to look worried hours before dinner."

"Well, take her to the temple and leave her there. They're vegetarians."

"She's a girl, remember? And the monks are much too bloodthirsty for her. They've vegetarians, not vegans. They wear *leather sandals*."

"Boy," Rafferty says. "I'm glad she's your problem, not mine."

"You don't really know a man until you marry him."

Mrs. Pongsiri comes into the room, heading toward the kitchen, a towel fastened over her shoulders with a big rhinestone hair clip. She mimes tilting a glass to her lips, eyebrows raised, and he shakes his head.

"In fairness to Miaow," Rose says, "I'd forgotten how boring it is here. The kids just stare at her with their mouths open and wipe their noses. *Everybody's* nose is running. People's houses leak, and it looks like the rice crop is ruined."

"Well, I'm sorry about that, and we'll send extra money to your parents if the crop fails. I'll even mail you some Kleenex, but I need you to stay away from Bangkok and to keep her with you."

"Oh?" She pauses and sniffles. "Me, too," she says.

"You too, what?"

"Nose running. Are you going to tell me what's going on?"

"I don't really know what's going on, so why don't I tell you what's happened instead?" And he does. He's halfway through when she says, "Arthit's got a girlfriend?"

"I don't know," he says, barely throttling his impatience. "How *would* I know? I'm a man."

"You were there."

"Okay, yeah, I think he does. I think they like each other."

"And she knew Noi? Did you like her?"

"Listen, I know I'm being all insensitive and male in wanting to talk about my problems when—"

"You care about Arthit, too."

"Well, of course I—Look, look. Here's the deal. These people think I know something, whatever it is, and that I might pass it on to someone else. And they don't really give a shit if they flatten a few bystanders. They can haul me in anytime they want—"

"How?"

"And they've got my gun."

A pause on her end. "How did they—"

"I was just about to tell you. They broke into the apartment and took the gun." The pause this time is so long that he says, "Hello?"

"I'm here. I can't believe I'm asking this question, but who was shot with that gun?"

He's been asking himself the same question from the moment the bag of coins hit the bed. "Madame Wing, but nobody's going to find her if they haven't already. Couple of Chu's guys, same thing. But the point is, I have no right to have it in the first place."

"It's not a big crime."

"Rose. This is a country that fired a prime minister because he made an omelet on television."

"No they didn't, they fired him for political—Okay, right, you're right."

"Plus, I'm under surveillance."

"That's why you're not using your own phone. Whose number is this?"

"Mrs. Pongsiri's. I want you to toss your phone and get a new one up there. When you've got it, hang on to it, and I'll figure out how to get you my new number."

"You can call my mother."

"You're not going to be at your mother's. Do you remember where you went after Howard Horner? Don't mention any names. You know the place I mean?"

"Oh, no," she says. "Yes, I remember it. Somewhere *else* where everyone's nose will be running. Why can't we go to . . . I don't know, someplace sunny?"

"Go to that village. Stay there until I get in touch with you."

"I'll go, but I don't know if they'll let us stay."

"They did before."

"I didn't have a twelve- or thirteen-year-old vegan with me before."

"They'll love her."

Rose says nothing.

"Pay them money," Rafferty says.

"And where am I going to get money?"

"Right, good thinking. No ATMs. Call those people's daughter on your new phone and tell her I'll be in touch with her to get your number, then ask her to send a few thousand baht up to you." The place he wants her to go to is the home of the parents of a woman nicknamed Fon. Soon after coming to Bangkok, Rose had taken refuge with Fon's family when she had to hide from one of the psychopaths who batter their way through the bars every now and then.

Rose says, "I *hate* this."

He doesn't know what to say, so he says, "I'm sorry."

"I should have married Walter."

"Who's Walter?"

"The little fat one with the rubbery lips who's lost most of his hair. You've met him three times."

"I don't remember him."

"That's the point," Rose says. "Nobody remembers Walter."

"Oh, well," Rafferty says, "if it's *safety* you want . . ."

"I'll call when everything is set." Rose hangs up, and Rafferty stands there with the phone at his ear, feeling like he's just stepped into thin air.

He puts the phone back on the table, and he's still staring down at it when Mrs. Pongsiri comes back in. She's got a glass of something dark in her hand, and she presses it upon him.

"Here," she says in a tone of command. "You drink." Her face is a masterpiece of the painter's art. It doesn't look natural, and it's obviously not supposed to. What it says is *skill*. What it says is *determination*. The makeup tells a customer everything he could want to know about a bar owner: She's attractive, meticulous, accomplished, in control. The women who work for her are going to laugh at a man's jokes, and in the right places. "Coke," she announces. "American always want Coke."

Rafferty loathes Coke, but he needs something and he accepts it gratefully.

"Problem?" she says. She's speaking English, as she almost always does with him.

"I think so."

"Sometimes we think have problem but not have."

"Maybe you're right," he says. He knocks back about half the Coke, which is room temperature, trying not to make a face.

She gives him a reassuring smile and starts to pad back into the bathroom but stops in midstep and holds up a hand, her face the blank mask of someone who's trying to hear something faint. "You have friend?"

"Jesus," he says. "I hope so."

"I mean now? You have friend come your house now?"

"No," Rafferty says with a sinking feeling.

"You listen," she says.

He listens. She has better ears than he does, but after a couple of moments he hears male voices in the hall.

Mrs. Pongsiri pats the air in his direction with her upraised hand: *Stay there*. She goes to the door and slides aside a little metal disk at eye level and peeks through the opening. Then she turns to him, puts a finger to her lips, and waves him toward her, fingers curved down.

"Special," she whispers, moving aside for him. "Super wide angle."

The lens is practically a fish-eye. Off at the far left, he sees three of them in uniform, as curved as the letter C by the edge of the lens. One of them, wearing a sergeant's chevron on his sleeve, is stooped slightly forward, unlocking the door of Rafferty's apartment. The other two have their weapons unholstered, hanging at their sides.

Rafferty says, without even thinking about it, "Shit."

"You move," Mrs. Pongsiri says, practically shouldering him aside. He looks down at her midnight-black hair, seeing the gleam of silver at the part and catching the scent of her, a scent so heavy she'd probably retain it after a sandblasting. He endures a cold wave of guilt for what she went through for him once before, for the danger she might be in right now. She's tiny, she's old, she's valiant, and she doesn't deserve any of this.

"He go in," she whispers. "This one." She draws the sergeant's chevron on her sleeve with her index finger. "Other two wait. One look in, one look at elevator. Both look stupid."

Rafferty wants to see for himself, but when he puts a hand on

Mrs. Pongsiri's shoulder, she shrugs it off. "He come out now. Talking, talking, door still open. Stand around. Cops so lazy, all same-same. Want everything free, act like big deal, sleep standing up, take money, money, money. Okay," she says. "He close door, they all stand around some more. They put gun away." She looks up at him. "You have trouble."

"Well," Rafferty says, "yes."

She gives him the dubious eye, the eye she's probably trained on a thousand customers who might or might not be deadbeats. Then she shakes her head.

"They waiting for you, yes?"

"Afraid so."

"Okay," she says. She goes into the living room and glances at her reflection in the beveled mirror that hangs over the couch. Yanks at her hair so a few long strands hang untidily over her face and then uses the heel of her right palm to smear her eyebrow makeup on that side, just a little. When she turns back to him, she looks like a woman who drinks away much of her day.

"You stay," she says, and goes into the kitchen.

"What do you mean, I stay?" He's whispering so sharply he's half afraid they can hear him. "What are you—"

"Cops," she says. "I no like. I like you, I like Rose, I like Miaow. Cops no good." She drops into an effortless squat and pulls open the cabinet doors beneath her sink. "*Okay,*" she says again, and it sounds like a mantra of commitment.

"Listen," he says as she pulls out a blue plastic trash bag, about half full. "I can take care of this myself."

"Yes? How?"

"I'm working on that, but you're—"

"When I come back," she says, closing the top of the bag with a knot a mariner would envy, "you tell me how you handle." She hoists the bag to her shoulder, Santa Claus style, and stands.

Rafferty blocks the door. "No way. I am not hiding behind an . . . an, uhh . . ."

"Old?" Mrs. Pongsiri whispers with a sweet smile. "Old woman?"

"No. I mean yes, a woman, I'm not hiding behind a woman."

"Why you marry such a big one, then?" She elbows him out of

the way, and he moves, mostly because he can't imagine getting into a pushing match with someone her size.

But he takes her arm before she reaches the door and says, "No. I'm serious. I don't want you to go out there."

"They still there?" she asks.

He goes to the peephole and looks out. "Yes," he says, and the door hits him in the forehead.

Mrs. Pongsiri pushes it open, and he has no alternative but to move with it, to stay behind it and not to make it obvious that she's in a fight with someone over whether she should go into the hall.

She leaves the door partway open, and Rafferty finds he can see down the hall, standing behind it and using the peephole. Mrs. Pongsiri takes wobbly little steps, shuffling in a way that adds years to her age. "Hello, hello," she calls gaily in Thai as she trundles toward the uniformed men. "They do something wrong?"

"Who?" asks the man who'd gone into the apartment, the sergeant.

"Them," she says, going toward the garbage chute next to the elevator. "The *farang* and his wife."

"You know them?" the sergeant demands.

Mrs. Pongsiri turns and looks at the sergeant long enough to make him fidget. "They live here," she says slowly, as though talking to someone who's challenged. "I live *there*. The elevator is *here*. How could I *not* know them?"

"How well do you know them?"

"I know the wife to say hello, how are you. The little girl doesn't talk to anybody, but she used to be sweet."

"And the man?"

"*Farang*," she says tartly. "I don't like *farang*."

"Why not?"

"Thailand," she says. "Thailand is for Thais. We have too many *farang*."

"You've been here all day?"

"I'm here every day," Mrs. Pongsiri says. "I go out once in a while to pick up a little something."

"Did you see them leave?"

"The wife and the daughter went together, two or three days ago. They went up north, Chiang Mai, I think."

"And the man?"

"Why are you hurrying me? I'm going to tell you." She blows some wispy hair away from her eyes and sways a bit, the picture of someone who's had a couple too many. Then she leans comfortably against the wall and smiles at them.

"So tell me," the sergeant says. "I haven't got the whole day."

"Come to my apartment," she says, and Rafferty starts looking around for a place to hide. "You're a handsome boy, we could have a drink and talk about it."

"No," the sergeant says. One of the men is laughing, and the sergeant starts to smile, too, but tucks it away before it can claim possession of his mouth. "It's very nice of you, but I'm on duty. About the man—"

"Go ahead," says the cop who laughed. "We'll stay here."

"The man who lives here," the sergeant says, looking like he wants to wipe his forehead.

"He left about noon. I came up in the elevator—I'd been down at Foodland, getting some rice and some chilies. I go through a lot of chilies. And I got two new towels also, very nice, yellow but not one of those awful yellows, a soft yellow, like . . . like butter. And they—"

"*The man,*" the sergeant says through his teeth.

"*And they were only forty baht,*" Mrs. Pongsiri says very fast, getting it in before he can interrupt again. "And he came out of the apartment and helped me carry the bags even though he had to put down his suitcase—"

"There's no suitcase missing," the sergeant says. "We went through this place last night, and there was only one suitcase in it, and it's still here."

"It was new," Mrs. Pongsiri says. "Still all shiny. A hard one, with wheels. It looked like the ones they sell at the Silom end of Patpong Two. But those are fakes, and this might have been—"

"Did he say where he was going?"

"Chiang Mai," she said. "With them."

"The . . . uh, the wife—"

"And daughter. Not a very pretty little girl, but smart as a whip. Do you have children?"

"No, I—"

"Of course not, you're practically a child yourself. Are you sure you wouldn't like some—"

The sergeant puts up both hands, palms out. "No, no. But thank you."

"Four days," she says. "He said he'd be back in four days. Said they'd all be back in four days." She brushes her hands together and pushes off from the wall again, stumbling toward the sergeant, who backs against the door. "Whoops," she says. "Well, bye-bye. I live right there," she adds, pointing. "Where that open door is."

Rafferty ducks into the kitchen as she swings the door closed. She goes straight to the mirror in the living room and begins to smooth her hair back, clucking at the state of her makeup. Her eyes find his in the mirror, and she begins to laugh.

Forty minutes later the cops are long gone, and Rafferty comes out of the elevator in the underground garage to find a silver Toyota waiting. The car's rear door is already open, so he's visible for just a couple of seconds. When he's lying on the floor in the back, Mrs. Pongsiri climbs in and rests her high heels on his ribs.

"Careful with that," he says.

"You not hide behind woman," she says as the car jerks into motion, "but hide *under* woman, no problem."

The driver laughs along with her.

7

I Try to Kill Him Many, Many Time

POWER IN THE dark.

Rafferty has always been fascinated by enormous power—power on an imperial scale—exercised in secret. He's spent much of his adult life traveling among the powerless, among people who generally are who they say they are and do what they say they'll do. People who have little and seem unwilling to become someone else in order to have more. In the past decade, this kind of behavior has become regarded by many as naïve and even quaint, behavior that identifies people who haven't figured out the new rules.

Power in the dark seems to Rafferty to be the defining form of evil in the twenty-first century. It's evolved from an occasional governmental tactic into business as usual, as the world's rulers find goals in common—usually economic goals that benefit the rich and strengthen the rulers' hold on power—and pursue them jointly, turning out the lights on the contradictions between what they say and what they do.

Rafferty can remember, hazily, a time in which getting caught in a lie was a career-threatening crisis for a politician, at least in the countries that retain pretensions of democracy. Now there's a whole thesaurus of euphemisms for lying, and it's opened daily.

It's the age of equivocation, the age of the press secretary, the age of entire ministries of spin, the age of collusion and obfuscation, the age when the future is on teleprompter and the script is kept in a vault. Anytime politicians talk about "transparency," Rafferty thinks, voters need to reach for the X-ray glasses.

Whatever compact of honesty was presumed in the past to exist between the rulers and the ruled is fast dwindling in the rearview mirror.

His own country is as bad as any of them and worse than some. Secret enterprise, stringently denied, is the order of the day. Which has created a boom market for people who are skilled at working in the dark.

What it *really* is, it seems to him, is the Age of the Spook.

When, he thinks, the day's agenda seems to have been carved into black stone in a dark room, when you feel as helpless as a penny on a railroad track, and when you glimpse spooks in your peripheral vision, it's time to go talk to some spooks.

IT'S PROBABLY NOT actually called the No-Name Bar, but no name is visible from the sleepy *soi* outside. Just a stretch of stucco the color of cream with dirt stirred into it and a pair of the smoked-glass doors that are ubiquitous among Bangkok's shadier business establishments. The *soi* itself is almost as featureless as the stucco wall: a thin seam of asphalt too narrow for two cars, framed by a sidewalk of tilting, badly set paving stones that are interrupted every now and then by one of those peculiarly Bangkok trees, wizened, largely leaf-free little spindles that look like they'd be more comfortable bent over a walker. Trees that look like they've got a cough.

The bar is just as he remembers it, which is to say it's more cramped than it appears from outside and as dark as a bat's theme park. He has the brief sensation that nothing at all has changed since he was last here, that the people inside have been frozen in place until he breaks the spell by opening the door.

It's a long, narrow room that gives the impression that all the right angles are subtly off. The front doors open directly onto the bar, which looks solid enough to repel a blast from a shotgun. The bar is U-shaped and protrudes into the center of the room like a stuck-out tongue, with two wary-looking bartenders in the center. The patrons all sit on the far side of the bar, facing the door. The rest of the room is occupied by a series of booths along the right wall, the dividers between them projecting out so far that the walkway that leads past them isn't much wider than a single heavyset man. A tiny transparent lightbulb, perhaps twenty watts, hangs like a distant, dying star over each booth.

The booths' occupants are shielded from view by the booth dividers, which are unusually high, about the height of the wall around a toilet cubicle in a public restroom. Rafferty sees only five people at the bar, three sitting on stools spaced well apart and the two working behind it, but there could be twenty more people in the place, enjoying their nice covert drinks as they hatch conspiracies or practice character assassination in smaller groups. He has a feeling the only reason the noise level doesn't drop when he walks in is that there *isn't* a noise level. If people are talking, they're talking in whispers.

Everyone he can see is looking at him.

The no-name is one of two spook bars to which Rafferty was brought by Arnold Prettyman, the putatively retired CIA man who was killed when he turned over the wrong rock while he was working on Rafferty's behalf. Rafferty has no idea whether his accidental role in Prettyman's death is known in this bar, but it very well may be. Information is the currency in the room. This is where the cloak-and-dagger friends and enemies of Arnold's shadowy youth and middle age gather to refight the old battles, from back in the 1960s and '70s, when they were outplotting and shooting at each other. The thawing of the Cold War and the shift of the global stress lines from Southeast Asia to the Middle East stranded a lot of spooks in the jungles where they'd been stationed, and a remarkable number of them rolled downhill to Bangkok.

And now they congregate day after day, night after night, in the no-name bar. It's a deadlier version, Rafferty thinks, of the Expat Bar, but just as sad.

One bartender looks at a customer, gets a minuscule nod, and comes to take Rafferty's order while the other bartender heads for one of the hidden booths. The three customers have swiveled their stools to turn their backs, but Rafferty can feel their eyes in the mirror on the opposing wall.

The bartender lifts his chin in a silent query, as though the sound of his voice is classified, and Rafferty orders yet another Singha beer, one of the big ones. The bartender makes no move to get the drink until Rafferty sees, in the mirror, a hand extend into the narrow aisle beside the booths and make the okay sign. The bartender examines Rafferty again as though he's checking for a hidden weapon or an ulterior motive and then slides open the cooler behind the bar. Rafferty is watching the man's movements when something heavy lands on his shoulder. A hand with a plenteous crop of black hair.

When he looks up, he sees a darkly shadowed chin, divided by a cleft that looks like it was incised with a hatchet. The chin and jaw are the widest parts of the head, which narrows as it rises toward a curly fringe of black hair, parted in the center and brushed over the forehead in very peculiar bangs. The upper lip is so long that Rafferty wonders whether the man can smell his food. Beneath a single solid hedge of eyebrow, a pair of tiny black eyes crowd as close together as a flounder's. The overall effect should be silly, but it's light-years from silly.

"You was friend with Arnold, yes?" The voice is liquid and heavy and saturated with melancholy; it sort of rolls around like mercury. The accent is Boris-and-Natasha Russian, but, like the face, deeply not comic.

"I was, yes." It seems natural to echo the question's structure.

"And Arnold." The hand on Rafferty's shoulder tightens, and the squeezed-together eyes get closer to him. "Arnold is now with the fishes?"

Rafferty shakes his head, not understanding. "I'm sorry—"

"Sleeps," the man says, turning it into "slips." "Arnold, he slips with the fishes?"

"Not unless they buried him at sea," Rafferty says. "Last time I saw him, he was dry."

"But not . . ." the Russian hesitates. "Not feeling good."

"Not feeling much of anything."

The eyes come even closer, and Rafferty smells a great many onions. "You killed him?"

"No," Rafferty says. "Not directly, at least."

"Hah," the man says. It sounds to Rafferty like he's indicating that he'd laugh if someone would only teach him how. The bartender pours half of the beer into a smeared glass and slaps both bottle and glass down on the bar. The noise makes Poke jump. The Russian straightens up and says "Hah" again.

"So," Rafferty says, hoisting the glass, "you knew Arnold."

"Long time, wery long time. Arnold and me . . ." He holds up his index and middle finger, close together, side by side. "Like this, you know?"

"I guess." This isn't the most comfortable news.

The man shakes his head fondly. "I try to kill him many, many time. Once I make honey trap—You know honey trap?"

"With a woman, right?"

"And such a woman." The man claps Rafferty on the shoulder again, and beer slops onto the bar. "Such a woman usually I kip for myself. But Arnold is problem. Arnold always is problem. So I make under bed, Semtex. Bed *wery* old, bend down when somebody sit on it, make two piece metal come together." His hands, palm to palm, are a couple of inches apart. "Make circuit, yes? *Booooom.*" His hands come together and fly apart. They're enormous.

"Boom," Rafferty says, mainly to show he's listening.

"Arnold, always he come elewen o'clock morning." A tap on the crystal of his steel wristwatch. "I put Semtex nine o'clock, when woman is go eat. But she like money too much, bring cook back from restaurant to make jiggy-jig fast before Arnold come. Cook wery fat, sit down . . . *Poh!*"

"'Poh'?" Rafferty says.

"Hah," the man says a third time, with something regretful in it. "Woman wery angry. Get cook—" He mimes brushing pieces of the cook off his sleeves. Then he picks up the bottle in front of Poke, which is still half full, knocks most of it back, does a basso profundo burp, and says, "You come." He turns away. Rafferty drops some bills on the bar and follows.

They pass four of the five booths. In each, three or four men, their faces pasteurized by the gloom, glance up at him with the impatient air of people whose conversation has been interrupted. To the men in the third booth, the Russian says, "You right, Arnold is dead."

One of the men in the booth raises his glass in a toast and says, "Good."

Two men wait in the final booth, the one to which the Russian leads him. Rafferty's eyes are adjusting to the darkness, and as he sits, he sees that one of them affects the ever-stylish Dr. Evil look, with a shaved head, a mustache, a goatee, and a single earring above a pale garment that might be the grandchild of a Mao jacket, while the other is simply part of the scenery, a man with no distinguishing characteristics whatsoever. A written description would read, "Medium everything." Like the man with the cleft chin, these two appear to be in their sixties or early seventies, but preserved in something potent and perhaps poisonous. Rafferty slides in beside Dr. Evil as the man with the Russian accent says, "You buy, yes?" and shouts something to the bartender without waiting for an answer.

"Vladimir," the man says, pointing at himself as he sits. "Pierre," he says, indicating Dr. Evil. "And, um . . ."

"Janos," says the man without any characteristics.

"Always I forget," Vladimir says. "This is why you genius."

Janos nods modestly, and everyone waits, looking at Poke.

"Ummm, Poke," Poke says.

"So this one," Vladimir says, tilting his head at Poke, "who says name is Ummm Poke, he was friend with Arnold. Arnold now he slip with the fishes, but friend who says name is Ummm Poke is here. Friend want something, yes?"

"Yes," Poke says. "And my name really is—"

"Poke," Vladimir says with the weary air of someone who knows much, much better. The bartender appears with a tray on which he has crowded a bottle of Johnnie Walker Black and three glasses, plus another megabottle of Singha, apparently to replace the one Vladimir drank. He slams the whole thing on the table, prompting a startled hiss from the next booth, and shimmers off into the gloom.

"I've got a description of someone," Rafferty says when everyone's glasses are full. "Someone about your age. I need to know whether any of you recognize him and, if you do, who he is."

"This is big job," Vladimir says automatically. "You have money?"

"Sure." Rafferty pulls all the bills from his front pocket and counts them out, with every eye in the booth following his hands. "Eleven thousand three hundred baht," he says. He pushes it into the center of the table and then cups his hands over it and waits.

"We need contract," Vladimir says. "Werbal contract. Ewerybody listen, ewerybody talk. Anybody know anything, we split up even, okay?"

"No," says Janos. "Whoever knows most gets half."

"We can do without you," Vladimir says. "Plenty other guys in here."

"Okay, even," Janos says.

Vladimir says, "Good." He mimes a handshake with each of them without reaching out very far, then takes a hundred-baht note and hands it to Poke. "For taxi," he says, turning it into "texi." "But why you think we maybe know him?"

"He's in your business, he's your generation, and his taste in clothes says he's been in the region for a long time."

Dr. Evil says, in a dry, wispy voice that reminds Rafferty of the dry rustle a T-shirt makes when he pulls it over his head, "Reason is always refreshing."

"He's American," Rafferty says, pocketing the hundred baht. "Maybe sixty-five now, short and thick, with a big gut. Red hair going gray, bright red face."

"You talking before about his clothes," Vladimir says.

"Right. Dresses awful. Jeans and a Hawaiian shirt. Wrinkled. Like a tourist who's spent ten years in a suitcase."

All the spies look at all the other spies. All that's needed for atmosphere, Rafferty thinks, is a ticking clock. The silence stretches out as he tilts his glass back and lowers the beer's level. Dr. Evil starts to open his mouth, but Vladimir shakes his head a quarter of an inch, one time. They look at each other some more.

"What else?" Vladimir says.

"Hair coming out of his nose. If he was Rapunzel, he could lower his nose hair to let the prince climb up."

Vladimir nods sadly and says, "More money."

"Where's the nearest ATM?"

"Around the corner," says Dr. Evil in his frayed voice. "I'll go with you."

Vladimir says immediately, "We all go."

"Nobody goes," Rafferty says. "First you tell me a little more, and if I decide I want you to keep talking, I'll go get the money."

Vladimir says, "You no trust us."

"Sure I do. I just don't want to have to get up if it's not necessary."

Vladimir nods at Dr. Evil, and Dr. Evil says, "Maybe Murphy."

"Maybe?" Rafferty says.

Vladimir fingers the cleft in his chin and looks disappointed. "Please," he says. "You think my name Vladimir? Him, you think his name Janos? This one Pierre? We think your name really Poke?"

"Of course not," Dr. Evil says. "But Murphy, that's what he called himself then. Sometimes Murph."

"Where? When?"

"Wietnam." Vladimir is watching Rafferty's eyes. "American in Wietnam, not always white hat, you know?"

"I know."

Dr. Evil leans in and lowers his rustle of a voice to the point where Rafferty has to strain to hear him. "Murphy was Phoenix." He straightens a bit, watching for a reaction. "You know about Phoenix?"

"Targeting?" Rafferty says. He read something about this years ago. "Targeting . . . targeting what? Collaborators, Vietcong sympathizers?" He knows he's about to hear something he doesn't want to hear.

"Arnold, he know Murphy," Vladimir says sleepily, his eyes half-closed. "Arnold say Murphy hard-core. Wery hard-core."

Dr. Evil says, "To be hard-core in Phoenix is to be very, *very* hard-core."

Silence falls again. The three men gaze at Rafferty as though they're waiting for him to wave his hands and materialize their dinner, and Rafferty says, "Back in a minute." He gets up.

"Thirty thousand," Vladimir says. "Ten, ten, ten."

8

Wery Bad

HE PLUNGES INTO the thickening dusk, the fumes of the beer clouding his head. Part of him wants just to keep going, not return to the dark bar and what he's about to learn. But instead he rounds the nearest corner to make sure he can't be seen from the bar, grabs a huge, anxious breath and blows it out, then pulls his remaining money from the hip pocket of his jeans. He's got forty-seven thousand left of his combined assets, plus a salad of small bills. With a quick glance over his shoulder, he counts out thirty thousand, all in thousand-baht bills. He puts the remainder back in his pocket, then pulls out five thousand more to cover the bar tab they're running up. Heading back to the bar, he wonders where he's going to sleep this evening and what he'll use to pay for it.

He nods at the bartender, who looks straight through him, and moves toward the booth. When he gets there, the three of them are huddled together over the table, all talking at once. They fall silent and sit back as he slides in. He makes a show of reaching into his pocket and counts out the thirty thousand, putting a stack of ten in front of each of them. Janos reaches for his, and Rafferty says, "Ah-ah. Leave them there for now."

Vladimir says, "Okay. I talking, everybody else keeping mouth closed. If I make mistake, Janos, Pierre, you fix." Vladimir puts his hands on the table on either side of the money, palms down, as though preparing for a magic trick, and clears his throat. "The

Phoenix Program," he says. "Some of it wery bad. Murphy maybe the most bad. Ewen some Phoenix guys, they tell boss, no, they not working with him no more."

"How would you know that? Phoenix was military, right?"

"Under CIA," Vladimir says. He touches the side of his beak with a straight index finger, a gesture that's apparently full of meaning that Rafferty doesn't understand. "William Colby, yes? Later head of CIA. Right now," he says, "we have two CIA here, in this bar."

"Maybe you should bring them over," Rafferty says, "and we'll split the money five ways. Six thousand each."

"Or maybe," Vladimir says, "you pay twenty thousand more." He smiles like a man braving pain.

"What do they know that you don't?"

"I was other side," Vladimir says. "Pierre was working with Chinese. Maybe we know more than CIA."

"I'm going to listen," Rafferty says. "And if I feel shorted, I'm going to start peeling bills off the stacks, and then we're going to get the CIA guys."

"You know," Vladimir says. He knocks back half of his drink and picks up the thought. "You know, when you talking, you not learning." He makes the other half of the whiskey disappear and refills the glass. "So. Looking for Wietcong supporters, yes? Problem in Wietnam is, nobody know who is this side, who is other side. Ewerybody Wietnamese, ewerybody have family ewerywhere, have family in north, have family in south. Ewerybody wear black pajama. Gowernment in South wery unpopular. So who is who, yes? Difficult question."

"Okay."

"The Phoenix Program, big project. America think big, always think big. So CIA decide, every month, find secret traitor. How many, Pierre?"

"Eighteen hundred," Dr. Evil says.

"Only eighteen hundred? In the whole south?" Rafferty asks.

"Ewery *month*," Vladimir says, tapping the table with his fingernail on each syllable. "Eighteen hundred ewery month. One year more than twenty thousand."

"And do what with them?" Rafferty asks. He gets a flat look from all three of them, and it makes him feel ten years old.

"Supposed to double some of them," Vladimir says, the tone of his voice making it clear what he thinks of the notion. "They work for Hanoi but supposed to be they work for U.S., but *really* you know they work for Hanoi, ewen if they take U.S. money. U.S. never get one good double in whole war. We have hundreds, you don't have none. You was on wrong side."

"So," Dr. Evil says, with an impatience that suggests he wants to pocket his money, "since they couldn't double them, they took some of them out of the picture."

"I see."

"No." Vladimir is looking at the center of the table, which has nothing on it. "You don't see. Not so nice like shooting. Not 'Hello, you are traitor,' *bang*. Nothing nice at all. Not Murphy. First, have problem, find Wietcong guy. Wietcong spy is name Nguyen, yes? And he live in this willage. Ewerybody in willage is name Nguyen. Have five willage same name. Ewerybody in all of them name Nguyen. So Murphy, he find somebody, maybe working in rice paddy, maybe walking with buffalo. Murphy and three or four ARVN—South Wietnam troop—they beat the guy up, hurt him bad. Then they say, 'You tell us what house is Nguyen or we kill you.' So man say, 'That house, ower there.' Maybe right house, maybe wrong. Maybe house is mother-in-law, maybe somebody guy owe money to. How can Murphy know?"

"Well," Rafferty says, "how could he?"

"He don't care," Vladimir says, waving the question away. "Somebody say, 'This is Nguyen,' okay, no problem. He can play game. He like game. Wait until dark, use makeup and make his face look bad, like dead for long time. Old clothes, many hole. Smell like dead animal. Puts around his neck—" He draws a broad U dangling from his shoulders.

"A necklace."

"Made from these." Vladimir tugs on his right ear. "Two rope full. Like Elizabeth Taylor, but with ear. Ewen ARVN soldier afraid. Murphy go alone into willage, make woices—"

Fighting the image of the ears, Rafferty says, "Woices?"

"Voices," Janos says. Dr. Evil is drumming his fingers on the tabletop; he's heard the story already.

"Many woices. Man woice, lady woice, ghost woice. Talk Wietnamese, talk English. Woice come from ewerywhere."

"Wait a minute, wait a minute."

"Ventriloquism," Dr. Evil says. It's nearly a snap. "This is the most famous part of Murphy's legend. He was the Voice Man."

"I am talking again now?" Vladimir asks from an affronted height.

"All yours," Rafferty says.

"Ewerybody run inside. Dead man in willage, ghost woices, bad smell, ewerybody run. Murphy goes to Nguyen house—maybe, maybe not—and kick open door. Then he kill ewerybody inside. Bababababa." Vladimir mimes a machine pistol with a jerky right hand. "Ffffft," he says, and blows on his finger. "Murphy goes home, makes line through name Nguyen."

"Seventeen hundred ninety-nine to go," Janos says.

"Helicopter," Dr. Evil says.

Vladimir says, "I don't think—"

"Maybe the CIA does," Rafferty says.

"He's just trying to pry a few more baht out of you," Dr. Evil says, leaning in again. "But you really should know all this, since the guy you saw is probably Murphy. Sometimes they don't want to turn Charlie or kill him. They want information. What does the double know? Any operations coming up? Where are the village's weapons hidden? Where are the supply trails? What's the chain of command? Who else should they be talking to?"

"Right."

"And let's say the old electric clips on the scrotum or getting beaten half to death doesn't open the man up."

"Cuts," Vladimir says. He sounds like he's sulking.

"Or cuts. Murphy loves to cut. He was the best America had at making very long, very shallow cuts that hurt forever. Some people who can handle being punched and kicked for days go all jelly inside when somebody takes a knife to their skin."

"Eyes," Vladimir says.

"More of the same," Dr. Evil says, "but worse. One thing

Murphy liked to do was try to frighten villagers out of keeping Charlie's secrets. He loved to cause fear. His favorite trick was to cut off Charlie's eyelids and then haul him into the middle of the village and announce, 'This man closed his eyes to what the Viet-cong is doing here. He closed his eyes when I looked into them to see if he was telling the truth. Now he'll never close his eyes again. Don't close your eyes, or I'll be back.' That was one of the things that made other people in Phoenix refuse to work with him."

"One of many," says Janos.

"Okay, helicopter," Vladimir says, reclaiming center stage. "Wietcong won't talk, yes? Nothing is working. So Murphy send ARVN for somebody, anybody, some farmer or carpenter. Take both men, farmer and Cong guy, up in helicopter, beat both of them up, ask questions, beat up some more. Other man, he don't know shit, don't know nothing, but Murphy still ask question, beat up more and more. And then open door of helicopter and throw other man out. Maybe one hundred, two hundred meters up. Scream all the way down. Take first man and drag him to door. Suddenly he talking. Tell everything, tell about soldiers, guns, wife, children, ewerything."

"So," Janos says, with an undercurrent of satisfaction. "That's Murphy."

Rafferty sits back against the wall between the booths, taking the weight off his spine, and shuts his eyes.

"Enough?" Dr. Evil asks.

"I'm thinking." His throat feels half closed.

"While you thinking," Vladimir says, trying for casual and missing by a wide margin, "Murphy. He is here?"

Rafferty opens his eyes and looks at the man for a long moment as he brings himself back into the room and out of the world Murphy had haunted. When he knows that his voice will be there when he wants it, he says, "You're asking me for information?"

Vladimir winces. Then he nods.

Rafferty says, "One more description."

"After," Vladimir says.

Rafferty says, "First."

Dr. Evil lets out a ribbon of air, his eyes on Vladimir's.

"Sixty-five, maybe a little older," Rafferty says. "Big, six-four or so. Light brown hair, not quite blond, going gray, cut military but longer. Blue eyes, wide, thick nose, maybe broken. Big chin. Fat now, but probably not when you knew him, if you did."

"Could be five hundred people," Vladimir says. "Anything more?"

Rafferty brings back the man's face but can't find anything distinctive. "No."

"My turn," Vladimir says. "Do you know who Murphy is working with?"

He can think of a million reasons not to tell them, but who else is he going to talk to? "You know a Major Shen?"

Vladimir says, in an almost-worshipful tone, "Shit. You are joking?"

"I'll give you that for free. No."

Vladimir taps his fingertips against his lips and says something that sounds like "Yooey, yooey, yooey. You have another question?"

"Where has Murphy been since Vietnam?"

Vladimir says, "This is not enough money for that question."

"It's what I've got."

"Then we trade."

"Okay. Where has Murphy been since Vietnam?"

"Here. Southeast Asia. Not usually Thailand."

"Where, usually?"

Vladimir seems to be weighing the value of the answer. "Other countries in the region. China, too."

"Doing what?"

"Fixing."

"Fixing what?"

"Major Shen," Vladimir says. "Him and Murphy. Working on what?"

"Fixing what?"

"I give you this instead," Vladimir says. He slips two bills off each stack and hands them to Rafferty. "Working on what?"

Rafferty waits, but no one objects to being short-stacked, and if they're willing to lose money, it's unlikely they'll tell him what he needs to know. They're all looking at him. "A guy who was killed yesterday."

Dr. Evil says, "The one who wasn't in the papers." It isn't a question, so Rafferty doesn't volunteer anything.

Rafferty puts one bill back on each stack. "Can you guys get me more information?"

"Not going near Murphy," Vladimir says.

"No. But you must know somebody who knows somebody who—You know." He holds out the remaining bills.

"We do." Janos says, staring at the money.

"Then I'll just top these up," Rafferty says. He looks Vladimir directly in the eyes. "And when one of you gets something or thinks of something, call my cell and leave a message." He writes his number on each of the three bills still in his hand and puts one on top of each stack. "Are we even?"

The men pull the money to them, and Vladimir says, "Until you owe us again."

Rafferty gets up, then leans forward and touches his fingertip to the cleft in Vladimir's chin. "How do you shave in there?"

"Not shaving," Vladimir says. "I hit them with hammer and bite them off inside."

As he opens the door, Rafferty hears Vladimir say, *"Hah."*

9

The Safest Place to Be Is Nowhere

The Diamond Sutra. He forgot the Diamond Sutra, the laundry ticket the dying man slipped into his shirt pocket. It's still in his apartment house, taped above the door leading to the stairs.

He gives the cabbie the address and settles back. He won't know whether he can get in if he doesn't try.

Money is an issue. He's going to have to get some, and it'll have to be right away, in case they put a stop on his cards. He's pretty certain that Shen's outfit could do it with a phone call.

Somebody who could squash you by snapping my fingers, Murphy had said.

Power in the dark.

What scares him most about Murphy is that he's an American and he had official American help, in the person of Elson. That means that Rafferty's Get Out of Jail Free card, the American embassy, is probably off-limits. Not that he'd ever go there; that would mean good-bye to Rose and Miaow and his life here, since the only thing the embassy could do for him, in an extreme situation, is to spirit him out of the country, and that's never been an option.

Still, part of him had been aware that the option was always there, and now it isn't.

Maybe he's reading the situation wrong. Maybe he's caught paranoia from Shen and the trio at the no-name bar, and this whole thing is actually blowing past him, not at him. After all, he really *doesn't* know anything. Maybe by morning he won't be on anybody's mind.

He hangs on to that thought like it's a life preserver until the cabbie makes the turn into Soi Pipat and he sees the red lights strobing—two police cars and a military van pulled up in front of his apartment house. He says to the driver, "Keep going. Change of mind. Take me down to the Indian district."

It's a long haul, and the driver's eyes, flicking to him in the rear-view mirror, don't make it any shorter. He'll remember Rafferty's face. The evening's traffic is in between waves, the business traffic thinning and the night traffic building, and the average speed is probably seven or eight miles per hour. Rafferty's legs are crossed, and his dangling foot bobs up and down mechanically. He stills it, and a minute later it's in motion again. He puts both feet on the floor for the remainder of the ride.

When he gets there, he pays the driver and hurries along the maze of dim alleys. The fragrance of spices and the tang of grilling meat hang heavy in the air. Along the right side of the fifth or sixth alley he enters, he sees a line of portable booths selling stolen cell phones. He checks his money and bargains back and forth from one shop to another until he buys the cheapest one on sale.

He moves on a few yards and uses the phone to call a policeman named Anand, one of the few cops Arthit trusts. When Anand answers, Rafferty asks him to go to Arthit's house and lend Arthit his phone, so Arthit can call the new cell number. Then he closes the new phone and waits, pacing the alleyways for almost half an hour, drawing some odd attention.

In fact, it's *very* odd attention. He can understand people looking at him the third time he goes by, but a few of them aren't just looking, they're staring. Two men in particular watch him pass, talking to each other in an energetic fashion.

After fifty very long minutes, the phone rings. Rafferty grabs it, ignores the person who is peering at him, and says, "Hello."

"Don't say anything," Arthit says. "If you don't have cash, get some immediately, because this is the last time you'll be able to use a card for a while. If they haven't been cut off already, I mean. Then go someplace no one will look for you and stay there. Stay off the street, stay out of restaurants."

"Why?"

"They aired the footage tonight, you and the other man, on three stations. The other man's face was blurred out, but the cameraman did a very nice zoom on you as you called for help, and they froze it there. You're famous."

"People are looking at me right now."

"Smile at them and get out of there, without hurrying. Get as far away as you can, as inconspicuously as you can. Taxis should be safe. For most drivers the shift hasn't changed since about four, and the clip aired at six-thirty. Get a cab, get money, and go someplace private. I'll call this number in three or four hours to see where you are."

"Got it." He's most of the way out of the warren of shops, holding the phone with two hands to mask the lower part of his face.

"Here's what's happening," Arthit says. "We just got an alert with your face, taken from the video, on it. The man who was killed yesterday—Warren Alfred Campbell, it says his name was—was shot three times. I doubt that's a real name, because they went to all that trouble to blur his face. The bullet that killed him was a through-and-through, nothing left for forensics to look at. But there were two other slugs in him, and they're saying they came out of your gun. Poke, the whole world is going to be looking for you."

He grabs a cab, no eyes in the mirror this time, and visits two ATMs within five minutes. One card yields forty thousand, one twenty-five thousand. He goes to a third machine, a few miles in the opposite direction, and uses the debit card for an emergency account he keeps in Miaow's name. It cheerfully gives him another twenty-five thousand. He thinks about emptying it, decides it might attract attention to the account and therefore to Miaow, and leaves thirty-something thousand in it.

His pockets bulging, he flags another cab and doubles back to the Khao San area, full of white foreigners, about a kilometer from backpacker central. He gets out a couple of blocks from his destination, walks in the wrong direction until the cab turns a corner, and then jogs to a short-time hotel where he can pay with cash and they won't ask for a passport.

The room is barely twelve feet to a side and painted a dirty mint green that his newly developed painter's eye automatically disdains. Two narrow beds claim most of the space. There's a built-in table poking out of the wall between them and a corroded aluminum lawn chair with nylon webbing at the foot of one bed. Cockroaches scramble when he opens the door of the plywood armoire that serves as a closet.

The first thing he does—after closing the armoire door so the bug party can resume—is collapse on the bed nearer to the door. For a long time, perhaps thirty or forty minutes, he lies on his back, his arm thrown across his eyes, partly to blot out the fluorescents and partly because the weight is somehow comforting.

His heart is pounding, and it's not because of the short jog. He's feeling waves of something so close to panic that it's not worth calling it anything else—black, gelid waves that climb his spine and squeeze his heart and make his skin prickle with sweat. When he finally turns on his side, the pillow is damp. He spends another ten minutes with his knees drawn up to lessen the tension in his gut, his arms wrapped around the dank pillow. His eyes are open and unfocused, all his attention fixed on the scenarios he's running in his head, one bad ending after another.

Things to do: one, two, three, *no good*. One, two, three, four, *no good*. Blind alleys everywhere.

He realizes he has one thing going for him: his mother's Asian genes.

In the bluish light of the tiny, damp bathroom, its grouting black with mold, he looks at himself in the peeling mirror. The hotel's sole gestures in the direction of amenities are a paper-thin sliver of soap in a plastic sleeve and a black plastic comb in a cellophane envelope. Experimentally, he wets his hair and uses the comb to part it in the middle and to bring it forward over his forehead on either side of the part, a fading hairstyle once favored by about 90 percent of young Thai men. His hair is shorter on the left because of the paint he cut away, but even given that, the new hairstyle helps a little. His black Asian hair won't draw anyone's attention, and it's a natural match with his smooth features and black eyes, heavily influenced by his mother's Filipina blood. At a glance, from a distance, he could pass for Thai.

Makeup, he thinks. He can darken his skin. The city is jammed with dark-skinned people at the moment, in from the countryside to get away from the flooding up-country. Tens of thousands of them.

Color is a dividing line here, as in so many other places. There are skin tones that make a person almost invisible. And he's been described as a *farang*. People won't be looking at a dark-skinned man, especially with this see-it-everywhere hair.

He can get makeup, he thinks, without even having to go into a store. It's not much—different hair, a new skin tone. But it lifts his spirits. He's *doing* something. He pulls out his cell phone and scrolls through his phone book.

"Hello?" says Mrs. Shin, Miaow's drama teacher.

"Mrs. Shin, this is Poke Rafferty. How are you?"

"I'm fine. Is something wrong with Mia?"

"No, she's okay, better than okay. Listen, I'm in a jam. Have you watched television tonight?"

"I never watch television."

"Well, you'll probably see it tomorrow in the paper. It's a big story, and it's bad, and I'm in the middle of it. I have to ask you to take my word that the whole thing is a setup."

"What whole thing?"

"Do you trust me?"

A pause, and then she says, "I've seen how you are with Mia."

"Good. Then I need you to trust me that what you'll hear tomorrow is a lie, and before you hear about it, I need you to go to the school and get some theatrical makeup. Dark, like a heavy tan."

"Foundation, you mean."

"Whatever it's called. Not for Othello but for—I don't know—Caliban. The stuff the kid who played Caliban wore. A couple of tubes."

"I can do that. You're really not going to tell me what this is about?"

"You'll know soon enough. It's bad, but it's not true. And

Miaow—Mia—is safe, and so is Rose. When you get the makeup, I need you to leave it in the bushes up in that planter to the right of the door to your apartment house. I'll pick it up later tonight."

"How cloak-and-dagger."

"I'll tell you all about it when I can."

"Give me an hour," Mrs. Shin says.

"When you need something done," Rafferty says, "Call a Korean."

HIS NEXT CALL is to one of the first friends he made in Bangkok, Dr. Ratt. Dr. Ratt, whose name is a shorter, modernized version of one with ancient royal connections, has founded a small empire by putting uniformed doctors and nurses into automobiles and keeping five or six cars on the move at all times, thereby defeating Bangkok's epic traffic by ensuring that medical help is usually in the neighborhood. They're good enough friends that Dr. Ratt listens without questions, although he must have dozens. Half an hour later, six blocks from his hotel and still waiting for Arthit's call, Rafferty climbs into the backseat of a Toyota Corolla with a doctor and a nurse, in full official regalia, sitting in front. They nod hello but ask him no questions.

After a stop to put three stitches in a patient, they drop him two corners from Mrs. Shin's apartment and circle the block while he cuts across a couple of *sois* to get to the building, where he reaches into the bushes and comes out with a brown paper bag. Then they return him to the place where they picked him up. He hikes back to the hotel, calls Dr. Ratt, and arranges to be picked up by another team at 7:00 A.M.

The safest place to be, he figures, is nowhere, and what could be more nowhere than the backseat of a car rolling through Bangkok at random?

Just another dark-skinned guy idling along in the back of a car. While he figures out how to live through all this. Whatever *this* is.

Part Two
EIGHT STORIES DOWN

10

Up Against the Night

FOR FIVE ENDLESS days, Rafferty sees the world through the wet windows of a succession of heavily air-conditioned Toyota Corollas, saying good-bye to each weary doctor-nurse team as they clamber out after an eight-hour shift and hello to the bright, fresh ones getting in. Dr. Ratt once told him that the doctors who drive his cars have all had what he described as "a little trouble" in their careers, or else they'd be working in some nice clean hospital that doesn't go anywhere instead of driving around Bangkok all day. If they get fired from this job, they'll be pulling the graveyard shift in some twenty-four-hour VD clinic. And they've apparently been told that any loose lips about having Rafferty in the car *will* get them fired. There's a conspicuous lack of curiosity.

He gets up before it's light outside and spreads Mrs. Shin's dark gel over his face and ears and the back of his neck. Last, he does the backs of his hands. He learns accidentally that if the tiny cake of soap supplied by his fifth-rate hotels sits in a little water overnight, it produces a gelatinous mass that he can spread on his comb. Applied to damp hair, it makes it even darker and holds it in place for hours. Dark-skinned, black-haired, center-parted, he walks the four or five blocks to the pickup point and gets into the first of the day's cars. He's passed from one team to another until the shift that ends at midnight drops him a few blocks away from the designated depressive fleabag of the evening. The routine has a deadening sameness to it, but still each day has some event to distinguish it.

On day one, Arthit redefines good fortune.

"You're in luck," Arthit says on Anand's cell phone. "The only decent picture they have is the one from your book."

"*Looking for Trouble in Thailand?*"

"That's the one."

"Why am I in luck? That's a pretty good picture."

"Every copy in Bangkok is apparently a bootleg from a photocopy. The contrast is so high that you could be anybody."

"They're not using the picture of me with Campbell, or whatever his name is, the one from the video? I guess they still don't want anyone to see his face."

"You're in three-quarters in the video," Arthit says. "Authority figures like full-face."

"And I'm not officially a suspect?"

"Not *officially*, no. But it's kind of hard not to connect the dots. The bullets the coroner pulled out of Mr. Campbell were supposedly fired by your gun, and the police want to talk to you. It doesn't sound like they want to name you *Farang* of the Year."

"What do they think they'll get out of this? Why would they take my gun and fire a couple of shots into a dead man?"

"I can think of two things," Arthit says. "First, they've got you hog-tied if they catch you and demand to know what the dead man said. Tell the truth, the line will be, and they'll make it all go away. Stonewall and you're in prison for the rest of your life, which probably actually means dead, since they won't want you talking to anyone else. So that's one thing: to force you to level with them."

"I did level with them."

"Yeah, well. Then there's the other reason. The country had problems, both political and religious, even before the flooding started. It's possible the government won't be allowed to serve its full term. It could get yanked if Bangkok floods badly, although this group had nothing to do with decades of bad or nonexistent flood planning. But even if we don't get wet, there's the situation in the south. We've got disorganized jihad going on down there, or maybe it's *organized* jihad and we're just clueless about it. And now a foreigner has been murdered, on the fringes of a demonstration over the violence down there. For the image of the country, not to mention the need to protect their own asses, Shen's guys need to solve that crime, even if one of them committed it himself. You're one way to solve it, and a way with no political or religious implications, since you're *farang*."

"Yup," Rafferty says. "I guess you could say I'm in luck." It's not time yet for him to meet the car, so he's gazing through the window of his hotel room, which looks onto a narrow, filthy alley much favored by rats. Sure enough, he sees a big one strolling right down the middle, ignoring the rain, as though it were in his own driveway. Poke envies it. "What would you do in my position?"

Arthit sighs into the mouthpiece. "I've been thinking about that for days. I have nothing that might make a real difference, and my instinct is that you shouldn't do anything at all until we've got a better idea. Do your rabbit thing. Keep still and stay out of their line of vision."

"So if you were me, you wouldn't go in and try to explain. You know, confront the problem head-on and all that."

"No," Arthit says. "If I could get my list of alternative courses of action up to ninety or a hundred, that would still be the one on the bottom."

After this conversation Arthit stops calling for a few days, which is fine with Rafferty; he's already as depressed as he can be without losing his ability to think straight.

On day two, waiting in the backseat while the doctor and nurse are tending to someone inside a fancy condominium, he calls Rose's new phone with his own new phone, just to hear the voice of someone who cares about him.

He says, "I'm lonely."

"I could send you Miaow. There are worse things than being lonely. What's going on down there?"

"I'm being nowhere. Riding around in cars all day and sleeping in boom-boom hotels at night. You'd like my new hairstyle."

"We're sleeping on folded clothes, half an inch thick. Oh, forget it, I'm sorry. I have no business whining to you about anything. Even Miaow's worried, during the brief moments when she's not feeling personally inconvenienced by the weather."

"Well, worry about me," he says. "Someone should."

"I do. And I love you. We're taking care of ourselves, we're fine. Forget about us. You just go be nowhere and work your way out of this. Whoops, I have to hang up—it's my turn for the shower." She hangs up.

Rafferty says, "You're the only person in Thailand who wants to get wet," but he's talking to dead air. He puts the phone down and sees a streak of light skin on the back of his hands. He's got to be on guard against sweating or brushing his hands against things. He rubs at the hand until the streak is smoothed out, then leans across the front seat and tilts the rearview mirror until he can see himself. He looks okay except for the end of his nose, which is a little pinkish. With the tips of two fingers, he tries to cover the pink spot, but the gel doesn't want to spread, so he licks his fingertips. The moisture does the job. He does the best he can to check his ears and the back of his neck, but it isn't much.

Makeup, he discovers, is more complicated than men think it is.

On day three he realizes that Bangkok is a city of fathers and daughters. He sees them everywhere, at all ages and in all sizes: fathers with infants they hold as though they've just been handed a soap bubble; fathers with toddlers, their hand clamped inside their father's hand as they claim the sidewalk, step by step; fathers with preteens, following obediently three steps behind their daughters in case school friends should happen to see them; fathers with the grim, desperate pride of someone who's sired a beauty and, unfortunately for his peace of mind, remembers what he was like when he was a boy.

He wonders for a moment how the men would look if he could see them through their daughters' eyes, then immediately banishes the notion. He gets glimpses of himself, occasionally, reflected in Miaow's eyes, and what he thinks he sees is the ruin of a statue placed on a pedestal that was too high for it, just chunks of anatomical rubble on a stone platform with recognizable bits and pieces—an eye, a smile, a strong arm—capable of provoking mild affection and somewhat more intense irritation.

And he asks himself, looking at the fathers, how anyone has the courage to embark on that voyage. To accept a child, not knowing the first thing about how much she can be shaped and how much of her character is set in genetic stone, to make the breathtaking assumption that you will always know what's best for her and are competent to guide her toward it.

Sheer hubris.

Miaow came to him and Rose preshaped by her years on the sidewalk, and in some ways that was probably an advantage. She had learned, within limits, what was necessary to her and what was superfluous, what she would put up with and what she wouldn't. He hadn't known then—he didn't know now, for that matter—whether she'd been abused sexually during those five or six wild-child years. But then, he thinks, every infant comes into the world trailing an infinite cloud of mystery behind it: where she came from, where she's going, who she really is, what she can do, what she can learn, whether she'll bring joy or heartbreak, whether there is darkness at her core. What landslide of karma has rolled her into this life.

Miaow is twelve or thirteen now. When they took her in, she was seven or eight. In those five years, he's tried every parenting approach he can, with little success, he thinks, before abandoning all of them in favor of two governing principles. First, to do no harm. Second, to place no limit on the amount of love he is willing to give. The ideas made sense when they came to him, but in the past year he's begun to wonder whether there's a third principle—the most *important* principle—he hasn't thought of. Or maybe Rose was right when she said if he wanted something that wouldn't change, he should have bought a table.

"Do you have children?" he asks the doctor behind the wheel and the nurse in the passenger seat.

The doctor grunts a negative, but the nurse says, "Four."

"How old?"

"The oldest is twenty-seven. The youngest is nineteen."

"Did you have principles? About how to raise them, I mean?"

"Yes. Keep them from killing themselves and don't try to turn them into me."

Rafferty says, "Those are good."

The doctor says, "My mother told me before she died that the biggest problem she had with my sisters and me was figuring out whether we had a compass. Two of us always knew what we wanted, my youngest sister and I. The middle kid was a rainbow, different every day."

"What did your mother do?"

"She gave up. She said it was the most valuable lesson she ever learned, giving up. Our middle sister is the happiest of us all."

"I guess in the end," Rafferty says, "happiness is the only thing that matters."

The nurse says, "That and making sure they live through their teens."

ON DAY FOUR, two things happen. First, he allows himself to admit how much he hates fast food. When the on-duty doctor and nurse take a meal break, they usually choose an American chain because that's the fastest, and he winds up with something to go, which he eats out of a bag, sitting on the backseat. His clothes stink of fried food. He's gaining weight. His knees and hips hurt from being seated for so long. He's perpetually damp.

He hates all of it. He will never eat another cheeseburger.

Second, he learns he can handle the sidewalk. At 4:00 P.M., in the open-air market mecca of Pratunam, Dr. Ratt pulls the car into a nearby *soi* and Rafferty ventures out into the crowds for a jittery experimental jaunt. The clouds have parted to allow the sun to drop by for a few hours, and it's remarkably bright, as though it's putting out extra effort to make up for a long absence. What's more, it seems brightest wherever he is. He has the sensation that a spotlight is trained on him, tracking him wherever he goes, as if he were the lead actor in a musical. He doesn't want to hold anyone's gaze for a beat too long, but he doesn't want to release it and miss the spark of recognition either. One girl of eighteen or nineteen locks her eyes on his as his heart rate skyrockets, but then she breaks into a wide Thai smile, lowering her head as she passes, leaving him gasping in her wake. He's powerless not to turn and make sure he's all right, and when he does, he catches her looking back at him. She sticks out her lower lip in a pout, shrugs, and goes on her way.

He spends more than an hour being a pedestrian without any alarms going off. He draws an occasional glance because of his height, but the Thais are growing taller at an extraordinary rate. As far as he can tell, no one finds him suspicious or familiar-looking or even interesting. He experiments with retracting his aura as he walks, just keeping his gaze on the middle distance and reeling in his energy. It occurs to him that this is a skill that Janos, the indescribable man at the no-name Bar, has mastered.

When he goes back to the *soi*, the car is gone. They're undoubtedly answering a radio call. He kneels beside a parked car long enough to check the makeup, which looks passable, then he heads for a real test. Moving with the crowd, he tries his hand with a couple of the vendors under the tarps, still bellied down beneath the weight of collected rain. Hoping that in the press of shoppers no one will actually pay attention to him, he buys a medium-size shoulder bag in artificial leather that's *so* artificial it's hard to tell what it's pretending to be. Into it, over the course of stops at several booths, he packs four T-shirts, two long-sleeved shirts, one pair of wash-and-wear slacks to alternate with his jeans, six pairs of socks, a travel bottle of liquid laundry detergent, and a small selection of essential toiletries, including some hair oil. He also buys a big pair of sunglasses, wondering why he hadn't thought of them earlier.

Finally he chooses a woman's compact, which is the nearest he can come to a pocket mirror. The vendor who sells it to him gives him an idle glance and says to him, in Thai, that she hopes his girlfriend will like it.

After a moment of panic, he answers her in English, with a sort of comic-hall Indian accent that used to make Miaow laugh. She nods and turns to the next customer. To test his new voice, he buys a decent cake of soap and two more disposable razors and strikes up a conversation, sounding to himself like a Taj Mahal tour guide. But the man in the booth answers pleasantly enough. Rafferty is apparently plausible as a sort of pan–Southeast Asian/Indian hybrid. It's not going to hold up for a second if the police stop him, but that's not what it's for; it's to keep the curious eye from pausing on him long enough for next steps to be taken.

On day five he makes his decision.

Dr. Ratt himself is at the wheel, with his wife and nurse, Nui, sitting regally beside him in one of her many custom-made silk uniforms. At Rafferty's request, Dr. Ratt drives him down the street where it all began, cruising past the splash of color as Poke tries to visualize where the crowd came from, where Campbell, if that's really the dead man's name, might have joined it, and why he might have been in that neighborhood.

How an American ex-soldier got caught up in a riot over the problems in the south. A bunch of farmers and villagers and people trying to run businesses, banding together and coming up to the capital as a group to protest the lack of effective action by the government as Buddhists continue to be shot, bombed, run over, and beheaded on an almost-weekly basis.

As though she's reading his thoughts, Nui, without turning her head, says, "How long can you keep this up?"

"As long as I have to, or as long as it takes them to figure it out."

Nui wiggles a little, seeking the next degree of comfort on her infinite scale, but doesn't honor his remark with a response. Her conversation is peppered with silences, usually indicating disapproval.

"To figure what out?" Dr. Ratt says, probably mostly to be polite.

"Either that they actually don't want to talk to me because the problem has gone away or that I'm the one behind this stupid disguise and they catch me."

"It seems to me," Nui says, "that you're taking a very passive course of action."

"That's occurred to me, too. But it feels like I'm up against the night, you know what I mean? This thing is so unfocused, its edges are so blurred, that I feel like I'm one person who's been ordered to keep it from getting dark."

"Or this rain," Dr. Ratt says. "Same thing. Nowhere to get hold of it."

"Really," Nui says.

They drive in silence for a moment, and then Dr. Ratt says, "When she says 'Really'—"

"I know," Rafferty says.

"It's not big and unfocused at all," Nui says, "even if you think you're up against the whole War on Terror. Actually, the entire thing comes down to three people, doesn't it? Whatever is going on, it's being pointed at you by three people."

"I suppose it is."

"This Thai secret policeman with the Hollywood uniform, the little redheaded *farang,* and that man from the American Secret Service."

"I don't think he's really involved."

"He was in that room, looking at you," Dr. Ratt says.

"A while ago he wrote some reports that named me," Rafferty says. "When he broke the North Korean counterfeit-money ring. My name is linked to his in some government computer. When Shen's people ran my name through the database after Campbell, or whatever his name is, got killed, Elson's came up, too. My guess is he was drafted into that observation room."

"Maybe he's where you begin," Nui says.

"Maybe he is," Rafferty says. "And maybe there's something to being passive for a while. At least until I can see three or four moves ahead. That's the rabbit strategy."

"Rabbits," Nui says, "usually get—"

Rafferty says, "Everybody tells me that."

Nui says, "You need to choose one of them and figure out how to make a move."

"Which one?"

This time she does turn around. "The most dangerous one," she says.

11

The Missing Sea

THE HOUSE STILL smells of Anna's perfume.

Pim opens the back door to let in some air and pads through the empty rooms to the front, which she also opens. For good measure she raises the windows in the living room. It's drizzling and cool, but at least it doesn't smell like *her* out there.

Gasoline and exhaust and wet dirt smell good to her.

She goes slowly through the dining room, not looking at the remains of the breakfast. It was bad enough to have to cook it and serve it; now she's supposed to clean it up, too. In the kitchen she stops at the table where she eats alone while *they* sit together, out in the dining room, and she picks up her half-drained mug of tea. After looking down into it for a few moments, she holds it over the center of the table and slowly tilts it, soaking the stack of paper napkins. Then she straightens the mug and repositions it over a full sugar bowl and pours the remaining tea into the bowl until it overflows.

When the mug is empty, she lets her arm hang loosely and stands there, looking at nothing, with the mug dangling from her finger. She glances down at it, goes to the back door, and throws the mug halfway across the yard, and then she sits down in the doorway and lets out a sigh she doesn't even hear. The flowers she's planted and nature has watered so plentifully are in full bloom, so gaily and brightly that it looks like sarcasm.

She's roughly scrubbing her cheek with the heel of her hand and sniffling before she consciously identifies the tickle of a tear.

He didn't need her help to stop drinking, and he certainly didn't need her to talk to. And he hadn't seemed any happier either, until . . . well, she thinks, swallowing—until a few days ago. When he met Anna. Before she came to the door, all he needed was food when he was hungry, and he did even that himself at first, forgetting she was in the house and then guiltily adding more rice or vegetables to whatever was on the stove to try to make her think he'd been cooking for both of them.

She has no business crying about any of this. He's just someone to work for—that's all he ever was—just someone to pay her money she can send home to her parents. One more sad, worn-down middle-class man, like the ones she'd gone to the hotels with, men who were baffled by their lives, who looked at them as though they were rooms they didn't remember having entered, who clung to some detail—a way of combing the hair, a mustache, a shirt far too young for them—something that made them feel that they still had possibilities. When it was obvious at first glance to any woman that it was all behind them and the only thing they had to look forward to was more, or rather less, of the same.

That's who she'd thought he was, one of *those*, until she began to understand the vastness of the hole his wife's death had blown in his life.

The missing sea, she had thought one night. She'd been in bed and on the verge of sleep, but the thought had pulled her up into a sitting position. What missing sea? And what about it? A picture, a picture in a book she'd seen at Poke and Rose's apartment: an enormous desert somewhere in the American West, ringed with spiky mountains, the farthest of them so distant they were like solid haze. The printing below the picture, Rose had told her, said that the desert was once the bottom of an inland sea, now gone for millions of years. And immediately it seemed to Pim that that emptiness was like the hole in Arthit's life, that he had filled it with love, and that all of it was gone now, evaporated into nothing. She saw him as a man who was capable of an enormous amount of love.

From that point on, she began to see his truthfulness, his decency, his fairness. The size of his heart. And then she was lost.

Idiot.

There are weeds among the flowers. All she has to do is turn her back for a minute and things go to pieces. She gets up with a grunt, makes a detour through the wet grass to pick up the cup, and at the border to the garden she sinks into a crouch and begins list-lessly to pull weeds. Some of her happiest hours here were spent crouching among these flowers as though she were back in the village. She'd believed that the flowers would . . .

She's been a fool, she thinks, tossing an armful of weeds out of the flower bed. She's too ugly, she's too young, she's too unedu-cated, she's a street girl. She could stay with him for years, take care of him for years, and she'd still be that dumpy little onetime whore who sweeps up and makes the beds.

She throws the weeds into the trash can and hangs the cultiva-tor on the nail driven into the weathered board where it always hangs. When she turns toward the door, there's a man standing there looking out at her.

She's inhaling when she sees him, and she produces an anguished little squeak and a spasm of coughing. The man holds up both hands, as though to show they're empty, and smiles at her.

"Please," he says, "please don't be frightened. I didn't mean to startle you."

"Why are you—" She wraps her fist around the handle on the mug, which is the only weapon she has. "Why . . . why are you in there? I mean, what are you—"

"I'm sorry," he says. He smiles at her again, and she sees this time what a nice smile it is. "I saw the door open in front. I called out a few times, but no one answered, and I was afraid something might be wrong, so I . . . well, I came in. I was hoping to talk to Arthit."

"Does he know you?"

"Does he—Of course he knows me. We work together." He shakes his head and steps back. "Look, I'm going to back up, and you can come in out of that wet. Wouldn't that be better, Pim?"

Pim doesn't take a step. "You know my name?"

The smile again, a wall of white teeth. "Well, of course I do. Arthit talks about you all the time. Come on, come on in."

"He does?" Pim asks. As he retreats, she goes up the steps

slowly, gripping the mug like a stone. At the top step, she pauses, still not coming into the kitchen.

"Oh, my, look at this," the man says, eyeing the dripping table. He's taller than most Thais, handsome almost in a movie-star way, with his hair combed straight back from a widow's peak as though to accentuate perfect cheekbones. The man takes a dishrag from where it hangs over the faucet in the sink. "Arthit says that you've made this place a home again." He turns to the table and begins to mop it.

"I'll do that," Pim says quickly. She puts the mug on the counter and starts toward him.

"Do you have paper towels?" he asks, turning toward her. "I'll use this on the table, and you can put some paper towels on the floor to soak up the—What is it? Tea?"

"The cup slipped," Pim says. Her eyes drop to the brimming sugar bowl. "Twice."

"Life is a chain of accidents," the man says. "I guess I just missed Arthit."

"Did he really say that?"

"What?" He's wringing the dish towel into the sink.

"That I—Never mind."

"Oh, that. Of course he did. Pim this, Pim that. He's been talking about you ever since he was smart enough to realize what he needed."

"What was that?" Pim asks, and she can barely hear her own voice. "That he needed, I mean."

"Someone like you, obviously. Someone with a good, generous heart who could bring his spirit back to him."

"Did he . . . ?"

"Say that? Yes. I'm telling you, we've talked about you a dozen times. More than a dozen."

Pim says, "Oh," and pulls a fat roll of paper towels from under the sink.

The man is mopping the underside of the table to stop the dripping. "How long ago did he leave?"

Pim stops unrolling the towels, thinking. "Fifteen minutes? Twenty?"

"Well, how far can he get in this traffic in fifteen minutes? He must have forgotten I was coming. Tell you what, you get the tea off the floor and I'll phone him. Maybe he can come back."

"Okay." She drops a wad of towels onto the puddle in the floor and moves it around with her foot as he turns away and dials his cell phone, ambling toward the dining room as though he's been here a thousand times. When the papers underfoot are sodden, she drops another handful, listening.

"No good," the man calls to her from the other room. "Voice mail." He lowers his voice to a conversational level. "Arthit, this is Prem. I'm at your house, talking to Pim. She's even prettier than you said. I have the information and the charts you wanted. I'll stay here a few minutes, and if I don't hear from you, I'll just go over to the station."

He reappears in the doorway and says, "Well, let's finish this up."

"Charts?" Pim asks.

"Yes, some things he asked for last night. You know, he's worried about Poke."

"Uh," Pim says. "He worries about a lot of things."

"You must be worried about him, too. That's a good technique, just pushing the towels around with your foot like that."

"I was . . . I was thinking." Her face is flaming as she drops to her knees and puts more towels down.

"I don't blame you. We've all got a lot to think about these days. Anyway, maybe Arthit will come back and you'll hear us talking, so—Oh, I don't know why I should keep secrets from you. He asked me to see if I could get a list of the cheap hotels our patrolmen were being sent to watch, and I got it and made a sort of chart of them. Just to make it easier for him to visualize them."

"Sent to watch," Pim says.

"Well, sure. The people who want Poke figure he's staying in some cheap place, probably a short-time hotel, where he won't have to show identification. So they're dispatching cops to keep an eye on places in a few areas where a foreigner wouldn't draw too much attention. Arthit wanted to know which hotels and where. Maybe so he could tell Poke. I don't know, and I didn't ask."

She gathers the wet towels and balls them up. "Where?"

"The Nana area," he says. Then, watching her closely, he says, "Around Khao San."

Pim's hands tighten on the ball of dripping towels.

"And around Soi Cowboy."

Pim says, "Ahh," and gets up.

"So he asked me to come by and show him this stuff this morning. I guess he forgot."

"He was busy," Pim says, dropping the towels into the wastebasket. "He had something on his mind."

"Like you do," he says, smiling again. "Like all of us, with this situation." He looks at his watch, which is made of gold. "I don't know what to do. He hasn't called back. Maybe I should just go to the station."

"You can leave the charts with me."

"No, I'd better take them so he can look at them. Otherwise he won't see them until tonight, and he said it was important." He looks at the table. "I think everything's fine except the sugar bowl."

"I'll fix that . . ." she says, but he's already leaving. She follows him down the hall to the front door.

Over his shoulder he says, "You should be more careful. Don't leave doors open like that. I could have been anyone."

"I needed . . . I mean, the house needed to be aired out."

"Well, it's nice and airy now." He stops at the door and looks down at her. He's wearing some sort of aftershave that smells like mint and lavender put together. "You'll remember to tell him, won't you? I mean, if he calls or you talk to him before I do?"

"I promise," Pim says.

He grins and holds up a crooked little finger. It takes her a moment, but she crooks hers through it, and they both give a little yank to seal the promise.

"About?" he asks, their fingers still linked.

"Those hotels."

"Good," he says. He lets go of her hand and touches her shoulder, and his smile broadens. "And where?"

She smiles back at him and says, "Khao San."

12

The Most Dangerous One First

NUI WAS RIGHT, Poke thinks. Go after the most dangerous one first.

He begins with what he knows. Helen Eckersley. Cheyenne.

A trip to Pantip Plaza, Bangkok's hub for stolen, cloned, and bootlegged hardware and software, buys him a lightly used, somewhat stripped-down netbook—total weight about four pounds—and an extra battery. It costs him a little less than twenty thousand baht, making a substantial hole in his reserves. Even with the money he pulled out of the ATMs on that last night, he's getting down to small money.

He'll have to do something about that.

But first he spends a little more on a second throwaway phone and some minutes to put into it. Now he's got two phones that can't be traced to him, and one of them is about to be used for something dangerous. After he's done it, he won't be able to use the phone to call anyone he cares about.

Before he can make the call, he needs information. He takes the computer into a Coffee World, feeling oddly exposed because all the shops in the chain resemble one another, and he's well known in the two he frequents near his apartment. He half expects to be called by name. A large cup of coffee and a hundred baht buy him the right to jack the netbook into one of their LAN connections for a lot longer than he hopes he'll need to.

It takes him about two minutes to get a phone number in Cheyenne, Wyoming, for Helen Eckersley.

It's a little after 8:00 P.M. in Bangkok, making it seven in the morning in Wyoming. Good enough, he figures; if he wakes her, he wakes her. He punches in the number on the new phone, closes the lid of the computer, steps onto the sidewalk, and presses SEND. The connection takes so long that he pops beads of sweat, envisioning airless rooms where men listen on headphones, but eventually a phone begins to ring on the other end: once, twice—five times in all. And then he hears a woman, a smoker's deep voice curlicued by some kind of accent. *"This is Helen. I can't come to the phone right now, but if you hang up without leaving a message, you'll break my heart. You wouldn't want to break my heart, would you?"*

He gives it a moment's thought and then breaks her heart. Feeling as though two electronic exposures—the telephone and the Internet—are enough for the moment, he goes back in, unplugs, pays his bills, and hurries off down the sidewalk.

This is the time of day he feels safest. The daylight is gone, and the neon is on, and the sidewalks are jammed. Tonight, for the first time, he'll return to the hotel room he left in the morning. He's never felt sufficiently secure until now to risk going to the same place twice.

It's the passage of time, he thinks. He's become old news.

He turns down a *soi*, thinking about money. He's definitely going to need money. Rose and Miaow are going to need money.

And although he doesn't want to contact him, he does in fact know someone with money.

It's still too early, so he goes into a bookstore, buys a paperback, and takes it into a small neighborhood restaurant, where he dares to sit in the window. He doesn't draw a glance. For the first time since he went down on that street under the dying man's weight, he loses himself in someone else's story. By the time he comes out, it's ten o'clock, which makes it 10:00 A.M. in Virginia.

The phone informs him it's got about forty dollars' worth of time on it. He dials a number he never thought he'd call.

"Speak now or forever hold your peace," a female voice says.

Rafferty says, "Excuse me?"

"It's the marriage liturgy," the voice says, "and if *I* know that, somebody who grew up in China, why don't you?"

"Ming Li," Rafferty says. "Are you engaged?"

"Older brother," she says, and the delight in her voice raises his spirits. "Oh, I *miss* you. Are you coming here, please, are you?"

"Afraid not. Why are you fixated on the marriage liturgy?"

"It's so civilized. It's such a good idea. We should hear it every time somebody suggests something life-changing. Someone neutral should have to step forward and say, 'Before this stupid girl makes up her mind to buy that car or kiss that hulking boy, does anyone know better? If so, speak now or forever hold your peace.'"

"Are you regretting something?"

"Why am I here?" she asks in a modulated wail. "I'm *dying* here."

"Everybody has to die somewhere."

"Don't sprain your sympathizer."

He finds himself grinning at the phone. He hadn't even known he had a half-Chinese half sister until his father dragged her out of China and into his life during one hair-raising week a couple of years earlier. And now, he discovers, he's been missing her. "So what's wrong? You don't like America?"

"These *kids*," she says. "They've got the fullest wallets and the emptiest heads on earth. My jaw has dropped open so often I'm holding it up with duct tape. This is like a desert, for . . . for conversation or thinking or anything except looking like a pop tart and hating on other girls."

"Why are you hanging around with kids?"

A very brief pause, and when she begins talking, she's picked up the pace, putting distance, he thinks, between her and an unexpected question. "Who else has any time? You know, China wasn't paradise, but I learned things. I had school, and I was thinking in two languages, and Dad was training me to be a spy or a crook all the time. And I was memorizing his invisible maps and his old grudges. It was . . . you know, a full childhood. The kids—I mean the people—here are label-literate, but that's about it. They wouldn't know a good book if one snapped closed on their foot, but they can spot Louis Vuitton at a hundred yards. And nobody ever, ever makes me laugh."

"I'm feeling really sorry for you. Is your—our—father there?"

"No," she says. "He's not. How's that for a change of pace? Dad's *not here*. He spends all his time over at the spy shop."

"Surely he's told them everything he knows by now."

"He makes up new stuff every day. Everyone just sits and soaks it up."

"I'll bet."

"He likes the attention. It's kind of sad. You've got a problem, don't you? I can hear it in your voice. Oh, you lucky, lucky thing. I'd give anything for a problem."

"No, things are just great here." It occurs to him he's been on the phone for too long. "I need some money."

"Really. How much?"

"Fifteen thousand dollars."

"I'll talk to Dad."

"I need it fast. And tell him he also has to figure out a way to get it to me without my needing to present ID anywhere official."

"Oh, *no*," Ming Li says. "You don't have a problem."

"Just ask him for me, okay? And don't call me. I'm serious about that. Don't call me for any reason. I'll call you tomorrow, okay?"

"Just so I've got it right," she says, "you need fifteen K as fast as possible, you don't want to have to identify yourself to get it, and don't call us, we'll call you."

"I've actually missed you," he says.

"Don't make me cry. I think that week in Bangkok was the last time I was happy. I know it was."

"I'll call you tomorrow," he says.

In the entire week that made Ming Li so happy, she's the only thing Rafferty remembers fondly. When his father barged into Rafferty's life, running from the Chinese crime lord whose retirement assets he had stolen, Ming Li was a teenager, although she claimed to be older, and she was already tougher than Rafferty; she'd had a lifetime of training as her father's secret weapon in his long, patient plan to liberate himself and his Chinese wife and daughter from the Triad he'd been working for. Without her, all of them—Rafferty, Rose, Miaow, and Rafferty's father,

Frank—would probably have wound up several fathoms down in the Gulf of Thailand.

But he hadn't been able to reconcile with his father, no matter how much Ming Li had wanted it to happen.

Will his father pony up the money? Certainly he will. Ming Li will give him no peace until he does.

In fact, Rafferty thinks, he should have asked for twenty. Frank has broken enough laws in his life to figure out how to get the money to Bangkok without leaving a trail. He'll get his money.

He says it to himself again to make it true. Money is the only guarantee that the person he's about to talk to won't just turn around and sell him.

THIS IS THE longest he's been out in public, not protected by the hard shell and tinted windows of the Toyotas, since he left his apartment building on the floor of Mrs. Pongsiri's car. But he's feeling more confident now; he's just another dusky-skinned guy who parts his hair in the middle, walking around Bangkok in the dark at ten-thirty.

He flags a taxi and gives the driver instructions in the mock-Indian accent Miaow used to laugh at. Every time he uses it, it makes him miss his daughter even more fiercely.

There are times when he looks back on his life before Bangkok and sees it as a rudderless drift across an expanse of water; any direction he took was potentially right and potentially wrong, and there were no guideposts or landmarks to say which was which. The boat he was in wasn't home, but it had familiarity, and that was enough to make him mistake it for home. It was more like home, anyway, than the stone house in the middle of the Lancaster desert he'd grown up in, a time he remembers as a series of explosions between his taciturn Irish father and his half-Filipina mother, who had been born with all her nerve endings exposed. In between the explosions, there had been silences as profound as the fading of a gong. Then, finally, the long, long silence that began the day his mother came home to find a note on the mantel telling her she owned more than a million dollars' worth of real estate. The envelope also contained a key to the safe-deposit box with the deeds in it and a short paragraph of farewell from her China-bound husband.

A few years later, Poke had chased his father across the water to Shanghai, had found the woman for whom Frank had deserted Poke's mother. He'd been turned away. After that he'd been alone in his little boat for years, bobbing along on the warm seas of Southeast Asia, distracting himself by writing facile books about cultures whose surfaces he'd barely scratched, until through some enchantment of navigation, he washed up on the island that had Rose and Miaow on it. Where he finally found out what home meant.

"We're here," the driver says.

Rafferty looks up to see the unlit wall of the no-name Bar, thanks him, and climbs out.

He stands there in the dark as the cab's taillights recede and almost converge down the *soi*, asking himself whether this is actually necessary. It would be easier, faster, and more painless, he thinks, to just walk up to a cop, pull a toy gun, and take a couple through the head. What he's about to do terrifies him to the point where his hands and feet feel numb.

But what's the alternative? He can't ride around in cars for the rest of his life.

If he's going to get out from under all this, he needs a specific kind of help. If he's going after the most dangerous one first, the person he has to trust is one of the least trustworthy people he's ever met.

13

Somebody Buys Me, I Stay Bought

THE BARTENDER'S HEAD snaps up, and he raises a hand that signals *Stop*, but Rafferty just nods and keeps moving. There's no way the bartender can get around the bar and catch up to him, so instead he drops a glass on the floor.

At the sound, men pop their heads out of every booth. The men in the first four booths check Rafferty's darkened face and dismiss him, ducking back in to resume whatever ancient battles they were dissecting. In the last booth, Vladimir, appearing even more unshaven than before, gives him a short look and then a longer one, does something with his face that would pass for a smile if anyone else did it, and watches Rafferty come.

"Let's go," Rafferty says when he's standing over him.

"Wery impolite," Vladimir says. "No hello, no how are you? You met ewerybody already. Except Alfred," he says, pointing the cleft chin at a short man who has apparently lived on doughnuts for decades. The rolls of fat around his neck are so pronounced that his earlobes float on them.

"Nice to see you all," Rafferty says.

Alfred purses his lips and gives Vladimir a Look of Great Significance.

"Like I said," Rafferty says impatiently, "come on."

"Is problem," Vladimir says, shaking his head regretfully. "Money problem."

"You don't even know what I—"

"Before, when you come here, we have not seen you on teewee."

"Teewee?"

"Television," says Dr. Evil. He smiles. Janos, whose name Rafferty doesn't remember at first, is doing his best to look like he doesn't know anyone at the table.

Rafferty says, "Bye," and turns to go.

"Wait, wait, wait." Vladimir's tufted knuckles close around his wrist.

Rafferty yanks his arm away. "I didn't come here to meet Alfred, and I didn't come to chat. In fact, now that I think about it, what I need is someone who used to be CIA."

"Shush," Vladimir says, leaping to his feet. "We can try, yes? They say maybe you not so smart, maybe we can bleckmail. I say to them no, no, he wery smart, but they say amateur, you are amateur. Look, look. Three of them, one of me. I am outwoted, yes?" He tries a smile, but the corners of his mouth weigh too much and the smile collapses.

"It's interesting that you raise the subject of money," Rafferty says, suddenly aware that all four of the men in the next booth are staring at him. When he looks at them, they lower their eyes in unison. "That's what I came to talk about, too. But maybe I came to the wrong place."

"No, no, no. Vladimir is here. You talk to Vladimir. These guys, they joking, always joking, but Vladimir, never joking. You think Vladimir funny?"

"No."

"You right. Vladimir wery not funny. Vladimir tragic. Only Russian is tragic, everybody else just little bit sad. You talk, I listen."

"Fine. But no committee. These guys stay here. If you want to bring them in later, there should be enough to go around. Or you could just sell me."

The men at the table Vladimir just vacated give him wide, innocent eyes, except for Dr. Evil, who says in his rustling-silk voice, "It could be very dangerous to sell you."

"It could be fatal," Rafferty says.

"So we'll all come," Dr. Evil says, putting both hands on the tabletop.

"No. If you guys are going to go conspiratorial, I'd rather you do it when I'm not around. I'm talking to Vladimir right now, unless Vladimir says different."

Vladimir says, "We talk."

"Good." He turns to Vladimir. "Coming?" and walks out of the bar.

Vladimir follows him down the sidewalk and around the corner. Once they're out of sight of anyone who might put his head out of the bar's doorway, Rafferty stops. They're midway between street-lights.

"That guy," Vladimir says, "That guy Alfred. Kill you easy, kill you for fun."

"I'd add him to my list, but I'm running out of paper."

"Just telling you. Some guy, no problem. This one, problem."

"And you, are you a problem?"

"I am mercenary." Vladimir shrugs. "Now Sowiet Union is dust, yes? Now all mafia, no room for honest spy. So you pay me, I am loyal. See? No bullshit."

"I need help."

"And I need money."

"I haven't got any."

"Then good-bye."

"But I will have."

Vladimir says, "Call me when you do."

"Here's the deal," Rafferty says. "It's a problem of chronology. I need work done now but I won't have money until later."

"This is problem, yes, but *your* problem, not mine."

"Look, if you've got other fish on the line, shine me on. If you want to take a chance on me, do some work now and I'll pay you later."

"How much later?"

"Two days, three days at most."

"And how much money?"

"Five thousand dollars, if you get what I want. If you don't, I'll pay you fifteen hundred for your time. But if you get what I want, there will be more money to come."

"This is gamble."

"That's what it is. But it's a gamble for me, too."

"How? I am working for free—"

"You may be free, but I don't know how that makes you trustworthy."

Vladimir shakes his head very slowly, the picture of someone who's just heard something he can't believe. "Then why you talking to me?"

"Because I don't have any choice."

"Sure you do. You have Pierre and Alfred and . . . and . . . and the other one."

"Janos."

"Janos." He mimes slapping his forehead. "Guy is brilliant. Why not them?"

"Just something about you."

He nods knowingly. "Is because I am tragic. Tragic people, *only* tragic people, know what is true, yes? We born, we get old, we die. Ewery now and then a little jiggy-jig. But at end, *poh*, dust and stink."

"And this is reassuring how?"

"Other people, they don't know. They little bit like the crow, you know? Want ewerything shiny. See money, they think, 'I can get new shoe, can get fency watch.' This make them happy, little bit, for short time. Then they want something new. But me, someone like me, we know shoe and fency watch, somebody take when I am dead, not even say thank you. We know only thing we can keep is in *here*." He strikes the center of his chest with a clenched fist. "I am mercenary, but I am not traitor mercenary. Somebody buys me, I stay bought. Unless they dead."

"When I'm dead, you can betray me with both hands." The two of them regard each other. "In or not?"

"What you are asking?"

"What Murphy's been doing since Vietnam. What brings him to Thailand."

Vladimir is shaking his head. "I don't know."

"Where he's living here."

"No. I am not going to be asking where Murphy is living. My life is not beautiful dance, but I like it better than death, yes?"

"Get somebody else to ask."

"This is cold," Vladimir says with an admiring expression. "'Get somebody to die' is what you saying."

"I guess so," Rafferty concedes. "Yes or no?"

"This person who will die. What do I pay them?"

"As little as you can get away with. And if you really think they'll get killed, pay them in installments."

"Hah," Vladimir says. "You think like spy. This is big compliment to you. How I get in touch with you?"

"Give me your cell number. I'll call you tomorrow."

"Wery disappointing. No trust."

"I'm changing phones every day." He takes out the current throwaway and keys in the number as Vladimir recites it. Then he says, "Good. I'll call you."

"Wait. Some things I can give you right now. But I am standing here too long. We go back."

"No, we don't go back. We go somewhere else. There must be another bar around here."

"Is," Vladimir says. "You follow."

14

I Gamble You, You Gamble Me

"MURPHY DISAPPEAR AFTER war in Wietnam," Vladimir
says. He's got an enormous hamburger in front of him, three layers
thick, accompanied by a deep-fried onion the size of a hand gre-
nade and beer in a sweating mug. They're in a restaurant that calls
itself the Philadelphia Hamburger Pub and is unconvincingly
decorated with old black-and-white pictures of a city that, Rafferty assumes, is Philadelphia. Kids in tattered clothing run
through sprays of water from hydrants. Black people on stoops gaze
warily at the camera. It's a little bit of America, even if it's not one
of the bits the State Department peddles.

"AWOL?" Rafferty has a beer himself, the first Budweiser he's
drunk in years. After the fat flavor of Thai beer, it tastes like carbonated butterfly urine.

A shrug. "Don't know. But many people looking for him."

"Why?"

"You kidding me, yes? For kill him. Many people want to kill
him. Ewen some people on his side want to kill him." He takes an
enormous bite out of the burger, chews on it for a moment, then
parks part of it in his cheek. "But no, not AWOL. When he comes
back, he is working with Americans. Maybe he is here all along,
but out of sight, working for Americans."

"Government?"

"No, no. I tell you, he is fixer, yes? He is fixer for business.
So . . . priwate." He tilts his head left, right, left. "Well, okay,
maybe little bit CIA."

"Fine," Rafferty says. "Fixing what?"

"You pretty young, but maybe you remember then, after Wietnam, Southeast Asia wery poor. Cities smaller, farmlands bigger. America look here and see, 'Hmmm, cheap labor.' They still not talking to China then, so cheap labor here look wery good to them."

"And."

Vladimir's eyebrows rise at Rafferty's tone. "And also they think, 'Southeast Asia, Communist ewerywhere. Domino, yes?' So they make long plan. Make business, make gowernment people rich—you know, kickback and stuff—make economic ally and then bring in army, make military ally. This is why here, Thai army and American army wery close, ewen now."

Rafferty sees Murphy, sitting like a king in that official interrogation area. "So. Murphy."

"Yes. Murphy. American company want to open, mmmm, garment factory in . . . in Cambodia. They go to Cambodia, find space, give money to owner. But then someone call and say gowernor need money. Police need money. People who make permit need money. Many, many permit. Company think, 'Hmmm. Maybe no good.'

"So somebody, somebody American, say to company, 'Talk to Murphy.' And Murphy, he say, 'Can do, give me money.' He go to Cambodia, pay ewerybody, pay not so much as company because he pay all these people many time, yes? They see him, they make big smile and open their pocket. Some money left ower, Murphy take. Okay, now American company need sewing machine, many sewing machine. Sewing-machine company, maybe in Indonesia, need to pay police, need to pay gowernor, need to pay ewerybody. Murphy, he take care of them all, keep some money. You understand?"

"Yeah. He's the navigator, and he pockets some change every time the ship has to make a turn."

"But not finish yet. He goes to Cambodia customs office and pays them to let the sewing machine in, takes some money. He goes to labor contractor, gets him to lower money per hour and split difference, some for him, some for Murphy. Not give lady one dollar sixty for hour, give one dollar twenty. Ewery hour, forty cent, split fifty-fifty. Three hundred girl, forty cent ewery hour, one hundred twenty dollar ewery hour, ten hour ewery day, sewen day ewery week." He closes his eyes for a second, lips moving silently. "So eighty-four hundred dollar ewery week, fifty-fifty. Small money, but ten factories, fifteen factories, not small anymore. Maybe forty, fifty thousand ewery week."

"Jesus," Rafferty says, looking for the waitress to trade in his beer. "He could buy a new shirt."

"And one more thing. Some small boss in maybe, Cambodia, gowernment boss, make problem. Murphy say, 'Let's talk,' small boss say, 'Fuck you.' So maybe he gets acid attack, not too bad, only half of face, maybe only one eye. Small boss say, 'Sorry, no more problem, ewerything your way.' If he make more problem . . ." Vladimir points an index finger at Rafferty's head and drops his thumb. "*Poh.*"

The waitress is leaning against the counter, gazing wide-eyed at the opposite wall, so Rafferty gives up on ordering. "All this is private industry?"

"Hah," Vladimir says, leaning back in his chair. "Sure, priwate company, but information is ewerywhere, yes? And Murphy have operation ewerywhere now. Forty year he been doing this. Probably he hear more than anybody. Who is up, who is down. Where army is building camp. Where harbor is being dug more deep. 'The business of America,'" he says, startling Rafferty, "'is business.' This is your Calwin Coolidge, yes? Business is the foot in the door. And eweryone buy information."

"You wanted to know who he was working with."

Vladimir says, "Sorry?"

"When I described him. You asked me who he was working with."

Vladimir shrugs. "People will pay to know. Small money, but they will pay."

"But when I told you, you looked very surprised."

"Of course," Vladimir says. "I think maybe you tell me DuPont or Ford or Reebok or something. But no. You tell me Major Shen." He sits back and pokes his index finger into the cleft in his chin.

"This is different," he says. "This maybe ewen important." He rubs at the cleft again, obviously thinking. "Tell you what: I gamble you, you gamble me."

"What's the bet?"

"I work first, you give me money later, this is okay. Like we say. But when you learn more about Major Shen and Murphy, about what they doing, why they come together, you tell me. Maybe I let you keep some of your money."

Rafferty says, "I trust you and you trust me."

For a moment Rafferty thinks Vladimir will smile. Instead he nods and says, "Yes. Like we friend."

IN THE BACK of the cab, he dials Helen Eckersley again, gets the same ring and the same request not to break her heart, which he again ignores.

Something in him wriggles uneasily at the fact that she isn't answering the phone. He waves it off and turns around again, looking through the rear window, trying to make sure that his new friend isn't following.

And it's only because Rafferty is looking out the back window that he sees them.

The cab is nearing Khao San, approaching the hotel where he slept the first night. As the cab passes it, two men come out of a doorway and watch the car go by. Then they turn and face the oncoming traffic.

"Turn right," Rafferty says. "Soon as you can."

The driver looks up into the mirror. He's been chewing on an unlit cigarette for as long as Rafferty's been in the cab, and it's turned transparent and brown with spit. "But you said—"

"I know, but I feel like turning right. Every now and then, I just need to turn right."

The driver says, "American?"

"How'd you know?" The cab sways as the driver cuts the wheel.

"I just know. Why do you keep looking behind you?"

"Same thing. Sometimes I want to turn right, sometimes I want to look behind me. I'm an American conservative."

There's another cheap hotel halfway down the block. Once

again he sees two men, just loitering, wearing everyday clothes, but something about them announces they're a matched set. "Tell you what," Rafferty says. "I'm not happy with my hotel. Why don't you drive me past two or three more, cheap but not too cheap. You don't need to slow down—I can tell at first glance." His imitation-leather bag and his changes of clothes are in the hotel room, and so, he realizes with a sinking sensation, is the theatrical makeup he uses to darken his skin every day. And his passport.

"Which way?" the driver asks.

"I don't care, as long as we pass some hotels."

"Turn right, then," the driver says. "Make you happy again."

They're waiting outside, he thinks. *And they're at two hotels at least.*

"On the right," the driver announces, "the Happy Palace."

The Happy Palace is badly named, if appearances aren't seriously deceiving. And this time the men are on opposite curbs, facing in different directions.

He also sees a dark, unmarked car parked a few spaces from the hotel.

Okay, three hotels, and probably more. They're covering multiple hotels. They know he's in Khao San but not where. And they're undoubtedly carrying photos and showing them in the hotels, so at least the desk guy at his current hotel hasn't identified him.

Yet. There are a lot of cheap hotels down here.

The pictures were bad, Arthit had said.

How did they learn he was in Khao San?

Another hotel, no one outside this time. Inside, talking to the desk clerk? Or perhaps they don't have enough men to cover all the hotels from outside, so they're taking them in stages.

If it's the latter, maybe he can . . .

"Go to the Regent, please." It's the hotel he stayed in last night and to which he had expected to return that evening.

"Anywhere you say."

"And please throw out that cigarette and start a new one. That one looks awful."

"Smells good, though." But the driver lowers the window and tosses the wet cigarette.

The block the Regent is on looks empty. "Drive past," Rafferty says, "and make the right."

"Sure. You speak Thai very well."

"Not really, but thank you." There's no one on the sidewalk on either side of the hotel. No parked car. The driver makes the right, and Rafferty says, "Let me out here."

When they've come to a stop, the driver says, "One hundred twenty."

"Fine." Rafferty hands him two hundreds and then shows him a five-hundred. "Drive around the block nice and slow, three—no, four—times. If you don't see me, stop here and wait for five minutes. I'll have you take me somewhere else, and I'll give you this as a tip. Okay?"

"Like a movie," the driver says. "No problem."

As he rounds the corner toward the hotel, Rafferty feels as if every pore on his body has opened. He can feel the faintest stirring of the air, he can hear the ticking of the rain on pavement and the legs of his trousers brushing each other. He keeps his head motionless, but his eyes scan the block. If they're here, Shen's men, they're out of sight and keeping still. The fact that they're not here now—if they're *really* not here—doesn't mean they won't be here soon.

All this anxiety for a couple of tubes of greasepaint and a useless passport. No, he corrects himself, it's to keep them from *seeing* the greasepaint. It's the color of his skin that keeps people's eyes moving, keeps them from looking twice. He'll lose that advantage if they get his bag.

And he might still need his passport.

But his body is arguing with him. His feet feel like they're encased in cement, and he seems to be walking into a wind. When he gets to the four steps leading up to the Regent's tattered lobby, he can't force himself to climb them. He keeps walking, all the way to the end of the block, and then turns the corner and collapses against the side of the nearest building.

He's breathing as though he's run a couple hundred yards, and his heart pounds in his ears like a drum at the bottom of a swimming pool. He wipes his face, and his hand comes away wet and brown with makeup. A car turns in to the street a block away, tires hissing on the pavement, and Rafferty pushes himself off the building and goes back the way he came, turning onto the street the Regent is on. He's a quarter of the way along when a sweep of headlight announces that the car has made the same turn, right behind him.

He thinks, despairingly, *Rose. Miaow.* The muscles at the base of his spine contract.

He slows, staggering a little bit ostentatiously, and wraps an arm around a lamppost, just a drunk whose world is turning too quickly, and lets his head droop in the pre-puke pose. The car hums past, not slowing in front of the hotel, glowing straight away into the wet night, going someplace where people probably aren't frightened, and Rafferty says to himself, *That's it. That's the sign I needed,* and he climbs the steps to the Regent Hotel. He pushes on the door, gets a squeal of protest that could wake the dead, and pulls instead. Pasting a smile onto his face, he goes in.

ANNA'S WEIGHT AGAINST his shoulder has already become familiar. Arthit is already comfortable with the brush of her thick, short-cut hair on his cheek. He could recognize her perfume in a crowd.

How in the world did he get here so quickly?

This is the fourth night in a row he's left work and driven to the school where she teaches. All the way across Bangkok tonight, he'd imagined the way her face lights up when she sees him, as though she secretly hadn't expected him to come.

She leans forward a couple of inches, turns down the car's air conditioner—which she thinks is a waste of money—then nestles against him again. She traces a question mark in the air: *Is that all right?* He says, "Yes," knowing now that she can interpret the vibrations.

She brushes his cheek with her fingertips and then draws a question mark on that, too. "Yes," he says again, and she laughs low in her throat.

He laughs, too. There's a quick contraction of guilt—*Noi*—but it passes. Noi wouldn't want him to mourn forever.

The first night, she'd chosen the restaurant, a white-tablecloth, Vivaldi-Muzak Italian place on Sukhumvit, the kind of place Noi loved but that always made Arthit feel awkward, as though he were moments away from dropping the four-pound fork onto the wooden floor and drawing the eye of everyone in the place, all of whom would wonder, *What's he doing in here?*

In fact, the staff of the restaurant had barely glanced at him, but they treated Anna like royalty. From the moment the maître d' walked right around a waiting couple to lead them to a flower-bedecked window table, they received a level of service that made Arthit feel almost important. A cool nod at the maître d' and a smudged glass had been swept out of sight and replaced by one that looked as if angels had been buffing it for days. It wasn't the kind of servile, resentful attention his uniform usually draws; it was more as though the restaurant had opened in the sole hope of attracting people just like Anna, and here one was at last. He felt throughout the meal like the obscure princeling of some minor but emerging royalty.

She'd seemed completely unaware of the staff's eager attention, and he'd thought, *This is how it is wherever she goes.*

He'd tried to avoid looking at the prices on the menu, felt his tension mount, and wondered what "piccata" and "tagliatelle" meant. Even during his time in school in England, he'd stuck to Asian and, when unavoidable, English food. Beyond a few obvious dishes, he had no idea what to order, and yet it seemed as though dealing with the waiter was going to be his job.

It became clear that she had the situation under control when she passed him her menu with her finger on something called "osso buco" and then put up a second finger and tapped the menu with them twice, just in case he'd missed the first sign.

After the waiter left, she extended a hand as though inviting him to cover it with his own, but as he reached for it, it was withdrawn, leaving a square of paper. His reflexes, for once, were operating, and he put his hand over the paper with almost no hesitation and drew it toward him. It said, *Meat, right? You look like you eat meat.* He'd raised his eyes to hers and burst out laughing.

She'd laughed with him and then widened her eyes and fanned her face as though to say, *Near escape.*

"I've eaten Italian before," he said, and then qualified it, "Pizza." She'd started to laugh again, and he'd added, "And spaghetti."

Her gaze on his lips felt like a cool breeze. He said, slowly, "A lot of spaghetti," just to prolong the feeling.

They'd traded spoken words and written notes through three courses, dessert, and a bottle of wine. In his memory the entire evening seems to have been candlelit. A high, silent room lit by candles with Anna in the center of it.

He still can't believe how much he learned about her across that table. It all felt so natural, so effortless that he can almost hear the tone of her voice as she told him about herself, although of course she never spoke a word. Forty-three, divorced, the mother of a twelve-year-old boy whose much richer and higher-ranking father had simply taken the child. The boy, she's told, is beginning to be a problem, but she's not being consulted on how to help, which seems to be the only aspect of her life that frustrates her.

Like Noi, she was born and educated in the city, first at schools for the deaf and then, defying all predictions, at Chulalongkorn University, Bangkok's best. Unlike Noi, who'd quit not only school but her entire family to marry a policeman, Anna had graduated and then won a doctorate from their school of education.

She's been deaf her entire life. Arthit's immediate reaction when she told him that was, *She's never heard music.* It was the only moment of pity he's had for her since they met. She's too capable and too complete to pity. And it occurred to him on their second night together that she's been spared the clashing, senseless, cacophonous sound that Bangkok is rich in. She lives, he'd thought, in a bell of silence.

The car purrs to a stop, and he waits for her to lift her head from his shoulder and tilt her face to his. She's done it two nights running, and tonight makes it three. He kisses her lightly on the lips, and she reaches up and squeezes his earlobe. He wraps his fingers around her wrist, turns her hand toward him, and kisses her palm, directly below the thumb. He says, in English, "Mount of Venus." Then, in Thai, "It tells me whether you have qualities

like kindness, harmony, love. And sensuality." He presses it experimentally with his fingertips and shakes his head. "Oh, well. You
could still go into politics."

She blows a puff of air at him, but it turns into a laugh. He opens
his door, patting the air with a palm, meaning *Stay there*, and gets
out. He goes around and opens her door, and she extends a hand,
half appreciatively, half in parody of the helpless, well-bred lady
who needs assistance getting out of the car. When she's standing
upright, she sags against him and taps her fingers over her heart.

They're halfway up the walk when the front door opens. Pim's
smile of welcome fades when she sees Anna, but she manages a
nod before turning around and retreating up the hallway and into
her room. Anna watches the girl go, looking perplexed.

Arthit says, "Coffee?"

Anna shakes her head, still looking down the hallway. And, as
if she'd felt Anna's attention, Pim sticks her head out of her door
and calls, "Did your friend show you the charts?"

Arthit says, "Which friend?"

Her forehead wrinkles. "Ummm, Prem? He works with you."

Arthit says, "Prem?" All the joy of the evening vanishes.
"Please. Come in here."

She moves reluctantly down the hallway toward them, stopping
without actually coming into the room.

"This man, Prem. Did he phone?"

"You didn't talk to him?"

"Pim. Tell me what happened."

She blinks at his tone. "He came here about ten minutes after
you—"

"This morning?" He steps forward but stops, seeing that he's
frightening her.

Pim says, "Yes."

"Describe him."

Suddenly Pim's face is white, and she's squinting as though she
expects a slap. "Tall," she says. "Handsome. Combs his hair . . ."
Her voice falters.

"Straight back," Arthit says, and Anna, reading his lips, releases
a sharp sigh that just misses being a cough. "What did he do?"

"I had . . . uhhh, I'd spilled something." She's tugging at her frizzy hair with one hand. "And he . . . he helped me—"

"What charts?"

"Charts, he said, he said you wanted—" Her chin crumples into a pattern of dimples, and a tear slides down her cheek. "Hotels, charts of hotels. He tricked me."

Arthit's face is rigid. "Tricked you how?"

"I don't know how he did it—"

"Did *what?*"

Anna can't hear the tone, but she sees Pim step back.

"I told him—I *think* I told him—that Poke was around Khao San. In a cheap hotel near Khao San."

"Which hotel?"

"I didn't know that." She's crying openly now, not even trying to hide it.

Anna puts a hand on Arthit's arm, but he shrugs her off.

"You're certain."

"Yes, *yes*, I don't know where he is, where he's staying. I mean, Prem acted nice, and he knew all about you, and he . . . he helped—" She backs up a step, and Anna follows her, a hand outstretched, but Pim looks down at it and then wails, running into her room and slamming the door.

Arthit says, in English, "Shit." To Anna, in Thai, he says, "Wait here for a minute. Right back." He goes down the hall and into the bedroom. When he comes out, a moment later, he has a transparent zippered plastic bag in his hands with what looks like oversize pieces of confetti in it.

"SIM cards," he says. "Out of confiscated phones." He sits on the couch and pulls out his phone and opens it. He slides the back off and tries to work the SIM card out, but his hands are shaking, and Anna takes it from him as she sits. She slips a nail under the edge of the card and pops it out, then holds out her hand with the card in it.

Arthit takes it and puts it on the table, then replaces it in her hand with one from the bag. A few seconds later, she closes the phone and hands it back to him with the new card in it.

Arthit takes a deep breath and says, "I hope this is the right thing to do," and dials the number of Poke's throwaway.

15

A Landscape of Broken Glass

THE KID AT the desk, who looks all of seventeen years old, barely glances at him.

Rafferty briefly considers the elevator, which is tiny, slow, and noisy. He's pretty sure no one has been here asking for him—the kid is totally absorbed in the Korean soap opera on the little television behind the counter. He's got no telltale jumpiness; in fact, his eyes are drooping a little.

Still, the elevator takes too much time, and he has a sudden vision of being trapped in it between floors. So he pushes the button to open the doors and steps in just long enough to punch the button that sends it to the top floor, the eighth, taking it out of action for three or four minutes as far as anyone down here in the lobby is concerned. With a last look at the kid, who has paid no attention to him at all, Rafferty walks in a leisurely fashion to the door to the stairs, and the moment the door closes behind him, he goes into a sprint, three steps at a time, as fast as he can manage it.

He's winded by the time he slows, halfway between the third and fourth floors. The steps haven't been swept in years, and the grit scraping underfoot echoes in the stairwell, so he tries to lift his feet as vertically as possible to eliminate the noise. After a few slightly-less-noisy steps, he just pulls his shoes off and lets them dangle in his left hand.

Not for the first time, he wishes he had his Glock.

Shooting anyone from Shen's outfit feels like a bad career

move, but at least he could threaten them with it. He's never wanted a gun so badly, even if he knows it's mostly psychological.

At the fifth floor, he pushes the door open a couple of inches and puts his eye to the crack. Same dim hallway, same luxuriantly greasy carpet, same sad reek of ancient cigarettes, same flickering fluorescent light. He counts to ten, and as he's counting, the elevator lumbers its way past, groaning toward the eighth floor at its usual funereal pace.

Nothing for it but to go in. He slips into his shoes and steadies his breathing.

Directly above the door he's looking through, he knows, a security camera points down the hall. He's 90 percent sure that whatever piece of equipment it's connected to either died or was stolen years ago, but to be on the safe side, he works up some saliva, spits on his fingers, reaches up, and swipes the lens. Then he slips through the door, eases it closed, and moves quickly down the hall. The key fights him, snagging on everything, as he pulls it from his pocket.

It's an old-fashioned key, and the lock is gummy inside, probably with nicotine. He has to wiggle it noisily to get the tumblers to move. If anyone is in there, they know he's coming, so he offers a two-word prayer and goes in.

The only light in the room falls through the window on the far wall, and he registers for the first time that there's a fire escape going past it. It eases the fist around his heart a little, although God only knows how rusted it is or how badly corroded the bolts holding it to the building are. It has to be fifty, maybe sixty years old.

Still, it's there. He goes to the window, gets his palms under the sill, and shoves up. It almost breaks his back. The window is painted shut, or possibly glued closed with the oil from a trillion cigarettes. He tries again and doesn't even get a creak of acknowledgment. He leans his forehead on the cool glass and looks down at the narrow alley, far below.

Time to move. Without turning the light on, he grabs everything that's his and stuffs it into the bag, which has its zipper stuck half open and is also beginning to give at the seams. With the strap over his shoulder, he goes into the bathroom and begins to feel around for his toiletries. He has a sudden vision of knocking the water glass to the floor and breaking it, so he turns on the light over the mirror.

And immediately hears a key being inserted into the lock of the room door.

He snaps off the light and pulls the door to the bathroom closed, not letting the tongue click into place. At almost exactly the same time, the door to the hallway opens and whoever it is turns on the light in the room, creating a bluish ribbon of light beneath the door.

Rafferty looks around frantically for something he can use as a weapon.

Whoever is out there, he or she says nothing, but Rafferty can hear the floor creaking under the person's weight. There might be only one person. A drawer is opened and closed.

So . . . one or two? And what does it matter? There will be at least one gun out there, and he's got—what? An imitation-leather bag with a stuck zipper. If he could open the zipper, he could use it as a cutting edge—shove it hard against a forehead, maybe, and saw with it. Might cause some bleeding, if nothing else. But, of course, even as pathetic as that is, the fucking zipper is fucking stuck. So scratch the zipper. And that leaves—

The intruder is walking. Coming toward the bathroom? Rafferty backs up a step and puts out a hand to steady himself, in case he has to jump in one direction or the other, and feels something bulbous and vaguely pear-shaped on the wall, just to the right of the sink. A cheap liquid-soap dispenser, probably from the 1950s.

That's what I've got, he thinks. *If I live through this, it will all have come down to a hotel too stingy to give me—*

The person is definitely coming toward the door. Rafferty pumps the dispenser five or six times into his cupped hand, and it makes a tiny noise. The person on the other side of the door stops, and the two of them stand there, with half an inch of wood between them, breathing at each other.

The moment stretches until Rafferty thinks it might snap. And then his cell phone rings.

THE FEAR ARTIST 131

The phone is still in the middle of its first ring when Rafferty kicks the bathroom door open.

It swings about two feet and bounces off the forehead of the man who is standing there, an automatic pistol in one hand and a two-way radio in the other. He stumbles back a couple of steps, and then Rafferty is on top of him, slapping the open palm filled with liquid soap across the man's eyes and scrubbing at them as the man brings the hand holding the radio sideways, into Rafferty's shoulder, and then the pain from the soap registers, and both of the man's hands come automatically up to his eyes, and Rafferty knits his fingers together, lifts his hands straight up, and puts all his weight into bringing them down on top of the man's head.

The man goes straight down, as though his legs are boneless, and his gun goes off, spraying half a dozen bullets across the room. Without really registering it, Rafferty sees the diagonal line of holes open up in the wall like stitches from some giant's needle, and then the man is all the way down, huddling against further attack and screaming. The gun is underneath him, and Rafferty's afraid to try to get to it. Even blind, the man could hit him dead center at arm's length.

Someone is yelling questions into the radio, and Rafferty takes that as his cue to leave. He kicks the man in the head, hoping for a few minutes' worth of unconsciousness, and opens the door to the hall.

The elevator groans past on its way down. It would take two minutes for it to make its way back up. He heads for the stairs.

As he starts to climb, he hears the first-floor door bang open, so once again he yanks his shoes off and takes the stairs up, as fast as he can without making too much noise. There's only one hope in his mind: that the fire escape goes all the way to the roof, or at least to the eighth-floor window so he can drop the single story from the roof to the landing.

Of course it does, he tells himself, topping the first flight and cutting it tight across the switchback. *Why wouldn't it? Even in Thailand, why wouldn't it? What sense would it make for it not to reach the top floor?*

Sixth floor. The bag over his shoulder makes a slapping sound as it bounces off his side, and he puts a hand over it to keep it still. Two steps at a time, no room for a stumble, the muscles of his thighs hot with strain. Seventh floor. Only the eighth and the final flight up to the roof to go. He finds energy somewhere, although he feels as though his lungs are tiny and he can't fill them often enough. Eighth floor, and past it, and halfway up the last flight now—and the door to the roof is in sight. It's steel, chipped and battered, and his heart leaps as he sees that it's ajar, open about an inch, just one inch of rainy darkness beckoning him into the wide, wet night beyond, with all of Bangkok to hide in.

He misses a step and almost falls forward, grunting with the effort to remain upright, and below him the hurrying feet stop. With all the strength he can summon, he hurls himself up the last four or five steps and slams a shoulder into the door.

And finds himself sitting on the filthy landing, looking up at the loop of padlocked chain around the pressure bar. The chain had allowed the door to open about six inches before stopping it, and Rafferty, dead.

Below him a man shouts in Thai for him to stop, and once again heavy-sounding shoes scrape against the gritty stairs, coming faster now. Rafferty gets up, pulls the door closed as far as he can without engaging the latch, puts the bag of clothes high on his arm to protect his shoulder, and runs at the door, which opens about ten inches and snaps back again, with a deafening sound.

The man below him fires a shot, the noise banging from one side of the stairwell to another. Rafferty grabs the door, yanks it toward him, then shoulders it again, and then again and again. He is rewarded by bits of cement falling into the opening. He manages it two more times, and on the second try the old screws securing the lock to the exterior wall pull free, and he falls through the door onto his side.

He hurts, he's gasping for breath, and there's a man chasing him with a gun, but he's on the roof.

It takes him a second to orient himself. The window in his room—which wall was it in? A fast survey shows him a wide street to the right, alleyways to the left and in front and behind. There was a switchback between each pair of floors, so it's behind him.

The roof is smaller than he imagined, just black tar ringed by a knee-high barrier with nothing beyond it but gasoline-saturated air all the way to the sidewalks. Behind him, about eight feet high and nine feet square, is the housing for the stairs. The door yawns open now, the chain with the padlock dangling from it, still connected to the anchor plate he'd yanked from the wall. Someone has put a small round metal table and a lightweight aluminum folding chair just beyond the door. Rising through the center of the table is an ancient umbrella, its cloth covering dissolved by the toxins in the air, its naked ribs tucked in protectively. It is anchored by a cylinder of cement that he can tell at first glance is too heavy to lift.

Useless. All useless. Even the chair, it's as light and flimsy as a flyswatter.

It's *windy* up here. The rain stings his face.

He can hear the man climbing toward him. He hears the feet on the stairs and the crackle of his radio, and then the man is calling for backup, trying to get someone up to the roof with him.

Is he coming all the way up or not?

Poke doesn't even have time to get to the edge of the roof to see whether the fire escape comes all the way up. If the man comes through that door, he's going to have his gun in his hand, and Rafferty, crawling carefully over the low wall and onto the fire escape, will look as big as a bus.

He pulls the door all the way open, tugging it against the wind, and positions himself behind it, holding his breath as he listens, becoming more certain with every moment that the man won't come onto the roof until he's got a whole posse with him. But then he hears the scrape of a shoe, and in the cold, milky fall of light through the door he sees a shadow: shoulders and a head. The shadow stops, and so does Rafferty's heart.

Radio static. The scratch of grit underfoot. The shadow gets a little longer.

Rafferty can hear the man breathe.

There's a distant boom, the door to the stairs being thrown open again on the ground floor, and shouting voices from below, echoes of unintelligible questions. The man standing only a few feet from Rafferty apparently draws courage from them; he calls out in response, and the shadow lengthens again. Almost the entire silhouette is visible.

Rafferty shoves the heavy door, using all his strength and all its weight to flatten the man standing on the other side of it. The door bounces back toward him, and he sees that the man has gone down outside the housing for the stairs. He's rolling away toward the front edge to escape Rafferty, the hand with the gun in it coming up, and Rafferty jumps as high as he can and comes down with both feet on the man's rib cage.

The momentum pitches him forward, and he lands on both knees, hard, as something skitters past him across the roof—the man's gun. He makes a despairing leap for it as it slides toward the low wall, and then the man's fingers are in his hair, yanking him back. As Rafferty topples backward into a pool of water, he recognizes that it's the smaller of the two men who took him from his apartment to Major Shen's interrogation room, the one he thought of as Smiley.

The man pulls himself to his feet and launches a kick, but Rafferty scrabbles back and it misses him by an inch. The man grunts, off-balance, and his momentum carries him backward, toward the gun and the roof's edge. Rafferty throws out a foot and hooks the man's ankle, and the man pitches back, falling, and makes a wild swoop with his arms to turn and stop himself. He takes one more automatic stumble back, and then his feet slip out from under him on the wet surface. The top of the low wall hits him at the waist, his chest and arms and shoulders and head hanging over it with nothing beneath him but concrete eight stories down, and he screams and his legs scissor and flail, and it's obvious that he's going over.

The next thing Rafferty knows, he has the man's shirt in his fists, and it tears away in his hands, and the man grabs at Rafferty's wrists and misses. Somehow Rafferty gets his fingers under the broad leather belt of the man's uniform. But the man is struggling frantically, every motion taking him farther over the side until Rafferty wedges both feet against the base of the wall, both his hands around the belt, and pulls until he hears another scream and recognizes it as his own as he wrenches the man back, over the wall, and then he's flat on his back with the man facedown across his legs.

The two of them lie there, wheezing, and then the uniformed man pulls himself to his hands and knees and crawls away from the edge of the roof. He's weeping, high broken sounds like a child's cries. When he stands, Rafferty can see his knees trembling. Flat on his back, his strength gone, Rafferty looks up at his captor.

The crying man keeps his eyes on Rafferty as he picks up the gun, his hand shaking so badly he almost drops it again. Then, with great care, as though he's navigating a landscape of broken glass, he backs up several steps and turns his back.

Rafferty waits a moment, partly because he can't believe it and partly because he's not certain he can move. Then he brings himself to a sitting position and from there to all fours. When he stands, he finds that his legs will more or less carry him.

And he hears the men coming up the stairs.

The fire escape is where it should be. It stops at the eighth-floor window, but it's only about nine feet down. He jams his feet into his shoes, grabs the leather bag and commits to the jump before he has time to think about it, going over the low wall on his belly and hanging by his hands before making the drop.

He's gone down two floors on the rusted stairs on wobbly legs, descending in a barely controlled fall, before the man on the roof fires his gun twice.

His cab is where it's supposed to be, the driver working on a new wet cigarette. Everything that just happened to him took less than eight minutes.

IF I GOT *away with that that*, Rafferty thinks, *tonight I can get away with anything.*

He gives the driver the address on Soi Pipat and leans back. He stinks with sweat and fear, and he finds the man looking at him in the rearview mirror.

"Would you sell me a cigarette?" Rafferty asks. He hasn't smoked in years.

"It's a present," the driver says, passing one back. "Looks like that was a rough visit."

"Easy to check in," Rafferty says, hearing his voice shake. "Hard to check out. Got a lighter?"

"Can't smoke in the cab." The driver leans right, his hand fishing for something, and then holds up a disposable plastic lighter. "Put your head out the window."

"Eat one yourself," Rafferty says. He's feeling light-headed, and the first lungful of smoke tilts the horizon alarmingly. For a ghastly, weightless moment, he thinks he'll pass out.

"Feeling better?" the driver asks.

"I must be," Rafferty says over the noise of the wind. "It's a big, surprising world, and it must contain at least one thing I feel better than. I'm alive, right?"

"And married," the driver says.

Rafferty brings his head back in but leaves the hand with the cigarette in it dangling out of the cab. "How can you tell?"

"In the eyes. You have married eyes."

"Really. That's amazing."

"Joking," the driver says. "The way you speak Thai, you must speak it at home. You don't have that up-on-tiptoes thing in your voice that most people have when they're speaking a foreign language. You speak it to somebody who's not going to laugh at you. So you're married to a Thai woman."

Rafferty says, "Very impressive."

"When you drive one of these things ten hours a day, you get good with people."

"I have a Thai daughter, too."

"Yes? Not fifty-fifty?"

"No. We adopted her."

"Was she poor?"

"Living on the sidewalk."

"Good for you. Good merit for your karma." He looks back again. "Who do you love most, the wife or the daughter?"

"How can I answer that? I love them both so much it makes my teeth hurt. What about you?"

"Four," he says. "Two sons and two daughters. I'm supposed to love the sons most, but I don't."

"And your wife? Is she beautiful?"

"Beautiful enough for me," the driver says with a grin. "Beautiful enough that I'm beginning to worry about my daughters."

"I know how you feel. They're babies, and then they're not."

"And we're all surrounded by boys."

Rafferty sees Andrew's earnest face, his black glasses, the anxiety in his eyes. "It's hard not to feel sorry for the boys," he says. "They haven't got a chance."

The driver laughs. "Girls can eat boys alive," he says. "It's a good thing they don't know it." He eases the car left, checking the outside mirrors, getting ready to turn. "So you're better off than a lot of people," he says. "Wife, daughter, love."

"I am, aren't I?" He leans back. "That was a terrible cigarette."

He's in and out of the apartment building in less than five minutes. He takes the elevator to his floor and goes straight to the door to the stairs. He's not worried about running into anyone, because Mrs. Pongsiri will be at her bar, lying to customers and keeping the girls in line. The smell of paint haunts the hallway like a ghost of his former life, when the color on his walls mattered. In front of the door to the stairs, he stretches up to work the masking tape free from the top of the doorjamb. When he's got the yellow ticket, he puts it in his pocket without looking at it. Then he goes into the stairwell and once again dials the number in Cheyenne, Wyoming.

This time he doesn't break her heart. "My name is Poke Rafferty," he says to the answering machine. "P-O-K-E. I'm in Bangkok. When you get this message, please call me at this number."

Then he goes down the stairs, thinking about Murphy.

Part Three
THE FEAR ARTIST

16

A Hand Grenade on a Pool Table

THE STEWARDESS WHO has accompanied Murphy from the first-class cabin indicates the express lane for VIP passports with an extended arm, fingers together and slightly curved, plus the hint of a bow at the waist. He walks on without acknowledging her, speeding up just enough to cut in front of a red-faced Korean businessman who starts to protest and then, looking at Murphy's jeans and wrinkled shirt, grimaces and slows to let him in.

The flight from Kuala Lumpur should have been only a couple of hours long, but a thunderstorm kept them on the runway for ninety minutes and its little sister made them circle Suvarnabhumi's sprawling runways for another forty, the city wet and dark below them. He'd looked down, checking to see whether the flooding in the low-lying areas was visible and not much caring one way or the other. As far as he's concerned, the river and canals could sink the whole city. Might clean it up a little.

Murphy is not good with delays. It takes him about two minutes to get to the woman who's processing the passports, and when she takes her time leafing through his to find a blank page—it's the thickness of a small-town phone book—he holds up his right hand in a loose fist and moves the thumb like a mouth so it appears to be saying, in Humphrey Bogart's voice, "Hurry it up, sweetheart."

The woman, startled, looks first at the fist and then at Murphy. He leans into the counter and says, in a conversational tone, "Either stamp the fucking thing or get your boss over here to do it. You may be on Thai time, but I'm not."

The woman's face reddens. She rises as though to call for assistance, but a flicker on her monitor draws her attention. She glances down at it and her eyes come up to his for a second and then down again, instantly. She straightens, grabs her stamp, hammers it onto a blank quarter page, and hands it back to him. She says, "Enjoy your stay, *sir*."

He's already on his way.

Murphy is traveling with nothing but a fat, battered briefcase—so full that the only way he can keep it closed is by cinching a belt around it—so he angles around the baggage carousels with their tiers of slowly rotating bags and all the schlemiels waiting for them, and he wonders for the ten-thousandth time why people buy black luggage that looks exactly like everybody else's black luggage. On cue, a tired-looking Anglo man wrestles a giant black bag halfway off the conveyor belt, sees the number on the ticket, and crossly shoves it back on. His wife, who hasn't moved a muscle to help, says, "Told you."

What we need, Murphy thinks, *is a selective battery law. He should get a hundred bucks from the Global Civility Fund for pasting her.* The thought cheers him slightly, and he bulls his way through the Nothing to Declare line, glaring down a questioning glance from the official behind the table.

He's headed to the taxi line when one of the uniforms from Shen's outfit materializes at his shoulder. "No bags, sir?"

Murphy hoists the briefcase and says, "Whaddaya call this?" and pushes it at him. "I didn't expect you. I'm a day early, and I didn't call anyone."

"Yes, sir."

"Shen's showing off, isn't he? Where's the car?"

"Right outside."

He follows the uniform, musing about whether Shen's insistence on having tall men in his outfit is a strategic decision or the expression of some sexual kink. Shen seems to be as close to sexless as any man his age Murphy has ever met. Maybe Nirvana for him is being surrounded by tall, identically dressed men. Murphy's come up against weirder glimmers.

"Do you think there's anything, however repulsive," he says to the man he's following, "that doesn't turn *somebody* on?"

"I'm a driver, sir." The man steps into the revolving glass door.

"What's that mean?" Murphy says when he's through the door himself. "They cut 'em off?"

"Here's the car, sir," the driver says, and sure enough there it is, a mirror-polished Lincoln Town Car guarded by a pair of airport policemen, who step away and offer two-finger salutes, touching just the index and middle fingers to the brims of their caps as both of them avoid Murphy's eyes.

"Nice to see you guys doing something," Murphy says in Thai to the one who holds open the rear passenger door. He slides in, and the cop closes the door. A moment later the driver's door opens and the driver gets in with a little difficulty, ducking his head as he squeezes through the door.

Murphy says, "You know where we're going, right?"

"Yes, sir, of course."

"Okay, then, where?"

The driver eases into the traffic loop. "Major Shen—"

"No, we're not going to see Major Shen. Fuck Major Shen. I'm going home. Do you know where that is?"

"No, sir, but Major Shen—"

"Major Shen isn't in the car, son. But I am. And right this minute I'm looking at the back of your neck."

After a moment the driver says, "Yes, sir."

"Aaaahhhh," Murphy says in disgust. He pulls out a cell phone and hits a speed-dial number. When it's answered, he says, "Hey, y'all."

Major Shen says, "Murphy? Is that you?"

"No," Murphy says in falsetto. "It's Dolly Parton. I was just sitting in the tub, lookin' down and watching 'em float, and I thought of you."

"I need you in here."

"And I need to go home. You tell me you got that little shithead tied up in a room with his feet on fire, I'll come in."

"We almost had him."

"Well, that's inspiring. What happened?"

"We put teams of men on cheap hotels around Khao San and found him in one of them."

"So. I guess he shot his way out? Kill a bunch of your guys?"

"No. Nothing like that."

"You don't have a lot of dead guys?"

"No."

"Then how the hell—"

"They chased him up onto the roof, but he jumped down a floor onto a fire escape—"

"You want to tell me how—No, wait a minute, wait a minute. I want whichever one of your violets saw him last, whoever had him on that roof, I want that man kicked in the gut until he's told you everything about how a fucking *travel writer* gets away from a trained, armed officer. A trained, armed officer *you* chose, remember? And you e-mail me the transcript, and if anything smells even a little, I'll come over there and talk to him myself. He won't like that. And even if it doesn't smell, break him. Put him on land-mine duty down south and make sure the word gets out. Next guy who fucks up will be digging the things up barehanded while fuzzy-wuzzies snipe from the woods. Do you doubt I could arrange that?"

"No," Shen says.

"And you're right. Not to be unpleasant, but it's Uncle's money that pays for those fancy uniforms, all extra-long."

"You're the only one arguing," Shen says.

"Why do you pick such tall guys?" Murphy asks. "Have you always wanted to be the shortest little boy in the room or something?"

"We'll talk tomorrow," Shen says.

"I want to hear that guy screaming all the way to my house, you got it?"

"Certainly, Murphy. Everyone here knows what you want." Shen disconnects.

"Hey," Murphy calls to the driver, "you want me to give you directions, or you gonna read my mind?"

TIME TO LIGHTEN up, he thinks. Time to shake loose again. Dump all the weight and break free. They're snarled in the perpetual Bangkok traffic jam, made worse by the flooded streets, the world just a blur of drizzle, taillights, and shining asphalt, with the occasional lightning pitchfork thrusting toward the city. He leans back and closes his eyes. How does this happen? Why do you *let* it happen? Every few years you look around and you've got all this shit. You've got a big fucking house with piles of expensive junk in it, you've picked up some women, and with the women there's usually a kid sooner or later, and you're living in some barn behind gates with people to drive your car and clean your rooms and wipe your ass. And a hundred people know who you are.

How many kids now, over the years? He can think of seven, five of whom he hasn't seen in decades, but he knows he's missing a few. No point in even trying to remember all the women. They were pretty much all the same woman anyway.

Some of the kids were okay. Some of them made it to college, and a couple are in the States. Had a few dominants in there. But some of them were eaten in the jungle.

Then, of course, there's Treasure. What the *hell* is he going to do with Treasure? The only kid he's ever had who he knows without a tenth of a drop of doubt is his. She's his from teeth to toenails.

And that's the problem. She's her daddy's girl. Leave her with some unsuspecting couple, she'd cook them over an open flame and serve them to their children. He can't put her with anyone, he can't let her mother have her, and he can't leave her alone. He needs to think about this, and fast, because he's got to move.

He's not having fun. And he's got a footprint a mile wide.

He grunts at the thought of how much effort it's going to take. The driver says, "Sir?"

"When I want you," Murphy says, "I'll say, 'Hey.' Got it?"

"Yes, sir."

"You just get me home and I'll see they give you another one of those pretty medals." Get rid of the house first, he thinks. Sell it under the name he used to buy it and leave the money in that account forever because the Thais hover like flies around a transaction that big. Bring in some fruitcake to buy all the fake antiques and all the real antiques and the fancy couches and rugs and

Song's goddamn mahogany table. Give some money to the little women so they can go home rich to Mudville. Pay off the help— enough so they don't complain but not so much that they brag about it.

Just like before. Except for Treasure. This is, what? The third time? But the first since Treasure—since it was clear who Treasure was.

Disappear and roll up the street behind him. Get a room some- where, just him and his briefcase and his jeans and his shirt and his brains and his reflexes, someplace shadowy in the middle of the concrete jungle, the lines laid out like a spider to tip him if any- one's looking for him. Tell everybody who matters that he'll be back when he feels like it.

Let the weekly money accumulate in the bank accounts. Let people begin to miss him so he can raise his prices when he's ready to start up again.

Find someplace for Treasure. Somehow.

Tuck her away under something very heavy with a high fence around it and then cut the strings, go rogue. Play some games, operate on his own without all these assholes looking over his shoulder all the time, doing the official *tsk-tsk-tsk* for the micro- phones while they urge him on with their hands. *Plausible deni- ability*, another concept born in 'Nam, using euphemisms like "action" for "killing" in case they were being recorded. Well, fuck plausible deniability, fuck the politicians, so busy covering their asses they'd blow a hand off if they farted, fuck the career officers with their eyes on the next star on their shoulder, who want the results but not the tactics. Fuck them all.

Do what he wants for a change.

Play without rules. Blow away some ragheads, maybe. Even up the odds down south. Operate the way he used to operate, back . . . back . . .

Back when he was young.

He hears himself groan and says to the driver, "No, I'm not talk- ing to you."

There are times when he sees himself as a hand grenade on a pool table. All the neat little balls rolling politely around according to the laws of physics, clacking off at their precious Euclidean angles, and here comes this kind of odd-looking ball that wobbles a bit and then blows all the balls near it to powder and creates a whole new order on the green felt, or what remains of the green felt. When the felt's ripped to shit and all the balls are banging back and forth and hopping off the table and hitting the floor and breaking apart, that's when a man can do some *real* work.

He had thought his time was over forever. People with his skill set and his experience were an embarrassment, like scraps of memory from an epic national drunk a few decades ago. America had fled the jungles and the rice paddies, it had abandoned the napalm and the Agent Orange and Phoenix Program tactics and entered into its World Policeman phase, and the way they played it, there was Good Cop and there was Gooder Cop. Benign capitalism pasteurizing the globe with blue jeans and shampoo and fine dentistry. Someone like Murphy, or an enterprise like Phoenix—which had taken out a couple thousand civilians a month, shredded the Geneva Conventions, interrogated with extreme prejudice around the clock on the faintest suspicion—well, as far as the new and improved United States was concerned, it was *shocking* to hear reports. The accounts of those things had been overblown, misreported, misinterpreted, or—if all the evidence hadn't been destroyed—they'd been the work of a few out-of-control individuals who'd twisted circumstances to their own personal purposes. Tragedies of war, never to be repeated.

So he'd kissed it all good-bye, disappeared for a while into Indonesia, and spent some of the money he'd taken from the people who paid not to be on the monthly Phoenix lists. When he reemerged, he'd settled into business mode, making his boring millions as the guy who knew who to pay and how much, where to get everything from steel wheels to bulk rubber, and doing the occasional bit of freelance wetwork when someone earned it. He'd maintained his connections to the spooks, since he had so many lines out and would be silly not to listen in. Sell information and plausible lies, get richer, get fatter, get laid, shoot someone once in a while, and dream of the old days.

Slow death.

And then those idiots flew into the Twin Towers screaming the name of God, and the President of the United States looked up from the children's book he was reading to a classroom full of kids and thought, Yikes. Terrorists without uniforms, children with grenades, an enemy without borders. Bad guys hiding in plain sight. Everyday people, people who look like everyone else, serving as double agents or actual combatants. In small, isolated, backward villages. In difficult terrain crisscrossed by secret paths. In countries where people hate us.

Jeez, the President thought, *what does this remind me of?*

So naturally the plan the Pentagon dusted off and revised and presented to the White House was based on the Phoenix Program, and it was accepted while Murphy was in the middle of complicated but boring negotiations for a pottery plant in northeast Thailand. The proceedings barely kept him awake, and his eyes were drooping in a meeting when he got the call he'd never thought would come.

How would he like, the suit had asked, to stick with the business as a cover and go back to doing what he'd been doing before, but also, from time to time, a little more? Or, whenever circumstances permitted, a lot more. Help the Thais deal with the Muhammads in the deep south and keep an eye open in case al-Qaeda or some other suicide club decided it needed to take things out of Camel World and into Bangkok or Yala, way down south, until things cooled off.

Fucking paradise.

The driver says, "What about the gate, sir?"

Murphy looks up. "Oh." They've come to a stop, and the gates designed to keep people like him away from houses like this gleam ice white in the headlights. "Hold on." He unbuckles the belt wrapped around the briefcase and fingers his way through the wads of documents, toiletries, and stray sticky notes until he finds the remote, which he points through the window at the gates.

"Wow," the driver says as the house is revealed: two and a half staggered stories with balconies everywhere, useless chimneys for useless fireplaces, a tiled roof gleaming with drizzle, water already standing in some parts of the yard. Manderley in the tropics.

"Do your work, son," Murphy says, "show up every day, stand tall, skim that graft, and you can buy the place. But you better do it fast if you wanna buy it from *me*." He automatically counts the lit windows: four. The pair of lamps behind the living-room curtain operate on a timer, so they don't tell him anything. The light in Song's room, on the second floor, is on, but the Humvee is gone, so she's out fucking around on him, which he should have expected, coming back early. The light gleams in the front window of the bathroom next to Treasure's room, but that doesn't mean anything either, because the kid has nightmares all the time, which is no surprise, since she has them when she's awake, too. And to the right of the house, light spills onto the lawn and trees from the big windows in his train room. Those shouldn't be on.

He wants to go back to the airport. Fly someplace with mud and thick greenery and short, smooth, brown women.

The light that shouldn't be burning. Which will it be tonight? Someone who wants to kill him or someone who can break his heart without even trying?

17

Treasure

"RIGHT, HURRY ME up," Murphy grumbles, getting out of the car before the driver can dart around to open the door. "Beat it," he says. "The gate closes fast, so don't hit the brakes when you're halfway through. I'd tell you to give Shen a kiss for me, but I think I'm too short for him." He gets a better grip, two-handed, on the gaping briefcase and wrestles it up the curving brick path to the double front door, his spirits and the shoulders of his shirt getting damp in the drizzle. The house rises up in front of him, a monument to bad judgment. Once on the porch, he blows out a long, heavy breath, feeling like a resentenced prisoner. He says, "'Home is the sailor,'" and keys in a code on a pad to his right. The lock responds with a discreet snap, and he's in.

The minute the door closes, he turns to the interior keypad, entering a five-digit code followed by two pushes of the zero key; if someone forgets to do this, as Neeni—the current wife number one—always does when she's been indulging in her whiskey and cherry-codeine cough-medicine cocktails, sirens wail and the lights all over the place blink on and off. And she stands there, mouth hanging open, trying to remember what to do until somebody comes to help.

She'll be able to buy a lot of cough syrup when he finally cuts her loose. She'll probably miss this place when she's in Mudville, but she'll have her codeine and her Jack. And *this* time he won't go back for her.

He puts the briefcase on the high-backed chair to the left of the door, a chair that exists for the sole purpose of giving him a place to put the briefcase. During his two years in the house, he has methodically broken or torn up anything anyone else ever put there, and he's finally got them trained, except for Neeni. Neeni can't be trained after, say, 4:00 P.M.

On the other hand, she's not out fucking someone, and Song is.

There's the light in his train room to think about, so he opens the drawer of an almost-antique marble-topped table and keeps pulling until he can reach beneath it and peel back the surgical tape that holds the knife on the underside. It's a Buck 119, one he's had since Vietnam, sharpened so often that the six-inch blade is probably a quarter of an inch narrower than it was new. The heft of it in his hand is deeply familiar. He lays it quietly on the table and leans against the wall to work his boots off. In his socks he moves lightly across the marble-floored entrance hall, the knife in his hand, his arm loose and relaxed. To his left, the living room is pale with the light from the lamps on their automatic timers, and in front of him yawns the formal dining room, now dim but dominated nonetheless by the silhouette of the enormous, six-hundred-pound mahogany table Song had insisted on, back when he still thought she was cute.

To the right, just his side of the stairs to the upper floors, an L-shaped hall leads to the doorway of a small den and then, a few yards later, turns left and ends in the train room. He could go through the dining room and then the kitchen to get to the train room, but those rooms aren't carpeted, and he's quieter on the carpet. At the turn in the hallway, an open door lets him look into Neeni's room. He'd moved her down here eight or ten months ago, after her third fall down the stairs. He can hear her snoring, and something in the shape of her body beneath the covers—always unexpectedly small, given how large she looms in his memory—calls him in. The glass on her bedside table is one-third full of a familiar reddish tan fluid. It's a big glass.

She's asleep or, more accurately, passed out, her long black hair fanned across the pillow, her arm bent at the elbow so that her open hand rests on the pillow, only inches from her face. The defenselessness of the slender wrist, the curl of the fingers, touches something deep inside him, and he bends down, studying the face that so drew him once, with its high, angel's-wing cheekbones and astonishingly fine nose, as perfect and surprising as a baby's. He'd been on his way home from an all-night drunk in a pig-shit village in Laos the first time he saw her, wearing a Tweety T-shirt and a wraparound skirt, coming out of the temple at about eight in the morning, gleaming in the honey-colored sun like some elegantly articulated, long-vanished exotic preserved in amber, just for him.

He can still see the colors the sunlight discovered in her hair.

She turns her head a few inches toward the light falling through the door, and the loose pouches beneath her eyes and the new softness under her chin become visible. Something heavy settles in Murphy's chest, some regret that he won't be able to return her to that village as she was when he took her out of it.

Back in the day, back in 'Nam, he'd never been able to kill the beautiful ones. Despite the business-as-usual betrayals: the working girls with big smiles counting the troops and memorizing the positions of the barracks when they were sneaked into the base for a short-time tussle, then pointing out officers in civvies in the street, targeting them for the knife from behind or the rolled grenade. The pretty village teenager filing reports with Charlie's artillery battalions. He could round up the women, he could bring them in, he could scare them till they pissed themselves, but he couldn't kill them if they were beautiful.

Well, he thinks, straightening up with a sigh, there was probably no one anywhere who didn't draw the line at something. He's faced down fifteen-year-old Muslim kids who fired automatic weapons into women and children in village markets without any apparent hesitation but who fought for their lives when a soldier was shoving pork into their mouths.

His shoulders sag. Maybe it's just the flight, the waits at both ends. He feels weary, and he has an impulse to crawl in beside Neeni. But she'd turn away from him, draw her legs up, make herself small.

And there's still the train room.

He looks away from her without any sense of loss; he had to learn to disconnect from her years ago, although the feeling manages to sneak back. At the door to her room, he pauses, looking down the hall toward the open door to the train room. He hears a faint clicking sound, regular and slightly syncopated, and he recognizes it. He relaxes, just a little. But he shouldn't hear it.

How tough should he be? More to the point, given what he's seeing in her the past two years, would it make any difference?

He moves on the balls of his feet, breathing silently, until he's standing a foot or two from the door, looking into the room. The clicking noise has stopped.

It's a big room, created by knocking together a maid's quarters and a breakfast area and moving the external wall out about eight feet. Evenly lit by pin spots recessed in the ceiling, it has a thickly carpeted floor in West Point gray and walls covered with shelving of blond wood, mostly empty but crowded in a few places by what look like mass collisions of cast-metal toys: trucks, cars, farm machinery, military vehicles, and trains—mostly trains.

Without looking right or left, he slips the Buck knife into a belt loop, snagging the top of the guard inside the loop so the knife won't fall out, and walks into the room as though he thinks he's completely alone. About two-thirds of the room is taken up by an enormous table, plywood on sawhorses, clamped together into a dependable flatness and covered with a two-inch layer of Styrofoam painted green. Carved and punched into the Styrofoam is a scale-model tropical world: four-inch hills, roads with little houses clinging to them like limpets, tiny villages, two-inch palm trees, rubber plantations with their military platoons of trees in straight lines, shallow, mirrored ponds, a narrow-gauge railroad. This is a precise scale model of a few square miles in Yala, the southernmost province of Thailand, just above the border with Malaysia.

The railroad is the key to it all.

A finger touched to the top of the transformer at one side of the miniature confirms that it's hot. He cranks the lever, and a small train, a golden yellow diesel that's a perfect model of several actually in use in the area, clickety-clicks its way along the track, nearing a small station. With the total concentration he devotes to everything he does, he brings the train to the exact point where it would stop to take on and discharge passengers, then breaks the current. In the absence of the train's noise, the room almost pulses with silence.

To the left and right of the big windows hang heavy, dark green, floor-to-ceiling curtains that he draws against the morning light when he's worked through the night in here. One of them bells out slightly from the wall.

Murphy sweeps several pieces out of the miniature world—buildings and trees, mostly—and they clatter against each other as they hit the carpet. While the sound is still ringing in his ears, he says in a low, animal growl, "I . . . smell . . . something . . . *ALIVE.*"

The last word is a roar. In the silence that follows it, he can hear an almost-inaudible sound, bone dry and fast and irregular: teeth chattering. The chattering gives way to something airy, high, and faint that could be a sob, a whimper, or even a nervous giggle. Or, since it's her, all three at once.

He crosses the room in a leap and yanks aside the curtain.

A figure in white, a single loose garment modeled on Wendy's nightgown in the animated *Peter Pan*, stands there, her back pressed to the wall. She's small, even for twelve, and almost emaciated, even though she eats like a wolf. Her arms are black with burned cork, as is her face, except for a straight horizontal stripe of brownish pink skin over the bridge of her nose, broken by two eyes, tiny circles of a wolfish amber completely surrounded by white, trained up at his face with an energy he can almost sense on his skin. Her hair, black with a reddish tint, is an uncombed tangle, shoulder length, and damp. She won't let anyone get near it.

"What are you doing?"

"Ghosting." Her voice is unexpectedly low-pitched, a boy's voice, and there's a tremor in it that could be fear or excitement or both.

"Where's the rotten meat? It works better if you stink."

For a tenth of a second, a pink tongue flicks across the blackened lower lip. "I'm on a, a, a sneak. If I smell bad, they'll know I'm there."

He puts a curled index finger under her chin and pulls it up, not particularly gently. "That's not what I asked you. I asked you where the meat was."

Her teeth chatter for a moment, and he feels her chin tremble. "Hwa threw it out. She thought it was just spoiled."

"That's Hwa's job," he says. "Protect us from spoiled meat. Protect us from you." He takes hold of a knot of hair and gives it a yank, and for a moment her eyes narrow, although she doesn't make a sound. "I ought to slap you," he says. "Some fucking ghost. 'My maid threw out the spoiled meat.' Oh, well, let's just stop the war until the little rich girl can age another porterhouse."

The child says, "You're right."

"You want to play this, play it real. If you don't want to play it, go be a little girl. I'm not saying you should stink right now, but if you want rotten meat, you keep it away from the maid." She's looking at nothing in the middle of the room. "Treasure? Listening or not?"

"In a, in a real war," Treasure says to the middle of the room, "if my, my maid figured out what I was doing, I'd kill her." She speaks her own version of English, flavored with Lao and Vietnamese.

"Then you'd have to get another one. And then *she'd* find the meat because you're so sloppy, and you'd have to kill her and hire another one, and a few months later you'd have so many dead maids you'd have to move out of the house. Dead maids stacked everywhere."

"I'd hide the meat better," Treasure says, still looking at nothing.

"Don't have maids," Murphy says. "Unless you can trust them with your life, don't have maids."

"Can you trust Hwa and Phung with your life?"

"They won't be with us much longer."

She ignores his response. "If you find out you can't trust them, are you going to—"

"We're not in a real war," Murphy says.

Treasure says, "Hwa couldn't protect you from, from *me*. Phung couldn't. Nobody could." She pulls the curtain over her lower half and edges sideways as though she expects a blow.

"In five years, maybe. I won't worry until then." He picks up the fallen model pieces, his back to her. He can hear her coming, and when he turns to look, she's a few feet from him, still holding the bottom of the curtain, dragging it away from the wall as though it's her connection to safety. "Have you figured it out?" he asks, looking down at the railroad.

"It's, it's, it's not the station."

"Let go of that thing. And don't tell me where it's not going to be. Tell me where it *will* be."

The curtain flops back against the wall, and she's standing beside the table, carefully out of arm's reach. He can smell the feral odor of her; she bathes only when she wants to, and she wears a nightgown until the seams are parting and it's stiff with dirt, when she replaces it with an identical one, maybe a quarter size larger, sewn by Hwa or Phung. She's refused to wear anything else since she saw the cartoon Wendy in flight, when she was seven. Neeni had sewn them at first, but these days it's dangerous to let Neeni near a sewing machine.

"There," she says, pointing a dirty finger at a length of track that borders an orderly stretch of rubber trees.

A little kernel of excitement flares in his chest. "Why there?"

"What you said." She looks up at him, but the moment he meets her gaze, her eyelids come down halfway. "Acc-access, escape, blame." She leans forward and touches the tracks, then traces the finger back across the treetops of the rubber plantation to a narrow road. "Park here, go through here, plant it here, go back and get into the car, and you can turn around and you go, you go this way." The finger stops at an intersection. "Here, you go right or left. No-nobody sees you twice." She lifts her face toward his but keeps her eyelids low, and he has the feeling she can see him through them.

"And?" he says.

"And here." Her finger returns to the track and follows it about five inches. "This is a Muslim village. Full of, of boys who have already been in trouble." She shuffles back a couple of steps, away from the table, her eyes on the miniature village, full of tiny, unsuspecting Muslims. Her head jerks right an inch or two and comes back, as it does sometimes. He's not sure she's even aware of it.

"That's good," he says.

He can hear her swallow.

"That's where I *chose*," he says. "Now tell me why I changed my mind."

She crosses her arms tightly across her narrow chest. Her head comes forward on her neck, a movement that always seems more animal than human to him. It brings her eyes two inches closer to the problem. He waits, and she puts her tongue just behind her upper teeth and makes a *tsssss-tsssss-tsssssss* sound.

He says, "I can hear that, and if you don't know you're doing it, you're dead."

"I *know* I'm doing it." The head jerk again. "Which way is the train coming?"

"Smart girl," he says.

"Because if it's coming *this* way"—she points her finger down the track toward the village—"and if it's going fast, all the stuff that blows off it will be going this way, too. And these houses—"

"And if it derails?"

"It's *here*," she says, and she shoves past him and knocks down some of the little houses.

He grabs her wrist, and, so quickly he doesn't see the move, she snatches her hand free, raking his forearm with her nails and leaving red welts. He steps forward and slaps her, hard enough that the tangle of hair snaps around. When it settles, some of it is hanging directly in front of her face.

Treasure doesn't back away or clear the hair. The eyelids are halfway down again, and he thinks—once again—that he wished he had that expression in the interrogation rooms. Then whatever was behind her eyes goes out, and she's so far inside herself he almost feels her leave the room.

"Don't break these things," he says, but he knows he lost his authority the moment he grabbed her. "That was good, though, Treasure, that was very good. Do you want to go with me when I do it?"

He waits, and he thinks she's gone to the deep place, as she does sometimes, occasionally for days, but then she says, "You know you won't take me."

He won't. "Make a deal. By tomorrow night tell me where it's going to be and why, and I'll think about it." He takes a quick step and puts his hand on the nape of her neck, feeling the shudder that rolls through her. "And don't *ever* break anything on this table again."

She says nothing, and he squeezes the muscles in her neck. Her mouth opens. He releases her, and it closes. He squeezes it again, four times, and as her mouth opens and closes, he says, in a good semblance of her voice, "I'm sorry, Papa."

Her eyes have closed. He lets go of her, and she moistens her lips.

"Go to bed," he says.

She turns her back to him and drifts slowly away, back toward the green curtain. "Hwa has a boyfriend," she says, almost singing it. "He's Thai. They meet each other in the pool house. I think she talks to him about us."

Murphy makes a note to talk to Hwa. "And you're not just making this up because she threw out your meat."

"Up to you," she says. "Mr. Smart Man." She leans back against the curtain and wraps it around her again. "Song had her Thai man here. I, I, I creeped them."

"What did you see?"

"In the living room. They had their hands all over each other."

"Why is the Humvee gone? If he came here, where's his car?"

"He came on a motorbike. In the rain."

"Well, Song has a taste for the lowest common denominator."

"He followed her out, her in the Humvee and him on . . ." Her voice trails away and she turns her face down slightly. There's a mirage of a smile on her lips.

"What else did you see?"

"They went up the hall to Neeni's room," she says. "They went in."

Moving slowly, he bends and retrieves one of the pieces he knocked to the floor, one he hadn't picked up. When he is sure his voice will be steady, he says, "Who went in?"

She pulls the edge of the curtain up beneath her eyes like a veil and gives him a skittering glance over it. "Both of them."

He knows his face is scarlet—even if he couldn't feel it, he can read the satisfaction in her eyes—but there's nothing he can do about it except let it flame. "What did you see? Wait, first, tell me *exactly* how you did it. Where you were and how you got there."

"When, when he came on his motorcycle, I was out front. Nobody could see, could see me because I had the night around me. She opened the, the, the gate from inside, and he went to the front door. I went fast to the back patio and watched them through the window in the living room. I got so close I almost laughed.

When they got up and went to the hall, I came in through the dining room and ghostwalked to the hall. I, I got down on the floor like you taught me and put just enough of my face around the corner so I could see."

"So you were at the other end of the hall. The living-room end."

She nods.

Twenty-five, thirty feet. "And."

"Song went in first. Then *he* went in. They both bent down, like they were looking at her or, or touching her, and then they laughed. After a while he straightened up, and I went somewhere else."

"How long were they bent over her?"

"I don't know. Not long."

Her voice is calm now. She's not really interested in what happened in Neeni's room, although Neeni was her mother, back before she got lost in her whiskey-codeine. What she's interested in is its effect on him.

She says, "I want to go outside now."

"It's raining. It's late." He's thinking how easy it would be to break Song's neck, beautiful or not.

"I want to go outside now."

"If you want to," he says, turning toward the door, "you will."

Walking toward the kitchen on his way to the stairs, he says, "Stay out of here for the rest of the night, and don't turn the train on. You can try to figure it out tomorrow, when I—"

There's a faint plucking at his waistband, and then a wasp stings him, hard, between the shoulder blades. He wheels to see her backing away, holding the Buck knife. He can see all her teeth, and she is not smiling.

"Phung," she says, her eyes enormous. "*Phung* will protect you."

Feeling as though his jaws are locked together, he says, "Put the knife on the table. Come here."

But her lids drop again, and she stands in the center of the room, arms hanging down and eyes half closed, swaying like someone at the end of a rope.

He takes the knife out of her hand and goes to the door and turns off the light. Leaving her there, swaying in her white nightgown.

He has no idea what to do with her.

18

The Diamond-Shaped Cutout

AFTER TWO DAYS holed up in yet another cheap hotel—on the outskirts of the city this time—Rafferty goes on the offensive.

The first good news of a dull, wet day is that the laundry that issued the yellow ticket, however many months or years ago, is still in business.

From across the intersection, Rafferty peers at it through the drizzle. It sits at the corner of two small, anonymous streets not far from the hotel where he'd kept Shen's man from falling off the roof. Its flyblown windows, ice blue from the fluorescents inside, face out from the bottom floor of yet another cheap hotel with an ersatz-fancy name, the Royal Residence. The hotel has a doomed look. For one thing, it's only five stories high, the kind of building that's not going to last long in the new Bangkok, where everything that can't go up gets torn down.

He's walked around the block twice, wielding a hundred-baht umbrella against the intermittent drizzle and using it to hide his face from time to time. Nothing has caught his attention. The days and nights since he escaped his apartment car have blurred into a new kind of marathon in which the runner jogs lethargically through wide, featureless stretches of boredom and then runs for his life from the occasional lion.

His head is almost too heavy to hold upright, and he feels that his control of his emotions is precarious. He has to go into the laundry, but he has a condensation of dread in his core. Not dread that something horrible will happen to him when he gets inside,

but a conviction that if anything at *all* goes wrong—any complica-
tion, no matter how minor—he'll burst into tears. He's been
alarmingly close to tears lately. More than anything in the world,
he wants to hug his wife and be ignored, in person, by his daughter.
He'd give anything to see their eyes.

In addition to everything else, he's out of money. He's called his
father's number in Virginia twice and had no answer, not even a
machine. He's got a couple of frugal days in his pocket, and that's it.

And he's left another message on the voice mail of the elusive
Helen Eckersley. He hung up feeling even spookier about her than
before. There's something wrong in the house that phone is ringing in. In his old life, he would have scoffed at such an intuition,
but after all his time with Rose he takes it much more seriously.

Ahhh, Rose. He looks both ways and steps into the street.

When he's eight or ten steps from the laundry door, one of his
new phones rings. He's carrying three at the moment, and he
juggles frantically through them, thinking, hoping, *wishing* it will
be Rose or Miaow. Eventually he works out which phone it is and
thumbs it open. Arthit says, "I'm looking at your new picture. It
just landed on my desk." He covers the mouthpiece with his hand,
and then he's back. "On everyone's desk."

Rafferty's been worrying about this. They have at least two
descriptions of him in his pathetically thin disguise now, one each
from the guy on the roof and the kid behind the hotel desk. "How
bad is it?"

"It's terrible. It's so terrible it's great. Shen's guy, up on the roof?
He must be *really* grateful. Your hair's three inches longer and
floppy, and you're very dark. You look like Hugh Grant playing
Gandhi."

Rafferty steps under the laundry's awning and tilts the umbrella
forward, so it's between him and the eyes on the sidewalk. The
building seems to ripple against his back, and he feels suddenly
seasick. He closes his eyes, then hurriedly reopens them. "That's
good, I guess. I'm so tired I halfway wish they'd catch me."

"Look," Arthit says, and clears his throat. "I haven't wanted to
bother you with this, but Pim's run off. Three days ago. She feels
guilty, I suppose."

"Oh, for Christ's sake. Are you looking for her?"

"She's not going to want to be found."

"Who cares what she wants? She's a baby. She's going to be somewhere around Soi Seven. She was working the sidewalk outside the Beer Garden when I found her. Where else would she go?"

Arthit says, "Home?"

"No. Tell me, did she ever have any money at all?"

"Never. I had to keep a few hundred baht in a bowl so she could go buy stuff when I called and asked for it."

"She sent it all home," Rafferty says. "Every baht. That's a big family up there. She's going to be working. Go arrest her."

"Poke. We've actually got bigger problems than Pim."

"Rose will kill me."

"I'm telling you, even if I find her, or you find her, she won't come back to my place. She's got a problem with—Poke, it was getting really odd around the edges. She's a sweet, good-hearted girl, but she's a *baby*."

"That's my point. She can't be hooking on a sidewalk, not there. You know who she'll be pulling? Drunks from the Beer Garden who can hardly walk, who'll take it out on her when they can't get it up. Guys who haven't got enough money to go to Nana."

"I know," Arthit says, "but I'm telling you, she's not going to go anywhere with me."

"Just a couple of minutes ago, I was thinking that one more problem would probably make me cry. I'm on the verge of getting weepy here."

"Where's 'here'?"

"Over near Khao San."

"Still? Isn't that kind of slow-learner behavior?"

"I have to be somewhere. You're changing the subject."

"I am. She came down to Bangkok alone, and she's going to have to take care of herself for now. She won't come back with me, and I haven't got anyplace else to put her."

"My apartment?"

"Think, Poke. Have a good cry and see if it clears your mind. Your apartment is almost certainly under surveillance. She'd be safer on a hillside in Afghanistan than at your place. I'll try to come up with something, okay?"

"Me, too."

"Anyway, you've had *some* good news today. The new picture is useless."

"Listen," Rafferty says, "I don't get it. About the picture. Shen is working with the Americans, right? I mean, that's who Murphy is, that's who Elson is. The Americans could get a good, current picture of me here in about fifteen seconds. Why haven't they?"

"I've been asking the same question. But for now they're looking for Hugh Grant. In blackface."

"Still, it's something to think about. Along with everything else, and Pim."

"I'll help her any way I can. From a distance. She'll bolt if she sees me."

"Thanks, Arthit. One more thing. Is there any way I can find out whether Murphy has been traveling?"

"Yes," Arthit says. "You can ask me, 'Arthit, has Murphy been traveling lately?'"

"What, you were saving this as a surprise?"

"I knew you'd appreciate it. And this is why, aside from general karmic reasons, you want me on your side. I wanted to keep this query away from Shen, so I requested a restricted-substances watch on him."

"Will that really keep the information secret?"

"Secret from everyone who's not paying for it, like narco bosses. But there's no reason Shen should be paying for it. Got a pencil?"

"Sure," Rafferty says, closing his eyes to listen.

"In the past ten days, he's been down to Yala twice. That was kind of interesting, because he used a chartered plane both times. The second time he filed a flight plan for Phuket and then diverted to Yala."

"Lot of Muslims in Yala."

"Majority population in places. Just today a buffalo stepped on a land mine and three kids were killed by automatic fire from a moving car. Buddhists are generally peaceful, but tempers are pretty short down there."

"Yala," Rafferty says. "In the south."

"Yes, Poke, Yala is in the south."

"Think it's been sunny down there?"

"Why? Do you want to work on your tan?"

"The man who was killed. The top of his head was sunburned."

"Hmmm. I don't know for a fact that it's been sunny down there, but I'd bet good money it's been sunnier there than it has been here."

"Where else has Murphy been?"

"Three nights ago he flew to Kuala Lumpur. Don't know why. Stayed one night and came back the next."

"Kuala Lumpur," Rafferty says with his eyes closed. He's so tired that he visualizes writing it so he won't forget. "Thanks, Arthit. Call on this phone for now and leave a message if it's off. If I toss it, I'll get you the new number."

He disconnects and looks up. The clouds have thinned enough to allow the afternoon sun to point a few shiny fingers down, picking out this car and that window and making them gleam unconvincingly against the gray of the day. Rafferty says, "Special effects," and pushes off the wall, tucking the phones into various pockets. A knot of girls go by, maybe eight of them, crowded beneath three overlapping umbrellas, taking tiny steps to stay together. They're laughing, and a couple of them eye him. He lets them pass, then falls in behind them, toward the laundry's door.

A chime rings as he pushes the door open. A woman of forty or so, Southeast Asian but probably not Thai, looks up from stuffing clothes into a bag and gives him a measured smile. She's behind a waist-high counter, one end of which is piled with unsorted garments of all kinds. As he nears her, he also sees an older woman, silver hair drawn back in a long, loose, shining ponytail, sitting in a chair behind the clothing. Her head is down, and she's doing something involving a skein of green yarn—crocheting or knitting.

"Yes?" This is the younger woman. She's not expending the energy most Thais put into a greeting.

"This ticket," he says, suddenly at something of a loss. "Someone gave it to me, and, uh . . ."

He fishes it out of his shirt pocket and hands it to her, still folded.

She takes it with a small, polite smile and opens it and stares down at it. When her eyes come up to his, they're terrified. She says, "You . . . you . . . who are you? Who gave you—"

The older woman says something in a language Rafferty doesn't speak but thinks is Vietnamese. Her tone is sharp enough to bring the other woman to a stop. She stands there, fingering the hole in the ticket, and the fear in her face turns with no transition at all to desolation and then tears. They're completely silent tears, and they gleam suddenly on her cheeks as the sun pokes another hole in the clouds outside. She brings her empty hand up, straight-fingered, to cover her mouth, but still the tears come, and still she holds Rafferty's gaze, although he's not certain she even sees him.

The older woman lifts her head and repeats herself more sternly, and Rafferty sees that she's blind, her eyelids two swirls of flesh mutilated in some terrible injury, a long time ago.

The crying woman closes her eyes and lets her head droop, an attitude of purest defeat. Her shoulders rise and fall with her sobs, but she still hasn't made a sound. She leans down and places her fingers gently on the older woman's wrist and turns her hand palm up. Then she puts the yellow ticket into the waiting hand.

The blind woman's mouth tightens. Something rough catches in her throat, and the work in her lap slides to the floor, the needles making a faint clinking sound. She passes her fingertips over the surface of the ticket, once, then again, and then—very slowly—again. She lets out a rasp of breath and tightens her hands into fists and brings them up so they meet in front of her heart, and she screams.

"How do we know?" the younger woman says. She regards him out of the corners of her eyes. "You could be anyone."

The door to the shop has been closed and locked, and the lights in the front room are off. They've all moved to the room at the rear, a big, raw room with unpainted walls and a cement floor that smells of starch and ironed cotton and has two walls lined with battered washing machines and dryers. The rain's pattering sound comes through a glassless, barred window.

He and the younger woman are sitting on folding chairs. The older woman is curled on her side, her back to them, on a cot beneath an enormous, almost painfully colorful calendar depicting some sort of festival in front of a Vietnamese temple. The younger woman has covered her with an old coat.

"I'm just me," Rafferty says. "He pretty much died in my lap."

"How many day?" the woman on the cot asks in English without turning. The words are heavily accented. They're the first words she's spoken since she released three screams that, Rafferty thought, could have brought her heart up with them.

"Nine," he says. "Or maybe eight."

"Why hasn't it been in the papers?" the younger woman asks. She's wide-faced, the lower half of her features overhung by extraordinarily prominent cheekbones. Now that she's not weeping, her eyes are difficult to read.

"I think you know why."

Both women are silent, but the woman on the cot stiffens.

"He was involved in something secret, something very bad," Rafferty says. "A long time ago. Looking at you, I'm going to say it was in Vietnam."

The woman on the cot says, "Who send you?"

"That ticket sent me. He gave it to me."

"You say so," says the woman on the cot. "True, not true, how do we know? You go now."

"Why would I lie to—"

"You kill him, take ticket. Friend of you kill him, give you ticket. You go."

"He talked to me," Rafferty says.

A pause. Then, "He say what?"

Rafferty sits back and crosses his arms, realizes how defensive it looks, and uncrosses them, but the sudden chill of caution remains. "I don't think I'll tell you. You don't trust me, and I'm not sure I trust you. I'm at risk here, too."

The woman on the cot rolls onto her back and turns the brutalized face to him, and he has an uneasy feeling she can see him. She says again, "He say what?"

Rafferty gets up. "I'm sorry I've caused you so much sadness. I didn't know the ticket was . . . was bad news." He goes to a small desk and takes a pencil and a piece of yellow paper. "If you want to talk to me, call this number. I won't answer it, but leave a one-word message on the voice mail. Don't say who you are—the word will tell me. If it feels okay to me, I'll either come back here or call you."

"What word?" asks the younger woman.

Rafferty looks at the older woman and says, "Helen."

The older woman says, "Wait."

"No." He puts the pencil down. "Let's *all* think about this."

"When you come back," the younger woman says defiantly, "we won't be here."

Rafferty says, "I don't blame you. I wouldn't be here either, if I had a choice. If you want to talk again, call and say 'Helen,' and we'll figure out a way to meet that makes all of us feel safe."

The older woman sits up and releases a stream of Vietnamese at her daughter—Rafferty suddenly sees beyond the savagery of what's been done to her face and finds the resemblance—but he keeps moving, through the door, through the shop. The younger woman follows him, putting a hand on his arm, but he shrugs her off and twists the lock, eager to be out of the shop and back in the cleansing, softening drizzle in the streets.

HE'S GONE THREE slow, careful blocks, the umbrella pulled low to cover part of his face, when the phone in his shirt pocket rings. He steps out of the flow of pedestrians, up against a shop window, and does a quick street survey in the time it takes him to close the umbrella and retrieve the phone. No one seems to be paying any attention to him.

This can't keep up forever. Sooner or later he's going to look up and find the eyes that are trained on him.

He doesn't recognize the number on the display. He scans the block again and says, "Hello."

"Where are you?" It's a woman's voice.

"Who is this?"

"Older brother, shame on you, not recognizing my voice. Where are you?"

"I'm in Bangkok."

"Well, *yeah*, but where in Bangkok?"

A terrible conviction seizes him. "Where are *you?*"

"I didn't want to go to your apartment in case it was uncool or something," Ming Li says, "so I'm standing around in the rain with a bunch of money in my pocket. And I'm hungry."

"You're in *Bangkok?*" Rafferty says. "But the phone number—"

"Hopeless, you're hopeless. You need me *so badly*. It's a global phone, silly. And it is *soooo cool* to be here. Asia, I smell Asia again. I thought I'd never smell anything except America as long as I lived. Fabric softener and frying fat, mixed together, that's what America smells like. Come get your little sister. Buy her something to eat."

19

Not a Creepy-Looking Solo Guy

"Oh, my God, I'm here," Ming Li says. They're in a tiny restaurant off of Silom, empty but for them, and she's got four entrée dishes and a bowl of rice in front of her. Two of the dishes are already empty, and the one that's currently claiming her attention is a hellacious mix of stir-fried basil, crisp pork, and enough tiny red chilies to bring moisture to her brow. "Nothing in America tastes like anything. It's like *reading* about food, not eating it."

He feels like he's still catching up with the fact that she's here. And he can't stop looking at her. She was a striking girl two years ago, and she's turning into a beautiful young woman. "So, you got through immigration with no problem?"

"I'm eighteen. It says so on my passport." She breaks off and looks quickly down at the bowl in front of her. The tips of her ears are scarlet. "*Boy,* this is good," she says. "Nothing like it in, um, America."

Rafferty says, "Eighteen. Chinese eighteen or American eighteen?"

"Chinese," she says to the tabletop.

"So. That makes you seventeen, counting the American way." He watches her make piles of food at the edge of the bowl. "And when you were here almost two years ago, you were twenty-two."

She says, "Would you have let me help? If you'd known?"

"Probably not.

She looks up at him for the first time. "And did I make any mistakes? Did I screw up?"

"No."

"See? I spared you a lot of unnecessary worry. And anyway, you bought it."

"Actually, I didn't. I checked it. I asked your—sorry, our— father, and he said . . ." He breaks off. "Sure," he says, "*Dad* said. I should have known right there."

"Before you beat up on Dad, *here*." She reaches into a purse so big that Rose would envy it, pulls out a well-worn American passport, and slides it across the table. "Hello, Bob."

Rafferty opens it and finds the picture of himself from the back of his books—a good copy this time—and the name Robert Delacroix. It expires in seven months.

"Courtesy of some people in his shop," Ming Li says. "Although they don't know it. It'll be good for hotels and stuff, but I wouldn't cross any borders."

Rafferty is flipping through the pages to see where he's been. "Delacroy or Delacwah?"

"How would I know? I'm from China."

"Maybe old Bob is from Louisiana."

"I wouldn't know that either." She stops the spoon halfway to her mouth, fans herself with her free hand, and says, "So. Good or no good?"

He smiles at her. Every now and then he catches, in her Asian features, a glimpse of his own, courtesy of their father. "Good. Very good."

She empties the spoon, then turns it upside down and licks it. "And are you glad to see me? No matter how old I am?"

"I'm . . . surprised."

"Don't go overboard. I fly a hundred thousand miles to bring you a stack of money and a passport, and you don't even hug me."

He kisses the tips of his fingers, reaches across and plants them on her forehead, then gives a little shove. He gets a basil-green grin in response. "I'm very, very happy, okay? I'm a little perplexed, because this is a dangerous place."

Her eyes widen. "Bangkok? You mean, the flooding? It doesn't seem so—"

"No. Sitting at this table. Being near me."

"Look," she says, holding out a rock-steady hand. "I'm shaking. You haven't actually asked about Dad."

"How's Dad?"

"Ehhhhh." She swivels the hand back and forth. "Fifty-fifty. I just wanted you to ask."

"And your mom?"

"She's better than he is." She picks up the dish and pours a pool of cooking oil, all that's left of the basil and pork, onto the rice and shovels it into her mouth. Around it she says, "She found a Chinatown somewhere near us, and she goes there on the bus every morning. She plays mah-jongg with a bunch of old ladies, and they cheat her, and then she buys a whole chicken from a Chinese grocery, one they've killed in front of her, and brings it home and uses it for soup. She's very heavily into soup these days."

"What kind of soup?"

"Who knows? They've all got chicken in them, though. *Healthy* soup. They're black, mostly, and they've got cloud's ears—that's a fungus—in them and some shells and I suppose whatever was wearing them and some stringy greens, and they smell kind of awful. They're good for reducing heat and wind, she says."

"Well, that's nice, I guess."

"It would be if I were hot and windy. But I don't eat them, and Dad doesn't really eat them, and—oh, well, it's all pretty sad. They don't even talk to each other."

"He didn't talk to mine either."

"So you've told me. Over and over." She leans forward and puts her hand on top of his. "Older brother, how would you feel if he came back here to live?"

"I'd feel like moving."

"He misses Asia even more than I do." She gives his hand a businesslike pat. "Think about it for a while. Get used to the idea."

"I'm already used to it. Asia's a big place. There are lots of continents available to him."

She puts her spoon aside for practically the first time since they sat down, and he feels a little pang of guilt. "All right, all right," he says. "I'll think about it, but don't get optimistic."

"Don't you want to know how much he sent you?"

"Why, yes, I would, Ming Li. How much did he send me?"

"Twenty K."

Rafferty says, "Well, well."

"I played on his guilt," she says, grabbing the spoon again and sorting through a mound of pad thai as though she's counting the shrimp. "He *does* feel guilty, you know."

"I'm sure it's eating him alive. But the money is welcome. Where are you staying?"

Her eyebrows vault toward her hairline. "With you."

"But where's your stuff?"

She pats the big purse. "In here." She pulls out a couple of folded shirts, a pair of jeans, and a little bag of sample-size soap and shampoo and puts them on the table. "Tourist cover," she says, and she shows him a small silver digital camera and a spiral notebook. The notebook says MY TRAVEL JOURNAL in bright yellow letters. "Smile," she says, and takes his picture. "Got a little computer and everything."

"Ming Li," he says, trying to see through the black hole in his vision where the flash went off. "When did you land in Bangkok?"

A shrug, the same shrug Miaow does to indicate a question not worth answering. She's putting things back into the bag. "I don't know. Three hours ago?"

"Well, turn around and go back. This isn't going to work. The people who are looking for me don't play nicely."

"That's exactly why you need me." She offers him a dripping spoon, and he shakes his head. "An extra pair of eyes, a messenger no one's ever seen before, someone who can do one thing while you're doing something else, a trained surveillance artist who could follow a flea across a dog, a trained surveillance *spotter* who'll pick up on a watcher way before you do. . . ."

"No."

"*And* someone who instantly turns you into half of a couple, not a creepy-looking solo guy with dark makeup and a hairstyle even Hugh Grant gave up on years ago."

"I know," he says. "I know about the hair—"

She drops the spoon in the pad thai. "And the other thing about me is that I look like everybody here. Someone arrests you, I just take a step back and they won't even see me."

THE FEAR ARTIST 173

"No."

"And I've got computer skills that make you look like someone who's just learning to work a calculator."

"All right," he says, gratified by the surprise in her face. "Computer skills I can use. For the moment anyway. Have you finished eating?"

"I eat when you want me to," Ming Li says, pushing the plate away and standing up. "Let's go save your butt, older brother."

HE'S NOT EVEN halfway through his coffee before Ming Li says, "Whoa."

While he was still ordering, she had pulled a little MacBook Air out of her bag and logged into Coffee World's router, and from that point on she'd been lost to him. He'd put down her tea and sweet rolls and stood there, feeling large and aimless, as she ignored him. A couple of young men looked at her and then at him, and he could almost see them dismissing him as competition: *Guy thinks he looks like Hugh Grant.* He finally said, "Well, just call if you need anything else," and went to sit facing the window as the dusk wrapped itself around the drizzle and lights popped on. And then she'd said, "Whoa."

"Whoa what?"

"Whoa the *Wyoming Eagle Tribune.* You need to read this." She gets up, grabs one of the rolls, takes out half of it with a single bite, and then passes him the computer one-handed. It's even lighter than his netbook, back in the hotel room.

He's looking at a headline that reads CHEYENNE WOMAN KILLED.

He'd known it, he'd known it almost all along. That phone was ringing in a bad house. He opens his eyes, which he hadn't realized he'd squeezed shut, and goes back to the screen.

Helen Eckersley had been discovered in her living room by her maid. Eckersley had, the local sheriff said, "been beaten repeatedly over a period of twenty-four hours or more with a poker from her own fireplace set."

"They hurt her for a whole day," Ming Li says, leaning over his shoulder. "They had questions."

According to a department spokesperson, the paper says, the killers broke all the bones in her arms and legs, as well as her collarbones, before shattering her skull. Some of the injuries were almost a full day older than others. The newspaper's description of the murder is "merciless, prolonged, and brutal."

"I'm glad they tell us it was brutal," Ming Li says. "We might have missed it."

Rafferty can feel the pulse thumping inside his left wrist as he finishes reading. "Any updates?"

"Not on this site. I'm going to look in a few other places."

Reading, Rafferty says, "And good luck to him."

"Who?"

"The mayor, who's the usual local gasbag. Says the killers will 'be pursued tirelessly.' They have no idea what just hit them."

Ming Li is running her fingernail lightly down the screen as she reads the end of the story. "What did?"

"The same thing that's after me right now. Notice what's not here?"

She leans closer, as if he's challenged her to spot something very small. "No. What?"

"Her age. Her family. Her marital status. Anything that indicates that she didn't just materialize unnoticed in Cheyenne from some other dimension. None of the inevitable neighbors seem to have come forward to say the things they always say: 'She kept to herself.' 'I never thought anything like this could happen here.' She seems—I don't know—disconnected. There's no background information: 'A native of Purdue, Indiana, Ms. Eckersley worked at the Cheyenne Public Library, and raised hydrangeas'—that kind of stuff."

"Maybe she wasn't from there."

Rafferty remembers the little curlicues in the way she spoke. "I'm pretty sure she wasn't."

Ming Li says, "Nobody deserves to die like that."

Rafferty says, "A lot of people have died like that."

A LONG, COLD cup of coffee later, it's 9:30 P.M. and Rafferty's reached the point where the caffeine is actually making him sleepier when Ming Li says, "Nothing much more. I've been through everything I can find, and they're still looking for whoever did it, and the sheriff is still saying they'll get him."

"What time is it?"

"You have a watch."

"What time is it in Wyoming?"

She looks at her own watch and bangs the keys for a second. "About eight-thirty A.M."

"Well, I suppose morgues open early."

She cocks her head to one side, waiting for the rest of it.

He takes out his newest cell phone, the one he hasn't used, and hands it to her. "Get the phone number for the morgue in Cheyenne, or call the sheriff's office if you can't find the morgue and ask them for it."

"I'll find the morgue."

"Give yourself an accent. You're calling from Bangkok to see whether Helen Eckersley's body has been claimed. If they ask who you are, you say something like, 'I'm calling on behalf of the family of a woman from here, a Thai woman who called herself Helen, who ran away from her husband in America several years ago and took a new last name, which the family doesn't know. The last anyone heard, she was in Wyoming. They're worried because she hasn't called them or returned calls for ten days or so. If someone has claimed Ms. Eckersley's body, or if she's not Asian, then she's not the woman we're looking for.'"

"'And if no one has, and if she's Asian,'" Ming Li says in a businesslike voice, reading a number off the screen and pushing the buttons on the phone, "'maybe we can help you identify her.'"

"Good."

She looks up at him, waiting for the phone on the other end to ring. "You need me," she says. Then she says, "Hello?" and goes into her pitch.

Listening to her voice without even hearing the words, he realizes again what their father has turned her into. Living in China, at the mercy of the Triad he worked for, Frank Rafferty had transformed his half-Chinese daughter into an asset. By the time she was eight, she was following people. At ten she was running low-level cons and forging signatures. At twelve she was helping to plan their escape, carrying in her head secrets that would have killed her father, her mother, and herself if someone had wormed them out of her. He'd worked with her, Frank had, until she had a coat of solid brass and her English was accent-free and she was fluent in Mandarin *and* Cantonese, and in her spare time he had her throwing fastballs in their courtyard in preparation for their annual ritual of watching the World Series on satellite. When Poke met her, she was capable of pegging him with a hard, wet lychee pit at sixty feet, and she had.

And Frank, self-exiled in Asia, had talked to her endlessly about his lost son. About Poke, whose mother he'd abandoned to flee to China when Poke was seventeen. When Frank and Ming Li had emerged from China for an unexpected and unwanted reunion a few years back, Poke had been surprised and even touched to learn how much she knew about him, this girl whose existence he'd never even suspected. He'd softened slightly toward his father, begun to think there might be a relationship there after all. And then Poke's father had pulled yet another con.

Even her body language, as she works the phone, is efficient, precise, persuasive. Instead of her usual teenage sit-on-the-lungs posture, she's perched bolt upright, her spine an inch or two from the back of the chair. Her free hand pats at her hair, as though she's moments away from getting up and going into a meeting. There's a half smile on her face; she obviously knows that people can hear a smile even if they don't realize it.

Her eyebrows go up and her eyes widen in misleading candor as she asks a question. He turns back to the window, not sure how he feels about any of this. She's seventeen, no matter what her passport says, and her father has turned her into a professional, a con artist and a premature cynic who finds the entirety of American civilization wanting. Miaow, at twelve or thirteen, has reservoirs of scorn, but as someone who was abandoned on the sidewalk at the age of two or three, she's earned it.

Ming Li is the only sister he's ever had. What has his miserable father done to her?

Reflected in the window, he sees her stand up, and he opens his mouth wide to clear his face of whatever expression he'd been wearing and turns to face her.

She says, "Helen Eckersley was Asian."

20

Boom in Yala

THERE ARE TWO places he could go, but it's 10:00 P.M. already, and the laundry will be closed. So at least he's spared that. For the moment.

With some misgivings, then, he calls Vladimir and tells him to come get his money. And thinks of a way to put Ming Li to work.

An extra pair of eyes, she'd said. Well, why not?

He'd told Vladimir to go to the closed Asia Books on Sukhumvit and then call him. A thumb on the phone had cut short Vladimir's protest that he could be trusted with the actual destination. He'd hauled Ming Li out onto the sidewalk, the guys in Coffee World drooping in disappointment, and grabbed a cab for Sukhumvit. The drizzle had lifted, but the streets still shone like obsidian and the air smelled almost fresh, or at least wet.

According to the driver's radio, water from the rising river is being diverted into several canals, and residents of the areas intersected by those canals are being advised to get their belongings—and, presumably, their asses—to higher ground. The cabbie says to Ming Li, in Thai, "It's going to be bad."

"*Poot Thai medai,*" Ming Li says. I don't speak Thai.

"There's already flooding around the Temple of Dawn," Rafferty says in Thai.

"My house is near there," the driver says. "My wife's taken the kids to her parents. Where do you live?"

"Silom."

"Never happen," the driver says. "Silom is a rich area."

"Yes, but does the water know that?"

Ming Li is ignoring the chatter. She seems entranced to see Bangkok again. Her nose is practically pressed to the taxi's window.

"The guy," Rafferty says to her in English. "He's six-two or so, getting a little paunchy, with a long face, a black mustache, and eyebrows that almost meet over his nose. And a cleft in his chin deep enough to be a national park. Head shaped like a bullet, black hair—"

"Got it," she says. Her breath fogs the window.

"Practically oozes melancholy."

"I said I've got it."

"He looks the way a Gypsy violin sounds."

"Tall, narrow-faced, dark hair, cleft chin, unibrow, mustache, depressive. Looks Russian, in other words." There's a lot of patience in her tone.

"Oh, right, I forgot. He's Russian."

"I *said* I've got it."

"Good. You just stand a few stores down and wait for me to call."

"I'm seeing a lot of girls on this street," she says.

"Oh, good Lord," he says, remembering Pim.

"Well, if *you* don't mind depraved tourists hitting on your little sister, *I* don't."

"They'll survive the encounter," he says.

He lets her out a few blocks from the store, tells her to be careful, and gets a snort in return. The cab takes him another quarter of a mile to a small *soi* with a cluster of Arab restaurants on it. He goes into the second one back from the boulevard and orders a Diet Coke. One swallow into the second can, his phone rings.

"I am here," Vladimir says. "You are not."

"Okay. Face Sukhumvit so the store is at your back. Got it?"

"This is not difficult."

"Turn left and start walking. Call me in two blocks."

"You are not trusting me."

"Of course I trust you. We're friends." He disconnects, and the phone rings instantly.

"He's towing somebody," Ming Li says.

"Does he know it?"

"Yes. The guy was about twenty feet past me, so I was in between them, right? Fighting off prospective husbands right and left."

"Come on, come on."

"So he put the phone away, turned and looked past me, and gave the other guy what I'd call a 'significant glance.' You know, melodramatic countries shouldn't even try to spy. Russians all think they're in an opera."

Rafferty signals the waiter and makes a scribbling motion in the air. "Can you tamp down the adrenaline a little? So they're both coming toward me, right?"

"I don't know where you are, do I? Sorry, it's just that it's so much fun to be doing this again."

"Vladimir turned away from you, and he and the other one are going in that direction."

"Yes."

"Well, that'll lead you to me, unless I move. Describe the other one."

"Mmmm. That's not easy. He looks like every Caucasian gene in the planet was put into a blender and—"

"Never mind. I know who it is." He hands the waiter some money and waves off a halfhearted offer of change. "Okay. Where are you?"

"Crossing a big, insane intersection with a street coming in at a diagonal and—yikes!—buses going in the wrong direction in the lane nearest the curb."

"Right. Okay. Dawdle a little. Hang back. Look both ways. Stop for a minute or two."

"I'm very popular when I stop."

"Dazzle them. Burn off some of that energy. I have to hang up."

His call-waiting signal beeps again. "Vladimir," he says. "You're being a bad boy."

"Always," Vladimir says. "But why you telling me now?"

"What's-his-name—I mean, Janos."

"Oho," Vladimir says. "You are looking, yes? Where?"

"Why is he here?"

"He is not trusting me. You are not trusting me, he is not trusting me. Good thing Vladimir is not sensitive."

"I asked why he's—"

"You owe him money. He is not wanting to have to kill me to get it."

"Money for what?"

"Ah-ah. We talking when we see each other."

"Okay. Keep walking. In about three blocks, there's a hotel, the Alpine Suites. Go through the lobby and into the bar. I'll be in a booth at the back. Bring Janos."

"You buy me drink?"

Rafferty says, "Oh, for Christ's sake," and turns off the phone.

ON THE WAY in, he stops at reception and asks for three standard letter-size envelopes. He takes them into the men's room, claims a stall, and closes the door, then does some quick sorting with the hundreds and twenties Ming Li brought from America.

The bar is empty. At this hour most of the businessmen who stay here are out experiencing the more vivid aspects of Bangkok life. He calls Ming Li and says, "I'm in a hotel up ahead of you, the Alpine Suites. They'll be going into it, if they haven't already. Just walk past it, twenty or thirty yards. The guy Vladimir is towing is going to come out in a few minutes. Make sure he goes all the way away, and then come in and go through the lobby into the bar."

Ming Li says, "I'm not old enough to—"

Rafferty hangs up and waves across the room to Vladimir and Janos, who is two steps behind. Vladimir crosses the room as though it's a minefield, eyes everywhere, and slides into the booth. When Janos starts to follow, Rafferty holds up an envelope and says, "Take this and go away."

Janos crinkles his generic forehead and says, "Why should I—" and then hefts the envelope and changes the subject. "How much?"

"One thousand, U.S."

"Ha," Janos says. He pops the flap on the envelope and looks inside. "This one, this Vladimir, he is so cheap. You I can work for."

"And you probably will, but right now go away. All the way out of the hotel and then into a cab and somewhere else. I have someone watching, and I'll know."

"You learn fast," Janos says. To Vladimir he says, "Bye-bye, cheapskate."

Watching Janos go, Vladimir sags back against the booth and says, "Five hundred. I tell him you can only pay five hundred. You Americans, you throw money ewerywhere. And *still* nobody love you."

"What did he find out?"

"Oh, no, no. Do not reduce me to laughter. First I am seeing some money. Already you owe me."

"Well, gee," Poke says, taking out another envelope. "I don't know. Now that you've told me I'm overpaying—"

"*Him*," Vladimir says, both eyes on the envelope. "You pay *him* too much. Me, I am contractor. Always you pay contractor good." He lifts the cleft chin in the direction of the envelope. "How much?"

"Two thousand." He puts it on the table. "For everything you told me last time, and for getting things moving."

Vladimir shrugs and reaches for it. "Good." He uses his fingertips to square the envelope precisely with the table's edge and folds his hands over it.

"Not going to count it?"

"I trust you." He surveys the room lazily, and Rafferty figures he's memorizing everything in it. "I count it later. One more small information for you. Murphy has first name. Heskell."

"Heskell?"

"No," Vladimer says. "*Heskell*."

"Oh," Rafferty says. "*Haskell*."

"I tell you two times, Heskell." His eyes lock on something and follow it. He reaches up and smooths his hair. "This is pretty girl," he says, and Rafferty looks up to see Ming Li.

"Get you guys something?" Ming Li asks. "You must be Vladimir."

Vladimir says to Rafferty, "She is yours?"

"How Old World," Ming Li says. She looks down at Poke. "Scoot over, whoever you are."

"I'm Poke," Poke says as Ming Li sits. "Vladimir knows my name. Vladimir, this isn't Minnie Lee. Minnie, this isn't really Vladimir."

Vladimir says, "Poke is not a name."

"If you'd told my father that thirty-seven years ago, I'd have been spared a life of shame."

"Poke is better than Philip," Ming Li says. She looks at the envelope. "Is that what I think it is?"

Vladimir puts a protective hand on the envelope and says, "Depends what you think—"

"Money," she says. "You going to earn it?"

Vladimir straightens up an inch or so and looks down his considerable nose at her. "Is already earned."

The two of them examine each other in a way that makes Poke feel he's in the next room.

Into the silence he says, "I wonder how you get a drink in here."

Vladimir says, "You have wery interesting eyes."

Ming Li says, "You've got a nice kind of aging-Borat thing going yourself."

"Was a time," Vladimir says mournfully, "you would have chased Vladimir through the woods."

"And caught him, too," Ming Li says.

"Would either of you like a—"

"But your eyes," Vladimir says, sliding the envelope back and forth with his fingertips. "Yes, pretty, wery pretty, but interesting."

"I'm just your basic hybrid."

"Glad you guys are getting along," Poke says.

Vladimir says to Poke, "She is baby spy, yes?"

"I'm his bankroll," Ming Li says.

"Yes? And you are knowing him how?"

"I've heard about him my entire life." She laces her fingers together and clasps her hands over her heart. "This is a dream come true."

Vladimir's lower lip comes out half an inch, apparently propelled by doubt. "You are young," he says. "You will have better dream later."

"Hey," Rafferty says. "My life is in danger."

"You guys talk for a minute." Ming Li gets up. "What do you want?"

Rafferty asks for a Singha. Vladimir says, "Wodka. The bottle, please," and watches her cross the room.

"A million dollar, she would be worth to me," Vladimir says. "Two million. Already I have a hundred ideas."

"Not for sale."

"With fifty like her, look like her, smart like her, I could have won war in Wietnam."

"You did."

"No. Wietnam won. We lose ewerything. We lose whole world. We were killed by American telewision." He puckers as though to spit but instead says, "*Dallas.*"

"Back in the present tense." Rafferty takes out the third envelope and hits it against the heel of his hand. It makes a nice, thick *thwack* that gets Vladimir's attention. Rafferty puts the envelope down and says, "Three thousand."

"For what?"

"Murphy's address."

Vladimir picks up the envelope and slides it into his shirt pocket. He fumbles in the pocket with two long fingers for a moment and then extracts them. There's a folded slip of paper between them. He holds it out to Rafferty. "Is here. But wery difficult to get in."

"That's *my* problem." He opens the paper and sees an address in a part of Bangkok he never visits. "How did you do this?"

"Janos. You already pay him for it. I have him waiting outside Shen's, two day, three day. People look at him, forget him, look at him again. Follow Murphy two time. Both time go this house. Wery big, with gates."

"Good. That's good."

"You go there, he will kill you."

"He'll kill me anyway."

Vladimir shrugs acceptance. "For two thousand dollar—what you pay me already—I tell you more things." He opens the flap on the envelope in front of him and peeks in. "U.S. Not so good these days."

"It's what I've got. Give it back and I'll write you an IOU in yuan."

"Coming up," Ming Li says, sitting next to Poke. Vladimir looks at her like she's a veal chop.

"You can't have her," Poke says to Vladimir. "Tell me what else I've bought."

"In the house, Murphy's house. Is two women, maybe both Mrs. Murphy. And one girl."

"Two Mrs. Murphys? What do you mean, a girl?"

"One Mrs. Murphy come from Wietnam, other one maybe Laos. Girl is twelve or thirteen. Daughter of Murphy. Wery strange, my friend say."

"Strange how?"

"Wery dirty. Wears always same thing. Hair like snake in a ball. Maid is afraid of her."

Ming Li looks impressed. "You've been talking to the maid?"

"Not me. Poke owe me five hundred more. Have friend, wery handsome Thai boy, talk to maid in supermarket, make some kind friend with her." He glances at Ming Li and leans toward Rafferty and lowers his voice. "You understand, 'some kind friend'?"

"I think I get it."

"So they"—he makes a rolling gesture with his hand—"*talking*. Thai boy and maid. House have two maid, two women, one girl, and Murphy."

Ming Li asks the question that's on Rafferty's mind. "Dog?"

"No. Maid says girl—" Vladimir breaks off as a waitress arrives with a big tray. She puts Rafferty's beer in front of Vladimir, Vladimir's glass and bottle in front of Ming Li, and Ming Li's Coke—Rafferty guesses—in front of Poke. She gives them all a blinding smile and retreats.

"Says girl kill two cat," Vladimir says.

Nodding acknowledgment, Ming Li rearranges the drinks in an expert fashion. She unscrews the cap on a small bottle of vodka and pours for Vladimir, her free hand supporting the hand with the bottle in it, laying on the formal Asian etiquette. Vladimir watches her so intently that Rafferty half expects a long tongue to dart out and snatch her across the table.

To distract him Rafferty pulls out a short stack of money and counts off five hundred. He starts to hold it out and then pulls back. "What do you know about Yala?"

"Yala? Ewerything is in Yala." Vladimir wrenches his eyes off Ming Li and drinks. Then he puts the glass down and gives Rafferty his full attention. "If Murphy is working with Shen, he is thinking about Yala. If he is thinking about Yala, he is thinking Phoenix, yes?"

"What's Yala?" Ming Li says. "What's Phoenix?"

"Tell you later," Rafferty says. His beer is heart-shrinkingly cold. "But Phoenix, that was against an invisible enemy. The people who carried it out didn't know who was Vietcong and who wasn't. Everybody knows who's Muslim down there."

"I am disappoint in you. You are thinking like American. Most Muslim wery peaceful. Have Buddhist friend, maybe even Buddhist husband or wife. Is the center of the problem, yes? If all Muslim is dangerous, solution is easy. So same problem like Wietnam. Which is which? What is command infrastructure? Who is giwing order? Are crazies from outside running ewerything? Don't be so straightforward."

Rafferty had mentioned Yala mostly to see Vladimir's reaction, whether he'd been withholding information about Murphy's trips down there. He still doesn't know the answer, but what he's getting is interesting anyway. "Straightforward how?"

"You are liwing here long time," Vladimir says with an undertone of reproof. "You can see what happens. Many people die, Thai gowernment sits around. Send soldiers, soldiers sit around like gowernment, except they get shot at. Newspaper don't talk about it so much. Maybe, if Murphy is working for Uncle Sam, Uncle Sam would like to see more action. Think Wietnam. Maybe time for Gulf of Tonkin."

Ming Li says, "I am *so* lost."

"American operation, long time ago, when I am young," Vladimir says with a glance at his glass. "America want to support gowernment in South Wietnam with troop, so they make phony incident. They say North Wietnam ship make bang-bang at American ship. Not true, but now America can send in many troop. Self-defense, yes?"

"Provocation," Rafferty says.

Vladimir fills his glass, holds up the bottle, and checks the level. "Why not? Many people, Thai people, want big show in south. Now five thousand, six thousand Buddhists dead and nobody do nothing. America, too, America probably want something big. You ewer see kid make sand painting?"

"Yes," Ming Li says.

Rafferty shrugs.

"Kid take paper," Vladimir says. He holds up a finger, knocks the glass back, and then uses the finger to blot his mustache. He puts down his glass, and with his long hands he frames a rectangle on the table. "Paper. Put line of glue on paper—maybe doggie, maybe house with tree. Draw with glue, yes?

"I actually am following this," Rafferty says.

"Then pour sand all ower paper." He mimes a big shaker. "All, all now under sand. Cannot see paper, cannot see lines. Then take paper and shake it back and forth and turn ower so sand falls off. And now sand is only where lines of glue were. Doggie was always there, yes? But only wisible now."

"Because it got shaken up," Ming Li says approvingly.

"Same in Wietnam, later," Vladimir says. "Phoenix use many Wietnamese, prisoners from Saigon jails, bad guys, will do anything to stay out of pokey. They dress like Wietcong, blow up willage. America and South Wietnam troops go in to protect peasant. Maybe move them to 'strategic hamlet,' just houses in mud, like prison camp. Then watch to see who needs to get out most, because they probably Wietcong, have to talk to boss." He touches his fingertip to the bottom of his glass and licks it. "Shake paper," he says.

"So," Rafferty says, "it would make sense to you if Murphy were going down to Yala from time to time."

Vladimir's eyes float to a spot in the air, which he studies with the concentration of a man trying to count money in a strange currency. Ming Li slurps her Coke. After a moment he says, without looking up, "You are saying he goes there?"

"I was asking."

"Mmm-hmmm." He picks up the glass and puts it to his lips, but it's empty.

"If you're thinking about selling this," Rafferty says, "it would be a very good idea to reconsider."

"I tell you, I am honest mercenary."

"Let's say you are. Let's say I didn't ask you about Yala. Let's say I asked you about Kuala Lumpur."

"He is flying around? Maybe this is why you not dead yet. Give me." Vladimir waggles his fingers at the five hundred, and when Rafferty gives it to him, he drinks. Then he brings the glass down on the table with a bang. "*This* is how good Vladimir is," he says. "You pay attention, Baby Spy, maybe you get better role model. In Kuala Lumpur is one wery famous American, Eddie Bland."

Rafferty says, "And Eddie Bland is—"

Vladimir holds up three fingers, a benediction. "After I tell you this, you trust me forewer."

"We'll see."

"When they blow up willage? When Murphy's guys blow up willage?"

"I remember."

"Eddie Bland was sergeant in Wietnam. Sergeant for Murphy. Is the guy who makes things go boom. Almost he kill me once." He points at the glass and says to Ming Li, "Hurry, hurry."

"Don't get used to this," Ming Li says, but she pours.

"So," Rafferty says, "Murphy, Yala, Kuala Lumpur, Eddie Bland, provocation. Adds up to what, from your perspective?"

Vladimir raises his glass to Ming Li and drains it in one toss. "Same as for you. Maybe soon something go boom in Yala."

21

Enough to Break Your Heart

DAENG HAS BEEN dragged into these rooms twice since the night he almost went off the roof at the hotel near Khao San. The same questions, over and over: How had Rafferty gotten away without a bullet in him? Was he armed? If Rafferty took the fire escape, why hadn't Daeng chased him? Why hadn't he radioed the men in the street to tell them Rafferty was coming?

Had Rafferty bribed him? How much? Where was the money? Was someone else there, someone who helped Rafferty? If Rafferty got away from Daeng, how come he, Daeng, was uninjured? How could he just have been standing on the roof with his gun in his hand when the other officers arrived?

Was he working with Rafferty? Where is Rafferty now? What wasn't he telling them?

What wasn't he telling them?

But tonight was different.

They'd been watching him somehow, actually looking into his house. At the precise moment he sat down to dinner with his wife and their two children, the men had banged on the door with boots and fists as though they'd been waiting for the signal. There were six of them. They hammered hard enough to splinter it around the top hinge. He'd told the family to stay put and gone to open the door. His feet had been swept out from under him, and then he'd been manhandled onto his stomach as plastic restraints were cinched over his wrists and his children stood screaming in terror.

When they pulled him up, they'd wrenched his shoulder sockets and he'd cried out. His wife had run at the men, trying to help Daeng, and one of them had shoved her hard enough to put her on the carpet. He'd been dragged downstairs, thrown headfirst into the back of a wagon, and hauled down here, his questions unanswered, then slammed into a chair. Two of the men had stood behind him. Waiting for something.

That had been four hours ago. Since then no one has spoken. Two hours or so after his arrival, the two men behind him left the room in unison and were replaced by two others.

Daeng's hands are completely numb. He's certain they're swollen to double their usual size. He can feel the pulses slamming in his wrists, trying to pump blood in and out, the veins crimped by the tight plastic cuffs. And his nose has been itching for hours. He's never realized what agony it can be not to be able to scratch his nose.

He has to pee so badly he's got a cramp. He crossed his legs against it, and one of the guards reached down and pushed the upper leg to the floor.

He's damp with fear.

The door opens, and a short *farang* in a bright, terrible old shirt comes in. Someone outside opened the door for him, because he has a paper cup in each hand, and Daeng smells coffee.

In no hurry at all, he plants one haunch on the edge of the table. He looks down at Daeng.

Daeng says, "Hello."

The red-haired man says, in Thai, "Coffee or tea?"

Daeng says, "Tea, please."

"Fine," the red-haired man says. "Catch." And he throws the contents of one of the cups in Daeng's face.

It's scalding. Daeng's legs straighten convulsively, the chair almost going over behind him, and the red-haired man says, "Take the coffee, too," and hurls that at him, cup and all. One of the guards yelps in pain. While Daeng is still gasping, his eyes squeezed shut, the red-haired man says, "Get him up."

Daeng is yanked to his feet. The red-haired man says, "Spread him out." Holding him under the arms, the guards kick his feet far apart. He hears a grunt of effort from the red-haired man, and his testicles explode.

"Drop him." The guards let go and step aside as Daeng crumples to the concrete floor and vomits and urinates at the same time. A kick to his cheekbone knocks his head aside. He lies there, choking and—to his shame—weeping.

The red-haired man says, "Hello."

"Where are we going?" Ming Li calls from behind him. "Shouldn't we be getting a hotel?"

"I have a hotel. We're probably not going anywhere. I just need to check up on someone. This has nothing to do with anything."

"Well, as long as it's important."

The women on the sidewalk have taken refuge in the doorways, and they smile at Poke. Ming Li catches up and grabs his arm. The women's eyes glaze over, and they look back upstream, scanning the oncoming faces for a possible short-time.

"Is he any good?" she asks. "Vladimir?"

"According to a former spy named Arnold Prettyman, he was the best, back in the seventies."

"Where's Prettyman?"

"He got killed. When you were here last, actually." He doesn't say what he's thinking, which is, *Collateral damage from your father's impulsiveness.*

"If he's dead, maybe he wasn't the best judge."

"Vladimir is what I've got. It's hard to recruit a team when the other side is a steamroller."

"When are you going to—"

"Whatever it is, I'll do it tomorrow." He stops at the corner of Soi 7. "Go get a hotel. Go back to the—" He motions down the street.

"The Alpine Suites. But why don't you come with me?"

He counts the reasons impatiently, on his fingers. "I have a hotel, my stuff is in the room, it's too much of a dump for you, and I have something to do."

"Then I have something to do, too."

He says, "No."

People are bustling past them: men coming alone into the *soi* from Sukhumvit and men going out with young women.

"Oh," Ming Li says, watching the crowd flow by. "I see."

"No. No, you don't see. Okay, don't look at me like that. This is an attempt at an errand of mercy, and it'll probably be a bust."

"Right," she says. "Well, you go earn your gold star, and I'll—"

"Oh, come on," he says, and sets off down the *soi*.

Despite the rain there are a lot of people. It's after midnight by his watch, and the Beer Garden is popping at the seams. Groups of women go in beneath shared umbrellas, arms linked or holding hands with one another, and come out hanging on the darling of the hour. Rafferty and Ming Li take folding chairs across a sticky plastic table in an open-air restaurant on the opposite side of the *soi*. This is the second time Rafferty has sat here watching for Pim. The first time, eight or ten months ago, he'd met her only moments earlier, and she had bandaged a bad cut on his arm while he wrapped her sprained ankle. They hadn't so much met as collided. He orders another beer for himself and a Coke for his sister, and for the first time since he caught sight of her that afternoon, Ming Li yawns.

"Jet lag?"

"Nah." She blinks the tears away. "I just didn't sleep on the plane." She brushes at her chin with her fingertips and then points at his. "Mirror reflection," she says. "Your makeup is streaking."

"I know. It does that in this weather. I don't worry about it so much at night."

"Oh," she says, and then she sits upright as though her chair has shocked her. "*Ohhh*. Mr. Delacroix, on the passport? He not wearing, I mean, he doesn't look like . . . I don't know, Gunga Din, or whoever you think you are now."

"It's okay. The sketch they've got out now looks like this, so I've been thinking about getting rid of Gunga anyway. Tomorrow I'll look like me again."

"It's not very convincing."

"It's not supposed to be. It's just to keep the moving eye moving, so to speak. *You* looked past me, if you'll recall."

"I guess I did." She yawns again. "How's the errand coming?"

"Haven't seen her. Let's give it ten minutes, and we'll pack it in."

"Then use the time. Tell me what I don't know: Phoenix and Lala, and—"

"Yala. Okay. Look at me. I want to see if your eyes close."

"I'll stay awake. You watch your awful little street."

"Before I start," he says, "I want to tell you that it's great to have you here."

"You're kidding." She breaks into an enormous grin. Then she punches him on the arm. "*Told* you."

"Okay now, listen, and you'll know why I'm only going to let you help me so much." He fills her in on Murphy's background—at least according to Vladimir—and the kinds of things he did under Phoenix. He's describing what happened in the laundry when she holds up a hand.

"The little thing cut into the ticket?" she says. "It was there for her to feel it, wasn't it?"

"I think so."

"That's really sad. He carried it, whoever he was, figuring he might get killed. And if he was, that little hole would tell the story to someone he cared about, someone blind. Sooner or later someone would take it to the shop, but only she would know what it meant."

"We need to talk to them tomorrow. Both of us."

"It's enough to break your heart," she says. She sips at her Coke and then rests her forehead on her fingertips. Looking at the table, she says, "Dad had a system for me, so I'd know if he got killed. Back in China. He carried a postcard with an address and a stamp and a written message. All ready to go, but not mailed. He figured if he got . . . you know . . ."

"He didn't," Rafferty says.

"But if he had, I'm saying, he'd designed a way to get word to me. His daughter." She exhales heavily and looks back to him. "So who are they to him?"

"I'm guessing, but think the blind woman is his sister-in-law. I think Helen Eckersley was his wife and the blind woman's sister."

"Why? Maybe the blind woman was his wife."

"Maybe. But what he *said* to me, the only thing he wanted to say, was 'Helen Eckersley' and 'Cheyenne,' and both women looked stunned when I said the name Helen while I was talking to them. And Helen had an accent, like her sister's."

Ming Li leans forward and rests her forearms on the table, then feels the stickiness and purses her mouth in distaste. She unwraps the napkin that her Coke has been sweating into and uses it to scrub at her arms. "What are your *big* questions?"

"Okay." He takes a pull on the beer and lets his eyes rove the street while he thinks. "Helen Eckersley was killed in America four days before the dead man bumped into me. That's fourteen days ago. Why, and what's it got to do with what's happening here? Second, why was the dead American in that crowd of protesters— or, to look at it from another angle, how did Murphy and Shen *know* he'd be there? They had troops on hand, cops with barricades to block traffic, a sniper—everything. No way someone spotted him in the crowd and they put all that together on the fly. That was a setup. Probably the only accident was that I was on that street."

"How could they set that up?" Ming Li says.

"That's why I'm confused. It seems unlikely that they created a whole demonstration somehow and then sent him an invitation. And one other question, just something that's been bothering me. Let's assume that it *was* a setup, that that's the reason everybody was there. The whole point was to catch, or take out, the guy who died in my arms. That's information you'd want to control. That's something they'd want to keep secret."

She's unaware she's put her arm back onto the table. "Yeah?"

"So what was a TV news crew doing there? This is Bangkok. They couldn't have gotten there in time any more than the cops with the barricades could. And the very first thing Shen's guys did—before they even talked to me—was try to get the tape. Took off after the cameraman like their lives depended on catching him. That crew was not wanted. So what were they doing there?"

Ming Li says slowly, "Maybe somebody isn't completely on the team."

Rafferty says, "From your lips to God's ears. And maybe it's who I think it might be."

"You're not asking the questions I'd be asking. Who was the man they killed, for one."

"I know who he was. I mean, I don't know his name, but I know, or at least I'm pretty sure, that he was a grunt in Vietnam when Murphy was there. Something happened there that was completely off the charts, even by the standards of the Phoenix Program. Something that threatens Murphy and his operation here."

"And here's a little question," Ming Li says. "Why don't they have a good picture of you?"

"Yeah." Rafferty goes back to surveying the *soi*. "I've been asking myself the same—"

His eye is drawn to a bright patch of color: A handsome Thai man in his early thirties comes up the street, holding an umbrella to shield several hundred dollars' worth of clothing—white slacks and a peach-colored shirt under a short black leather jacket. With him, ignoring the umbrella, hanging on to his arm, and talking a hundred miles an hour, is Pim.

He sits forward, and Ming Li follows his gaze. "Her?" she says. Then, before he can answer, she says, "Boy, look at her. She's flying."

"Is she?" Rafferty tries to see her through Ming Li's eyes. Pim's free arm is making short, meaningless gestures, like a charade of stuttering. The half of her that's not under the umbrella is wet enough to shine. Her steps are so approximate she's almost falling over her feet. She's back in sidewalk-tart clothes—tight, glittering shorts, an off-the-shoulder T-shirt with a big red lipstick mark on it, the ghost of a giant's kiss. Her hair has been frizzed out in all directions and sprayed, and it sparkles.

"Stay here," he says, and gets up and goes down the steps to the *soi*, heading into the middle of the street to intersect them. He can hear Pim's voice now, high and slightly shaky, broken by an occasional burst of laughter. She's not just flying. She's pasted.

He says, "Pim."

The Thai man stops, but Pim takes another step and stumbles, and he tugs on her arm. She squints at Rafferty and starts to smile, but the expression dies on her face, and she takes a step back.

Once again the Thai man restrains her.

Rafferty wipes water off his face and says, "Pim," again.

"Not Pim," says the Thai man. "Name now is Angel."

"I'm talking to her, not you."

Pim pulls at the Thai man's arm, shifting from foot to foot in her eagerness to leave. The man yanks her arm sharply, and she stands still, looking down at the street, heedless of the rain.

"You want her?" the Thai man says.

Rafferty says to him, "Go away."

The Thai man steps to the side and gives Pim a little push. "Go in, Angel," he says in Thai, "and I'll see you back at the room after three. Not before."

Pim makes a wide circuit around Rafferty, eyes down, and hurries into the Beer Garden.

"You give her the pipe?" Rafferty asks, also in Thai.

"We share. She likes it more than I do."

Rafferty turns to follow her in, but the man says, "She won't go with you. Not unless I tell her to. And if you go in there and make a problem, guess who will get beat up."

Rafferty stops, feeling Ming Li's gaze from across the street.

"But if you want to talk to her," the man says, "pay me forty dollars for a short time. I'll go get her for you. Talk as much as you want for an hour. Forty dollars."

"How about I pay you fifty and just break your nose?"

"Go back home," the Thai man says. "Where you understand how things work."

Rafferty stands there looking at the entrance to the bar. He mentally runs two or three chains of events and can't find one where he'd have the time to get involved and stay involved.

He's about to turn and go when the man says scornfully, "Big talk."

Rafferty turns and nods at him. So furious it feels as though the road is rippling beneath his feet, he takes a few steps toward the side of the street where Ming Li is waiting—standing now—and as he passes the handsome Thai man, he folds his right arm, brings it as far across his chest as he can, as though he's scratching his left shoulder, sets his feet, and swings the point of his elbow into the man's throat. He scores a direct hit on the larynx. The man makes an agonized rasping sound and goes down on his back, both hands to his throat. He lies there coughing and hacking, rolling from side to side in a puddle, knees drawn up, and Rafferty bends over him and says, "I'll be back. If I see a bruise on her, if I see a Band-Aid on her finger, I'll have you torn into small pieces and fed to *soi* dogs. I will find your mother and make her watch them eat you. Nod if you understand."

He waits, and the man nods. Rafferty leans closer. "And keep her away from that pipe."

He straightens and sees a ring of watching people, mostly men. One of the women from the Beer Garden, a familiar-looking one, gives him a covert thumbs-up.

"Something wrong with his throat," Rafferty says. "*Listen* to him. It might be contagious." He keeps walking as Ming Li comes down the steps and falls in beside him.

"If that's mercy," she says, "I can do without it."

DAENG IS ON the floor again. He's come to prefer the floor. When he's there, at least he knows he's not going to fall.

He'd never imagined he could hurt this much.

"Up," says the *farang*—Murphy, his name is Murphy—and the two men yank him upright. They shove him back into the chair, and Daeng squints through his one open eye at Murphy.

"I'm not going to play with you anymore," Murphy says. "Did you know Rafferty before that night?"

"No." He's answered this a dozen times.

"Did you arrange to be the first man on the roof?"

"Ask the others."

Murphy goes to the little table, knocked crooked and spattered with blood now, and picks up the box cutter.

Daeng's bowels loosen. His forearms are already scored with shallow, intensely painful cuts.

"Did you arrange to be the first man on the roof?" He wiggles the box cutter. "Yes or no."

"No, no, no."

"Did he tell you anything while you were up there with him?"

"No."

"You didn't talk about anything."

"I told you. We fought, he hit me with the door, I stumbled. I was falling off the building, and he stopped me, he grabbed my belt, and—"

"And he saved your life, and you repaid him by letting him go."

"Yes."

Murphy holds the box cutter vertical, inches from Daeng's face. He says, "Stick out your tongue."

Daeng says, "Uhhhhh, uhhhhhhh," and then he's weeping again.

"This is the third time you've been brought in and questioned, but you've never told the story about him saving you before, have you?" Murphy makes a quick movement and nicks the end of Daeng's nose.

Daeng is sobbing too hard to answer.

"So you've had a lot of time to think this up. Maybe you and Rafferty worked it out together. How many times have you talked to him since that night?"

"Ne-ne-never, never."

"I told you to stick out your tongue."

A huge shudder racks Daeng, but he puts out his tongue.

"You know how much it hurts when you bite your tongue?" Murphy says. His voice is calm, even gentle, like an adult explaining something to a child. "Just full of nerve endings, the tongue is. Imagine what it would feel like for me to start at the tip and saw back an inch or so. Give you a forked tongue."

One of the guards makes a choking sound.

Murphy looks up at the man behind Daeng. He says, "Are you in the wrong room?"

"No, sir."

"Do you think this piece of shit has told us everything he knows?"

"No, sir."

"Well, what would you suggest? Tell me what to do to him. Come on, be creative."

The guard clears his throat.

"Sorry? You said what? Pull his hair? Call him names?" Murphy nods. "Good idea. Do it."

"Sir?"

"It's kind of crude, but who knows? Ball up your fist and punch him in the face. And I want to see you put some back into it."

Daeng pulls his tongue in and squeezes his eyes shut. He hears the guard come around the chair, hears the feet stop in front of him. The guard's breathing sounds ragged.

"Well?" Murphy says. "You waiting for him to bloom or something?"

Daeng hears feet scuff the concrete, and his head explodes. The force of the blow takes him off the chair and onto the floor again. He curls himself up against kicks and hears the guard hissing with pain.

"Broke your knuckle," Murphy says. "Poor baby. Get him into the chair again."

For what feels like the hundredth time, Daeng is lifted into the chair, hearing the gasp from the guard with the broken knuckle. The entire world is a pillow of pain Daeng is sinking into. The cheekbone on which the guard broke his knuckle beats with a hot red pulse, and blood is trickling down the side of Daeng's neck. The swelling from the cheekbone pushes against his one open eye.

"Cuff his ankles to the chair," Murphy says. "We're down to it."

The guards drag his feet up against the chair legs. Daeng doesn't even try to resist. He hopes they'll kill him. His wife and children flash in front of him, and he silently says good-bye, hoping their spirits will hear. He feels the warmth of the tears running down his face.

"Look at me," Murphy says.

Daeng opens his right eye as far as he can. Murphy has the box cutter in his hand again.

"This is it," Murphy says. "You tell me right now whether there's anything more we need to know about you and Rafferty. I want you to talk, and clearly. To give you some motivation, here's what I'm going to do if I'm not satisfied: I'm going to cut off your lips. You," he says to the guards. "Grab his lips. You take the top, you take the bottom. Pull them as far away from his teeth as you can."

Daeng tastes salt and sweat on the men's hands, and then his lips are almost torn from his face.

Murphy's eyes are boring into him. "You know, if I do this, nothing will happen to me. No one will even speak sharply to me. Not a frown in the hallway. You, on the other hand, will terrify everyone who sees you, and you'll spend the rest of your life trying to keep your teeth wet."

He brings the box cutter closer. "Trying to pronounce the letters *b* and *p*," he says. "And *f*."

He stops. He's still looking at Daeng, but his face has gone slack, and it feels to Daeng as though Murphy is seeing straight through him. Then the gray-blue eyes lift to a point just above Daeng's head and wander slowly to the right. Murphy stands up straight and backs up until he bumps the table, and then he sits, the box cutter dangling from his hand. "Or *w*," he says to no one. *Or m.* He closes his eyes for a moment. Without opening them, he says to the guards, "I don't want those lips to move at all, is that clear?"

Both guards say, "Yes, sir," and pull even harder on Daeng's lips.

Murphy gets up and comes back over. He leans down so he's only inches from Daeng's face and says, "I want you to say something for me. Okay?"

Daeng tries to answer, but all that comes out is a vowel.

"Exactly," Murphy says. "Now, here's what I want you to say. I want you to say 'Helen.'"

Daeng says, quite clearly, "Helena."

"Wait, wait, wait," Murphy says. He bows his head and closes his eyes. Without looking up he says, "Now say 'Cheyenne.'"

Daeng begins to speak, but Murphy says, over him, "'Eckersley,' say 'Eckersley.'"

It's a difficult word because it's nothing Daeng has heard before, but he says, "Eckersley."

Murphy whirls and flips the table so it lands legs-up, the sound ear-popping in the small room, "Mother*fucker*. The worst-case scenario, in three-fucking-D. No, no. Wait." He turns back to Daeng. "Say 'Cheyenne.'"

Daeng begins the word, but Murphy's not listening. He tosses the box cutter onto the floor, pulls out the cell phone in his pocket, and speed-dials a U.S. number. He glances over at Daeng and the guards and carries the phone into a corner, with his back to them. Daeng hears him release a quiet laugh, just a single, una-mused syllable, and say, "Paul."

Murphy listens for a second and then says, "Have you been in her house since you had your visit with her?" He turns, so Daeng is looking at his profile. Murphy's eyes are closed. "Well, *go* in. Use her phone and download her voice mail. I want to know who's called her. Especially from over here." Impatience tightens his face. "Yes, yes, from Bangkok. . . . Of course Bangkok. Just do it." Murphy punches at the phone with a stubby finger and winces as he looks at Daeng, as though just registering the injuries. "For Christ's sake, let go of him. You," he says to Daeng. "You'll be fine in a week or two." He picks up the box cutter and slides the blade back in. Then he goes to the door, moving like an old man. "Just fine."

"What should we do with him?" asks the man with the swelling hand.

Murphy puts a hand on the doorknob and turns back to face them. "Daeng," he says. "Means 'red,' right? Same nickname I had, back when I was a kid. Red." He looks down at the floor. As the guard is about to speak again, he says, "Bury him in solitary. As deep as you can. The most solitary solitary you've got. A week at least, until I say he can go. He talks to nobody."

He puts the phone into his pocket. "You're lucky, Red," he says. "You'll get to kiss your wife again."

22

The Red Man

THE ROOM IS a faded green not found in nature, pale and spectral in the overhead fluorescents. All the way around the room, about three feet from the floor, are tiny, grimy handprints, hundreds of them, as though left by an army of invisible children. They seem to jump and twitch in the lights' flicker.

Sitting on a pillow, Rafferty can't keep his eyes off the handprints. He keeps asking himself where the children are.

The sobs have subsided to irregular gasps and sniffles. The two women lean against each other, a limp pantomime of grief. The older one has collapsed against the younger, her arm thrown heavily over the other woman's shoulders. And yet it seems to Rafferty that the older, with her terrible, devastated eyes, is the one who is recovering more quickly. In the last half minute or so, her hand has grasped the loose fabric of her pajama-style trousers and formed a fist around the cloth. Ming Li sits on the floor in front of them, face submissively down, her little MacBook Air closed to hide the screen shot of the newspaper from Cheyenne. She keeps her eyes on the floor, giving the women the invisibility they need to recover themselves.

The older woman coughs, so suddenly and loudly that the younger one flinches. She says, without lifting her head toward Rafferty, "How you find us?"

"My sister," Rafferty says with a nod at Ming Li. "She followed you when you left the shop."

Ming Li says to the older woman, very formally, "I am sorry."

"No matter," the woman says. "Name you, child?"

"Ming Li. This is my older brother, Poke."

"We're both sorry," Poke says. "Sorry to bring you terrible news."

"Twice," says the older woman. She sniffles percussively. "My name is Thuy. This girl is my daughter, Jiang."

Jiang, who is in her forties, shakes her head in the negative, although it's hard to tell what she's objecting to.

Rafferty says, "What was Helen's name?"

"Bey," Thuy says. "Means 'baby.'" She coughs again and says, "Baby sister for me."

"The man who was killed," Rafferty says, "gave me—"

"Billie Joe," Thuy says. "Billie Joe Sellers."

"Well . . . um, Billie ran into me—"

"Billie *Joe*," Thuy says.

"The last thing Billie Joe did was stick that ticket in my pocket." Rafferty tugs at the edge of his pocket. "It was very, very hard for him to do that. He didn't have any strength left. But he did it because he wanted me to have that ticket."

"Stop," says the younger one, Jiang. She releases a sharp barrage of Vietnamese, and when she stops, Rafferty tells the rest of the story.

When he's finished, Thuy puts her hand across her mouth, as though trying to hold something in. Her shoulders shake several times, and she sniffs twice.

"That night cops came to my apartment and dragged me down to an interrogation room. I saw a man there, an American."

Thuy could be made from stone, but Jiang's eyes widen. She glances away quickly and translates.

"I'm going to tell you what he looked like," Rafferty says. "He was short and—"

Thuy says, in English, "Red."

THE RAIN HID them when they came.

The monsoon had hit with fury that year, rain so thick, so dense that people disappeared into the gray, two or three meters away. The rains dragged an unusual cold front behind them, and for people whose skin was always wet, the cold seemed to reach straight through and scrape at the center of their bones.

All the huts leaked. It was a season of dripping water. The rice was rotting, and green mold grew on clothes that were folded and stacked. The paddies had overflowed the dikes so that water ran ankle-deep through the mud street of the village.

They sat in the huts day and night and shouted at each other over the rain. The hut that Thuy and Jiang shared with Bey had a corrugated tin roof the rain struck like hammers. The hut had belonged to Thuy's husband, but he'd gone to fight against the Saigon government and the Americans, and he'd been killed in an ambush only thirty kilometers away. He'd been nineteen when he died, and she'd been seventeen. She'd been carrying the child who her mother, who was never wrong about a baby's sex, had assured her would be a girl. Bey and Thuy's mother was dead now, but Thuy had her daughter, whom she named Jiang.

Now only women, children, and old men lived there. But some of the village's men—and women, too—had fought and been captured and had been made to talk before they died. In Saigon's eyes the place was a nest of traitors, and in the end they paid for that.

It was very late. The village was asleep, and the rain had driven even the dogs inside, so there was no warning when seven heavily armed men came up the path: three Americans and four Vietnamese troopers. The Vietnamese were scum, tattooed and drug-raddled, released from the worst of the city's prisons to earn their freedom by killing the men and women who were trying to reclaim Vietnam for the Vietnamese. It took the team only a few minutes to kick in the village's doors and drag the terrified people out of their houses and into the downpour, making them squat in a dark field of mud at the edge of town.

There they waited for hours as the rain pounded down, all sixteen of them: eight grown women, six children, and two very old men—one of whom was crippled—cold and shaking. Their muscles cramped as two of the uniformed Vietnamese troopers systematically found and shot every dog in the village and tore most of the huts apart, looking for arms.

The leader of the group was an American, short even by Vietnamese standards, with hair the color of fire. He paced in front of the soaking, terrified villagers, shouting and cursing at them as one of the Vietnamese troopers tried halfheartedly to translate. It would have been clear even to someone who spoke neither Vietnamese nor English that the translator was putting no effort into his task, but the red man never slowed the flow of words. A demon controlled him, pushing him from one fury to another: He screamed at the villagers when he learned there were no young men there, he slapped the ear of one of the Vietnamese troopers for accidentally getting in his way, he raged at the skies and the trees. When a buffalo emerged curiously from the rain, he shot it for no reason at all.

Where were the men? he wanted to know. Where were the men? The more he raged, the more his rage grew. He grabbed a sopping, sobbing child of five by the arm and hoisted her in the air, demanding to know who the mother was. The dangling child was Thuy's daughter, Jiang.

Thuy instinctively began to stand, but Bey pulled her down and rose instead. For years afterward Thuy was ashamed that she'd let her sister face the beast.

The red man, still holding Jiang in midair, called Bey to him like a dog, pointing at her and then at a spot in front of his feet. He made her kneel there and demanded to know where her husband was and where the weapons were hidden, and when she couldn't give him the answers he wanted, he pulled a short, ugly gun and aimed it at Jiang as she twisted and kicked in his grip. When Bey said again that her husband was dead and there were no weapons there, the red man swung the back of the hand with the gun in it at her jaw and hit her, and she'd gone down on her side with a splash, and he'd thrown Jiang at her.

And then, as Thuy watched Bey creep back to the circle of squatting villagers, trying to quiet the sobbing Jiang, the morning sky began to lighten and three young men—boys, really—blundered down the path and into the village, having heard nothing over the rain's roar. They were just children, boys of twelve and fourteen from the next village, but they tried to scatter when they saw the soldiers. The red man shouted at his Vietnamese troopers, and within moments the boys had been brought back, their hands tied.

The red man stood them about a meter apart near the tree line, and one of the Vietnamese troopers pulled an automatic pistol and pointed it at the forehead of the boy on the left. The trooper was only a few paces from the boy, and he held the gun steady, obviously waiting for instructions. But the red man turned his back on the trooper and the boys and left them standing there, motionless, to walk toward the field where the villagers squatted or knelt.

He walked among them, zigzagging between them, the only person standing. Most people kept their faces down, not wanting to attract the demon's attention. From time to time, the red man would pull someone to her feet and ask questions, but he was never satisfied with the answers, and he ordered each of them down again. After a few minutes of this, he stood still, looking at the ground, and then he cleared his throat to spit, just missing one of the village's oldest women. He raised a hand and pointed it at one of the other Americans and then pointed to the nearest hut—one they had left standing—and the American picked up his pack and went to the hut. The first thing he removed from his pack was a spool of thick cord. Barely visible through the curtains of rain, he began to circle the hut, paying out the cord and looping it through the bamboo uprights on the walls.

RAFFERTY SAYS, "DID you hear his name? The man with the cord?"

Thuy says, "Eddie. Red man call him Eddie."

At the name Eddie, Ming Li's eyes swing to his, but she says nothing. She wraps her arms around her upraised knees and turns back to Thuy. In this room she's the obedient child.

Rafferty says, "Sorry to interrupt." He has never been less sorry to interrupt any story in his life.

THUY HAD BEEN looking at the red man through a haze of terror, without seeing him clearly. Now, as he passed her on his way toward the trembling boys, she saw the things that were hanging around his neck, thick and meaty as a string of sliced dried fruit. And she smelled the odor of death they trailed.

He turned his head and glanced back at her as though her thought had touched him, but he kept moving until he reached the boys. He stepped up to each of them in turn—their eyes following him the way they'd have followed the movements of a cobra—and lifted the thick, black hair from the sides of their heads. When he'd done it to all three, he waved two of the Viet-namese troopers over and had them hold up the boy in the center, and then he drew a short knife and sliced off the boy's left ear, as easily as Thuy might slice crackling from a roast pig. The boy let out a wail, his knees folded beneath him, and he went down. The troopers picked him up, one by the shoulders and one by the feet, and held him so that his head was lower than his feet, as a ribbon of blood ran from the place where his ear had been, mingling with the rain as it fell. When he came to, shrieking and wailing, and they put him down, the boy couldn't stand. He was crying like a small child. One of the troopers pushed him to his knees, between the two standing boys, whose faces had gone blank, motionless.

Thuy knew they were waiting to die.

The red man put the ear in the pocket of his shirt. The pocket was already mottled with the rust brown of old blood. He wiped the knife on his pants and put it away. He didn't have to look down in order to slip it into its sheath.

The third American had stayed apart from the red man and the others, keeping an eye on the villagers. His eyes came again and again to meet Bey's eyes, and then Thuy's. He'd looked away when Red cut the boy's ear off. Thuy thought she saw disgust in his face.

The red man stepped up to the boy on the left. He held his left hand in the air, like someone who is about to signal a group of men to move forward. The boy looked at the center of Red's chest, unwilling or unable to meet his eyes. Red shouted, in accented Vietnamese, "What's the name of your village?"

The boy hesitated, and Red said, very loudly, "Too slow," stepped to the left, and lowered the upraised hand. The trooper shot the boy through the forehead, the bullet pulverizing the back of the boy's head and lifting him off his feet, throwing him back-ward. By the time he landed, the red man was in front of the second boy, the kneeling boy.

He said to the boy, "Did you see that?"

Thuy could see the boy say "Yes," although she couldn't hear his voice. He was swaying on his knees, forward and back, and he'd clasped his bound hands at chest level, fingers interlaced in a position of prayer. The shoulder beneath the remains of the sliced ear was pink with blood, diluted by rain.

Red said, loudly, "Good. Fast answer. What's the name of your village?"

The boy shouted the village's name, his voice breaking at the top of his range.

"Quick," Red said. "Who's the highest-ranking cadre in the village?"

The boy opened his mouth, and Red, without waiting, dropped his hand, and the trooper fired. The boy fell flat on his back. His knees, which had been folded beneath him, came up for an instant and then sagged sideways. Thuy found herself staring at the soles of his sandals, so worn down that she could see his pale heels peeking around them. Then the rain began to fall more heavily, and she couldn't see him so clearly.

The third boy was screaming names as fast as he could, incriminating everyone he could think of. Red slapped him, and he stopped as quickly as if he'd been shot, too, his eyes closed and his mouth still open. Red said to him, in Vietnamese, "Wait."

He turned to the third American and shouted, "Sellers! Move them into the hut." He waved one of the Vietnamese troopers toward the man named Sellers, and the trooper walked around the squatting villagers, swinging the barrel of his automatic rifle from side to side as people cringed away. Then Red and two of the troopers took the boy who was still alive into the trees, and Thuy could hear the shouted questions.

Their departure left the American who was wiring the hut—Eddie—and the trooper he'd called to assist him, plus the man named Sellers and the fourth Vietnamese trooper, who was shouting for everyone to get up.

The man named Sellers put up a hand, and the shouting trooper went silent. Sellers stood there, glanced again at Bey, and then kept his eyes on the hut until the man who'd been laying the cord backed out of the door. The man with the cord said something in English, and Sellers nodded at the trooper, and the trooper began to shout orders again. The man who'd been laying wire backed off, trailing some other kind of cord toward the trees. The trooper who'd been working with him came out of the hut and followed him, stepping carefully over the cord that had been laid down.

Sellers made scooping motions with his hand, meaning *Get up*, and the villagers did. Their faces, as far as Thuy could see, were empty. They'd seen what had happened to the boys, and they knew these were their last moments. Two women went to the old men and helped them up, one staying beside the crippled man so he could use her as a crutch. Three other women brought the children together into a silent group. Somebody began to weep, and then there were three or four of them, and someone else—a bossy woman named Ngoang, whom Thuy had never liked—called, but not unkindly, for them to be quiet and to remember that the children could hear them. The sobbing stopped, and slowly the group was herded toward the hut.

Thuy felt a touch on her shoulder and was startled to see Sellers right behind her. He glanced at Bey and said very quietly, in barely understandable Vietnamese, "Your sister? Her child or yours?"

Thuy said, "Mine."

Sellers said, "Fine." He looked over at the trooper, who was shouting at the women shepherding the children, telling them to hurry up. Then he said, again quietly, "Nod if you understand. You and your sister and the baby. Stay near the door. Right at the door. Do you understand?"

"Yes."

"When you see me, you come *fast*. Understand?"

"Come . . . ?"

"To me. Fast, as fast as you can. Tell your sister. She should be holding the child."

He was getting the tones wrong, muddling the words, and Thuy said, "What?"

"Sister hold child," he said, his eyes flicking back and forth over the group. "Stay by door." The trooper was holding open the door of the hut, motioning people inside.

"Go on," Sellers said to the women who were nearest them and grabbing the back of Thuy's blouse to slow her. "Let them go," he said softly. Bey lagged, holding Jiang's hand, looking at them questioningly. Then Sellers released Thuy and brought up the rear as the villagers crowded in. One woman turned to try to break for freedom, but Sellers shouted and fired a shot over her head, and she wailed in terror and got back into the group.

That cry was a signal: Suddenly everyone was weeping and calling out, and Sellers and the trooper were motioning the remaining people in, sometimes grabbing and shoving them. The rain was hammering down now, and as Thuy and Bey and Jiang were pushed into the hut—the last villagers in—they smelled wet cloth, sweat, and shit; someone, or several someones, had fouled themselves. The door was swung closed on them, the hut so full that the door hit Thuy on the back, and something was thrown across it or against it to keep it closed.

The woman Thuy had never liked began to pray. Others joined in, some praying to the god of the Catholics and the others begging Buddha for mercy and courage.

Outside, Sellers shouted, "Okay. Give us fifteen seconds to secure and get clear."

Then the force of the rain tripled, and all the water that heaven held seemed to pour itself over the hut. Thuy tried to push at the door, but it was jammed from outside, and then, over the roar of the rain, Thuy heard a sharp sound and something heavy falling, and a moment later the door was yanked open and Sellers was standing there, the Vietnamese trooper slung over his shoulder like a bag of seed.

He grabbed Bey and yanked her to him, and Thuy picked up Jiang and followed, and as the villagers surged forward, Sellers threw the dead trooper at them and stepped back, but two children came flying through the air, literally thrown at him, and he stepped aside to let them pass and slammed the door, and Thuy and Bey grabbed the children and watched openmouthed as he propped a pole against it.

"You can't—" she began, but he snatched up Jiang and another child, Jiang over his shoulder and the other child under his arm, grabbed Bey's hand, and said, "*Run,*" and they were charging through the rain toward the tree line, Thuy hauling the second thrown child behind her, all of them going in the opposite direction the red man and the others had taken. The rain was so heavy they couldn't see six feet in front of them. From that direction there came a single shot, probably the third boy going down, and just then they reached the tree line. Sellers put Jiang down and opened his mouth to say something.

But the hut blew, an eruption of orange flame and a bottomless *whump*, so loud that Thuy thought the wave of it might knock her over. When the sound had died, Sellers was thrusting the children at them and waving them away, saying, "Run, run, run," and then things began to land around them, crashing through the leaves of the trees, and Thuy saw they were flaming lengths of wood and palm fronds and pieces of people, badly burned and barely recognizable, and she picked up her child and pushed the others ahead of her and followed her sister into the forest. Another, smaller explosion made her turn her head, and something full of bright fire was blown into her face and into her widened, terrified eyes.

"Your sister led you out?"

"Bey and Jiang," Thuy says in English. She shifts back to Vietnamese, her daughter translating as she goes. "They each took a hand. We were slow, and I couldn't stop crying, but no one came after us. Later Billie Joe said they went looking for the missing trooper. Troopers ran off all the time. Murphy wanted to kill him as an example to the others. "

"Are they still alive?" Rafferty asks. "The other two children?"

Thuy says, "Yes."

"I don't want to know where they are. Could you find them if you needed to?"

"Of course. They became our children that day, Bey's and mine. Jiang's brother and sister. We could never lose them."

"So Sellers came back to Vietnam—"

"Twenty-two years later. In 1997. When Americans were welcome again. We were living in the same village, or the same place anyway, since nothing was left from the first village. The government assigned us a bigger house because of the children and because of my injury. They made me into a hero, as though I'd been fighting instead of running for my life."

Jiang finishes translating and speaks for herself for the first time in half an hour. "No," she says, "you were running for *my* life." She rests a hand on her mother's shoulder.

"He found us. Bey recognized him the moment she opened the door. He had been preparing for the meeting the whole time he'd been gone. He had learned to speak Vietnamese almost perfectly, he had learned how to propose marriage. He formally apologized to us for the people he left in the hut. If he hadn't done that, he said, the red man—Murphy—would have known, because there would have been no body parts, and we would have been caught. Everyone would have been caught, everyone would have been killed. He said he traded the people in the hut for us. He said he had to choose between many of us dying and all of us dying.

"He stayed near the village for a month in a small hotel, but he came to us every day. On the fifth day, he asked Bey to marry him. He said he'd thought about her—" Thuy's voice breaks, and she passes a forearm across her face. "He'd thought about Bey every day since he left Vietnam. Every day. He . . . ahhh—" She sniffs again. "He showed her pictures of his house. He proposed very formally. But Bey said she had to stay and take care of me."

"And I said I could take care of you," Jiang said. "Not that you need to be taken care of."

Ming Li says, "Aww," and wipes her cheeks.

"She said yes. How could she not say yes? He'd saved us. He could have been killed himself. Murphy would have blown him to pieces if they'd seen him helping us, but he did it. So she said yes, and he said he would work things so she could go to America with him. Because they were married, right? And then he told us he had a way to get Jiang and me out of the country when he came back in four months and that we should let him do it. We should go wherever he wanted to put us."

Knowing the answer, Rafferty says, "Because."

"Because Murphy had probably learned we were alive. Because he had become very powerful. Because some reporter had written about our village from an interview he did with one of the Vietnamese troopers, and he'd said there were survivors. Because the story of the village was being denied. Because the truth of what happened could destroy Murphy. Because Murphy would be coming for us."

23

They Stay with Us Now

THEY'D BEEN IN Bangkok for twelve years, arriving after spending two years in a village in the northeast, learning some Thai and staying out of sight. While they were there, Americans, obviously former soldiers—not Murphy, but probably working for him—had come to the reconstructed village in Vietnam several times, asking about survivors who had lived there during the war. But no one knew where Thuy, Jiang, and the two now-grown children were, just that Bey had gone to America with her husband.

And because no one had warned them not to, they told the men Bey's husband's name, making the mistake that, years later, would result in Bey's being beaten to death in a cold little house in Wyoming.

"What can you do?" Jiang asks. "They're just people. They don't know how to lie."

Rafferty says, "You have a very good heart."

Billie Joe had bought the dry-cleaning shop for them before he brought them to Bangkok, and he'd taken the lease on the apartment. The name on the lease was a Thai name, no way to trace them through that. The shop was in the same name.

"Did you know that Billie Joe was in Bangkok this time?" Rafferty says. He is folding a piece of paper on which Jiang has written in Vietnamese two words he asked her to write.

"No," Thuy says. "He never call or come say hello."

Jiang says, "What will you do?"

"Well," Rafferty says, "I don't think I have any choice. I'm going to try to destroy Murphy."

Both women look down, unwilling to show him the doubt in their eyes.

"It's okay," Rafferty says. "I barely believe it myself."

He puts the folded paper into the pocket of his T-shirt. "Are you going someplace new?"

"Yes," says Thuy. "Back to the northeast."

"Good, good. Don't tell me any more. Does the shop have voice mail?" He turns to Ming Li and reaches down to give her a hand, but she tucks her feet under her and rises in a single, smooth movement, her bag already in her hand.

"Yes," Thuy says. "Have."

"I'll call here and leave a message if I make it, if Murphy is finished. If you don't hear from me, I guess you'll have to figure that Murphy won."

Ming Li says, "He's smarter than he looks. My brother, I mean."

"He look pretty smart," Thuy says kindly.

"Thank you for talking to us," Ming Li says. "We're very sorry to have made you so unhappy."

Thuy says, "Truth is always best." Then she starts crying, full out, as though she's just this moment heard the news of her sister's death.

At the door Rafferty looks around again. They live very sparely: a bed that doubles as a couch, a threadbare chair with a deeply dented cushion, a small television on a low black table that's ornately inlaid with abalone, a two-burner hot plate, and a waist-high refrigerator. Another bright calendar on the wall, this one from last year. A few books in Vietnamese. The bathroom, where they probably wash the dishes, is just a tiny box of a room with a sink and a showerhead dangling at the end of a length of flexible tubing. It hangs on a hook above a damp concrete floor that slopes down to a central drain.

The awful green walls.

Rafferty asks Jiang, "Who made the handprints?"

Jiang says, "They're from the family who lived here before us. My mother bought this paint very cheap, and we put on two coats to hide them, but after a few months the little hands came through. Cheap paint, it doesn't cover anything. I wanted to paint again because this color is so ugly, but she wouldn't let me. She says the handprints are really—"

"The village," Thuy says, rubbing an arm across her ravaged eyes. "The children in the village. They stay with us now."

Since Thais love an excuse for a party, most Western holiday celebrations have found fertile soil in Bangkok, and Halloween has done even better than others. It takes Ming Li about six minutes with her iPhone and Google Translate to find a Halloween store, near enough for them to get there before closing.

They ride through the monotony of the rain without speaking, their ears ringing with the story Thuy and Jiang told, with the images of the three captive boys and the children in the hut. The cabbie has Thai pop on the radio instead of the flood news, although he cranks it down when they get in. Ming Li wrinkles her nose at it and stares out the window, looking like someone studying a landscape of regret. Staring out his own window, Rafferty hears her sigh.

It's almost eight o'clock, the hour when one Bangkok turns into another Bangkok, folding the worn-out day neatly and putting it away, amping up the energy for the night. Some neighborhoods disappear into gloom while others suddenly flower, as streets that were nondescript in daylight put on their feather boas and bright sequins, and bloom revealed in their true colors, like some mousy male bank clerk who goes home, rinses off the dust, changes clothes, names, and sexes, and emerges as Fabulosa, Queen of the Night.

"Bangkok may not be glamorous," Rafferty says as they pass a pink-lit bar, the door flanked by hostesses shivering in cheap, shiny gowns and elbow-length gloves, "but it's got lurid down cold."

Ming Li doesn't even grunt. Ten minutes into the ride, she says, "It would be nice if something really terrible happened to that man."

"I can but try," Rafferty says.

"I want to be in the middle of it." She sounds like someone in an argument that's been going on so long it's become chronic.

"We'll see."

"*You* couldn't have followed those women home."

"I could have if they hadn't already seen me."

"Yeah, and if your grandmother had wheels, she'd be a tea cart."

"Frank," Rafferty says. "Frank used to say that."

This time Ming Li does grunt.

"Does it ever worry you?" he asks. "How he's shaped you, what he's turned you into?"

She turns her back on Bangkok and gives him her eyes, full bore, and he's pierced by the thought that she's becoming a beautiful woman. "Are you shitting me?"

"What kind of language is . . . ?"

"I've seen the alternatives. Hanging around with girls just like me, picking on girls who *aren't* just like me, buying ugly clothes with famous names to appeal to boys who talk through their noses and think tattoos are really daring. Whoa, dude, take your life in your hands, light a cigarette. Hey, man, let's rebel by refusing to learn anything. Let's be dull, stupid, ordinary kids who are looking forward to being dull, stupid, ordinary adults. No thanks, and with change. And by the way, I don't see *you* living in some plaid-shirt American town and flashing your junk at Builders Emporium all weekend."

"You can thank Frank for that, too."

"Oh, of course, you poor baby. You chased your terrible runaway father all the way to Asia, such a sad story. And look how badly it's worked out. You're living here, married to the best-looking woman in the world, with a daughter who's—"

"Okay, okay."

"Lighten up on Frank. He gave me that money for you, he stole that passport. And you know what else? We could *use* him. I'd take him over Ivan the Useless, or whatever that guy's name is, any day."

"Not me," Rafferty says. "I know Vladimir's a cheat and a liar and that he'd sell me out in a minute. But I keep expecting Frank to be something else."

"Like what?"

He feels silly as he says it, but he can't *not* say it. "A father."

"Oh, you're *so* breaking my heart. Tell you what. Let's just ignore each other."

"We're both upset," Rafferty says.

"Gee. You think?" She looks at her watch. "We should be there by now."

"You here now," the driver says, angling sharply to the curb. And there it is, a big, brightly lit store with a bunch of creatively melted and fractured mannequins in the window and the word ZOMBIETOWN in letters that look like the Hollywood sign. Ming Li reaches across the seat and jabs Rafferty with her forefinger.

"Sorry."

He hands the driver the fare. "Both of us. Imagine living through that."

"Why did he kill her?"

One of the fluorescents in the store flickers out, and Rafferty says, "Later. Let's get in there so they can close up and go home."

The store smells like a freshly opened box of latex gloves. The young salesgirl who hurries to help them wears a fraying bedsheet, a stringy wig of dead white hair, and two ounces of face powder. She's drawn a gruesome red scar down her left cheek, with stitches of black thread glued in place. After the green apartment, it's so innocent it makes Rafferty want to weep. She looks at both of them, clearly trying to find a racial classification, and gives up. In careful English she says, "Welcome to Zombietown. I am the Mistress of the Night."

"Whoo," Rafferty says, rubbing his arms with a shudder that surprises him by being real. In return he gets a grin, rich in plastic fangs. In Thai he says, "I want something, a mask, that wears glasses."

"Of course," says the Mistress of the Night, in English. "Glasses."

Ming Li says, "Why do we want glasses? Actually, what are we doing here?"

"One thing at a time." They follow the Mistress of the Night toward the back of the store. She calls out to someone, putting a little edge into it, and the lights snap back on. The Mistress of the Night turns dramatically and raises an open hand in a sweeping gesture that takes in a segment of wall hung with plastic masks of the full-size, pull-over-the-heard variety.

She looks at Ming Li and says, in English, "For your daughter?"

"Sister," Rafferty says. "No, bigger. For me." He points at a goofy-looking face with buckteeth, sleepy eyes, a lopsided grin, and a pair of black-framed glasses hanging from ears like cup handles. "Him."

"Mortimer Snerd," the Queen of the Night says doubtfully. "Not very scary."

"Really?" Rafferty says. "I think he's terrifying."

IN YET ANOTHER cab, Rafferty fumbles with the X-acto knife the Mistress of the Night sold him. The fourth time the driver hits a bump, Ming Li says, "Oh, give it here." The cab reaches the bottom of a ten-degree grade and plows into a temporary lake, hydroplaning briefly and skewing sickeningly to the left, until the driver slows and the tires find the pavement again. The moment the cab loses contact with the street, Ming Li lifts the knife's point an inch above the surface of the mask and waits.

Rafferty says, "Don't cut yourself."

"You know," she says, going back to working the knife very precisely through the rubber, "if you hadn't said that, I *absolutely* would have cut myself. 'Don't fall down the stairs,'" she says through her nose. "'Don't hit your thumb with that hammer.' 'Don't crawl into the refrigerator and pull the door closed and die there.' Welcome to the Useless Warnings Brigade."

"I had to say something."

"If you have to say something, tell me why he killed her."

"Right." He settles back and closes his eyes for a second. "Well, the first thing is that I don't actually know anything. This is all guesses."

"Guesses are a beginning."

"Okay. Okay, okay, okay." Now he's gazing through the window, trying to assemble the chronology. "I think Murphy was looking for Sellers and Helen—sorry, Bey—off and on for years. Practically ever since he found out about them, after Americans were allowed back into Vietnam. But it got really important in the past four or five years, as his stock started to go up with the American spooks and he had even more to lose. The Islamic unrest started here, and the Americans needed someone who could do dirty work but be deniable. He's perfect for them. He's former Phoenix Program, so he knows the drill, he's even had a security clearance, and he's in business all over Southeast Asia. He's the ideal listening post, and he can go operational, too. So one day some aging general in Washington says, 'What about old Murphy?' and they pick up the phone and give him a call."

Ming Li is holding the knife still and watching the windshield wipers lose their fight with the rain as she listens. "Yeah?"

"So for Murphy it's the golden ring. Suddenly he's got the government helping with his business, making his cover look even better, throwing contracts at him. But there's a problem, and that's what happened in that village. Given to the wrong media, the wrong administration, it could destroy him. So all of a sudden, catching up to Bey and Billie Joe moves way up his to-do list."

"And," Ming Li says, "he's got new resources now. To help him find them."

"And he did," Rafferty says.

"And they hurt her for twenty-four—"

"Trying to make her tell them—"

"—where Billie Joe is."

"So about five days before Billie Joe runs into me," Rafferty says, "she tells them what they wanted to know—"

"And what she says is, 'He's here, in Thailand,' except they can't pin down his exact location. But they've got some sort of pipeline to him, and to draw him they set up that thing you got in the middle of. *And* it does draw him, and they do the dirty. And Murphy thinks he can relax, except that suddenly you're there and Billie Joe talked to you."

"And let's not forget, there may be something in Yala, which probably has its own calendar. So Murphy might be getting squeezed from three or four directions at once."

They both think for a moment. The driver says, "At once," and Ming Li jumps, but Rafferty shakes his head. The guy's just trying out the phrase.

"You said the government might pay him through his company," Ming Li says, lowering her voice. "Why would they do it that way?"

"You tell me. Vladimir wouldn't have asked that question."

Ming Li gives him a sour smile and finishes her work on the mask. She sheathes the X-acto carefully and says, "So it looks legit if the money transfers are revealed. So they can deny any spook connection."

Rafferty says, "Let's hope so. Plausible deniability. Keeping him at arm's length. If there's no daylight between him and them, we're—*I'm*—probably dead."

"Coming up," the driver says, and Rafferty looks out through a slant of rain at the high walls the Southeast Asian rich use to help the poor keep their distance. A moment later Murphy's gates slide into view and the cabbie slows, but Rafferty says, "Keep going. Go to the corner and make the turn and wait for me."

"You get wet," the cabbie says.

"I'll get dry again."

"Here, stop here." Looking at Ming Li, he points to the ground: *Stay here.* She gives him a frown, but he lifts his chin toward the driver and mimes him turning the wheel and driving away, and Ming Li makes a face he chooses to take as acquiescence.

When he opens the car door, the rain is a roar. He's soaked before the door closes again. He realizes that the glue might not hold, that the ink might run, that Murphy might miss it altogether if the rain gets any heavier. He realizes that he never seems to have a backup plan.

The glue *doesn't* hold. The plastic slides over the surface of the wet wood as though the glue were grease. But the ink that forms the Vietnamese words Jiang had written is thick and black, from an alcohol-based Sharpie, and it reads dark, hard-edged, and clear. He shoves his single pushpin through the bit of the plastic mask and then through the paper, and pushes the point deeply into the wood of the gate, hammering it once with the heel of his hand, the one he scraped on the pavement when he went down beneath the weight of Billie Joe Sellers.

He backs up, shaking the hand to get rid of the pain, and sprints for the cab. Ming Li pulls away from him when he climbs in, dripping profusely, and the driver makes a tsk-tsk sound as he puts the car in gear.

"It's up?" Ming Li asks.

"It's up."

God turns the rain off, and the sudden silence makes Rafferty's ears pop. He opens his mouth wide to equalize the pressure.

Ming Li says, "And what exactly is it you think this will accomplish?"

"What do I *hope* it will accomplish, you mean."

"Fine. What do you hope it will accomplish?"

"Well," he says as the cab swings back onto a busy, four-lane boulevard, "I'm hoping it'll shake the paper."

24

That Night

THAT NIGHT SOLDIERS and emergency workers slap another hundred thirty thousand sandbags on the dikes in the city's lower-lying areas. The river rises silently, running fast between its banks. More water is diverted into more canals, and more canals overflow. The national death toll from the flood is estimated at more than three hundred and, like the water, rising.

THAT NIGHT ROSE opens her eyes on the thin mat of folded clothes she and Miaow use as a bed and realizes she's alone. She gets up silently, not wanting to wake Fon's parents, and tiptoes outside. Through a clearing in the clouds, a half-moon gleams, sharp-edged and pockmarked in the clear night air, and fifteen meters away she sees her daughter, sitting against the town's biggest tree, with her knees drawn up and her head down, misery in every curve of her body.

Miaow doesn't look up as Rose sits beside her on the wet earth, but she leans against her mother, and Rose can feel her shoulders shaking. Water drips musically from the tree.

When she's gotten herself under control, Miaow wipes her nose with her index finger and says, "I'm so sad."

Rose hugs her a little closer. "I know, baby, but we'll go home soon."

Miaow swallows loudly and says, "I want . . . I want a steak."

"Well, that's easy—"

"Why do I have to pretend I'm *special* all the time? I'm not a vegan. I was just trying to be different, to be . . . be . . . be special—"

Rose strokes her hair, something Miaow normally won't permit. "Everyone tries to be special, Miaow."

"No they don't," Miaow says. "You—"

"Sweetie, Poke and I aren't any different—"

"Not you and *Poke*," Miaow says, and Rose feels her own eyebrows climb. "It's *Andrew*. He doesn't pretend to be anything. He's just dweeby and weird with his stupid glasses and his . . . his . . . his pants too high and his—oh, his hair. He dyed his hair to match mine because it never occurred to him I'd dye *mine* to match his. Ohhhh," Miaow wails, throwing her arms around her mother's neck, "I miss Andrew *so much*."

THAT NIGHT PIM'S second customer passes out on top of her, in the middle of saying something. She waits politely for him to finish speaking, and when she realizes he won't, she rocks him back and forth, using her elbows against the mattress for leverage, until he rolls off, landing on his back on the edge of the bed, his knuckles brushing the carpet.

Pim shakes him twice, saying, "Hello," because she doesn't remember his name. He begins to snore.

She gets up and pulls on her clothes, looks around the room, and sees his trousers on the carpet in front of the bathroom door. The wallet is in the right-hand back pocket, and she eases it out, looking for her sixteen hundred baht. What she sees is a stack of American twenties as thick as a comic book. She works two out, and then the nameless man snores again, loudly enough to make her jump, and she takes five more, and then five after that. She jams the money into the back pocket of her jeans and quietly lets herself out.

Thirty minutes later she's sitting in an alley off Sukhumvit with her back against a fence made of chain-link and big sheets of rippled green plastic, with her legs crossed and a flimsy plastic Ziploc bag in her lap. From the bag she takes an aluminum-foil pipe and a big, crumbly pinch of crushed *yaa baa* tablets. She pushes the speed into the bowl of the pipe, being careful not to bend the pipe so sharply it'll crimp the air flow, and then—with the pipe dangling loosely from her mouth—she breaks a wooden match, licks it to get it wet enough that it won't catch fire, and shoves the sharp end into the jet of a disposable butane lighter. A flick of the wheel shows her that the flame is still fat and yellow and soft, so she turns up the flow and wiggles the splinter of wet wood to close the opening some more, burning her fingertips, until the lighter produces a blue needle of flame. Then she points the needle into the pipe and hits the smoke, and her heart rises eagerly to greet its new friend. This is the first time she's done it alone. This is the first time she hasn't had to share.

As she exhales and hits it again, she sees Arthit's sad, disapproving eyes. She slams her own eyes shut and fills her lungs until they feel like they'll explode.

In less than a minute, the Earth, with Arthit and her family and everyone else pinned helplessly to its surface, is a thousand feet below her and, all alone in the sky, she can look down on the dark, folded world with cities gleaming in its seams. It's so beautiful she thinks she might cry.

THAT NIGHT VLADIMIR uses his teeth to unscrew the cap from his second bottle of vodka. He's in his same old room but sitting on the new Kirghiz carpet he bought with the money Rafferty paid him.

He reaches for his empty glass, but it dodges at the last moment and he knocks it over. He closes one eye and fixes the glass with a glare until he's wrapped his fingers around it. As he pours, he asks himself for the thirtieth or fortieth time since he opened the first bottle how much he could earn by telling what he knows—from a safe distance, of course—to Murphy. He asks again the corollary question: Who is more likely to be alive in a few days, Murphy or Rafferty? When this is over, who will he have to share Bangkok with? He gets the same answer he's been getting all night long. It's not the answer he wants, but if there's one thing Vladimir has learned in a lifetime of betraying and being betrayed, it's that winning is all that matters.

The rain hits the window, hard as a handful of nails.

But there remains the problem, he thinks as he raises the glass. There remains the problem of Baby Spy. He could not do this to Baby Spy. So much youth, so much promise, such a beautifully devious nature. He could do nothing to harm her. His soul, his magnificent Russian soul, would not permit it.

His eyes fill up in admiration of the oceanic vastness of his soul, even as the dry clockwork of his mind says, *There must be a way to get her off the stage, just for the amount of time it would take.*

THAT NIGHT ANNA awakes with a start, breathing fast, feeling as though she's been in free fall. It's the second time in a few days this has happened. She finds herself wrapped in Arthit's arms again; he's been hugging her in his sleep as though he's afraid she'll dissolve before he can wake up.

She eases herself loose, hearing him murmur a protest, but he's still asleep. His breathing is deep and regular, his face—when she turns to look at it—is soft, relieved of the tension it harbors all day, tension that really abandons it only when he sleeps.

And, she thinks, with a tiny pinch in her heart, when he looks at her.

His hair always gets flattened by the pillow. The second morning she woke up with him, she went to the kitchen and got him some coffee and then steered him to a mirror and wrote a note saying it looked as if someone had ironed him. He had laughed a mouthful of coffee onto the mirror, and that sad little maid, whatever her name was, had come running at the sound

A thousand things had gone through the girl's face. She'd been happy and amazed to hear him laugh, but she hadn't known Anna was there, and the girl's head was made of glass. Anna could see everything.

The poor kid.

Anna has one of what she's come to think of as her *moments*, when she feels as though all the strings that run through her life, the ones that attach her to her work, to her son, to her future and his, to the promises and commitments she's made, the bad decisions and the good, have tangled inside her into a giant, misshapen knot she'll never be able to untie and isn't allowed to cut. She knows that whatever she does next will be wrong.

In a whisper even she can barely hear, she says to Arthit, "I had no idea this would happen. Please," she says, "you have to believe me. I never thought it would turn out like this."

THAT NIGHT AT 4:20 A.M., Murphy's headlights illuminate the opening gate, and he stops the car with a jerk. Unsure of what he's seeing, he hits the remote again to reverse the gate's course. Then he turns on the high beams and gets out of the car, leaving the engine idling and the door open. Ignoring the rain, he moves quickly to the gate, keeping to one side so his shadow in the headlights doesn't obscure what's stuck there.

It's not until he's practically on top of it that the object resolves itself into what he actually knew it was at first sight: a human ear. The hairs that rise on the back of his neck don't go down again until he touches it and realizes it's plastic.

He rips it from the gate and finds himself automatically beginning to slip it into his shirt pocket. Time folds around him, and he's back *there*, with the old blood on his pocket and the weight of the reeking necklace bumping against his chest. His heart galloping, he pulls the folded, sodden piece of paper off the thumbtack that secures it. Tilting it toward the headlights and opening it up, he sees, in thick black lines, two words in Vietnamese that he automatically translates: *Four survivors.* He backs away until his shoulder blades touch the gate, folding the paper as though to hide the words from prying eyes, and slowly turns in a half circle, looking for the enemy.

Back in the car, he watches in the rearview mirror as the gates close safely behind him. When he's pulled in to his usual parking space in front of the house, he shuts off the engine and sits there, his hands still on the wheel, feeling the muscles in his shoulders and back bunch and jump like those of someone who's been wired to a field generator. He waits until it's stopped and his breathing has smoothed out, and then he gets out of the car, leaving the note and the plastic ear on the passenger seat.

He's just keyed in the front-door combination and pushed the door open when something cold touches the back of his neck, and for a second his heart slams itself shut so hard he thinks he's dying. But then he smells her.

As he turns slowly to face her, Treasure backs away, out of arm's length, holding his automatic in both hands, in the approved shooter's position. It's pointed directly at his heart. Her face is blackened except for the narrow, skin-colored strip that contains the bridge of her nose and her wide, wide eyes. When she smiles and takes another step back, he sees that she's also somehow blackened her teeth.

"If this was a real war," Treasure says, shivering with some unreadable emotion, "you'd be dead now."

In the house the alarm begins to shrill.

THAT NIGHT, A little before five in the morning, Rafferty snaps awake to a high, repetitive bleat, coming from the clutter of cell phones on the bedside table. He rolls over, spots the one that's blinking, and picks it up. Presses the button to answer but says nothing.

"Hello?" a woman says. She's American. "Hello? Is anyone there?"

He says nothing. He doesn't know the voice.

"Are you there? Is this voice mail, is that it?" She waits as Rafferty silently counts to three. "Well, if it is, I'm calling Mr. Rafferty? You've phoned me several times, but I wasn't able to return the call, and I'm sorry about that, but here I am at last. Sorry about the time, too, but I just landed. You've got my hotel number in your phone now, and I'm in Bangkok. Oh," she says, "silly me. This is Helen Eckersley."

Rafferty waits until she's hung up. He powers the phone off and pops out the SIM card. Then he pulls the battery from the back, just to be sure. With a loud sigh, he gets up and crosses the room, slides the water glass out of its clear plastic sleeve, and drops the card and the battery into the sleeve, knotting it so they can't slip out. He goes into the bathroom and turns on the hot water, letting it run to get it as hot as possible as he flips on lights in the bedroom and opens his deteriorating shoulder bag. Throws in the plastic sleeve and then wads up the day's T-shirt and stuffs it in, too.

When he's finished with the bag, he pours both the room's packets of instant coffee into the glass and totes the glass into the bathroom, where he runs the hot water into it, stirring with his finger. Two minutes later, wearing a mustache of powdered coffee, he calls Ming Li's room and gives her five minutes to pack and meet him in the hall.

At 5:28 A.M., they check into a third-class hotel several kilometers away. Rafferty slides the Delacroix passport across the desk, expecting the clerk to reject it, but all he does is look quizzically at Ming Li, photocopy the page with Rafferty's photo on it, and hand it back, along with a room key. Aside from the two of them and the clerk, the huge lobby is empty, and Rafferty feels the man's eyes on them all the way to the elevator.

Up in the room, Ming Li offers to take the couch, since she's the shorter of the two, but Rafferty claims it, and as she snores daintily on top of the still-made bed, he gazes down at the predawn lights of Bangkok and realizes—for the first time—that when someone thinks he's looking at city lights, 90 percent of what he sees is darkness.

Part Four
SHAKING THE PAPER

25

The Murder of Children Does Affect Me

AROUND SIX THAT morning, the rain breaks, and small, ragged patches of blue open up and glide slowly from south to north as though they're the clouds and the gray is the sky. Low in the west, the horizon has the dull metallic shine of pewter. To the east Rafferty can see a dark, vertical curtain of rain.

He's spent an anxious and mostly sleepless night. He seems to have sand beneath his eyelids and cotton wrapped around his brain; thoughts come slowly and shapelessly, and he has to force them to hold still while he examines them for usefulness. His center of gravity has risen uneasily to the region of his lungs and his heart, forcing him to sit low in the backseat of the cab with his knees jammed against the back of the driver's seat.

"We're doing this in order of availability, not importance," he says to Ming Li, mostly to see whether he can compose the sentence out loud. He looks at the list in his hand and then at his watch—7:10. He sighs yet again and dials Arthit.

"*There* you are," Arthit says. He sounds relieved.

"Here I am," Rafferty says.

"To cut to the chase, the drug people have a line into the airlines that fly here from Kuala Lumpur," Arthit says. "Your Mr. Bland, Edward Bland—"

"Eddie," Rafferty says.

"Ah. Well, the ticket says Edward."

"What ticket?"

"The one he bought last night. To Bangkok. This afternoon."

Rafferty makes a writing pantomime in Ming Li's direction, and she ransacks her bag.

"What time? What flight number? Which airport?"

"Wait. Okay, here we are. Flight 21, arriving at three-twenty P.M. at Suvarnabhumi, which is a good thing since the airport at Don Mueang is flooded out."

Rafferty repeats the flight information as Ming Li jots it down. Into the phone he says, "Can you have someone there?"

"I could have Kosit call in sick."

"I think it would be worth it. Bland's coming either to blow something up or to finalize the plan to blow something up."

"I'll get him on it. Anything else?"

"Yes. Do you remember what channel shot the tape when the guy was killed? By the way, his name was Billie Joe Sellers."

"How do you know that?"

"I was right when I said all this has to do with Vietnam. I found someone who knew him."

Arthit says, "He was USA, right?"

"Right."

"Okay. It was Channel Seven."

"Could you call the news department and go all official and find out who tipped them to send the crew?"

Arthit says, "I've been wondering about that myself."

Poke says good-bye and dials another number. "Vladimir. Get up now. Get Janos up, too."

"Mʀ. . . . Mʀ. *Rafferty?*" Andrew's hair is wet and slicked back, and his face is shining with soap and water. His school clothes are honor-student immaculate, and when he opened the door, he'd had the penny-bright *Oh, boy, it's morning!* look that only children can manage, but it changes to dread the instant he sees Rafferty's face. He glances at Ming Li, but then his eyes jerk back to Rafferty's. "Has anything happened—" His voice breaks, and he licks his lips. "Is . . . is Miaow okay?"

"Anh Duong," a male voice says, a no-nonsense voice with extra starch. Its owner asks a question in Vietnamese.

"It's . . . ummm," Andrew calls in English, and immediately

lowers his voice and says, through his teeth, *"Miaow?"*

"She's fine," Rafferty says, and the man snaps his question again, in a tone that suggests long familiarity with command.

"It's Mr. Rafferty," Andrew says, a bit wildly. "Miaow's . . . you know. And . . . and a lady."

Ming Li says, "A *lady?*" and the door is pulled the rest of the way open.

The man who stands there isn't much taller than Ming Li, but he seems to have a very high density. His face is almost square, wide-cheekboned and sharp-jawed, with small, hard black eyes and a mouth that pulls down, drum-tight, at the corners. He wears a white shirt and a dark, small-patterned tie, tightly knotted, over very fine navy blue slacks. His feet are in black socks. "Andrew," he says in English. "Finish your breakfast."

Andrew is gone so fast that Rafferty can barely see him move.

"And you are?" Andrew's father is looking at Ming Li.

"I'm Miaow's aunt," Ming Li says. "Kind of."

"I am Nguyen." No name, no title. He steps back to allow them in, glancing down at a glittering steel watch as they pass. "I have coffee if you want some."

Poke says, "Thank you. Have you got fifteen minutes?"

Nguyen says, "Does this concern my son and your daughter?"

"I wish it did."

"Really," Nguyen says. "Please go left, into the living room."

"Can I help with the coffee?" Ming Li asks.

"No, Auntie, you cannot. Just go sit with your . . . whatever Mr. Rafferty is to you."

"My half brother."

"Yes, of course." He shakes his head. "I'll be back in a moment. And please. Speak softly. My wife is in bed with a migraine."

Ming Li looks over at Poke as Nguyen turns abruptly. She fills her cheeks with air and lets it escape slowly between her lips. "Poor kid," she whispers.

As she and Poke turn the corner from the hallway into the living room, she says, "Sheesh." The room is larger than Rafferty's entire apartment. But despite the sweep of space and the floor-to-ceiling windows, opening onto an expanse of gray sky and glinting buildings, the room feels rigid and cold. Rafferty has a sense that things he can't see are whispering in corners. He instinctively dislikes the pale blue upholstery and the spotless white carpet, the permanent bouquets of silk flowers dead center on the dark, heavy tables. The whole place cries out for someone to come in and mess it up, and the reason for Miaow's lie about Rose's parents becomes even clearer.

"I'm not clean enough to sit down," Ming Li whispers, her eyes on a sky-blue sofa. Along the longest wall, just a few feet from the windows, is a round table with three blue-silk-covered chairs pulled up to it and a fourth at a precise forty-five-degree angle. On the table in front of the angled chair are several newspapers, folded and stacked military straight. Rafferty lifts his eyebrows at the table, and Ming Li tracks him across the soft carpets to it. They sit, just as Andrew takes a speedy diagonal from what Rafferty supposes is the kitchen, heading for the entrance hall. His head is down, and he doesn't look at them. They hear the outside door close, presumably behind him.

Five or six minutes drag past. Rafferty is tapping his foot and looking at his watch when Nguyen comes in with a teak tray in his hands. He's put on his suit coat and buttoned it, a gesture that increases the distance between them. Ming Li scoots back in her chair to give him access to the table, and he puts the tray in its center. It contains a carafe, two cup-and-saucer sets in a thin, filigreed china with tiny blue flowers on it, and cream and sugar in matching containers. Nguyen pours for each of them, indicates the cream and sugar with his left hand, and sits, undoing the lower button on his suit coat as he does so.

The three of them face one another for a moment, and then Nguyen inclines his head and lifts his eyebrows. Ming Li spoons sugar into her coffee as Rafferty jumps in.

"Andrew says you have something to do with the Vietnamese diplomatic corps here."

Nguyen nods once, as though to say *Go ahead* without necessarily acknowledging the fact.

Rafferty says, "Well, is that right? There's no point in my wasting everyone's time."

Nguyen crosses his legs. "My son, Anh Duong—or Andrew, as he prefers—is an honest boy. As to whether you're wasting my time, I'd need to know more to decide on that."

"All right. Well, to come to the point, would you be interested in learning that someone who committed an atrocity against Vietnamese citizens, noncombatants, during the war—more than one atrocity, probably, but one I can absolutely prove—is here in Bangkok?"

Nguyen starts to speak, but Poke cuts him off with a lifted hand.

"And if you wouldn't be interested in that, can you send me to someone who would?"

Nguyen says, "The person is American?"

"Yes."

Nguyen looks out the window. "There have been a lot of Americans." His English is perfect, if a bit prim. "There has been a lot of war. We are the only country ever to defeat America, China, and France. If we spent our time thinking about past wars, we would lack the energy to meet the needs of the present."

"On September seventeenth, 1975," Rafferty says, biting down on the words, "in the middle of the rainy season, two American soldiers and a CIA adviser, plus four Vietnamese troopers, entered a small village in the Delta, not far from Ninh Kiều. There were only two men living in the village then, both in their late sixties. Everyone else was either a woman or a child. By the time the squad left, five or six hours later, everyone in the village was dead. They forced everyone into a hut and blew it up."

Nguyen continues to look out at Bangkok.

"They were herded into the hut like cattle," Rafferty says. "Before the explosives went, off the people in the hut prayed to Buddha and Jesus."

"So, obviously," Nguyen says, "if you know that, not everyone died."

"They also killed three boys," Ming Li says. Her cheekbones are flushed with color. "They shot them point-blank through the forehead. They cut an ear off one of them. They were children."

"Yes," Nguyen says colorlessly. "I can see how that might affect you more than the deaths of the adults."

Ming Li puts her cup down noisily and stands up. To Rafferty she says, "Come on."

"Please," Nguyen says. "Sit. More coffee?"

Rafferty inclines his head toward Ming Li's chair, and after a moment she sits and says, "No."

Rafferty says, "No, thank you."

Ming Li's mouth tightens, but she says, "No, thank you."

Nguyen turns away from the window to face them and stretches his legs out in front of him, crossing one sock-clad ankle over the other. He sits back in his chair an inch or two, unbuttons his jacket the rest of the way, and studies Ming Li long enough to make her fidget. "You're what—sixteen?"

"Eighteen," Ming Li says.

"I think not."

Ming Li shrugs and dips her index finger into her coffee and puts the finger in her mouth. It's a tiny insult.

With his eyes still on her, Nguyen says, "Does my son have that?"

"Have what?" Rafferty asks.

"I am not an entirely unintimidating man," Nguyen says. "Not many people have stood up to walk out of the room during a conversation with me. Telling me, in essence, to go fuck myself. You know my son, apparently. Would he do that?"

"Would he do what? Be brave? Rude? Impulsive?"

Nguyen looks down at his tie and straightens it a tiny amount. Without looking up at them, he says, "Unconventional."

Rafferty says, "I don't know. There are things we *can't* know about people until the time comes and they either have what's necessary or they don't."

"It's a terrible thing to be a father," Nguyen says. "There are so many ways to do it wrong." He glances again at Ming Li. "So yes, the murder of children does affect me."

"He's a good kid," Rafferty says, surprising himself. "I love my daughter more than life itself, and I'm glad she chose Andrew."

Nguyen gives him a quarter-inch nod. "Thank you. But I think he chose her."

"I suppose that's possible," Rafferty says, "but I doubt it."

"I've been unhappy about it, to tell you the truth. Miaow is . . . perhaps *too* interesting. And not Vietnamese, obviously. And her family situation, if you'll excuse my saying so, is irregular."

"But it's solid," Rafferty says.

"And this is why it's so difficult to be a father," Nguyen says, as though Poke hasn't spoken. "On the one hand, I want my son to obey me. It's his filial duty. On the other hand, I'm secretly pleased when he behaves in a way that, as I said before, essentially tells me to go fuck myself. I worry about him being too docile. The world wipes itself on docile people."

"He dyed his hair to match hers," Rafferty says. "I'll bet he didn't ask permission."

Nguyen almost smiles. "I wondered where the color came from."

"It's Miaow's way of trying to be different."

"Actually," Nguyen says, and this time he lets the smile all the way out, "I don't think that being different is going to be one of life's problems for your daughter."

"I don't mean different from other people," Rafferty says. "She's got that aced. I mean different from herself, different from who she sees herself to be."

Nguyen closes his eyes for a moment, then opens them again. "Of course."

"This is all really sweet," Ming Li says, "but we've sort of got an agenda?"

Nguyen looks at her again, leaning forward slightly as though to see her better. "You're . . . what, little Auntie?" he asks. "Half Vietnamese?"

"Half Chinese, half American. Poke's part Filipino. We share a father. What else do you want to know?"

"If you grew up in America," Nguyen says, "your attitude is typical. If you grew up in China, you must know that you're being extremely rude."

Ming Li sits up and puts her hands in her lap and inclines her head. "I'm sorry."

"On the other hand," Nguyen says, "I admire you for it. But still, a conversation must be allowed to shape itself, to allow each of us to discover whom we're talking to. Don't you agree?"

"You're completely right. I forgot myself."

"Well, we're past that now. Who were the survivors?"

"Two women and three children," Rafferty says.

"How did they escape?"

"An American soldier got them out."

"A white knight," Nguyen says. "Or perhaps a black one. It's a shame there weren't more of them." He looks down at his legs, uncrosses his ankles, and recrosses them the other way, with the left on top. "This was a terrible crime, but it happened decades ago. In wartime. Even if there's no legal statute of limitations on war crimes, there's an emotional limit. I have to tell you that I don't know whom you should talk to. Vietnam is a different country than it was in the 1970s. And, as you may know, the snatch-and-snuff teams, as your soldiers called them, were partly an imitation of tactics used by the army of North Vietnam. Neither side had a monopoly on terrorism."

"Well," Rafferty says, "that's a very even-minded attitude."

"The heat of passion has cooled," Nguyen says.

"Let's see if we can't strike a match," Rafferty says. "About a week and a half ago, one of the survivors was murdered in the United States."

Nguyen lifts his eyebrows. In a face as controlled as his, it looks to Rafferty like a tectonic shift.

"By the same man," Rafferty continues. "Or, rather, by people working for him."

"Can you prove that?"

"I can make an excellent case."

"Was she still a citizen of Vietnam?"

"I don't know. But her sister and her sister's daughter are. And the two children who got away. And this man is after them, too. Now, today. Here, in Thailand."

Nguyen fingers the knot in his tie, and Rafferty is certain he has no idea he's doing it. His eyes are on his feet but focused about halfway down, on something only he can see. "And what do you want from me, Mr. Rafferty?"

"I may lose this fight. If I do, I just want to know that somebody else is going to kill him."

"You must want it very badly."

Rafferty says, "I do."

"When I saw you at the door," Nguyen says, "my first impulse was to make you wait for coffee while I called the police."

"Yeah, I was getting a little antsy out here."

"It would have been difficult for me to explain to Anh Duong why I turned Miaow's father over to the police."

"It's not exactly the police."

"No, it isn't. And the implication of that—of the people who are looking for you—is that you've somehow brushed up against the War on Terror."

"That's the implication."

"And then you talk to me about someone who was involved in the Phoenix Program. I'm assuming that what happened in that village was the Phoenix Program."

"It was."

"This is freshly interesting, since the Phoenix Program is one of the blueprints for the War on Terror."

"Something done badly is worth doing badly twice. An American saying."

"The man in the village is the man who's after you?"

"He is."

"I'm sure there's a simple explanation for that, but I think I'll dispense with it and go with my conviction that you're in the right." He looks at Ming Li. "Which is, in turn, based on the way you've presented yourselves—both of you—during this conversation. Instead of talking to my colleagues about you, I'll focus on the recent murder of a current or former citizen of Vietnam and a present-day threat posed to other Vietnamese citizens, living here in Thailand. By a man who also happens to be a war criminal." He shifts his weight onto one hip, reaches behind him, and pulls out a slender black wallet, which he opens to reveal a notepad and a thin gold pen. He removes the pen, clicks the point into position, and says, "Name?"

Rafferty says, "Murphy. Haskell Murphy."

Nguyen puts the pen back without writing anything. He says, "Well, of course."

26

If People Do Business with Rats

"DID WE JUST accomplish anything?" Ming Li says. The rain is back, and whoever sat on the cab's backseat before them was very wet. The damp has already seeped through Rafferty's jeans.

"I can only stir the pot," Rafferty says, beginning to dial the phone. "And see what comes to the top."

"You sound like Charlie Chan."

"The Vietnamese are efficient people," Rafferty says. "Nguyen's official diplomatic nonsense notwithstanding, they're not known for turning the other cheek. And he's already heard of Murphy, so yes, at the very least we've created an awkward situation for Mr. Murphy, turned a few more eyes on him. Hang on."

"Before you push those buttons. Are you frightened?"

"Scared senseless." Rafferty punches in the final numbers and presses SEND.

Ming Li watches the plume of water thrown up alongside the cab as Rafferty says, "Hello, Jiang and Thuy, this is Poke. Hope you're both okay. Someone will probably call you from the Vietnamese embassy. You'll know the call is the one I'm talking about because they'll say they're calling about Helen. Then it's up to you whether to call them back, but I think we should try to shine light on Murphy from as many directions as possible." He glances over to Ming Li, eyebrows raised.

"Just tell them hello."

"Ming Li says hi," he says, and disconnects. "What I want to do right now," he says, keying in another number, "is make Bangkok feel very small to Mr. Murphy."

He checks the number he's dialed against the one on his list, but before he can make the connection, the phone rings in his hand.

"Yes, Arthit."

"Well, this is interesting," Arthit says. "The man who called the TV news director spoke English, and the news director was pretty sure he was an American."

"And the name. I'm assuming he got a name."

"He did," Arthit says. "His name was Frank Rafferty."

"Is TRAP," VLADIMIR says, making it rhyme with "pep." He's shiny with alcohol sweat, and his eyes are so glazed he looks like a baked fish. Across the table Janos does his chameleon act, blending into the upholstery.

"Of course it's a trap," Rafferty says, putting down a mug of weak coffee. "The woman is dead, and she wants to meet me. The question is how close we can get to her without stepping in it."

"Why you want to get close to her?" Janos asks.

"Look," Rafferty says, "and you look, too," he says to Ming Li, "whatever your name is supposed to be—"

"Minnie Lee," Vladimir says with a ghastly attempt at a smile. The door to the restaurant opens, and all eyes go to it and look away as a stranger comes in. A gust of air strikes the table, rich with the fatty smell of frying bacon. Vladimir's eyelids drop as though in self-defense.

"You look, too, Minnie," Rafferty says. "I haven't got a master plan, okay? The goal is to pull Murphy offside, to get him into territory where he's vulnerable. To create a *lot* of territory where he's vulnerable. To get a bunch of people thinking about him and wondering whether he should be here at all."

"And this woman fits in how?" Ming Li asks.

"She's an opening. She's something he's investing energy in. If he hangs her out there somewhere, she's going to have a hook in her. And Murphy's going to be on the other end of the line."

"And you'll have a hook in your mouth," Ming Li says.

"Maybe not. Maybe we'll steal his bait."

"And after you make him uncomfortable? After you steal his bait? And then?" Vladimir says.

"Well, ideally," Rafferty says, "we kill him or put him in the position where someone else will do it. That seems like the simplest solution."

Vladimir shakes his head, very carefully. "They will still be looking for you. Shen and his people, they will still—"

He breaks off as the waitress sets down a plate of fried eggs for Rafferty and a stack of pancakes for Ming Li. To Janos she says, "Oh, sorry, I forgot about you," but as she turns, Vladimir grabs her sleeve.

"Beer," he says. "Big one."

"This is Breakfast House," the waitress says, pronouncing it "Hout." "Beer not have."

"Here," Vladimir says, holding out a bill. "Is twenty dollar. You go across street, buy beer, bring here, keep change. You do this, you go to heaven."

The waitress takes the twenty, turns it over to check the back, and shrugs. She heads for the front door.

"Drinking last night," Vladimir says apologetically. "But Shen—"

"I'm not thinking about Shen yet." Rafferty leans forward, his elbows on the table. "I have to do this one step at a time. Right now Murphy's what I need to think about. He's driving this train, and, what's more, the son of a bitch is overdue."

"Getting personal, no good," Vladimir says.

"Me?" Rafferty cuts into his eggs. "Personal?"

"Speaking of personal," Ming Li says, "I want to try something out on Vladimir and . . . and this gentleman."

"Janos," Janos says.

"Thank you." Ming Li gives him a smile that makes him smooth his shirt and sit straighter, and Rafferty realizes she's got it calibrated, and that was about a 6.8. He thinks, *God, what's she going to be like at twenty?* She says, "I've been wondering about the time they almost caught you in that hotel near Khao San. It doesn't feel right to me."

"Ahhh," Vladimir says, nodding. "This is talent."

Ming Li says, "You, too?"

"How could I not?" Vladimir says. He passes an open hand over his brow, reducing the shine somewhat. "It doesn't work."

Rafferty says, "What doesn't?"

"This is the way it's *supposed* to look," Ming Li says. "This is what you're supposed to think happened. Shen watched the house until Arthit left, and then he went in and tricked the seventeen-year-old maid into telling him which neighborhood you were hiding in. Is that about it?"

Rafferty nods.

"And the maid knows this," Ming Li continues, "because *nothing* is kept secret from her in that house, even though Arthit's contact with you could put him in jail. It's nothing he'd keep from a maid."

"Well," Rafferty says, feeling uneasy, "Pim and I have a history. I put her there."

"Baby Spy wery smart," Vladimir says. "This is not something Shen could know. That you and small-girl maid have friendship. How? What record is this on? What paper, where?"

Ming Li says, "Ventriloquism."

Janos says, "Obviously."

"What?" Rafferty says. It's almost a snap. "What's obvious? It doesn't do me any good if all you spooks sit there nodding sagely at one another and looking wise. What's ventriloquism? I mean, other than that parlor trick Murphy can apparently do."

Ming Li says, "You're not going to like this."

Rafferty says, "I'm getting good at living with things I don't like."

"This is a lecture from Frank, almost word for word. Let's say you have a piece of intelligence you want to act on. You can't be completely sure it's going to bring your problem to an end, and if it doesn't, if the problem isn't solved, then the fact that you *have* the information will tell the other side who your source is. And you don't want that, because if the plan fails, you need that source to remain in place."

"So you pick dummy," says Vladimir. "Same like wentriloquist."

"Wait a minute," Rafferty says.

"They set Pim up," Ming Li says, so deliberately that she seems to be laying the words on the table one at a time. "And they did it so well that even *she* thinks she gave you up."

"She did give me—"

"When all along," Ming Li says over him, "there was someone else in the house. Someone who heard all of it. Someone, in fact, who came straight to Arthit from Major Shen and didn't even pretend otherwise."

Rafferty says, "No." And feels a deep throb of certainty that says, *Yes*.

Everybody looks at him. Their eyes, the clatter of silverware, the noise and the smells of the restaurant, the bright yellow of his egg yolks—it all crowds in on him. He hauls himself to his feet, fighting a wave of nausea. "I'll be back." On the way out, he pushes past the waitress carrying Vladimir's large Singha back to him.

Out on the street, he goes half a block before he registers that it's still raining. He edges toward the storefronts on the theory that rain doesn't fall straight down and there's at least a possibility that it's slanting away from the buildings.

The strategy's failure distracts him from his panic about Arthit and Anna. By the time he makes the first right, having apparently decided subconsciously to walk around the block, his clothes are already clinging to him. He thinks about buying an umbrella and then forgets about it, seeing in his mind's eye Arthit, how happy he looked with Anna; seeing Pim, the loss and the devastation in her face outside the Beer Garden. The pimp and, waiting for her later, the pipe.

What can he do? What can he do for anyone?

And while he's at it, what can he do for himself?

He can't find a way around it: Ming Li and Vladimir are almost certainly right. Shen's visit with Pim was an ice-cold act of ventriloquism. Pim was dropped out a window to keep the secret that Arthit, lost in the long loneliness following Noi's death, is falling in love with someone who has been inserted into the household, into his heart, to betray him.

But at the same instant, he questions the whole thing. Why? Why would Anna Chaibancha, well born and well raised, financially comfortable, someone who has turned her disability into a career, helping others to overcome the same challenge—a long-ago friend, for heaven's sake, of Arthit's dead wife—why would she allow herself to be put in this position?

Does it even matter why? The fact is there, blunt and ugly and unarguable. She's a spy, she's working for people who are enemies to both Poke and Arthit. She could break Arthit's heart all over again and probably will. And she's responsible, at least in part, for what's happened to Pim.

By the time he reaches the second corner, he's stopped noticing the rain again, and he's turning the situation over in his mind, trying to bottle up the anger so he can think coldly.

When the idea comes, it's beyond cold. To make it work, he'll have to lie to the best friend he's ever had.

"SHE'S STAYING AT the Chiang Palace," he says to Janos before he's even seated. "I called her back this morning, and that's how they answered the phone. I need you to get in there, find out what room she's in, and get a look at her."

"How do I find out what room she's in?"

"I have to tell *you* this?"

Vladimir says, "This is why you get contractor," and Janos says, over him, "No, no. I can handle it. But what then? After I know what room—"

"Then you find a way to get a look at her. They'll have photocopied her passport when she checked in, so see if you can get a copy. Get police ID or bribe the desk clerk."

"After that?" Janos says.

"After that I pay you fifteen hundred U.S."

"That's good, but, what do we do next?"

"You wait around, being invisible, and the moment you see her come down, you call me. If she's leaving, you follow." To Vladimir he says, "Can you get a car?"

Vladimir looks longingly at the empty bottle in front of him. "Can buy one."

"Next option."

"Rent, can rent one."

"Good. Use the money I've already given you. Once you've got it, I'll replace it and give you more." He leans back in his chair and closes his eyes again, and he's rewarded by the room tilting and whirling slowly to the right. He reopens his eyes, looking for something stationary that will help him stop the room's spin, and sees the concern in Ming Li's face. "I'm okay," he says.

"You and Frank," she says. "If someone chopped off your leg, you'd say, 'No problem, I've got another one.' What are we going to do about that woman with Arthit?"

"Nothing," Poke says. "Not now."

"Then when?"

"A long time from now. The next ice age. Maybe tonight, maybe tomorrow. Let's throw some more stuff at the wall and see what sticks. *Then* we'll worry about her."

"Mr. Elson's office."

"Is he there?" Rafferty says. He's standing in the doorway of a closed shoe store, not far from his apartment. All he wants in the world is walk over there, take a shower, take a nap, and start painting the walls.

"I'm sorry, he's in a meeting." From the vowels, she's come straight from Georgia, the American one, with the peaches.

"Please tell him Frank Rafferty called, from the TV station."

"Does he have your number?"

"No. I've got a stack of calls to make. I'll call back later."

"He has a lunch at noon. You might try him a little after one. He's always back by one."

"Thanks," Rafferty says. "That's very helpful."

He hangs up and leans against the door of the closed shop, feeling the tightness across the tops of his shoulders. By now Janos is manufacturing some plausible reason for hanging around in the lobby of the Chiang Palace, although with the rain, no excuse is really necessary. He'll be wearing a nice, unremarkable suit, just another interchangeable *farang* businessman, dazzled by the City of Angels. No one will look at him twice. Vladimir will be scouting for a car.

Or, he thinks, talking to Murphy.

Does Vladimir have the nerve? There's no question that he's afraid of Murphy. If Rafferty's the one who ends up dead and Vladimir is on the wrong side, Vladimir is going to spend the next four or five years looking over his shoulder for Murphy. If he were in Vladimir's shoes, Rafferty would give it some thought.

Eleven-fourteen A.M.

How is he even going to stay awake? He feels like he hasn't slept in days. He closes his eyes against the gray day, and what he sees is his living room, with all of them in their usual places: Rose and Miaow on the sofa, himself on the white leather hassock, facing them over the glass table. Nothing special, just three people in a room, a moment with nothing to make it memorable, maybe even a little boring, maybe Miaow would rather be with Andrew, maybe Rose is fretting about business falling off at the domestics agency, maybe he's thinking about money, worrying about the bills for Miaow's school, about the bank balance. Maybe they're all preoccupied, in their own separate worlds, maybe even wishing, for the moment, anyway, that they were somewhere else.

And he would give everything he's ever owned and might ever own in the future to be in that room right this moment. Bored, irritated, apprehensive, hungover, angry—it wouldn't matter. It would be the three of them. It would be his world, back again.

"Wake up," Ming Li says.

He opens his eyes, and she's standing there under a new black umbrella. She hands him another, still rolled up, purchased two doors away.

"You know what?" he asks.

"I know how," Ming Li says. "I know whether. But I don't know what. Sorry, Frank used to say—"

"Here's what." He pushes himself away from the window and opens his umbrella. He takes her by the arm and turns her, and they step out onto the sidewalk. "Murphy can't do this to me. The son of a bitch isn't going to know what hit him."

AT YET ANOTHER Coffee World, he types everything he knows about Murphy, except for the names of Thuy and Jiang, on the keyboard of Ming Li's little computer, and she pays a few baht to get the boy behind the counter to print out two copies for her. Following Rafferty's instructions, she picks them up with a napkin, avoiding both the paper's surface and the boy's curious gaze, and takes them back to the table. Using the napkin, she folds one of the copies and opens a boxful of envelopes that she bought when she bought the umbrellas. She uses the napkin to take the envelope out, too, and when she's gotten the printed page into it, without touching either, she dips one of the napkins into a glass of water and slides it over the mucilage on the flap. With the napkin she pushes it across the table, untouched, to Rafferty, who uses another napkin to pick it up and yet another to wrap it. Then he slips it into the pocket of his jacket.

She says, "Now what?"

"Now we take that one with us," he says, indicating the second copy, "in case it becomes useful."

"How might it become useful?"

"I have no idea," he says, standing up for what feels like the ten-thousandth time that day, "but humor me."

"Who was that?" Ming Li asks as he shuts off the phone. They're side by side, umbrellas overlapping, as the rain pounds down.

"Floyd Preece, a reporter at the *Bangkok Sun*. I gave him the best story of his life three years ago, about beggars and gangsters and a baby-selling ring, and it made his career. I just gave him another one."

"You kind of misled him. All those witnesses you were throwing around."

"I'll get Thuy and Jiang to talk to him. If he calls me back and says his editor is interested, I'll leave a message for the two of them to call me, and we'll work it out. He'll do anything they want, including not mentioning their real names or their locations, to get them to tell the story. This is front-page stuff." He frames the words in the air with his free hand. "'PROMINENT AMERICAN BUSINESSMAN TIED TO VIETNAM MASSACRE.' And under that, in upper- and lowercase, 'U.S. War on Terror Connection Suspected.'"

"That'll make the American embassy happy."

"Fuck them," Rafferty says. "If a government can't carry out its policies in the light of day, it should make new policies."

Ming Li stops walking. "Do you know how many people would be put out of business if that happened?"

"Well, at the risk of being repetitive, fuck them, too. My wife and child and I are threatened by all this nonsense because we're too small to matter." He takes her arm and tows her along. "It's like some clodhopper with thick boots stomping on a bee. 'Oh, you mean lots of little things that don't sting got killed, too? Well, gee, too bad. They're collateral damage. How do they expect me to tell the difference from way up here?' This is not what America was supposed to be."

"I don't talk politics," Ming Li says. "It's a principle."

"Politics is supposed to be a delivery system for food, security, and freedom."

"Oh, my God," Ming Li says. "No wonder you're so disillusioned."

"What time is it?"

"Look at your watch. Okay, okay, sorry. Male prerogative and all, ask the little woman. It's about seven to one."

"Perfect. Keep your eyes open for a very skinny American in a dark suit. Short hair, glasses, walks like his spine won't bend."

"We're on a sidewalk in Bangkok, which has fourteen million people in it, and you think we're going to run into a single, specific person."

"I'm in the zone."

"Well, warn me next time, and I won't ask stupid questions."

"It's the end of lunch hour. For this guy lunch hour is sixty minutes, minus ten for walking, five in each direction. He absolutely will be back at his desk one hour after he left it. And when he first came to Bangkok, I searched his suitcase and he had a stack of receipts from the restaurants on our right."

"Then this is the Secret Service guy, right? Poke, I *know* him. He's the one Frank bargained with, the one who got him out of here."

"Sorry." Rafferty lifts his shoulders and lets them drop, then turns his head from side to side. "I'm forgetting things. This isn't a good time to be—"

She puts her fingertips on his arm. "You're not forgetting anything that matters, so relax. You're just focusing. It's like taking a test in school. You don't need to remember your math if the question is about history."

He looks down at her and is surprised all over again at how young she looks. "I hope Frank appreciates you."

"He does. Of course, he thinks he created me." She gives him a sharp elbow. "There's your boy."

Ten feet ahead of them, Elson has come out of the door to an Italian restaurant and is fighting with his umbrella, which seems to have a broken rib.

"You stay back," Rafferty says. "I don't want him to know you're here." He picks up the pace. "Here, fellow American," he says, coming alongside Elson and offering half of his umbrella. "No point in getting wet. That awful suit might shrink."

"Poke," Elson says, his lips even thinner than usual. His eyes scan the street. "I can't talk to you. I can't be seen talking to you. You know that."

"Not Poke," Poke says. "*Frank.* Frank Rafferty. You know, news organizations tape their incoming calls. And these days even someone like me can order up a voiceprint, if he's got the money."

"Lower that umbrella," Elson says, moving away. Rafferty brings his down in front of him, and Elson continues to fight with his own until they've got their backs to a building and he succeeds in opening it. He holds it beside Poke's, effectively masking both of them from view.

"I had no idea you'd be involved in this," Elson says. He's almost whispering. "You were the furthest thing from my mind, or I'd never have used that name. I didn't like the way things were shaping up, and I thought having a news crew or two on hand would keep them from going too bad. When the woman at the station asked my name, I blanked."

"'The way things were shaping up,'" Rafferty repeats.

"*You* know." Elson lowers his umbrella a couple of inches, does a quick survey, then brings it back up. "With Murphy. I don't like

Murphy. I don't trust him. I had a *feeling* he was out to kill that man."

"Sellers."

"Yes. He told us Sellers was operating in the south with the insurgents, that he'd been engaged with militants in three countries—here, the Philippines, Indonesia. All countries that Sellers had traveled to, according to the records. But I didn't like the way things smelled. I wanted to talk to the guy, but Murphy said he didn't have a location. Just said he—I mean, Sellers—was guaranteed to come to the demonstration because he was organizing it, so Murphy got Shen to put his guys out there, and they charged the demonstrators, or so they said—this is how it got back to me anyway—and fired tear gas at them, and in the melee Sellers got shot."

"With me underneath him."

Elson shakes his head. "Who knew you'd be there? I mean, who *could* have known?"

"But you knew, after it happened, that they'd go nuts if they found out the name of the person who called the station and asked for the crew and it turned out to be my father. Makes it a little harder for Shen to believe I was there by accident."

"I don't think they did," Elson says. "It never got back to me, and it would have. Murphy wanted everything about you, but the relationship between you and your father is down a few levels. He wouldn't have turned it up unless he already knew what he was looking for."

It's begun to rain again, and the two of them are getting wet, since Elson is using the umbrellas as a wall to hide behind. "Why is it down a few levels?"

"He's living right there in Virginia," Elson says, "in a nice, expensive house, on Uncle Sam's tab. And he was a high-ranking criminal in a Chinese triad. We're not going to put him on a billboard."

"Plausible deniability."

Elson shrugs. "If you like."

"I don't like anything. There's a coffee place right down here. Got a second floor, where no one on the sidewalk will be able to see us. Come on."

"I have to get back."

"Dick. If I do what I'm about to do without telling you about it, without giving you a chance to get in position, you'll regret it for the rest of your career."

"I'd love a cup of coffee," Elson says.

"THE VIETNAMESE? THE newspapers?" Elson has his forehead in his right hand.

"The Phoenix Program returns to Southeast Asia. And the explosion down south, don't forget the explosion. That'll look good to the *New York Times*."

"We don't know anything about the murder in the States. We don't know anything about an explosion."

"Who's 'we'?"

"Good point. I'm not in the chain of command. He just wanted me at your . . . um, interview so I could tell him if you were lying."

"Who *is* in the chain of command?"

"That's the question. The ambassador, undoubtedly. They're not going to run anything in the country without him knowing about it. The CIA guys at the embassy. But it might not be the ones you'd expect. They keep all this kind of nebulous."

"Sure. This is shit nobody wants on his shoes."

"It's a different world, Poke."

"And we helped to make it that way."

Ming Li comes up the stairs with a cup in her hand and sits down at a table behind Elson. She doesn't glance at them.

Pulling at his sodden suit coat, Elson says, "Jesus, I'm sick of being wet."

"Yeah?" Rafferty says. "How's your rice crop doing? Your house been swept away yet?"

"Fine, fine." Elson lifts his hands, showing Rafferty his palms. "Guilty of thinking of myself."

"That's sort of what we do," Rafferty says. "We Americans. A tsunami hits Japan and we start worrying about radioactive flounder off Santa Monica."

"What do you want me to do? Agitate for a change in global policy?"

"Let's start with this," Rafferty says. He puts on the table the second copy of what he wrote in Coffee World. "Read it. And while you're reading, tell me why you guys never put up a decent picture of me."

The look he gives Rafferty is almost guilty. "We didn't request one," he says. "I didn't pass the request along, and Murphy probably didn't want to do it himself, didn't want the embassy to realize that it was he, not Shen, who was looking for an American. And there are virtually no good pictures of you on the Internet. Just your author picture, over and over."

"So I have you to thank. Well, what you're about to read isn't going to seem very grateful."

Elson squeezes his eyes closed and rubs at the bridge of his nose. Then he lets out a deep, melancholy breath and pulls the page to him. Rafferty drinks his coffee, and his eyes briefly meet Ming Li's. It's comforting, he decides, to have her there.

Shaking his head in disbelief, Elson runs the tip of his index finger down the edge of the page. Halfway down, he says, "*Beat* her to death?" but it's not a real question, just another way of exhaling. When he's finished, he folds the paper with great precision and stares at it.

"All true?" he finally says.

"To the best of my knowledge." Poke thinks for a second. "Yeah. All true."

"And you've given this—"

"To the Viets and a newspaper here in Bangkok."

Elson says, "I don't know what I can do with any of this. If I go to anybody who *is* in the chain of command, the first question is going to be, who gave me the intel? And then they're going to want to nail you to the floor until they've verified everything, which could take months, and they might even give Murphy a crack at you to see who comes out on top."

"Here's what I want: I want you to say you received this anonymously today." He puts two fingers into the bottom of his T-shirt and uses them to pull the napkin-wrapped envelope from his jacket pocket. "It's the same thing you just read, everything from the Vietnam massacre to the murder in Wyoming and Murphy's role here, including the names of Shen and Sellers." He tugs the napkin, and the envelope falls to the table. Elson pushes his chair back as though he's afraid his DNA might jump from him to it. "You're going to have to handle it, Dick. You can't give it to them without touching it."

"How did I get it?"

"Did you hang up your raincoat in the restaurant?"

"Sure. It was dripping."

"Well, somebody put it in your pocket while you were eating. You found it when you got back to the office, and you knew they'd want to evaluate it."

"That's ridiculous."

"So figure out something better."

Elson shakes his head. "But . . . I mean, what's your objective? Do you actually care whether we—they, whoever they are—are embarrassed, or whatever, by being linked with him?"

"If you really want to know, I don't give a shit. If people do business with rats, they should expect to get the plague. On the other hand, if something should happen to Murphy, I just think this is information that you—or they, whoever they are—should have, before they make a big stink about it and call attention to the connection, to the fact that this guy was essentially their boy, on their payroll, doing their bidding. Before people figure out how dirty the bidding was."

Elson starts to pick up the envelope and then pulls his hand back. "There's no telling how they'll react if something happens to him."

"I understand that. But it seems to me, as a good citizen, that they should know about the massacre in Vietnam and the murder in Cheyenne and the murder here in Bangkok and the possibility of a major newspaper story and the interest of the Vietnamese before they go out and do something that will have the whole world looking at them."

Elson picks up the envelope. "I'll think about it. But Jesus, Poke. You're supposed to be a travel writer, as far as I know. How does someone like you get this devious?"

"I'm just writing," Poke says. "I got stuck in somebody else's story. All I'm trying to do is write my way out."

27

The River Spirit

HE JERKS AWAKE as the car begins to move, ripped from a dream in which Miaow was back on the sidewalk, her clothes and face filthy. She was running from someone, a shadowy shape looming behind her. His mouth tastes foul, and his heart is hammering, pumping pure panic through his veins.

"What?" he says. A rattle of rain hits the windshield.

"We going," Vladimir says, turning on the wipers.

"Who? Oh, you mean—"

"Lady. Janos just give me one ring. Means she going."

"Time is it?"

"You have watch."

"Right, right. Ahh, twenty to six." Through the windows the city is gliding into the terminal stages of dusk, hurried by the heavy cloud cover.

"The hotel's coming up," Rafferty says.

"I know, I know. Don't tell me things I know, yes?"

"But you're going to pass it."

"I will be in front of them. Janos will be behind. If they looking, they will see Janos. Nobody looks at car in front when they think they being followed."

"So," Rafferty says, rubbing his face with his palms and wishing he had some coffee. "They see Janos, and—"

"And then I tell him go away. Then I let them pass me, but no problem because I was in front before. I do this many, many time, okay? When you were boy, I was doing this."

"Fine."

Vladimir moves his lips before speaking, as though rehearsing the line. "Where is Baby Spy?"

"She's running some errands." He's not about to tell Vladimir that she's in Chinatown, visiting a little old Chinese lady named Mrs. Ma, who sells illegal handguns.

"She is really your sister?"

"Half sister."

"Ahhh," Vladimir says. Then he peers through the window and says, "This your lady, I think."

They're creeping past the hotel as the traffic builds up to the nightly post–6:00 P.M. snarl, and Rafferty sees an attractive, tall, blond woman in a gray business suit, late thirties or early forties, coming through the revolving door and getting a big-tipper's salute from the doorman. He springs to the side of an idling white sedan and pulls the door open for her. The hotel's driveway is a looping curve up and down a gentle hill with the entrance at the top, and coming on foot down the left side of the curve, signaling a taxi, is Janos.

"Tell him to forget it," Rafferty says.

"Why? We all in position. Why?"

"Look at her. She's as Caucasian as Finland. I was hoping maybe she was a daughter, some sort of relative, but she hasn't got any Asian blood."

"So?"

"Well, if it looked like she might be for real—even if it only looked a little bit like that—it would have changed things. It might have meant she doesn't belong to Murphy. But Jesus, look at her. Why is Janos talking to himself?"

"Talking to me," Vladimir says, tapping the ear farthest from Rafferty.

"Take that thing out," Rafferty says. "Put the phone on speaker."

"I think we quitting. You say we—"

"Well, we're here. Let me hear him."

Mumbling to himself, Vladimir puts the phone beside him on the seat and pushes a button.

" . . . car has been waiting almost half an hour," Janos is saying. "Rented by the concierge in her name, Eckersley."

Rafferty mutters,

"I wish I had someone to search her room."

"Baby Spy."

"She's busy." He slumps back in the seat. "All right. Let's do it." He pulls an envelope out of his pocket and puts it on the seat, beside the phone. "That's another two thousand."

Vladimir grunts acknowledgment and cuts the wheel toward the curb, just squeezing past the car in front of him as the sedan with the woman calling herself Helen Eckersley comes down the curve of the hotel driveway. In the passenger's mirror, Rafferty sees Janos's cab slow to let her in. When he looks back at the seat, the envelope is gone.

"Good," Vladimir says. "If they are professional, now ewerybody looking at him."

On the phone Janos says, "This is her first time out of the room since I got to the hotel this morning." Then he says, probably to his driver, "No, never mind. I'm on the phone."

"She waiting in room for your call," Vladimir says.

"Maybe." Rafferty yawns hugely, watches the windshield in front of him steam up, and wonders why he's here.

"You know today, Thai gowernment—Bangkok Metropolitan Authority—tell ewerybody in office to come to City Pillar Shrine for ceremony to Ka Kang. You know Ka Kang?"

"No."

"Goddess of riwer, spirit of Chao Phraya. Ceremony to ask her to lower lewel of water before city floods."

"Makes sense."

Vladimir glances over at him and says, "You been here too long."

"See, that's the problem with America," Rafferty says. "We don't have enough gods. Our plane is late, we blame the president because of all the security nonsense. The price of bread goes up, we blame the president for the economy. The president, whoever it is, is just some schmuck in the White House who has no idea what to do about the price of bread, no idea what to do about the planes not taking off on time. But Americans don't have a goddess of flight schedules or a patron saint of dietary staples, so we vote out the president and his gang of robbers and vote in some other idiot and a bigger gang of robbers, and two years later we're all demanding to know why everything hasn't been fixed."

Janos says, over the phone, "But the river spirit can't lower the Chao Phraya."

"Neither could the president. Point is, the Thais know who to blame. The river spirit. If it rains too much, they don't take it out on the ballot box."

Janos says, "So you don't think the government is responsible for anything?"

"Oh, it's responsible," Rafferty says. He draws Miaow's favorite doodle, a round-headed cat with six whiskers, on the steamed window. "It's responsible for the sloppiness and imprecision of the War on Terror, for example. It's responsible for taking people's tax dollars and spending the country into debt on useless wars and pointless pork projects to buy votes. It's responsible for bailing out the banks instead of standing up for the people the banks cheated. It's responsible for plenty."

"American people," Vladimir says, pronouncing it "pipple" and dividing his attention between the rearview mirror and the car in front of him. "American pipple all baby. Ewery pipple except American know what is gowernment. Gowernment is machine rich people inwent to take more. Same when we have king, same when we have pope, same when we have Communist. Is no graw-ity, no Isaac Newton, in gowernment. Money go up, up to rich people. Power go up, up to people with power. Always same."

"Her driver is looking back at me," Janos says.

"Good."

There's a whiplash of lighting, and the phone sputters, and Janos can be heard saying, "Left-hand turn signal."

"Good. You follow, but slow. Then turn and come around block so you behind us."

"Why are we bothering?" Rafferty asks.

Vladimir says, "Is information. Maybe is lie, yes? But you see lie, and maybe sometime you see through it, like window, to truth." He makes the left and slows to pull over until the sedan is past them. Three cars later he eases back into the traffic.

Rafferty lengthens the whiskers on Miaow's cat face and says, "I want to go home."

"Open window," Vladimir says. "You make front all cloudy."

"Maybe you can see through it to the truth," Rafferty says, but he opens his window.

"You think this is funny," Vladimir says, "but is life. We newer see ewerything. Life is looking through cloud, try to see who is your friend, who is your lover, who is wanting to kill you. What is true, what is not. God makes insect look like stick, make fly look like bee. Poison mushroom look like good one. Child killer look like schoolteacher. People show teeth when they smile, show teeth when they bite. Baby Spy, Baby Spy wery lucky. She learn early to look for real thing. You, you cannot tell. Snake tell you he is horse, you probably look for saddle."

"Yeah," Rafferty says, "it's swell to doubt everything. It's a great way to live, holding everything up to the light all the time, checking every label, looking for the spider in your pocket."

Vladimir makes a clucking noise. "You are in bad mood."

"Gee, you think?" He sits up, his exhaustion gone. "Hold it, I know where she's going."

"Where?"

"They're going to turn up here. You keep going, two more turns, then you turn, same direction as them. Tell Janos to wait at the corner. He can follow them again when they come back down."

"Maybe you wrong," Vladimir says, but at that moment the sedan's turn indicator begins to blink. He says, "Huh."

"Nyaaa-nyaaa," Rafferty says. "Skip this turn and the next, then make the one after. You'll go uphill and then take a right, and we'll be looking down at them."

Vladimir barks orders at Janos, and then he and Rafferty ride in silence until the second turn comes up, and Rafferty says, "One more," and Vladimir snaps, "Yah, yah, yah." He takes the turn and points the car up a gentle hill.

"At top?" he says.

"Yes. Kill your lights just before you turn right and then pull to the left curb."

"Street is one-way?"

"It is."

"This part Bangkok, I don't know."

"You haven't missed much. Turn coming up."

When Vladimir switches the lights off, Rafferty realizes that it's gotten darker than he thought. "Go down half a block before you pull over," he says.

"Cannot get close with no lights." Vladimir is peering through the windshield. "They see car with no lights, they know we looking."

"It's dark," Rafferty says. "It's raining. Tell you what." He picks up the phone and says, "Janos. Go to the next turn and then come up here and go right. I'm pretty sure you'll drive past them, and when you do, hit your brakes for a second, slow down, and then drive away."

"Wery good," Vladimir says grudgingly.

"I'm learning," Rafferty says. "Just hanging around with you, I'm learning."

Vladimir says, "Peh," but he looks pleased.

They make the turn, and a glance along the street tells Rafferty he was right; between the rain and the darkness, they can't see more than a block. Vladimir pulls to the curb and puts the car in its lowest gear to slow it. Half a block down, the rain eases, and Rafferty says, "Stop," and Vladimir uses the hand brake so the brake lights won't come on.

The white sedan is idling at the curb on the opposite side of the street, in front of the paint store. The blond woman gets out and opens an umbrella, then takes a few slow steps until she's dead center in the pale stain that Rafferty's spill of paint left on the sidewalk. She stands still for a count of eight or ten and then closes her umbrella and hangs it over her left wrist. She bows her head in the rain and brings her hands up, palm to palm, to the center of her chest. She remains motionless, head down as her suit gets wet and heavy, and her hair drips with rain, until Janos's car makes the turn and rolls past. He taps the brakes, but even the sudden gleam of red light doesn't crack her concentration. Rafferty is asking himself whether he's wrong as Janos's car goes on down the hill, but then, when Vladimir says, "Look at car,"

Rafferty does, and he sees the driver put his head out the window, watching Janos's taxi.

Vladimir says, "Driwer. Driwer is professional."

"BECAUSE YOU CAN'T," Rafferty says. "Because I don't want Anna to see you."

He and Ming Li are in her room in their new hotel. It's functional but not fancy, not even a little bit cleaner than it needs to be, and the carpet and bedclothes smell of old cigarettes. On the center of the bed, making little dents in the mattress, are two small automatic pistols, scratched and nicked, and a couple boxes of ammunition.

"I understand that," Ming Li says, although she's clearly not happy about it. She's claimed the room's armchair, which is too big for her; her feet barely graze the carpet. It makes her look like a child. "But I want to be close, just in case. I know you're not going to call to say you're coming, but I mean, what if she goes in the other room and uses a phone, 'Come get him'?"

"An even better reason for you not to be there. If anything happened to you, Frank would kill me." He's leaning against a wall, letting his clothes drip, and he puts one foot up against it. One more scuff won't ruin the decor.

Ming Li says, "You think he would?" She gives it a moment's thought, lips pursed. "Anyway, you'd already be dead."

"Well, good, then at least I won't have to worry about Frank."

"He called me," Ming Li says casually. "While I was buying the guns."

Rafferty says, "What did he want to know?"

She runs her fingers over the napped fabric on the arm of the chair, leaving five parallel lines, like sheet music. "Listen to you. Not, 'What did he say?' Not, 'How was he?' No, it's 'What did he want to know?' He wanted to know how you were. How I was. He wanted to know if we needed help, if there was anyone here he should call."

"And you said."

"I said everything was fine, that there were no problems, and that I'd be coming home in a few days."

Something in her tone catches Rafferty's ear. "And?"

"And he . . . um, he asked me again how you'd feel about him moving back here."

"To Bangkok."

There's a spark in her dark eyes. "If that's what 'here' means."

"I thought you guys had it cushy back in the States. To hear Elson tell it, you're living like royalty. What would he do for money if he came—if you all came—here?"

"Is that really the issue?" Ming Li says. "What he'll do for money? He's your father, not your child. He's not going to sponge off you."

"I suppose—"

"But that's not the point, is it? It's that you're doing the big tough-guy cowboy act: This town's not big enough for both of you."

"I'm not sure it is."

"*I'd* be here," Ming Li says.

"And that would be great," he says.

A silence claims the room. She's curled up in her chair, looking at him. Her head is pulled back on her neck as though she half expects him to take a swing at her.

"You know," he says, "if it was okay with Frank, and if it wouldn't bring him across the ocean, I could probably work out a way for you to stay here."

Her eyes widen, and she doesn't make a sound, but when she blinks, a tear slips down her cheek. Then she's up, and her arms are around him. "You don't know," she says, "you *can't* know, how much that means to me."

"It's just an—"

"I don't belong anywhere—not America, not even China, not anymore. I'm a nuisance to my mother, and Frank . . . well, Frank doesn't need me. He'd go anywhere in the world that appealed to him and never even ask if I wanted to go. He'd forget to pack me."

Poke says, "Vladimir is crazy about you."

She laughs and backs off, wiping her nose. "I know. But he's not exactly what I have in mind."

"And I'm crazy about you, too."

"Thank you," she says. She squares her shoulders and rubs her face with her forearm. "I won't hold you to it, but thank you. All right, I won't go with you to Arthit's. I'll be around the corner in the car, with the motor running, just in case."

"Can you drive?"

"Better than you, in a pinch. Nobody drives like a teenager."

He nods. A moment ticks by. He says, "And you *can* hold me to it."

"Well," she says, and takes a shaky breath. Then she abandons the sentence and goes to the bed. "You wanted small," she says, all business. "Mrs. Ma had a lot of Chinese guns, but Frank always called them 'three-finger specials' because they blow up all the time, so these are both Colts. They're kind of beat up, and this one fires hot, Mrs. Ma said, but they work." She picks up the smaller and racks it, the slide smooth and precise-sounding. "Forty-five. Kicks like a horse, according to Mrs. Ma, so I figure this one is yours." She taps the barrel on a box. "Ammo here. And the other one is mine." She drops the gun back on the bed and licks her lips, looking down at them. "She said hello, by the way. Mrs. Ma did."

"I couldn't have gotten through this without you," he says.

"I know that. But don't make me cry anymore. It messes up my self-image."

"Fine." He pushes off from the wall. "I'm going to put on a dry shirt, and then we'll go."

"I'll drive."

"No," he says. "Let's save that weapon until we need it. Which we probably will."

28

Tangled Web

"I WENT AROUND the block half a dozen times," Rafferty says. There are candles burning on the living-room table, and Arthit clearly hadn't been expecting anyone. He feels very much like the uninvited guest, so he's making small talk to soften his entrance. "Nobody seemed to be watching the house."

"It's kind of surprising," Arthit says. He blows out the candles and glances at Anna, who immediately drops her eyes in a way that probably looks demure to Arthit but to Rafferty looks like a plain old guilty conscience. "I keep checking," Arthit says, turning on the lights. "It's been that way for days, which is odd. There's nothing my superiors would rather do than hang me out the window in the rain."

Anna holds up her pad, aiming it at Poke. It says, *You've been careful?* When she glances up at Poke, she catches him staring and gives him a tentative smile. He smiles back, his face as stiff as cardboard.

"Careful as I can be," he says.

Arthit hasn't sat yet. He says, "You want a drink?"

"Beer would be nice."

"Fine." He turns toward the dining room, but Anna is up and on her way, motioning Arthit back to the couch.

"I feel guilty," Arthit says as he sits down.

"About what?"

"All this." He raises his chin in the direction Anna took. "I'm here, feeling like I'm living in a greeting card, while you're out there with half the world looking for you."

"I'm doing okay," Rafferty says. "And you have a life to live."

"I hope so. I mean, I know so. And I know that this will be over soon, and we'll all be back to normal. But I wish Rose had been around to get used to . . . this . . ." he says, with a vague circular gesture that takes in the two of them and Anna, in the other room. "I wish she could have gone through it in stages, like I did, instead of being presented with it in full bloom, so to speak, when she gets back." His tone is light, but his eyes hold Poke's. "She loved Noi so much." He stops and swallows. "Will she be okay with it?"

"I can't say," Poke tells him. "We'll have to let time sort it out." He feels the coldness of the answer. "Everything is . . . good with the two of you?"

Arthit says, "I don't know what I've done to deserve it." He turns his head a few inches toward the dining room and continues. "She's not Noi, I know that, but no one is. No one ever could be. But she's not like anyone I've ever known, and—" He looks down at his knees and crosses his blunt, dark hands in his lap. The lamp makes his gold wedding band gleam. He shrugs. "And I think she loves me."

There's no way around it. "I'm sure she does." His throat feels so tight he's surprised Arthit can't hear it.

"I didn't mean to talk about this," Arthit says, "You've got all these problems, and I'm rattling along about being in love. Please forgive me. You've got something important to talk about."

"It's all important," Rafferty says, automatically. While Anna's still out of the room, he asks, "Did Kosit follow Eddie Bland from the airport?"

"Straight to a big house that turns out to be Murphy's. Still there. And he's booked back to Kuala Lumpur at midnight, so he'll probably stay put till then."

"I guess Kosit can go home, then," Rafferty says, getting up as Anna comes into the room, a middle-height, sturdily built woman who moves like a very light one. The businesslike chop of her hair bares her face, her smooth brow, her wide-set, guileless eyes. She hands him the beer in a bottle and smiles, then closes her eyes and screws up her face with effort.

Arthit watches with an expression halfway between apprehension and fierce pride.

Anna, her eyes still closed, says, slowly and tonelessly, "No . . . glass." Her eyes fly wide open and go to Arthit's, and he's beaming from ear to ear. She drops her head to hide her own smile and turns deep red, and Rafferty wishes lightning would strike him where he stands.

Anna gives him a shy, quick glance and hands Arthit a glass with a good four fingers' worth of whiskey in it. Then she mimes wiping sweat off her forehead and collapses beside him on the couch, letting her head drop onto his shoulder.

"We've been working on that," Arthit says. He rests his free hand on her thigh. "She thinks she sounds ugly when she talks. But she doesn't." He catches himself and shakes his head. "Please. Let's talk about your problems."

"Well, first," Rafferty says, sitting, "I'm very happy for both of you."

Anna says, out loud, "Thank you." She drags out the *a* on "thank" a bit experimentally and gives both words the same pitch and the same stress, but her voice is low and pleasant, coming from someplace in the center of her chest. Arthit's face, as he watches her, is as transparent as water.

"So," Rafferty says, mostly to break the moment, because it's too painful to look at, "I want to bounce something off you."

"Anything," Arthit says. "And if I can help, tell me."

"No, I don't want to involve you. But you can give me an opinion." He tries not to glace at Anna and fails. She smiles encouragingly.

"Helen Eckersley," he says. "The woman in Cheyenne." For a wild, panicked moment, remembers that when he talked to Anna last, he said, "Helena," but she hasn't noticed the change; perhaps it's the difficulty in lip-reading either word. And Arthit doesn't know that Eckersley is dead, that she was Vietnamese, a survivor of the massacre in the Delta, but he knows he hasn't. They've barely spoken, beyond immediate needs, for days. It's Ming Li he's been talking with. "I called her in the States, starting a few days back. Left three or four messages on her machine. I never talked to her. But she called me a couple of days ago. She's here. She wants to meet me."

Arthit says, "Mmm-hmm," but there's nothing in his face. Anna's eyes, on the other hand, are sharp with interest.

"So I'm thinking about doing it."

Arthit looks over Poke's shoulder, in the general direction of the front door, and Poke knows he's thinking. "For what purpose?"

"She was the last person on Sellers's mind. She was *important* to him. Part of my problem is that I don't know who he actually was or why he was killed." He's never lied to Arthit before, and every sentence makes him feel more counterfeit. "She might be able to tell me—I don't know—who he was, beyond his name, what he was doing here. What his relationship was with Murphy."

"What if she's a plant of some kind? What if Murphy—"

"They didn't know her name, remember? That's why they were after me in the first place."

"Suppose they figured it out somehow," Arthit says. "Suppose it's not even really the same person. Suppose it's a trap and she's just some floater, just some burnout he's picked up and paid a few hundred bucks to call you and try to set up a meeting."

Anna is writing, and when she lifts the pad, the words startle him. It says, *No. Too dangerous.*

"I followed her today," Rafferty says, and Anna sits just a tiny bit straighter. "She went to the place where Sellers was shot. Stood in the rain in the middle of the spilled paint, praying."

Arthit says, "Doesn't mean anything. Maybe it was a show. Maybe they knew you'd be following her."

They certainly did, Poke thinks. "Maybe. But maybe she's got something I need to know to get myself out of this. It's pointless to pretend they're not going to find me sooner or later."

"I still don't think you should do it, but if you do, where?"

"The new shopping mall on Rama IV. At the peak of business, about eight-thirty tomorrow night. We—I—spent part of the day checking it out."

Arthit says, "'We'?"

"A friend."

Arthit nods, but he's obviously stored the evasion to question it later. "So there will be people around."

"Thousands of them. Not the kind of place to make a big fuss."

"Good and bad both," Arthit says. "It also means they can salt the crowd. And getting out can be a problem."

The comment catches Rafferty unprepared, since he's given no thought at all to how he'll get out. "If there's anyone there, they'll be watching her," he says. "What I'm planning to do is get there two, two and a half hours early so I can look the place over again. Then I'll go into the business center on the fourth level with a couple of books for them to copy, so I have a reason to stay there. It's got a big window, but it's away from the heaviest traffic. I'm going to ask her to meet me at the fountain on the first floor. I can see it from up there." Up to this point, he's rehearsed it mentally, but now he's off the map. "When she shows," he says, "I'll go back into the business center and call her and tell her to go out through the front. If anyone is watching, they'll see her answer the phone and trail along after her. I'll go down the interior stairs and out the other way." As he invents it, it feels almost plausible. "Then I'll call her again and tell her to walk toward the back of the lot, and I'll pick her up in my car. If there are people behind her, I'll just keep driving."

Arthit says, "You have a car?"

"Rented." He's startled again by how little he's told Arthit. "Got it this morning."

Arthit shakes his head. "You can't use your ID or your credit cards. Who rented it for you?"

"The same friend. You've never met him." He gets back to what he came to say. "So. I'll get there about six-thirty, stay mainly in the business center, wait and keep my eyes open for the opposition, and then leave through one door while they're following her through another. What do you think?"

"I think it would be better if you had someone to watch as she leaves and make sure she comes out alone, not trailing some posse."

Anna holds up her pad. She's written *Don't do it* and underlined the words twice.

"I agree," Arthit says. "I'll go. Instead."

Anna's face freezes. She looks like someone who's seen lightning and is waiting for the thunder.

Rafferty says, "You wouldn't recognize her."

"Describe her to me."

"No. No, it's not possible." He gets up, just to do something. "I can't put you in that position. Suppose you're right, suppose she really is a plant, suppose it's a trap and Shen's people are there with Murphy. How could you explain it? You'd be committing suicide. Your career would be over."

Arthit looks at his glass and swallows most of what remains, and Anna watches every move as though she's afraid she's seeing him for the last time. He lowers the drink and looks up at Rafferty. "I'm not sure what you might get that's worth the risk."

"I'm not sure of anything," Rafferty says, sitting again. He closes his eyes and rubs them with the heels of his palms. "Except that this can't drag on much longer. They're going to catch me sooner or later, and if they don't, I'm going to die of exhaustion. And I'm *lonely*. I want my wife and daughter back. I want my life to be ordinary again, the way it was before. When I barely appreciated it. I just want to get through this and put things back together and then be grateful for everything I have, everything I *had*, before all this began. Honest to God, Arthit, when I get through this, I'll never be bored again. If you ever hear me complain, you have permission to kick me. Hard."

Arthit says, "Why does it take something terrible to make us understand how blessed we are?" He leans forward, and Anna shifts away slightly. Rafferty thinks, *She's frightened*. But then he pictures Pim, blistered on speed and hanging on a pimp's arm, and the moment passes.

"If you have to do it," Arthit says, "just think it through a few more times. I'll do the same, and we'll talk tomorrow. Maybe we can find a way to improve it."

Rafferty wants to tell his friend the truth, that he'll be nowhere near the shopping mall, but he can't. And it feels like he's lost something else, something almost as precious as his wife and child, and the anger he's been carrying gives him a sharp shake. "I'll do that," he says, getting up and avoiding Anna's eyes. "Listen, one other thing. Maybe this doesn't mean anything, or maybe it does, I don't know. I think Murphy has been misrepresenting how close he is with the U.S. people here, how much they know about what he's doing. I think he's lying to Shen."

"Why? What makes you say so?"

The instant he looks at Anna, her eyes skitter away, but they snap back to him the moment he begins to speak. He talks to Arthit, but he feels her gaze like warmth on his cheek. "I had a talk with someone who's with them—the U.S., I mean—and I'm not mentioning a name, okay? You never heard a name from me."

Arthit's forehead wrinkles in a question, but he says, "Sure."

"And this guy seemed to be worried that Murphy has gone off the tracks, the way he did in Vietnam. They're not hearing much in the way of reports from him, and they're getting worried that he's . . . well, overenthusiastic in the way he does things. The bottom line is, the newspapers are taking an interest in Murphy, thanks in part to me, and if there's a bad story, I'm pretty sure Shen doesn't know that the Americans are going to deny any direct involvement. Shen will be left holding the bag. You know the drill: 'We've used Mr. Murphy as an intelligence source from time to time, but no one here authorized anything beyond that.' So who else is responsible? Shen, that's who."

"That's interesting," Arthit says. "There's a space between them. You might be able to get a lever in there, especially if Shen thinks he'll to be the scapegoat in case anything goes wrong. But you'd have to find a way to get the word to Shen."

"I'm working on that," Rafferty says. "Maybe you can think about it, too." He smiles and directs the smile at Anna as well. "So there are two things to consider until tomorrow."

"Turn your enemies against each other," Arthit says. "Very Sun-tzu."

"It'll be interesting to see who turns up at the shopping mall tomorrow," Rafferty says. "If this woman is a plant, if Murphy set her up, maybe Shen's people won't even be told about it. Might just be Murphy and a thug or two if his plans for me include stuff he thinks Shen might draw the line at." He picks up the beer again and knocks back about half of what's left. "Is it just me, or is this complicated?"

"'O, what a tangled web we weave,'" Arthit says, and Rafferty feels a sharp pang of conscience, but his friend's eyes are direct and clear; he's talking about Murphy. "But it all seems simpler if we just keep the end in mind. Getting you out from under."

"Right," Rafferty says. "Thanks for everything." To Anna, who has sprung to her feet, he says, "And thanks for the beer."

She nods, and Rafferty surprises himself by reaching for her hand and saying, "And take good care of my friend. He needs it."

She looks at Arthit, at her own hand clasped in Rafferty's, at the floor, at everything in the room, before she looks at him. When she does, he sees that her eyes are moist. She says, in her low, uninflected voice, "I will."

IT'S RAINING AGAIN when he comes out; he can almost feel the weight of the swollen river rushing by several miles to the west. He has an impulse to lift his head and scream curses at the sky. Instead he turns left and takes the sidewalk to the corner, realizing he's lost yet another umbrella. He makes the right, and there's Ming Li, waiting for him behind the wheel of the little Toyota.

He gets in, and she starts the car without asking whether it's okay if she drives. The tires hardly squeal at all as she pulls away from the curb. He doesn't say anything, just sits back with his eyes closed.

She says, "And?"

"And I'd like to kill myself. But since that wouldn't accomplish anything, let's go get something really good to eat and then sleep for twelve hours. I think we're going to need it." He pulls out the cell phone he used when he called America. "But first." He presses SEND and a moment later says, "Helen Eckersley's room, please."

29

Women Are Like Cave Paintings

BUT HE DOESN'T sleep.

They eat at a Chinese restaurant Mrs. Ma recommended to Ming Li after selling her the guns. The food lives up to her hopes, but the two of them pick at it. The sidewalks are almost empty, the rain blowing down in sheets, and every time a customer climbs the three steps to the door and drips his way in, the waitress mops mud from the floor. People talk anxiously in Cantonese, and Ming Li says they're discussing the welter of contradictory instructions issuing from the government: stay, go, get your belongings and/or yourself to higher ground, just sit tight—everything's fine. Through the streaked window, the streetlights gleam below them, reflected in the fast-flowing water that fills the street.

After a few minutes of trying to talk about something—any-thing—other than what's coming, they give up and discuss it: what they'll do, what they'll have the others do, what they hope to get from it.

The ways it can go wrong and kill them.

"You know," Ming Li says, "you can't worry about protecting me. You can't divide your attention. It's too dangerous. Believe me, I'm not going to be thinking about you when things get moving. I'll be focused on myself. You need to do the same."

There's a dark, shapeless cloud in his chest, something that feels like a million swarming insects. Everything he's planned, every-thing he's trying to do, seems transparent, clumsy, amateurish, unconvincing. It wouldn't fool a child. These people, Murphy and

Shen, they're not idiots. Nothing is going to work. He says, without meaning to, "They're not idiots."

"They want something," Ming Li says, following his thought. "Dangle the right purse in front of an American high-school girl and watch her run into traffic to get it." She makes a motherly gesture with her chopsticks. "Eat the duck before it gets cold. Colder."

"If I did, I think I'd heave it all over the table."

"Take some with you." She raises the hand with the chopsticks in the air, and the waitress is there instantly. "Wrap this up, please."

"All?" the waitress asks.

"You'll wind up eating it," he says to Ming Li.

"I know." She says to the waitress, "And could you throw in an extra order of rice?"

They sit silently again, both of them looking out the window. "It's kind of unfair," Ming Li says. "This weather, I mean, the flooding, all the rest of it. There are cities that could use wiping out, but this isn't one of them."

"Makes perfect sense to me," Rafferty says. "We're caught in a meaninglessness node. The weather is just as meaningless as the situation we're in. If the city drowns, if we get hurt or killed, it'll all be collateral damage. Nobody, anywhere, is directly responsible for this, but that didn't stop them from setting the forces in motion."

"Older brother," Ming Li says, "with all due respect, please shut up. You don't have to bring down the world order to stay alive. I mean, we don't. It's one guy, or maybe two, and we're doing something about it. Doesn't it make you feel better to be doing something about it?"

"It keeps me from being frightened," Rafferty says, "but fear isn't the only bad feeling there is, is it? There's anger, loneliness, self-pity, anxiety for others, the confusion of being overwhelmed, the sense of outraged justice because none of this is right, none of it even makes sense. I've got all of those."

Ming Li is wiping her chopsticks on her napkin. "That's good," she says. "You're probably going to need them."

•   •   •

IT'S THE SECOND night in their hotel, since Rafferty couldn't face the thought of moving again. There's something almost comforting in the act of closing the door behind him and seeing a room he knows, with the bed in the same place and the bathroom right where he left it, and his awful fake-leather bag on the chair, and his change of clothes, wet when he put them on hangers in the bathroom the previous evening, waiting for him all dry and orderly, the wrinkles hung out of them.

He considers booting up the computer he bought. He's barely opened it since Ming Li showed up with hers, but he can't think of anything he wants to look at except the weather forecast, and a glance out the window gives him that: wet and then wetter, with the chance of a biblical deluge. He shucks his wet shoes, pulls out the laptop anyway, and powers it on for about a second and a half, after which it powers itself off. Dead. The power brick is at the bottom of the sodden fake-leather bag, so he pulls it out and plugs it in to charge.

There, he thinks, he's done something. Lesson for tomorrow: no assumptions. Call everyone first thing in the morning and go over all of it. Go over it twice.

Of *course* he's worried about Ming Li, even though she's probably already asleep in her own room. How could he not be? He's dragged her into this, even if sometimes she makes him feel like it's the other way around, since she's so clearly braver than he is. Going up to the second floor of that coffee place, for example, just to make sure Elson hadn't overpowered him and put in a call for the marines. He feels himself smile at the thought, the first real smile of the day. The smiles at Arthit's had been heavy as stone.

What in the world is he going to do about Arthit? How can he repair all that dishonesty?

Not that he's necessarily going to be in a position to repair anything after tomorrow night.

Since there's nothing for him to do, he kicks his discarded shoes against the wall so he can't trip on them in the dark and falls on his stomach on the bed. Naturally, the moment he's comfortable, he has a pressing reason to stand up again.

It takes him a moment to choose a phone that hasn't been used for anything dangerous. He launches himself at the bed again, pushes some buttons, and closes his eyes in prayer.

Rose says, "Hello, you."

Instantly he has tears in his eyes and all his muscles loosen. "That's what I wanted to hear."

"Should I ask how you are?"

"No." He sniffs. "Okay, ask."

"How are you?"

"You don't want to know. But I'm doing what I can, and that's what I can do."

"I have faith in you. Just keep your head clear."

"I'm clearing it as we speak."

"Meditate. Tonight. Before you go to bed. You know, no one in the history of the world has ever done harm while meditating."

"I promise."

"*You* know," she says. "All those little monkey voices that start chattering in your head when you have to decide something. You need to shut them up so you can hear the calm voice."

"Got it," he says. "Meditate."

"Is it going to be dangerous?"

"Maybe."

"Is there a way to avoid it?"

"Not that I can think of. Not if I want all this to end."

"How dangerous will it be?"

"No, no, I take it back. Not so dangerous. The only person I have to be afraid of will be miles away. I should have an hour or two, easy."

"Then what are you worried about?"

"Murphy's Law." He hears the words after he speaks them, and the hairs on his arms stand up.

"What does that mean? What's Murphy's Law?"

"It's an . . . it's an old joke." He looks up at the ceiling, trying to frame an explanation that won't frighten her. Frighten both of them. "From the army, I think. Murphy's Law says that anything that *can* go wrong *will*." She says nothing, and he adds, "But it's just a joke."

She draws a deep breath. "We'll go to the temple tomorrow, Miaow and I."

"Good," he says. "That would be good."

Rose says, "It will, you know."

"I'll tell you what," he says. "At the very least, it'll make me feel better." He rolls over onto his back and looks down at his feet in their wet socks. "How *is* Miaow?"

"In love, to hear her tell it."

"Well, so is Andrew. He's come by looking for her, as though this whole thing is a plot to separate them. He looks completely lost."

"I'll tell her that. It'll make her feel better."

"To know that the guy she loves is unhappy? That'll make her feel better?"

"Of course."

"I give up," Rafferty says. "Women are like cave paintings. You know what they look like, but not what they mean."

"This isn't mysterious. She's stuck up here, missing someone who's probably forgotten her, who's cutting a swath through the girls of Bangkok—"

"*Andrew?*"

"And to learn instead that he's lonely, maybe even a little heartbroken, wandering around, lost in a gray cloud—"

"He is."

"Good," she says. "He should be."

He's using one foot to peel a soggy sock off the other. "I can't tell you how much I miss you."

"Sure you can," she says. "You haven't even tried yet."

"Let me think. Okay, so here you go: A spirit appears before me—"

"Male or female?"

"Male. With a mustache and long, curving blue teeth. And he says, 'I'm going to give you two choices. You can have one or the other, but you can't choose neither and you can't choose both.' Are you with me?"

"Of course. A million stories begin this way."

"The first thing the spirit offers me is, I get to see you for an hour. The second thing is, it will rain as long as I live, and I'll live for centuries."

"And which one would you choose?"

"Well," he says, "if my socks weren't wet—"

"I'd choose the same," she says. "I'd rather be with you right now, wet socks and all, than anything else in the world. Do they smell?"

"Of course."

"Send them up to me. I need them."

He rolls onto his side and comes face-to-face with the little automatic that Ming Li bought him that afternoon. "Whatever happens," he says, "I want you to know that I love you more than the rest of the world put together."

"What about Miaow?"

"Miaow's a special exception."

"She certainly is," Rose says. "Right now she's sitting outside under a big tree, very dramatically getting wet."

"Give her a kiss from me. Tell her it's from Andrew."

"No," Rose says. "Let her get wet. I'll keep the kisses for myself."

HE RACKS THE gun and dry-fires it a few times, trying to get used to the feel of it in his hand. It's not as heavy as his Glock, but it's bulkier and more awkward. Then he pops the magazine in and handles it some more, getting used to its loaded weight. He doesn't like it much, but he figures it'll put down anything it hits.

The loaded gun and the remaining shells go on the bed table. He gets the hotel hair dryer from the bathroom and sticks it into his socks, one at a time, watching them balloon and steam until they're dry. Then he uses it on the inside of the fake-leather bag until a sort of chemistry-is-not-your-friend smell makes him stop and let it cool for a while. He uses the time to assemble his clothes for the next day: his better-looking pair of pants, his still-wet belt, and a big shirt he can wear outside the trousers to hide the gun.

He takes the hair dryer to the bag again, getting it mostly dry before it starts to go toxic, then waves the dryer around inside his shoes, getting them warm and wet instead of cold and wet. In the interest of readiness, he puts on the clothes for tomorrow, stashes the gun inside his belt, and practices getting at it until he can clear the shirt most of the time, until his hip has memorized the gun's position and his index finger has memorized the location of the trigger guard.

He takes the clothes off again and lays them on the armchair, along with the dry socks and the gun and the bullets and the fake-leather bag and the hotel's umbrella, which he removes from the closet. He makes a semifinal pass through the room to double-check that he's got everything, because they won't be coming back the following night. Recognizes that most of what he's doing is just nervousness finding an outlet and leans against the wall.

All I wanted to do, he thinks, *was paint my apartment.*

By now, or at the latest by tomorrow morning, Anna will have gotten word to Shen, who either does or doesn't already know about the arrangement at the shopping mall, depending on whether Murphy saw fit to share it. It's academic one way or the other, since Rafferty will be on the other side of Bangkok while they wait for him at the mall, but it will still be interesting to see whether the opposing team is intact.

In any case, there's nothing he can do about it now. There's really nothing he can do about anything now, except worry about Ming Li. Which, of course, is exactly what she told him not to do.

So he worries about Ming Li until a little after four, when he finally falls asleep.

30

I'm Not Actually One of Them

"THIS GUN IS a pig," Ming Li says, pointing it through the glass of the passenger window. "Did you ever use a steak knife that's got all the weight in the handle, and every time you lay it on your plate, it falls off?"

"No." He works his way into the turn lane.

"Oh, you did so."

"And this gun is like that, is it?"

"Yes."

"Compared to what?"

She glances at him quickly. "To a good gun."

"What make? What caliber?"

"A Burpmeister," she says through her teeth. "Thirty-three-and-a-third caliber."

"Boy, *that* was a gun," he says. "How many guns have you actually fired?"

At first he thinks she won't answer, but then she says, "Three. No, four. All three-finger specials. But I promise you, they balanced differently than this one."

"Ever shoot one *at* somebody?"

"Trees," she says. "A few bottles. But I'll tell you something, and you can believe it or not. There are people for whom there's a big difference between firing at a tree and firing at a person. And I'm not actually one of them."

He makes the turn. The day is drawing to a dark, wet close, and the street has three or four inches of water in it. "Unless the person is firing back at you."

"That's a different issue," she says. "That's not getting killed. Killing is different. I'm already good at not getting killed, and I don't believe I need practice at killing. A person is a target, same as a tree, only it moves faster."

"Let's hope we don't have to find out whether that's true."

"You're such a sexist," she says. "There was a time in your life when you hadn't killed anybody, right?"

"Obviously."

"And then, all of a sudden, you had to, and you . . . you what?"

"I killed her," he says, although he still doesn't like to think about it.

"And you don't think I can do the same? Why?"

"It's not that I don't think you can," he says. "I just hope you won't have to."

"You are *so* lying," she says, and the phone in Rafferty's shirt pocket rings.

"Thai kid is waiting," Vladimir says. "Where you are now?"

A flock of black birds breaks from the trees in front of them and swoops over the car, so low it looks as if the windshield wipers will bat one aside. "Almost there. Let the kid wait, he's getting paid. Where is he?"

"With me. I should be in backseat. With you and Baby Spy."

"Stay where you are. Keep the kid with you. We're not doing anything until we hear from Janos."

"I should be there, too," Vladimir says. "With Janos. I should be ewerywhere."

"You're where I want you. Just stay there. I'll call you if you have to move." The phone beeps to signal an incoming call. "Stay off the phone," Rafferty says, punching the button to bring up the new call.

"This is interesting," Janos says.

"Please," Rafferty says, "don't make me ask questions."

"I'm up on the fifth level of the mall with a cup of coffee, looking down at the business center."

"And?"

"And maybe five minutes ago, two men showed up. About the same height and weight, short hair, big black shoes, looked like they'd be happier in uniform. So they walked together, all the way around the fourth level three times, looking in every window except the business center. They're starting another circuit now."

Rafferty says, "What time is it?" and both Janos and Ming Li tell him it's six-fifteen.

"And there are three more down on the first level," Janos says. "They wander around alone and then regroup every few minutes."

"No Shen," Rafferty says.

"Not yet, but these are his men."

"No one else?"

Ming Li makes an anxious popping sound with her lips.

"No. But these guys look nervous. I'd bet money the brass is coming."

"The moment you see Murphy," Rafferty says, "you call me. No waiting to see what happens or what he does. 'Murphy's here' will be considered a complete report, are we clear?"

"Sure."

"I want your finger on that SEND button from now on. We need to be talking within ten seconds of your laying eyes on Murphy."

"And Shen?"

"Take your time. Twenty seconds will be fine."

Ming Li says, "Here's the turn."

THEY'RE TWO BLOCKS away from Murphy's compound, parked under the drooping, water-heavy branches of a tree. Big, rambling houses line the street on either side, most of them behind walls, and a barrier of sandbags, about eight bags high, has been laid out along the perimeter of the road's south side, where the lots slope gently downhill from the pavement. The most direct route from Murphy's house to the main boulevard is behind them, so he won't spot them driving out, although Rafferty is sure it doesn't matter. He's certain that Murphy's already left.

"Two maids, two wives, and the little girl," he says again. "One of the wives is apparently almost never home, and the other one is some kind of invalid, spends most of her time in bed. From what the maid told Vladimir's boy, I'll never catch a glimpse of the daughter. She'll be spying on me."

Ming Li says, "So if that's what happens, you'll be bringing me the two maids and the sick wife."

"I'm hoping I don't have to bring the wife. Apparently she self-medicates quite a bit. Maybe she won't even turn over the whole time I'm in there."

"And maybe the clouds will open and a shaft of light will shine on you and a voice will say, 'All is forgiven.'"

"Could be."

"Three is a lot. Two I can just cuff to the steering wheel. The third one—"

"The armrest in the backseat. It's got an opening in it. You can pass a cuff through it, and she won't be going anywhere."

"She might be able to yank it off."

"That'll be the invalid."

"Okay." She shifts her weight, looks at her watch, and says, "Unbelievable. We've only been here thirteen minutes. Are you sure about the noise?"

He says, "Get out."

"It's raining."

"I'm *so* sorry."

"All right," she says. "But if this takes the curl out of my hair . . ." She fluffs her perfectly straight hair at him, a Thai gesture of dismissal, and climbs out, and Rafferty puts the windows all the way up. When Ming Li is eight or ten feet away, he begins to shout. She puts a hand to her ear, and he shouts more loudly, and she shrugs and comes back to the car. Once inside, she swivels the rearview mirror toward herself, combs her bangs with her fingers, and says, "Better than I hoped. The rain helps—it's noisier than you'd think. You're sure they won't be able to reach the door handles."

"Yes, I'm sure. Would you like me to cuff you to the—"

"No thanks."

"Anyway, you're staying with them unless something—" The cell phone rings. Rafferty glances at it, says, "Janos" to Ming Li, and then, "Yes?" into the phone.

"Shen's here."

"Where?"

"Ground floor. The three cops down there all answered their phones a minute ago and met over in front of the mall shrine, and Shen showed up. They're in a huddle."

"And the two on the fourth floor?"

"They're looking over the railing, watching."

"How does Shen look?"

"Pissed off, and the other three look like they'd like to turn and run. Here come the fourth-floor boys, heading for the escalator. I've got to go into a store for a minute. One of them glanced at me."

"Call me back when you can." He puts the phone in his pocket and wishes he had a cigarette. How many nights ago was it that he smoked the cabdriver's, after Shen's guy almost went off the roof? "I don't suppose you have a cigarette?"

"I'm young," Ming Li says, "not stupid. No Murphy?"

"Not yet. But he's there, I'm sure he is."

"Then let's go in."

"I'm not *that* sure." He opens his door. "I need to walk around a little."

The rain is a fine sprinkle, nearly body temperature. He hasn't gone ten steps when a mosquito whines in his ear, and then another. He waves a hand around to clear them, feeling the weight of the gun under his shirt. His shoes, soaked again, squelch in the mud. An image of Murphy in his awful shirt, his face red with anger, pops into his mind, and at that precise moment the phone rings.

He grabs it, snaps, "Hold on," and sprints for the car. Ming Li looks up, startled from some reverie as he jumps into the seat. He says, "Murphy?"

"Let me tell you," Janos says. "It will interest you, I promise."

"Do it, do it, but make it short."

"So Shen goes up to the fourth floor with the two boys who were doing circles up there and goes into the business center. He comes out a minute later, actually scratching his head. For a second I thought he knew he was being watched and he wanted to demonstrate—"

"Get to it."

"He was scratching his head," Janos continues implacably, "and then he looks down at his shirt. He pulls a cell phone out of his pocket and has a short conversation, very grim, and then starts running up the escalator. He keeps looking up, as though he's going all the way to the top, and I'm scrambling to the stairs at the rear, and as I get up to the fifth floor, I hear voices above me, so I go out on the fifth level and walk the length of the plaza, and when I turn, I see Shen up on the sixth level, the top, heading for the stairs as though the place is on fire, and he pulls the door open, and Murphy pushes him away and comes through the door with a woman following him."

"The woman from the hotel." In one part of his mind, Rafferty is regretting that he was right about Anna. There can't be any doubt now.

"Yes, her. Anyway, Shen practically jumps on him. Shouting and waving his arms and—"

"Can you see Murphy now?"

"They're still going at it."

"Thanks. Call me if anything changes."

"If Murphy disappears, you mean."

"He's not going to stay in sight. Try to see where he goes, and call me if the woman disappears."

"Got it."

Rafferty disconnects and starts the car. Ming Li is looking straight out the window, but he can feel the intensity coming off her in waves. She seems to be heating the car. He says, "You like this, don't you?"

"Compared to Virginia? This is heaven."

"Here goes." He pushes speed dial for Vladimir. "Have your boy call the maid in two minutes," he says. "He should tell her to open the gate for him. Oh, and it's raining, so she should come out with an umbrella. Think she'd do that for him?"

Vladimir says, "Is wery handsome boy."

31

Murphy's Law

WHEN RAFFERTY STEPS through the half-open gate, the maid lets out a squeak. He's wearing the one-eared Mortimer Snerd mask.

He says, "Quiet. No one will hurt you.' He takes her upper arm and tugs her toward the house, slowing for a moment when he sees that the yard is under several inches of water. He says, "Is there a way not to get our feet soaked?"

"You could leave," the maid says. She's pale-skinned and Chinese-featured and hard-eyed. Her accent sounds Vietnamese, although the English comes quickly. The squeak aside, she's handling the situation as though it happens every week.

But she does turn to look back over her shoulder as headlights hit the front of the big house, bringing it sharply out of the darkness and creating an upside-down mirror palace on the water's surface. Ming Li pulls the Toyota in very slowly, trying to avoid running it off the invisible driveway and into the mud.

"Should she go straight?" Rafferty asks. "And if you tell me a lie and she winds up stuck on the lawn, you're going for a swim."

"Straight another two meters," she says. "Then left to the front of the house."

"Get in front of the car and guide her in." He takes the umbrella from her hand.

The two of them back up as the maid waves Ming Li forward, the car churning twin wakes to the right and left. When the Toyota is clear of the closing gates, Rafferty holds up both hands and the car stops. He takes the maid's arm. "How many people inside?"

"Two. Neeni and the girl."

"Where's the other maid—Phung? Where's Wife Number Two?"

"Phung has the night off. Won't come back until tomorrow morning. The missus, who knows? Shopping, maybe. Maybe in some hotel with someone she's known half an hour."

"You don't like her."

"I don't like any of them except Neeni, the poor thing."

"Where are they? Neeni and the girl?"

The car door opens, and Ming Li gets out. She's wearing a Morticia Addams mask they'd picked up that morning at Zombietown, its long, black nylon hair hanging over a loose white blouse and dark jeans.

"Neeni is in bed," the maid says, looking at Ming Li. "The girl, who knows? Cutting worms in half, maybe. Or she could be watching us right this minute."

"Okay. I need you to get into the car."

She shakes her head impatiently. "No. What you *need* is for me to open the door. I have to key in the alarm and then go in and enter the code that resets it, or it'll go off." She shakes her arm free and heads for the house.

"Yes," Rafferty says, "that's what I meant," and splashes through water at least three inches deep.

Catching up to him to get under the umbrella, Ming Li says, "I told you to get a scarier mask."

"He doesn't need to scare me," the maid says over her shoulder. "I only work here, and I won't be doing that for much longer. Just don't hurt Neeni."

"I'm not going to hurt anybody," Rafferty says.

"Well," the maid says, "good luck with that."

They step up onto the porch, the surface of which is about half an inch above the water, and the maid keys in a combination of numbers on a pad to the left of the door. The door clicks, and she pushes it open.

"What's the code?" Rafferty asks. He steps in and leans the

umbrella against a big chair, making a mental map of the hallway, the large living room, the dimly lit dining room. In the rear wall of the dining room are a bank of windows and a pair of double doors with big panes of glass in them.

"Three-six-one-six-nine," the maid says. "Then you hit zero twice."

"Three-six-one-six-nine," Ming Li repeats. "Zero-zero."

Rafferty says, "What happens if we leave the door open?"

"Alarms. And alarms go off if I don't key in the inside code, too, right about now."

"Go to it."

The maid punches up some numbers and then pushes a button with ALT under it and another above a tiny black telephone icon. She holds the telephone button down for a count of three and then steps back, hands folded in front of her.

"What's that button?" Rafferty asks.

"If you don't hold it down, the alarm will go off anyway. That way, even if someone has the combination, it probably won't work."

"What's the code in here?" Rafferty asks.

"I'll write it down for you." She crosses the hall, opens the drawer in a marble-topped table, and pulls out a pen and pad. "For outside," she says, writing *3616900*. "In here, this one." She writes *43892*. "Then hold down the little phone button for a count of three."

"And when I open it from inside?"

"No problem. You only need the code for closing it after it gets opened from out there."

A telephone begins to ring, straight ahead in the dusk of the dining room. Then another, from somewhere to the left, and another. "Let it ring," the maid says. "It's for him, and no one who calls him will talk to anyone else. They won't even leave a message. If there's no answer here, they call his cell phone."

It seems as though phones are ringing all over the house. Rafferty automatically counts the rings until, at six, they stop.

"Good," he says. He swallows. The ringing telephones have made it real, somehow. Everything he wants in the world right now comes down to the next few minutes. "Now you go with Morticia here."

"And if I don't want to?"

"Then Morticia will shoot you," Ming Li says. She pulls up her shirt to display the gun stuck into her pants.

"I'm not getting shot," the maid says. "The car?"

"The car."

Rafferty says, "Where's Neeni?"

"Down the hall. Last room before it turns left."

"Thanks. Go with Morticia."

He watches them cross the porch and step down into the black water, now dappled with widening concentric circles as the rain gains strength. When Ming Li opens the door of the car and steps aside for the maid to climb in, he hears a metallic click behind him, and he whirls.

Nothing. No one is there. The heavy dining-room furniture stands there like massive, browsing herbivores. Nothing seems to have changed.

Turning back to close the front door, he replays what he saw and realizes what was different. Ignoring the urge to double-check, he very deliberately shuts the door and makes sure it's engaged, all his attention trained on the open space at his back. Only when the door is secure does he turn, unhurriedly, to face the back of the house.

The double door at the rear of the dining room is open an inch or two. Not enough to admit a telltale draft, but not actually closed either. Closing it would probably have made the latch engage with another, louder click.

Rafferty says, "My, my." His face is cool with perspiration. He touches the gun through his shirt, just making sure it he'll get it on the first try, and moves down the hallway.

The living room is sunken two steps, carpeted in an oyster white with a random gray fleck, mercilessly overfurnished in gray leather and distressed, whitewashed wood. It is the work of a professional designer who thought the room was bigger. The room smells of damp, most likely water seepage from the storm. Bangkok's emerging upper-middle class has created a boom market for new, semipalatial houses built of soda crackers and promises, and Rafferty is pleased to see that Murphy has bought one.

There's nowhere for anyone to hide in the living room, so he puts it behind him and goes into the dining room, looking at everything except the open door. Twelve high-legged chairs surround the big table, and a mahogany sideboard towers almost to the ceiling on the left. Jammed into the corner is a card table, inlaid with stylized face cards of agate and jasper and other colored stones. Four cane-bottomed chairs lean against it, price tags still visible on the backs. Everything he can see looks like it arrived on the same truck. It's a big room, but there's barely space to move.

The phones begin to ring again: one in the room he's in, one from behind him in the living room, and at least two others, one faint enough to be upstairs. The insistency of the noise increases his uneasiness. He counts six rings again, standing still, until they stop.

Ahead of him, through an eight-foot archway, is a blinding kitchen, all reddish saltillo tile, pale beige granite, and white appliances, as brilliantly lit as an operating room. He stands in the archway between the dining room and the kitchen, listening. Now that the phones have gone silent, he hears rain on the windows and the *pat-pat-pat* of a leak, water dripping onto fabric.

And then he smells something. It's faint and sharp at the same time, like urine on a floor two or three rooms away, or the germy odor of dirty clothes that have been piled damp in a hamper for days. The door creaks behind him. He turns, but it's swaying back and forth by itself, obeying the air currents that ghost through the room.

He leaves it ajar and goes back toward the entrance hall, thinking about calling Ming Li, but what's he going to say? There's a spook in here with me? He knows who it is, and he's pretty sure he's not afraid of her.

So he takes the stairs, two at a time, stands at the top for a moment, and decides to start with the most distant door and work his way back. The door at the end opens into what is clearly the master bedroom, the size of a small ballroom with a vaulted ceiling. It looks to him like it was decorated by the birds who drape

Disney heroines in badly designed gowns: an acre of shell pink organdy hangs from a towering frame above the king-size bed, which is mounded with enormous pastel pillows, like big Valentine candies. The wall to the right is mirrored from floor to ceiling, reflecting an ambitious home gym: treadmill, rowing machine, and a couple of hinged and counterweighted contraptions whose function he can only guess at. An overstuffed couch and a table jostle each other under the front window. Money—quite a bit of it—has been misspent here.

The newer wife, he thinks.

He angles across the room, smelling sachet and face powder and the raw, jangly perfume of hair spray, into a bathroom so prettied up it seems like an architectural euphemism for the natural functions it was built to accommodate. A connecting door opens into a smaller room.

Clearly this is where Murphy recharges his prodigious, murderous energy. The carpet was either never laid or has been peeled back, baring a floor of gray, industrial cement. A narrow single bed has a paper-thin pillow and two rough blankets thrown over it. At the foot of the bed is an olive green, army-issue trunk, securely locked, and on the opposite wall is a rough, barely finished wooden dresser with white china knobs on the drawers. Above the dresser, set into the wall where a mirror might be, is a gun safe, which is locked as tightly as the chest. The furniture is dented and scratched, and as Rafferty looks around the room, he has the sense that this value-free assemblage of chipped, hard-surfaced junk has followed Murphy from place to place, while a succession of newly graduated village girls filled the other rooms of houses just like this one with the imitation lives they'd seen on television.

Being in Murphy's room brings back the sense of pressurized fury he'd experienced when he saw the man face-to-face. He has an impulse to call Janos, but instead he looks at his watch—6:52. He's been inside for only fourteen minutes. Murphy doesn't expect him to show up at the shopping plaza until eight or eight-thirty. He's got plenty of time.

Then why is he so frightened?

•   •   •

MURPHY IS PACING the rear office area of a sixth-floor cloth-ing store, fighting a case of the jitters and telling Andrea Fallon, the aging Khao San junkie posing as Helen Eckersley, for the third time what she's supposed to do when Rafferty finally shows up. He knows he's repeating himself, but some little animal in his chest is clawing to get his attention. Andrea is just barely not rolling her eyes when his cell phone rings. He glances at the readout, which says ALARM.

As he looks at the word, the little animal in his chest begins to use its teeth. "Yeah?"

"Mr. Murphy, we've got an entry at your house, but someone there diverted the alarm to the telephones. No one is answering."

"How long ago?"

"How long—"

"How long since the relay came through your office to ring the phones?"

"A little less than fifteen minutes."

"What the *fuck* have you been doing for fifteen minutes?"

"We didn't have this number in the main file. We had to look at your forms—"

"You dumb shit." Murphy punches the DISCONNECT button so hard he cracks the screen. "Get out of here," he says to Fallon. "Call me tomorrow for the rest of your money."

"Yeah, right," Fallon says, "and you'll mail me the check." She holds out her hand, palm up. "Gimme."

"Oh, sure," Murphy says. "Sure thing." He grabs her upper arm, pinching the area between the bicep and the bone viciously enough to make her gasp. With his other hand he seizes her wrist and brings her open hand up into her face, with enough force to send her staggering back to the wall, blood streaming from her split lip. "Clean yourself up and get out of here."

He leaves her leaning against the wall, swearing at him, and goes out into the store. Despite the external display of anger, there's a kind of glee at his center, and his vision and hearing are amplified. He feels like he could hear a whisper a mile away. It's a state of consciousness he loves.

The immediate problem, of course, is getting out. If Rafferty's not here, he's got someone else here, on the lookout. The store is obviously being watched. The only way out without taking the escalator, in full view of a thousand people, is the staircase he came up. The entrance to the stairs is about eight meters from the door to the shop. Left, from his perspective.

As always when he's in this state, ideas announce themselves to him complete and fully formed.

"You," he says softly to the woman who seems to be in charge. "Don't say no, don't give me any shit, don't attract any attention, just do what I tell you to do, or three days from now there'll be a toy store in this space. Are you listening?"

"Yes," she says, and a part of him registers the thick, badly applied makeup, the sickly perfume with the pampered-animal smell beneath it, the fragility of her neck.

"That one, over there," he says, pointing at a salesgirl who, like the manager, is as tall and lean as a fashion model. "Get her."

While the woman scurries to do his bidding, Murphy puts his hands under one of the heavy rods the dresses hang from and pushes up. As he hoped it would, it lifts easily from the wall bracket. He pulls it down and steps behind the counter, where he tilts the rod until all the clothes slide to the floor, leaving him holding a round bar about seven feet in length. To the two approaching women, their eyes on the spill of clothes, he says, "The longest things you've got, dresses, coats, I don't care what they are, but they've got to be long. Understand?"

The manager starts to say something, but Murphy feels his eyes widen, and she retreats, calling instructions in Thai to the other woman. Customers are beginning to pay attention as the two of them scoop clothes from displays everywhere in the store, throw them over their arms and shoulders, and hurry back to Murphy, who holds the pole horizontal.

"Hang 'em up. Jam them together. I want a wall, you got it?" He holds the bar by one end, the other end slanted up slightly, and the women hook hangers over it until it's about three-quarters full, the clothes sliding down to his end to be smashed together by gravity. Murphy says, "Fill it up."

The saleswoman says, "The *clothes*," and Murphy whirls on her so fast that some of the hangers fly off the other end of the rod. *"I'm not going to tell you again."*

A customer backs out of the store, followed by another.

The saleswoman takes off at a run. Fifteen seconds later the rod is packed with hanging clothes. Murphy shoves the garments on the near end together to bare about a foot of rod. "On your shoulder," he says to the manager. Then he clears the other end and sets it, not particularly gently, on the salesgirl's shoulder. "Put your hand on it, stupid. If it falls off, you'll be sorry for the rest of your short, shitty life. Now, stay there."

He goes toward the door of the shop, turns his back to it, and pulls a revolver out of the holster at the center of his spine. "Hey!" he shouts, although everyone in the shop is staring at him. "This is a national security incident." He repeats the words "national security" in Thai. "We have a threat, but nobody's going to get hurt if you do what I say." He holds up his cell phone with his free hand. "I want to see your cell phones, right now, and I mean everyone. If you don't show me a cell phone and I find one on you, you won't go home tonight. Get them out and hold them up."

Every person in the store—five customers and three employees—holds up a phone. "Put them on that table full of T-shirts, near the front door. Do *not* go out of the shop. You, you, you. Go to the table and drop your phone on it, then come back. Keep your hands in sight. Good. Now turn around and go through that door in the back. He waves the revolver at the door. "You'll stay there for five minutes. In five minutes come out. Everyone understand?"

A few people reply automatically, but most of them head for the door, moving fast, as though they're anticipating a bullet in the back. When the door has closed behind the last of them, Murphy shouts, "Five minutes!" Then, to the two women, he says, "I'm going to get behind these clothes, and when I say 'Walk,' we're going to walk at normal speed. Outside the door we'll turn left, all moving together, until we get to the stairs. Then we're going through that door, all together. Both of you got it?"

The women nod, and the store manager clears her throat, licks her lips, and says, "Yes."

"No hurrying, nothing out of the ordinary. You're just a couple of women carrying a lot of clothes, okay? There's a truck waiting down there, and you're just taking them down the stairs, right?"

"Fine," says the manager.

"Keep me in the middle, same distance from both of you. Go at the count of three. Carefully, so nothing happens to the clothes. Ready. One. Two. Three."

They're both taller than he is, but he hunches down anyway. He knows he's invisible from below. It's a watcher a level up that worries him.

AND THAT'S PRECISELY where Janos is, drinking his third cup of coffee, shifting from foot to foot and wishing with some intensity that he could take a bathroom break. He's been staring for almost twenty minutes at the front of the store that Murphy went into, and it feels like an hour. The woman has gone into the store, too, and she hasn't come out yet, so he's stuck here. He has no idea where Shen is, although Rafferty hadn't seemed worried about Shen. But it's sloppy. He needs half a dozen people, with radios, to do this right.

He's pulling out his phone to give Vladimir a piece of his mind when the women come out, carrying what looks like a whole rack of clothes. He goes up on tiptoe to see whether he can look over it, but he can't; he'd have to be practically on top of them to do that.

So they're moving clothes—they'll take them to the escalator. Except that they turn left, heading for the stairway, the stairway Murphy came up. Maybe it's nothing, maybe the people who run the mall don't want that kind of shop business done in sight of the customers. Or maybe Murphy's got himself an escort.

Rafferty's not due to arrive for ninety minutes. Why would Murphy be leaving? And would he be leaving without the woman?

If it's not Murphy, and Janos goes out of position to check, he could miss it if Murphy actually does move. This might be a diversion to draw whoever's watching, leaving the area clear for Murphy to walk out two minutes from now, big as life. Janos leans forward, elbows on the railing. He's forgotten about pissing. The shop attendant in front pulls the door to the stairs open, toward her, and gives it a shove; it's the kind that swings closed automatically, and they'll have to hurry to get through before it shuts on them. And they're not going to make it. The woman in front is through, and the door is closing on the center of the rack, and then it's pushed back again, and it opens and starts to close, and the woman at the back pushes it open again.

Two people, three shoves on the door. The woman in front could have kicked back at it, or . . .

Vladimir and the boy are at the front exit, waiting for word. *Why would Murphy leave the woman?*

Janos makes a decision and takes the down escalator in a kind of swan dive.

THE THIRD BEDROOM is small and dim and smells like a sickroom. Rafferty flicks on the wall switch, but nothing happens. The only light comes through the door in the hallway. He stands there, letting his eyes adjust, listening for the sound of movement behind him, and gradually he sees a milky line of light beneath a door in the room's far right corner.

To open that door, he'll have to go through the bedroom, and he realizes that he doesn't want to. Rose, he thinks, would take one look and back away, saying, "Bad place."

The rumpled bed, the sheets creased sharply, as though the person who sleeps there perspires heavily, a lemon yellow, edgy smell that Rafferty associates with fever, the absolutely bare walls—not a picture, not a poster, not a mirror—all fill him with a deep uneasiness. His eyes go to the ceiling. The area above the bed has been attacked with paint: spirals and loops and jagged, shapeless lines, random as roughly torn paper, in dark reds and chromium yellows and a lot of black. Years ago Rafferty had seen video of a spider spinning a web under the influence of lysergic acid, and that web had the same uncontrollable, fractured energy. Imagination as broken glass. He looks away, feeling vertiginous, and then up again. This is what the person on the bed, lying on her back, would have seen: a ceiling full of cracks and fault lines, a solidity on the verge of flying apart, but to what end? Would something come down—was that the meaning of the slashes of red and yellow?—or would the person on the bed be drawn up? And up to what?

Holding his breath, he enters the room and walks swiftly to the door with light beneath it, which he pulls open. It's a bathroom, very long and narrow, with a window at each end, looking out on both the back and the front yards. Other than the peculiar shape, it's purely functional: small and plain, with a single fluorescent tube running almost the full length of the ceiling. The bathtub, located below the back window, is piled full of white, an irregular, cloudlike surface of white cloth. He reaches over and tugs a fold close to him, and what he's holding is a filthy white nightgown. He looks again. There must be thirty of them in the tub.

The nightgown smells of damp and sweat and dirt. It's the same smell he'd caught downstairs, standing in the archway to the kitchen with the open door behind him.

From nowhere Miaow's face suddenly swims up at him with its usual mix of hope and apprehension, and he finds himself on the verge of tears. He wants to be anywhere in the world but here.

He tosses the nightgown back into the tub and looks around to find a reason for the room's shape. And there it is, a door in the wall opposite the small bedroom, closed and locked. Feeling the pressure of time, he goes quickly through the bedroom and into Murphy's room. It takes him about four minutes to find the ring of keys; he begins by pulling out the drawers in the dresser and feeling their undersides. The bottom drawer comes out completely, and there it is, on the bare concrete floor beneath.

The first key on the ring opens the door.

The room is as long as the bathroom and twice as wide. It's unfinished; there's no drywall, and the floor is bare plywood. A small cache of firearms, including holstered sidearms, automatic weapons, and what seem to be wooden spears, fills one corner. Old uniforms hang on hooks set into the two-by-four uprights in the wall, and a low table, the size of a single bed, is piled with papers and photo albums. He opens one and sees a much younger Murphy and two other Americans in camouflage fatigues grinning at the camera. They flank a stick, much like the ones he sees in this room, on which is impaled the wide-eyed head of a young Asian male.

He pulls out Ming Li's little silver camera and photographs the page. And the next. And the next. They get worse by the page. By the time he goes downstairs, he's moving much more quietly. He doesn't want to wake the dead.

He's halfway down when he hears the noises from below, a whirring and a faint, repetitive clicking.

JANOS IS SLOWED by the crowd on the main floor and has to push his way to the entrance and then run, as fast as he can, around the entire structure to reach the door at the bottom of the stairs. It's heavy steel, and he pulls it open with both hands, only to hear the indignant voices of the two women climbing back up.

He's missed Murphy. If it *was* Murphy.

And now he's out of position, not watching the girl, not watching Murphy, not watching Shen. He can almost see the thousand dollars he's been promised floating away, above the roofs of the parked cars. He can't just go back in and hope everything's fine. He has to know whether he was right, and he has to know which exit Murphy will take. If it *was* . . .

He bats the doubt away and stands still, letting his eyes go soft and unfocused, trying to keep the entire scene in front of him in sight. It's dark and raining, which doesn't help. When he's got the gaze he wants, he very slowly turns his head, taking in the part of the lot that's visible from this side of the building, looking for nothing but movement.

He gets it, three parking rows away, a short man in a hurry, zigzagging between wet, gleaming cars, not paying any attention to him at all. Janos takes off at a run, up on the balls of his feet to avoid making scuffing noises, trying not to catch up to Murphy but to get a look at which way his car is going, so he can direct Vladimir and the Thai pretty boy who romanced Murphy's maid. Then he's to alert Rafferty on the phone, and Vladimir will call to confirm or deny that Murphy is headed home.

Janos slows and stops. He's a row of cars beyond the one he spotted Murphy in, but he can't see the man. To his right he hears a car start, and he turns toward it.

And hits his cheekbone on the fast-moving barrel of a gun.

It's a revolver, Janos registers instinctively, and the sight on the end of the barrel has torn the skin over his right cheekbone. He raises a hand to touch it, but the revolver comes down on top of his wrist, very fast, and Janos knows that a bone has been broken.

Not until then does he look into Murphy's blue eyes, eyes the color of the sky on a hazy day. Janos steps back, banging into the car behind him, and Murphy says, "Where's Rafferty?"

Janos says, "Who?"

Murphy lifts the gun until it's pointing directly into Janos's left eye. He says, "See this?" and immediately brings the edge of his left hand down on the bridge of Janos's nose, which breaks. Blood pours over Janos's chin and onto the front of his shirt, and he coughs and begins to bend forward, but Murphy grabs his hair and pulls him upright. He takes a step back, the gun still pointed at Janos's eye, and says, "Put your finger under it and push up a little. It'll hurt like a son of a bitch, but the bleeding will slow. Where's Rafferty?"

"Your house." He blinks away the tears, but all that does is show him the gun and Murphy's eyes more clearly, and he can't look at the glee in Murphy's eyes; he's seen people who enjoyed this before, but not like this. He lets his eyes water. He lets his nose bleed.

"What's he doing there?"

"Looking for something. I don't know what."

"Who else is here?"

"Nobody."

Murphy raises his left hand again. "You can't imagine how it'll feel if I hit it again."

"Vladimir. And some Thai boy."

"Vladimir." Murphy does a little two-syllable laugh. "Talk about the big guns." He leans in toward Janos, and Janos flinches. "I've forgotten your name."

"Janos."

"Right, Janos. So, Janos, where's your cell phone?"

"Shirt pocket."

"Don't be stupid now." Murphy touches the gun to Janos's fore-head and lifts the cell phone out of his pocket. "Rafferty's number in here?"

"Speed dial two."

"And Vladimir?"

"Four."

"Great, we're making progress. Look, we're both pros, and I've got nothing against you, but I don't want you warning Vladimir and Vladimir calling Rafferty, so I'm going to need to slow you down a little. Lie down in between these cars."

That's when the coffee lets go, and Janos feels the wet heat on the front of his pants. "I . . . I don't want to."

"All I'm going to do is put flex-ties on your wrists and ankles. I know you'll get out of them eventually, but by then I'll have Vladimir under control. What's his car look like?"

"Gray Mazda. Sedan."

"So what you need to do is let me put the restraints on you and then promise me, one professional to another, that you'll repay my leaving you alive by not finding a way to get in contact with Rafferty."

"I don't know his number. It's in the phone, that's all."

"No problem, then." Murphy reaches into the pocket of his jeans and pulls out a plastic flex-tie. "Lie down and put your hands behind you, and we'll get this done, and then we're square. In fact, I might have work for you in a week or two."

"It wasn't personal," Janos says, going to his knees, and Murphy moves behind him, and their relative positions, the classic execution tableau, tell Janos that he's wrong, that it *was* personal all along, and he's just grasping that and thinking about standing when the bullet, the first of two, tears into the base of his skull.

32

Neeni and Treasure

THE WOMAN IN the bed is beautiful and tiny. She lies on her back, one hand dangling off the side of the mattress. Her eyes are half open, focused on the far edge of the world. Rafferty passes a hand over them, but she's either unconscious or so deeply intoxicated that she doesn't register the movement. The room smells stickily of artificial cherry from the two open bottles of cough syrup on the table. He lifts the glass beside them and smells the cherry again, floating against a background of whiskey.

This is Murphy's life, he thinks. This overstuffed, leaking house, the woman who's never here, the one dying slowly in the bed, and the child who sleeps beneath that schizophrenic ceiling. The narrow bed, the chipped dresser, the black-and-white memories in the locked room. Whatever it is that visits him when he sleeps. Murphy's life is all collateral damage.

Tikka-tikka-tikka-tikka comes the sound from the room at the end of the hall. He takes a deep breath, touches the gun again as though it's a talisman, and leaves the bedroom and its unconscious mistress, heading down the hall toward the light. The pressure of passing time pushes at his back, making him walk a little faster.

The room is big and brightly lit, and on a huge raised platform a small, golden train races around a curving track. The miniature landscape is Southeast Asia, someplace where rubber is grown. Standing just inside the doorway, watching the train click its way through the intricate loops and over the tiny hills, he says, "Hello."

No response, but he knows she's here. He can smell her, and it almost breaks his heart. No child should smell like that. No child should be here.

After a moment a voice says, "Who are . . . are you?"

"A friend of your father's."

Silence, except for the train. It negotiates a tight curve, just barely, and Rafferty says, "Should this be going so fast?"

"You don't, you, you don't know how to slow it down," the voice says, and this time Rafferty locates it; it comes from behind the open door to the kitchen.

"I can figure it out," he says. "I think."

"You look stupid," says the voice. "You're too stu-stupid to figure it out."

"Maybe," Rafferty says. "Maybe I'm smart enough to wear a stupid mask."

Another pause. Then, in an almost-musical tone, "You forgot something. When you were here before."

"Did I?"

"Look at the roof of the train station, Mr., Mr. Stupid."

He goes to the table, one eye on the door. It takes him a moment to find what he's looking for in the tiny world; there are dozens of isolated structures and two small towns in the landscape, but then he sees the station and the pink thing on its roof. "My ear," he says. "I lose ears all the time. I drop them everywhere."

The silence this time is so long he wonders whether she has an escape route of some kind. Then, very slowly at the edge of the door, a tangle of reddish black hair comes into view, followed by a cheek, an eye, and a nose. Precisely half a face, no more, dark as the night outside but for the strip, shockingly pale, that contains her eye and the bridge of her nose.

She can't be much older than Miaow.

"Ears don't fall off," she says slowly. "You have to cut them off."

"Mine do," Rafferty says. He reaches up and tugs his real ear, where it protrudes through the hole in the side of the mask. "And then they grow back."

"*No*," she says, and it's almost a shout. Her one visible eye, which has been fixed on his, wanders downward, going aimlessly left and right, as though she's reading something written on the air or on a falling page, and then the movement stops and she's looking at a spot on the floor about halfway between them. A pink tongue touches the center of her lower lip and then disappears. The energy that had been animating her face seems to have fled. Dully, she says, "They stay off."

"Why are your teeth black?" Rafferty asks.

She doesn't move, and she continues to stare at the floor, but a moment later she says, "What?"

"Why are your teeth black?"

The face disappears behind the door again. "So I can smile in the dark."

He feels the connection between them fraying, and he urgently wants to maintain it. He says, without a moment's thought, "Could you make mine black, too?"

"I don't get that close," she says without reappearing.

He moves carefully, making no quick gestures and not looking in her direction, to the edge of the train table and locates the transformer. "You're right," he says. "I don't know how to slow it down. Can you fix it?"

"You have to go away," she says. "Back to the door you came in through."

"Fine, here I go." He backs up. "I'm in the door. Do you want me to go farther?"

"No. Just stay there."

She comes out from behind the door. Beneath the dark charcoal, her face is beautiful, with a high, narrow nose, the full lower lip he'd seen on the small sleeping woman, and eyes that could be Lao or Vietnamese. But she's far too thin, her knees below the smudged nightgown swollen like parentheses. The skin of her legs is scraped, punctuated by bruises and insect bites. Her feet are muddy. One of them—the right—is bleeding, leaving little stencil marks of red on the carpet as she walks. Twigs and leaves are caught in the tangles of her hair. Her eyes look into his and beyond them, and he can almost feel her gaze scraping the back of his skull. She never looks away as she moves. Not until she stops, at the edge of the train table, do her eyes drift downward, and once again he has the sensation of something, a current or something, being disconnected. He says, "Are you sure I shouldn't back up some more?"

Instead of answering him, she turns to the train table and looks down at it until Rafferty actually begins to wonder if she's forgotten he's there. But then she reaches out long fingers and adjusts the lever on the transformer, and the train slows. She says, "Take off your mask."

"If you take yours off."

She turns her head partway toward him, but her eyes remain on the table. "It doesn't come off."

"Okay," he says. "I'll take mine off anyway." He pulls it over his head and waits, but she's not looking at him. He says, "Why are you by yourself?"

"Mommy One had too many cheerses," she says. "Mommy Three is out with a boy somewhere, fucking. One of our maids has a boy, too, the maid who let you and your friend in."

"Cheerses?"

"*You* know." She mimes holding a glass and lifts it toward him and says, brightly, "*Cheers.*"

"Why does she do that?" Rafferty asks.

"She wants to die, but she's trying to do it by accident."

"Has she told you that?"

The girl's lip curls. "I don't talk to her. She's weak."

"You said Mommy One and Mommy Three. Where's Mommy Two?"

"She went into the river," she says. "In Laos."

"How long ago?"

She doesn't look down at her hand, but first the thumb and then all four fingers curl under, one at a time, and Rafferty can almost hear her counting. "When I was seven."

"And now you're twelve."

Her eyes flick up to his and then away again. "How do you know?"

"I have a daughter. She's twelve."

She nods, fiddling with one of the little trees on the table and taking in the information. "Do you like her?"

Rafferty's voice feels hoarse when he says, "I love her."

Now she looks at his face, inspecting it as though she expects a test on what he looks like. "What are you?" she asks.

"A lot of things. Anglo and Filipino, mostly. What about you?"

"Lao, Thai, and what my, my, my father is."

"We're both mix-ups," he says.

She shrugs the topic away and looks back at the train layout. "If you're smart, why did you wear a stupid mask?"

"If people don't know you're smart, you can surprise them."

She sticks out her lower lip, possibly thinking about it.

"Why wear a mask that looks like you?" he says. He realizes he's talking because he half expects her to vanish, like smoke. "If you're stupid, you wear a smart mask. If you're mean, you wear a nice mask. That's what a mask is, something to hide who you really are."

She says nothing.

"What does yours hide?"

She pulls back her lips and shows him the black teeth, the gums above and below them a startling pink by contrast. "Nothing. This is me. Back up some more."

He takes three steps back, but she seems to have lost interest in him. Looking down at the world on the table, she says, "I can see things."

"I'm sure you can."

"I saw you and your girlfriend come in. I saw you surprise that stupid Hwa."

"The maid?"

"*Hwa,*" she says sharply. "Her name is Hwa. She's going to quit soon, but she doesn't know I know about it." She slows the train and speeds it up again. "I see all sorts of things."

"I believe you."

She leans over the train setup and moves something Rafferty can't see, just a rapid movement with her hand. "Do you see things?"

"Sometimes."

"*How* old is your daughter?"

"Twelve. Same as you."

"What's her name?"

"Miaow," Rafferty says. "Like the sound a cat makes."

She's looking at whatever she moved in the miniature jungle, but he thinks she knows to a millimeter how far away he is. "My name is," she says. She adjusts something on the table. She opens her mouth and closes it, opens and closes it again. "My name is Treasure."

"That's a beautiful name."

"My," she says.

He waits.

She turns her face partway to him again, but her eyes remain on the table. "My, my father named me."

"Aaahhh," Rafferty says, at a complete loss. "Well, you're the only—"

"My father did," she says. "Are you really my, my, my father's friend?"

Rafferty says, "What do you think, Treasure?"

She says, "I think he'll kill you."

What he wants to do is approach her slowly and put his arms around her, but he doesn't think that's a language she's learned. "Maybe he will," he says. "Can I come in?"

"Five steps," she says. "One, two, three, four, five." She backs away a step for every one he comes forward, and then she turns and runs to the wall with the big windows in it, windows that are bordered by long, dark green velvet curtains. She pushes one of the curtains aside and then wraps the lower part of it around her waist and legs. "You can't come here," she says.

"Fine." He says, "Look," and takes three steps toward her, and as she starts to step to the side, he comes to a sudden stop. Feeling like a bad mime, he puts his hands up and pushes them, flat and open, against an imaginary pane of glass. "This is as far as I can go."

She tilts her head to one side and startles him by emitting a short, very high syllable that sounds like *Eeeeee*. She says, "Do it again, do it again."

"If you want me to." He goes back to the table and takes the same three steps, and this time he not only stops but also pulls his head back as though he's hit it on something, then rubs his forehead and mimes the pane of glass again.

Treasure is leaning forward, one arm wrapped in the curtain, and she's biting on a thumbnail. She says, her voice high and the words tumbling over one another, "And I can walk through it and you can't, you can't, but I can."

"That's right." He moves to the right, and she counters warily in the other direction, her face suddenly stiff, but then he edges left again, always moving his hands over the invisible pane of glass. "And I can't get around it either."

"Only me," she says. "Only I can go through it. Even if you're mad at me, you can't go through it."

"I'm not going to get mad at you." He goes back to the table and looks around the room. "I can't go over there where you are, but is it okay if I look at the rest of this room?"

"Yes." She passes her tongue quickly over her lips. "If, if, if, if you want to come over here, you let me, me, move first, and when I'm somewhere else I'll tell you a magic word so you can get through."

"Awwww," he says. "Tell it to me now."

"*No.* Only when I'm somewhere else."

"All right. But over here is okay?" He indicates his half of the room. "You're sure?"

"If I, if I tell you to stop—"

"I'll stop."

"Fine."

There are bookshelves, the big table, and a door that he thinks probably leads to a closet. He checks the shelves first, but it's just stuff: a lot of metal toys including an assortment of train components, a few creased paperback books with nothing hidden in them, some more old china like the junk in the sideboard, a small coin collection on cotton under glass, with a Purple Heart in the middle of it. Improbably, a snow globe. On one end of the second shelf, a small, mud-daubed bird's nest.

Rafferty traces its shape in the air, his fingers inches from it, careful not to touch it. "This is yours."

"How do you know?" She's leaning far forward, her weight borne by the velvet curtain.

"You're the only one who would have seen it."

"I saw it. In a tree. Down there, too."

He looks at the shelf below and sees a paper wasp's nest. "How did you get this? They would have stung you."

"They did. Here and here and here. And on my eye. My eye was closed for a long time. I couldn't tell how far away he, he, he—"

"I had one when I was a boy. But I waited until they were gone."

"I *wanted* it," she says.

"It's beautiful." He goes to the closet and says, "I'm going to open this door."

"My, my father will be mad."

Rafferty jumps back as though he's frightened. "Is he in here?"

He gets the *Eeeeeeee* again, and she sways back and forth in the curtain. "He's not here. If he was here, I couldn't talk to you. I can only talk to, to, to him."

"Well, here goes." He turns the knob, but the door is locked.

"You *don't* see things," she says. She sounds disappointed.

"Not like you do. Can you teach me?"

"It's secret."

"Gee," Rafferty says regretfully. "I really wanted to look inside, too."

"Are you going to say, say thank you?"

"Of course."

"Go over there. To the train."

He does as he's told. Treasure steps back toward the wall and pulls the curtain over her until she's completely hidden, except for her face. Then she puts a hand over her eyes.

She says, "I can't see you."

He scans the miniature world frantically, but there is so much detail: hundreds of little trees, all those structures, the tracks, the towns, the train stations. One small one, one a little bigger, and one—

The biggest train station. There it is, brass dulled with use, on the floor beneath the ceiling of the train station. He has to slip a single finger in to fish it out. A Gardner key, the kind usually used to open safe-deposit boxes.

He picks it up and palms it, then says, "Thank you."

Treasure hums, a disjointed melody without a key.

She continues to hum as he goes back to the closet door and raises both hands above his head. The humming stops. Mumbling something he hopes sounds magical, he rubs his hands together and then brings them to the left side of his head and pretends to pull the key out of his ear.

She has spread the fingers of the hand over her face to look at him, but she doesn't say anything, so Rafferty unlocks the door and pulls it open.

He sees a few bright tropical shirts hanging on a rod, six medium-size hard-sided leather briefcases, and two bricks of something wrapped in dark plastic. Everything is very neat, the angles precise, the edges of the briefcases, stacked on their sides with the handles facing him, plumb straight.

He pulls one of the briefcases out.

"It's money," Treasure says. "They're all money."

"Can I open one?"

She says nothing, just sways back and forth in the curtain and begins to hum again. She seems to be losing interest.

He goes down on one knee and pops the clips on the briefcase. Hundred-dollar bills, all facing the same way, gleam greenly up at him. He does a quick estimate: sixteen stacks, maybe four hundred bills to a stack, is $640,000. Six cases. Four million dollars, give or take. He removes Ming Li's camera from his pants pocket, turns off the flash, and photographs the money. Then he closes the snaps and puts the case back.

"And this?" he says, touching the plastic wrap.

"Boom," she says. "Uncle Eddie."

"Uncle Eddie," he says. "Did you see him yesterday?"

"Yes. But he, he didn't see me."

"Nobody sees you," he says, "unless you want them to." Then he closes the briefcase and puts it back in the closet. He's about to pick up one of the plastic-wrapped bricks when she speaks.

"I know where the boom is," she says.

"It's here, isn't it?"

"It's there," she says. "Too."

He looks over his shoulder at her, but she's hanging by one hand from the curtain, looking at the train table.

"He, he, he moved it," she says. "From here to there and then here again. To fool me. But I, I, I know where it is."

Rafferty gets up and goes back to the table. It's not just Southeast Asia, he realizes. It's someplace specific. Positioning himself so she can't see what he's doing, he takes the camera out again and snaps three shots of the tabletop. As he puts the camera back, he says, "It's here somewhere, isn't it?"

"A *clue*," she says accusingly. "I left you a clue. You don't see *anything*."

"You're so smart," he says. Relatively close to him and a little to his left is a stretch of track that leads through rubber plantations, paralleling a two-lane road. It goes past the train station where he found the key and then skirts a small village. On the track, about ten inches from the train station, on the opposite side from the station, is the plastic ear from his mask.

"The train will be coming toward me, right?" he says. "There will be people in the station and people on the train."

"The boom is Plan A," she says. "The fire is Plan B. Plan C is the boom *and* the—"

Her voice breaks off. He hears the curtain slide over her, and then he hears a noise from the door to the kitchen that stops the blood in his veins.

"He doesn't need to know what Plan C is," Murphy says. He pushes Ming Li in ahead of him, the revolver in his hand pointed at the center of her back. "Treasure's not usually so friendly. You're lucky she didn't sink her teeth into you." He gives Ming Li another push. "Go over to your friend."

"Brother," she says, joining Rafferty at the table. She's not wearing the mask, and her eyes are all over the room.

"Treasure," Murphy says, "come out from there. Now. You don't want me to have to come get you."

The green curtain slides aside. Treasure's face hangs down, hidden by her hair. She seems to be looking directly at her feet.

"Go to the dining room," he says. "Get the magic chair. Now."

She runs across the room and out through the door. For that

moment Murphy's eyes are on her, and Rafferty raises his hand to put it on Ming Li's shoulder, but Murphy points the gun at him and shakes his head. Ming Li has turned her own head to follow Treasure, and when she looks back to Murphy, her eyes are as hard and black as onyx.

Murphy leans against the train table. The locomotive continues its *tikka-tikka-tikka* path past his left hand, its engineer unaware of the giant in the sky. "Where are your Viet witnesses?"

"I don't know."

"We'll see about that."

"I don't know. Not any more than Bey did."

"Bey? Oh, *Bey*. Right. In Wyoming. That was her real name, wasn't it?"

"It was."

"She didn't mention more witnesses. Maybe Paul didn't ask. Do they exist?"

"Four of them. But I don't know where they are."

Murphy says, "Mmm-hmmm." He seems to be thinking about something else.

"But Bey did say that Billie Joe was in Bangkok."

"On the wrong side again," Murphy says, "working for the poor, persecuted ragheads. All I had to do was get some people on the inside to put out the word about the demonstration, and there he was. And there you were, too."

"By accident."

"Looks like it. He told you Eckersley's name. Why didn't you just say so? I probably would have watched you for a little bit and then let you go."

"I didn't remember it."

"Doesn't matter now. Doesn't much matter about the witnesses either. According to Shen, you've fucked me good and proper." His eyes go to the open closet, and he shakes his head again. "Everything. This little shit just told you everything, didn't she? My little Treasure."

"If you hadn't walked in," Rafferty says, "I'd have taken her with me."

"That would have been good. She's a problem, she is." He looks toward the door that Treasure disappeared through. "So you found *survivors* of the *massacre*. Talked to the newspapers, the Vietnamese, the Americans. A trifecta. Guaranteed to give the pussy patrol the squits. Same as they get every time we're in a fucking war."

"Is that what this is?" Rafferty says "A war? I thought it was a license for you to fuck people up."

"You don't care that people are getting blown up down south," Murphy says. The cords at the side of his neck are beginning to stand out. "You don't care that they throw bombs into the market-places and the elementary schools and cut the heads off monks. You don't give a shit that the most powerful country of the twenty-first century can't figure out how to protect itself from a few illiter-ates who are still stuck in the ninth, still trying to get even for the fucking Crusades." He walks across the room, stiff-jointed with anger, until he has his back to the curtain that Treasure had wrapped herself in. "Just like you didn't care, or you wouldn't have if you'd been old enough, that nobody knew who the enemy was in Vietnam, that a sweet-looking old granny-san could roll a gre-nade at you without even saying hello."

Treasure comes slowly into the room dragging one of the spin-dly chairs that had been drawn up to the dining-room table, and Murphy points to her to bring it to him.

"No," he says, "what *you* need is a Nazi army, all in a uniform that says 'bad guy' from half a mile away, with blood on their teeth and dueling scars. Waste *those* people, you'd sit in front of your TV and applaud. Wave your flag and get all teary-eyed. But women? Children? Some twelve-year-old Muhammad with a suicide vest in his closet? *Ohhhhh, nooooooooo, Mr. Bill*," he says in a falsetto. "The weepy wailers come out in the papers and on TV, and when the weepy wailers come out, the pussy patrol gets the squits, and you know what happens then?"

Ming Li says, "Pussy patrol is a nice phrase." She sounds calm, but her eyes haven't left Murphy's.

"What happens then," Murphy says, and his face is suddenly scarlet, "what happens then is that we *lose the fucking war*." He's spitting at them as he talks. With his free hand, he snatches the chair from Treasure, who leaps backward and stands at an unconscious approximation of attention, with her feet together and her arms straight down, tight at her sides. Murphy turns the chair around and sets it in front of himself, leaning on its back. "Because here's the chain of command," he says, "here's how it works. A bunch of guys, and these days maybe a woman, in two-thousand-dollar suits and a uniform or two, sit around a polished table in some air-conditioned room so they won't have to get too warm or too cold and say things like 'measured response' and 'surges' and 'tactical support' and 'appropriate force,' and that's at one end of the chain, okay?" He holds his hands up, about two feet apart, the revolver pointed at the ceiling, and he moves them, still separated by a couple of feet, left to right in jerky increments, as if measuring something. "And at the *other* end of the chain is some poor asshole on his back in the dirt, swelling up in the sun, with his intestines tied around his neck. So, you know, all well and good, *that* guy's not going to cut off another head, and his friends will probably think twice about it, too, but then somebody takes a picture, and it gets into the papers, and the weepy wailers start up, and those people who were sitting around that table and sending down the orders in their nice, polite language turn into the pussy patrol, waving their hands and saying, 'Not us, no, no, not us, we never called for such a thing, we would never condone the indiscriminate use of lethal force against a civilian population.' And right then and there, they *lose the war*, no matter how many Americans have been shot to death and blown up trying to win it, and lost their arms and legs and dicks—do you know that castration from improvised explosive devices is one of the most common injuries in Iraq?—because these people in their suits and their fucking air-conditioning still haven't figured out that there's no such thing as civilians anymore."

"Let us walk out of here," Rafferty says. His mouth is so dry he can hear his lips sliding over his teeth, and his voice sounds thin in his ears. "You've got your money. You know how to disappear. You've done it before."

"Not that easy," Murphy says. "Not anywhere near that easy. I'm going to disappear, but you, you're a loose end." He sits in the chair, the gun loosely pointed at them. "Treasure."

Treasure doesn't move.

"Treasure," Murphy says again.

The child begins to sway back and forth, her head still down. She leans so far forward that Rafferty steps toward her to break her fall, but Murphy raises the gun so it's aimed at Rafferty's chest. Treasure slowly lifts her head until she's looking at her father.

"You two," Murphy says. "Pull up your shirts."

Rafferty does, followed by Ming Lee. Murphy's eyes drop to the gun at Rafferty's waist and then go to Ming Li, and he says, "Girl. Turn around." When her back is to him and the gun is visible at the small of her back, Murphy says, "Stop turning."

He leans back in the chair, and it creaks. "Both of you. Hands on your head, fingers interlaced, and don't neither of you move. Treasure. You get those guns."

"'Don't neither of you,'" Ming Li says, and Rafferty hears her swallow. "I learned English in China, and I speak it better than you do."

"You're prettier than I am, too, but that's not going to help you. Do it, Treasure. And bring them here."

The child remains still.

"Treasure," Murphy says. "Come here."

The girl remains where she is, and Rafferty sees her hands curl into fists.

"She's showing off for company," Murphy says. "If you're not standing in front of me by the count of three, you know what's going to happen. One . . . two . . . "

"Leave her alone," Rafferty says.

"Three," Murphy says, and by the time he's finished the word, she's standing in front of him. He lifts his free hand and slaps her face. Her head whips to one side and back, but her feet don't move. Rafferty involuntarily starts forward, but Murphy's gun returns to him. "Never get between a parent and a child. You just make things worse. Treasure has broken some big rules, and she knows it. *Treasure*," he says, a little more loudly, and she raises her head halfway, so she seems to be looking at his knees. "Go get the guns and bring them to me."

She turns, moving disjointedly toward Rafferty, her head still down as though she's presenting her bare neck to the blade, her feet sliding over the carpet and her back stiff. She pulls the gun from under his belt without so much as a glance at him, and then she goes to Ming Li and takes hers.

Ming Li says, "Poor baby."

"On the windowsill," Murphy says.

The child looks up at Rafferty, and he gives her a tiny nod: *Do as you're told.* The guns look enormous in her hands. She does that slow, sliding walk, never lifting her feet from the carpet, until she's at the window. Murphy turns his head slightly to keep her in sight, warily, Rafferty thinks. "Up there," he says. "Put them right there, on the sill. Now come here." When she's reached him, he puts his free arm around her as she squeezes her eyes shut, and he lifts her to his knee.

"We're going to do a little show for our guests," Murphy says. "Do you want to, Treasure?" He puts his hand on the back of her neck and squeezes the muscle, and when her mouth opens, he answers in an uncanny imitation of her voice, "Yes." He relaxes his pressure, and her mouth closes. He squeezes again, one time for each syllable, and the child's mouth seems to say, "Yes, Daddy, please." Her eyes are wide now, white showing all the way around her irises. Her gaze goes to Rafferty and bounces away with something like shame, looking everywhere in the room.

"What do I say to people when Daddy's not here?" Murphy says, and Treasure's mouth opens and closes again as that high, breathless voice says, "Nothing."

Ming Li says, "That's enough, you sick fuck. Just shoot us."

There's a movement at the edge of Rafferty's vision, and he turns to the door to see the small woman from the bedroom, wearing a T-shirt and shorts, the clothes she'd undoubtedly worn in her village, holding a glass of cherry-colored whiskey, and she shrills, "*Baby!*" and throws the glass at Murphy.

It hits him on the left shoulder and splashes on him as Treasure leaps from his lap, and he jumps up, swearing, but Neeni retreats down the hall, saying, "My baby, my baby," and Treasure grabs the chair he was sitting in by its legs and runs at the train table, swinging the chair over her head and bringing it down on the miniature world, and tiny trees and bits of buildings fly into the air. She lifts it again, emitting a high, thin, ceiling-scraping scream, and slams it into the train table again, and this time pieces fly several feet in the air.

Ming Li takes two quick steps toward the windowsill with the guns on it, but Murphy says, "Don't," and comes toward the ruined miniatures as Treasure, still screaming, raises the chair again. When Murphy's eyes go to the movement, Rafferty grabs the engine of the train and yanks it off the tracks. The last two or three cars break off and tumble free, but the rest of them remain attached, and when he swings it around, what hits Murphy across the face is the sharp-cornered end of a twenty-pound metal whip.

It rips skin from his forehead and snaps his head back and sends him crashing against the table, his gun arm hanging down, his elbow against the edge of the table, and Rafferty raises his right foot and puts all his weight into forcing his shoe straight through the wrist of Murphy's gun hand. Hears the change in the intensity of Murphy's scream and the muffled sound of the elbow snapping backward. The gun falls from Murphy's hand.

Treasure drops the chair and leans forward at the waist, fists clenched, screaming, "Do it again, do it again, do it again!" and Murphy pushes himself away from the table, his face a mass of blood and torn skin, and lurches toward the guns on the windowsill. But Ming Li is already there, and she fires twice at Murphy's midsection, and he folds in half with a long shudder of a groan and goes down.

Coming up with the gun Murphy dropped, Rafferty hears nothing but the echo of the shots and then, from the hall, a rapidly repeated prayer in Lao.

Murphy moans and rolls over.

Ming Li steps back, out of his reach, with her gun aimed at his forehead. Her face is pale, but her hand is steady.

"Always had trouble . . ." Murphy says. He grabs a breath and says, " . . . shooting the pretty ones."

Her voice shaking, Ming Li says, "You didn't even get close, fat man."

Murphy is losing a lot of blood, the stain spreading rapidly outward over the carpet. To Poke, Ming Li says, "What should we do?"

"We're going to let him die," Rafferty says. "And then I'm going to figure out how to deal with this." He takes a quick step toward her, puts his arms around her, and squeezes. To the side of his neck, Ming Li says, "Might be a good idea to start that now. Figuring out how to deal with this, I mean."

He pushes her to arm's length and looks at her, but she won't meet his eyes. "Are you okay?"

"I'll be better when I'm moving."

Murphy makes a noise that might be a cough, and Ming Li steps back, slipping out of Rafferty's grasp, and points the gun at Murphy's midsection.

Rafferty says, "Here you go, then. Get Neeni—that's the woman who threw the glass—and take her out to the car. Carry her, if you have to. The maid, whatever her name is, can take care of her."

"Where will she be?"

"In her room, I think, probably in bed. Straight down the hall, the door to the left. Grab some clothes for her. I don't think she'll be coming back."

"And?"

"And then come back in here and get three or four of the briefcases in that closet. Take them to the car. They're full of money."

"What about you?"

"I'm going to find Treasure."

He watches Ming Li go, moving quickly but not hurriedly, and thinks, *Frank taught her well*. His heart is hammering in his temples, and he thinks his knees might go out. So he kneels down beside Murphy and studies him. The man's breathing is shallow and irregular, and his eyes seem to be watching something projected on the ceiling. His face is white as paper, making the hair on his head and the tufts coming out of his nostrils seem a brighter orange, almost clownish. The smell of blood rises from the carpet around him. Rafferty is slightly surprised to find that he feels no pity for the man. When he stands up, he nudges Murphy's side with his toe. He gets no reaction.

He leaves the room through the door to the kitchen and sees the double doors at the back of the dining room standing wide, with rain slanting in to puddle on the floor, and he realizes he's lost track of time. It could have been a minute since Treasure ran out of the train room, or it could have been five.

He does a quick check of at the living room—unoccupied—and decides she's outside. From what he can see, she more or less lives outside. He takes the distance to the back door at a trot, then slows and steps through it into the night.

There's rain, but it's not heavy enough to impair visibility. The yards is as wide as the house, though not particularly deep, backing up fifteen or twenty feet to a white plaster wall that's got some kind of dense hedge growing in front of it, four or five feet thick. The foliage looks black, although it's probably dark green. Three trees spread their branches to create a sort of canopy over most of the ground.

The water back here is at least four inches deep. He starts by jogging to his left, his shoulder only a few inches from the wall of the house, slowing when he comes to the living-room windows, which permit a long rectangle of pale light to reflect on the standing water and shine off the trunk of the nearest tree. The hedge *is* a dark green, shiny-leafed, thorny-looking, and dense. At the end of the house there's a wall that runs straight back to create a corner with the hedged wall at the rear, so unless she's gone over the wall, this isn't where she came. He doesn't see a way over the wall.

Up, he thinks, and he slogs through the water to the nearest tree, but the trunk is smooth, the bark almost slick to the touch. He checks the branches anyway. No platform, no tree house, no fort. Squinting against the rain, he surveys the other two trees, but no straight lines, no paler shapes, reveal a structure in either of them.

He feels time passing. His anxiety level, the terror he deferred while Murphy had his gun on them, has been rising for the past minute or two, and he wills it down, breathing against the tightness in his chest and working his way back along the edge of the house. The wall here is vertical iron bars, and he can see the light from Murphy's train room shining in the water. Impossible for Treasure to have slipped between the bars.

Water-covered lawn, three trees, hedge. No Treasure. No place *for* Treasure. He realizes he's been expecting a structure of some kind, a place she can shut others out of. Someplace where she can be whatever she really is, when her father's not nearby.

But it's not here.

So it has to be in the hedge.

He splashes across the yard to the bushes and bends down; she's much shorter than he is. About halfway across the yard, almost straight back from the dining-room doors, he spots it: an opening in the bushes, perhaps three feet high. In front of it, he drops to his knees in the water and sees that it's a tunnel, neatly clipped into the foliage. It's very dark, but it seems to go in a couple of feet and then curve right.

Putting one hand on the lawn below the water, he reaches in and waves his other hand around, hoping to avoid coming face-to-belly with one of the extravagant spiders of the tropics. He's never lost the fear of spiders that made Frank call him a sissy thirty or so years ago, and he performs this check instinctively even though he's certain she's just crawled through here and there won't be any webs. *There won't be any webs*, he says to himself, and he crawls in.

Eighteen or twenty inches in, the tunnel turns sharply to the right. Following it, scraping his back and shoulders on the sheared-off twigs, he puts his hand on something hard, and his fingers turn into a bright orange, barbed-wire jolt of pain. When he yanks his hand up, it brings weight with it. It's clamped into a mousetrap. He pries the trap off and drops it, then crawls farther in, sweeping the dirt from side to side and finding four more traps, which he pushes out of his way. Suddenly he feels the space expand and rise above him. He stops and looks straight down at the black water, willing his pupils to open wider. He hears the rain pattering on something, but he's not being rained on.

He puts a hand up and finds smooth, heavy plastic, feeling the sticks and leaves of the hedge on the other side. He tries not to focus on anything, knowing that the peripheral vision is more sensitive, and out of the darkness a shape emerges, a bit farther in and to his right, rectangular and relatively light-colored. It's wood, his fingers tell him, finished wood with a smooth surface, and he finds the top and immediately knocks something over, small, light, and slick to the touch, and he knows what it is.

A plastic disposable lighter.

He's certain he's alone in here, but he doesn't know how far back the hollow goes. He picks up the lighter and flicks the wheel. And feels the blood leave his face.

Treasure has used pieces of plywood to create irregular walls, not so much walls as a gallery space. Color pictures from books and magazines cover every inch, overlapping here and there. There must be a hundred of them.

Ballerinas. Princesses. Girls in frilly, pale dresses. Girls holding hands with other girls, laughing with other girls. Girls at parties, giving one another presents. One wall is devoted entirely to a single large picture, twenty or thirty copies of it: a young girl in a loose white dress, her hair alive with sunlight, walking a dappled path in green, hospitable woods. The picture has been trimmed to the girl's left side, and the forest on the right has been left uncropped and the pictures placed seamlessly beside each other so she perpetually emerges from the green of the forest to the safety of her path. Again and again and again. A girl, floating through a world of green light. On a path.

Rafferty wipes his eyes fiercely and wishes Murphy could die twice.

On top of the table are rounded stones and dried thistles and another mud-smoothed bird's nest. A loose handful of wild grass splays gracefully from the top of what Rafferty recognizes as a cough-medicine bottle. Another medicine bottle holds a single, half-burned candle.

He takes a last look around, replaces the lighter on the table, and crawls out again, back into Treasure's other world.

33

Spirit House

AS HE STANDS up, his eyes go to it immediately, the brightest thing in his field of sight. It's a small window, high up, and it's lit, and the light flickers and then intensifies, and he realizes two things simultaneously: that it's the window in Treasure's bathroom and that it's on fire.

He starts to run, splashing toward the doors that lead into the dining room, but he slows at the sight of a small cabinet, about three feet high and four feet wide, built against the rear of the house. It's rough plywood, and its door lolls open. There, stacked neatly, are six one-gallon gasoline cans.

There is room for three more.

His feet nearly slip out from under him on the wet dining-room floor, and he sees that the living room carpet is on fire, flames inching up the sides of the couches. There's a foot of gray smoke trapped beneath the ceiling, and the smell of splashed gasoline is overpowering.

Almost thick enough, he thinks, to trigger an explosion. He goes farther in, to the stairs, to see how advanced the fire is.

The carpeting on the stairway is burning, too, but it's been burning longer than the living room and the flames are five and six feet high, licking at the banister and being drawn upward by the ravenous inhalation of the fire that's already raging upstairs.

He envisions it all in a second: beginning in her own bathroom and bedroom, pouring the gasoline on cloth and wood, tossing a match and running, spewing gasoline behind her, the flames following obediently along on the wet trail, the gasoline splashing from the can until the can is empty—there's an empty can at the entrance to the hallway that leads to Neeni's room—and grabbing another can and then another.

The L-shaped hallway is on fire, its carpet saturated. Neeni's room is dark and cool-looking beyond the flames. It's been spared.

He wipes his stinging eyes and coughs out a lungful of smoke, and then he knows where she is, if she's still in the house. He wheels around and runs back over the tile of the entry area and the bare wood of the dining room and the tiled kitchen floors and into the train room.

The train table is engulfed in flame. Murphy is still on his back below the window, below the green drapes that Treasure had hoped would protect her. The carpet near the hallway that leads from Neeni's room is blooming ripples of blue flame, not yet hot enough to turn yellow. Treasure, her back to him, backs away from the open, wet closet, drops the gasoline can, and pitches into the closet a chunk of bright metal—a heavy military-style Zippo, its little wick emitting a bright yellow light.

He shouts "NO!" and rushes at Treasure from behind, getting his arms around her waist as she turns and fights him with pure animal rage, tearing at his hair and clawing for his eyes and kicking at his chest and stomach, and he throws her over his shoulder, her head hanging down behind him, and runs for his life.

As he clears the kitchen, Ming Li runs in through the front door to meet him, and he waves her out and charges ahead, practically banging into Murphy's car, pulled up to the front porch, not stopping until he's halfway across the front yard, and he shouts to Ming Li to give him one of the briefcases. She pulls one out of the trunk of the Toyota, and he snatches it with his free hand, the story he will eventually tell taking shape in his mind. He tightens his hold on the kicking, screaming Treasure and runs back to Murphy's car, pulls the driver's door open, and tosses the briefcase into the backseat. Then he yanks the remote for the gate from the sun visor above the steering wheel. Moving away from the car, he's almost pulled off his feet by Treasure, who's clamped her fingers over the window of the open car door. He pries her loose, pushes the button to open the gate, and calls to Ming Li, "Start the car!"

Backing away as fast as he can from the flaming house, he hears breaking glass, and Treasure suddenly goes so limp he thinks she might have passed out. He bounces on the balls of his feet once or twice to jostle her and says, "Treasure? Treasure?" but she's dead weight.

He backs farther away, curling his other arm around her and taking her off his shoulder so he can look down at her face. Cradled in his arms, her fists clenched together at the center of her chest, she's looking at the right side of the house, her mouth half open and her eyes as luminous as those of a nocturnal animal.

And her mouth closes, and she begins to hum again, that same broken, disjointed "Mmmmmm mmmmm mmmmmm," tracing a melody as random as someone throwing stones at a keyboard. He looks away from her to follow her gaze, and something whines past him, and he hears the shot.

Bent half over, but holding the arm with the gun in it raised high, Murphy lumbers around the side of the house, firing twice more as he comes, but Rafferty can't hear the shots over the scream that's coming from Treasure, who shrills a single, glass-shattering note and somehow jerks herself upright, a convulsion seemingly involving every muscle in her body, and slips through Rafferty's arms, running for the wall behind him. She stops a few feet from it, staring at the barrier, and her arms go straight into the air, fingers spread wide. Then she wheels around and splashes toward the still-opening gate.

Murphy fires again, but Rafferty is barely paying attention. At the edge of the driveway, Treasure stops, shoulders heaving, looking out at the world beyond the walls. Rafferty hears a ragged, almost-imploring shout from Murphy, and Treasure stiffens, turns, and emits that piercing unbroken scream again, and as she runs, it trails away behind her like a wake. At the last moment, Rafferty sees where she's going and starts to follow, but Ming Li is suddenly there, with a foot hooked behind his, bringing him down into the mud. He watches, up on his elbows in the water, as Treasure runs directly toward the front door and through it, into the burning house.

Murphy stops his agonized shuffle, his mouth wide, the gun hand dangling down, and then he bellows *"Treasure!"* and breaks into a run. Seconds later he's a dark silhouette against the flames in the hallway, and then Rafferty, up on his feet, feels a drop in air pressure as though the planet has taken a breath, and the flames increase in brilliance for a blink's worth of time, and the house shudders and blows, sending pieces of burning wood and broken glass twenty and thirty feet into the air, deafening Rafferty and stunning him motionless as bits of fire arc lazily down through the limbs of the trees, and he sees the entire structure reflected upside down, the spirit house of the water gods afire on the surface of a lake.

34

No Wonder You've Been Sleeping in Hotels

FOR THE FIRST few miles, Neeni's sobs supply the soundtrack. Every now and then, she says, "Baby baby baby baby." She never says, *Treasure*.

Then the crying softens and gradually dies away, and Rafferty looks in his rearview mirror to see her lying on the backseat, her knees drawn up and her head in the maid's—Hwa's—lap. Hwa's eyes are on his in the mirror.

Ming Li is sitting as close as she can get to the passenger door, hugging her knees. Her eyes are partly closed, and she seems to be memorizing the dashboard.

The rain has let up again, but water is inches deep in the streets, masking the potholes, and he has to go slowly to avoid mishap. He doesn't think he could endure a mechanical breakdown right now; he has an image of himself disappearing screaming into the night, leaving all of them behind.

A tiny snore comes from the backseat. He looks in the mirror again and meets Hwa's eyes.

"You like her," he says. "At least you said you did."

"She's never hurt anybody."

"She's in for a rough time. Do you want to help her?"

No answer. Hwa turns and looks out the window. She says, "Help how?"

"Say yes and I'll give you two thousand U.S. tonight, when we get where we're going. Just for agreeing to try."

"Help how?" Hwa says again.

"She needs to get over this, and she needs to get well. Tomorrow I'll give you six thousand dollars, and you go out and find a nice two-bedroom apartment in the Silom area and rent it. Furnished, so you don't have to waste a day shopping for furniture."

"I like shopping for furniture."

"Then you can look for it after you move in, replace things if you want, but you need to find something you can move into right away, because I don't have room for you, and I think she needs to be someplace that will eventually feel like home. I'll pay the rent and expenses and give you two thousand U.S. every month. And I'll get you a doctor, a good doctor who's a friend of mine, to help with her. She needs to get off the codeine. I'll keep this up as long as he says she's making progress and as long as I think she's being taken care of. And the day the doctor tells me Neeni is over it, that she can live without it, I'll give you fifty thousand dollars."

Hwa strokes Neeni's hair. Without looking up, she says, "You must be rich."

"I've come into some money," Rafferty says.

"Fifty thousand is a lot," Hwa says. "Why don't we see what happens first?"

"You'll do it?"

"Why not?" Hwa says. "Poor thing. He took everything away from her. He took her out of her village, he took her away from her family, he took her daughter. Yes, I'll help her."

Rafferty says, "Thank you."

For a few slow, waterlogged miles, he drives to the sound of Neeni's snoring. He says, "She's going to want a drink when she wakes up."

"She's going to want a drink every moment of the day for months," Hwa says.

Rafferty makes the turn onto Silom, feeling the nearness of the apartment ease the tightness in his chest. To Ming Li he says, "What is it? What are you thinking about?"

"Vladimir," she says.

Some of the strain immediately comes back. "Yeah. Me, too."

"At first I thought he was just waiting for a chance to sell you out, but then he . . . he changed somehow, and I thought, well, maybe I was wrong."

"He likes you," Rafferty says. "He's got an eye for talent. And it doesn't hurt that you're beautiful."

"Whatever it was. I thought he was with us. But somebody told Murphy we were at his house, and I don't know who else—"

"Oh," Hwa says. "That was me. I did it."

Ming Li turns to her. "How?"

"I was worried about Neeni," she says. "I didn't know what you really wanted."

"The phone button," Rafferty says.

"And I lied about it. " Hwa looks again at Rafferty in the rear-view mirror. "I'm sorry."

"No problem," he says. "Keep taking care of her that well and everything will be fine."

MING LI PUSHES past him and stops, surveying the room. "God. No wonder you've been sleeping in hotels."

"Oh, no," Rafferty says, exhausted at the sight of the place. "I'd forgotten how bad it was. At least it doesn't still stink of paint." Feeling like he weighs a thousand pounds, he steps aside and lets Hwa in, leading a blinking, confused-looking Neeni by the hand. "Take her to the couch," he says. His voice sounds ragged, and his throat is raw. "It's the one thing you can get to. Beer?" he says to Ming Li without thinking, and then says, "Of course not."

"Of course yes," she says. "I've got it coming, after tonight."

"As long as we're breaking rules," Rafferty says to Hwa, "do you think a drink would help her? We've got some Crown Royal some-one gave us a few years ago, but I don't think it spoils. And would you like something?"

"Bring her the whiskey, a good big glass of it. When she' s lying down—Is there a bed somewhere?"

"There will be in a minute."

Neeni's eyes have come up at the mention of the word "whis-key," and she's looking from Rafferty to Hwa and back again.

"When she's lying down," Hwa says, "I'll make some tea."

"Fine." He looks around the familiar space, and all he wants to do is curl up and sleep. You want to help me, Ming Li?"

In the kitchen he pulls out his last two big bottles of Singha as Ming Li takes a drinking glass from the cupboard. She stands there, looking at the other cupboards, which are closed. "Whiskey?"

"To the left. Behind some cans of stuff, in a blue sort-of-velvet bag." He opens the drawer, takes out the bottle opener, flips it into the air, closes his eyes, and puts out his hand. The moment his eyes close, the floor dips beneath him, and as he opens them, the bottle opener lands with a flat, reassuring smack, dead center in his palm. To Ming Li, who is staring at him with one eyebrow raised, he says, "My luck is back."

Twenty minutes later Neeni and Hwa are set up in Poke and Rose's room, and he and Ming Li, whose face is turning stop-sign red from the beer, have put new sheets on Miaow's bed and moved things around to create a path to the door. "Bathroom's on the left," he says as she follows him into the living room. He hears Hwa clanking the teapot in the kitchen and takes a quick peek into his bedroom, where Neeni is sitting on the far side of the bed, her back to the door, drinking.

"I'm not going to sleep in Miaow's room," Ming Li says. "You are."

"Wrong. I'm sleeping here."

She gives the couch a disapproving look and drains the rest of her beer. "It looks too short."

"I've slept on it before."

Ming Li yawns enormously. "It's not too short for me."

Hwa comes out of the kitchen with the mug Rose always uses, steaming away like a witch's kettle. She says, "Do you have some socks I could wear?"

"Second drawer of that . . . that thing in there." He waves his hand at the bedroom. "The dresser."

"I like to sleep in socks," Hwa announces, and goes into Poke and Rose's room, shutting the door behind her.

Rafferty collapses onto the couch and folds himself forward like someone fighting a faint. The events of the past hour or so, which he's been holding at bay with action, swirl in his head, a jumble of color and noise and blood and eyes: Treasure's eyes, Ming Li's eyes as she stared at Murphy. He breathes slowly and regularly, staring at the carpet, and lets the feelings catch up with him. A noise brings him back into the room. Ming Li is looking down at him.

"You okay?"

"Getting there," he says. "That awful leather bag. Can you bring it to me?"

She picks it up beside the door, where Rafferty dropped it, and hands it to him. He pulls out cell phone after cell phone until he has his old one, the one he used before everything began. Holding it again, back in his own apartment, he begins to believe that it might actually all be over.

As he dials, Ming Li says,

"Older brother, not to doubt your judgment, but is it safe here?"

"We'll know in a second. Okay, shhh." He looks up at her, scoots over to make room on the couch, and then says, into the phone, "I need to talk to Shen. Tell him it's Rafferty."

Ming Li says, *"Shen?"*

"Now or never," he says to her. He waits a moment, until he hears, "Hello."

He closes his eyes, grabs a deep breath, and says, "I wanted to tell you I'm at home, and I'd appreciate your letting me stay here. And there are reasons you should."

Shen says nothing.

"Murphy is dead. Do you want to hear about it?"

"It's eleven-thirty at night. You've had people wake me up. What else do I have to do?"

"He pulled me out of that mall, the one you didn't see me in, and cuffed me and took me to his house. He was pretty crazy, talking about how I had screwed him over and that the best thing for him to do would be to disappear. His daughter was in the house—" Rafferty stops for a second and clears his throat. "She was having some sort of breakdown."

"That poor child," Shen says.

"He took a briefcase full of money out of a closet and put it in his car, I guess. Anyway, out through the front door. Then he poured gasoline all over the place and set fire to it, then hauled the girl and the maid and that sedated wife of his out. I got my hands free—"

"How?"

"An ancient yoga technique that took me years to learn," he snaps. "Do you want me to explain it to you?"

The couch shifts. He opens his eyes to see Ming Li getting up, shaking her head, and going into the kitchen.

"No."

"And I broke the side window. There were two guns on the windowsill. I took one and went through the window, and when I came around the house, he shot at me. I shot him, maybe twice, and then the little girl screamed and ran into the house, and he followed her, even though I think he was hit pretty bad. And I backed the hell away, and the place blew up."

Shen lets a moment or two pass. "That's quite a story."

Rafferty hears the refrigerator open and close.

"I know. I'd barely believe it myself, except that the witnesses— the maid and the wife—saw it the same way."

"Did they." It's not a question.

"They did, and that leads me to my second point. I know you've been told about the things I did regarding Murphy during the past week or so, because I intentionally said them to someone who would tell you. They're all true. The U.S. embassy will abandon him in a heartbeat, deny any connection at all. But I didn't tell your friend everything. For example, I didn't tell her that there are four living witnesses to the worst thing he did there during the war, a rampage that killed nobody except women, children, and old men. Those survivors will be available to the papers, if it comes to that. When Murphy added all that up, he said that the best thing for him to do would be to disappear. What I think he meant by that was—"

"I know what he meant by it."

There's a clinking of glass on glass in the kitchen.

"So here he is, disappeared, in a sense. And I have a present for you. I'm e-mailing you some photographs. The first three are snapshots from Murphy's War, his time in Vietnam. No one who ever helped him would want them to appear in a newspaper."

"Is he recognizable?"

"Some people don't change. Second, if you saw Treasure, if you were at his house, you saw his train set."

"I did."

"Well, this may surprise you, but the train layout was a model of a real place, somewhere in Yala. If you take the pictures I'm sending you and get someone to look at them and compare them with Google Earth pictures of Yala, down where the rubber plantations are, I'm sure you'll find it. In the picture you'll see a pink thing, the ear from a rubber mask. Where that ear is, a little bit north of a train station, there either is or isn't going to be a cache of explosives, if it hasn't been blown before your men get there. If it hasn't, if you get there first, you'll be a hero."

Shen sighs. "The ear from a rubber mask."

"It's a long story."

"When I get to the house, will the physical evidence support your version of events?"

Ming Li comes in with a glass in her hand that's got a couple inches of whiskey in it.

Rafferty says, "I don't know what'll still be standing. But I think you'll be able to see the broken window in the train room, and the gun should be on the windowsill, and the place will reek of gasoline. Oh, and there will be money in his car, so you might want to get someone out there before the fire crew goes through it. And also, I don't know if there'll be anything left of it, but there was a cabinet built against the back of the house, full of cans of gasoline, so I guess he had this possibility in mind for a while."

"It's a somewhat drastic measure, don't you think?"

"He was a drastic guy. So yes, the evidence will be a good enough match, I think, especially compared to the alternative, which would be opening up the whole thing with Murphy through the newspapers and probably raking up what happened in Vietnam, complete with pictures, and the Vietnamese government getting involved, and the U.S. disclaiming a connection with him, and—"

"Yes, yes. The little girl," Shen says. "You say she died in the fire?"

"She ran in before the house blew up. She didn't come out."

Shen says, "Probably for the best."

It stops Rafferty for a second. What he hears in Shen's voice might be genuine sympathy. He has to force himself back on track. "Maybe so," he says. "My guess is that you'll find a rifle in the place that matches the bullets in Billie Joe Sellers."

"We might."

Ming Li tilts the glass of whiskey and drinks. Rafferty makes a grab for it, but she snatches it out of his reach.

"So," he continues, "I guess the headline tomorrow or the next day would be along the lines of 'AMERICAN BUSINESSMAN DIES IN FIRE,' something like that. Leaving me out of it, since including me would open up all these cans of worms. Maybe 'ARSON SUSPECTED.'"

"I can practically see it now."

"And then, a day later, a story about the heroic action of your unit, discovering the explosives in Yala, preventing a massive loss of life and—"

"I could write it myself," Shen says.

"And finally a modest little squib somewhere about a correction in the ballistics in the death of Billie Joe Sellers and an exoneration of anyone previously considered a person of interest. No names, so as not to drag anyone through the dirt again. Maybe a courtesy call to the American embassy just to say you've cleared it up and I'm not on anyone's list."

Shen says, "And of course the rifle is in plain sight."

"I don't know," Rafferty says, his energy suddenly abandoning him. "I can't tell one rifle from another. But I'm sure you'll be able to put your hands on it." Ming Li plops down on other end of the couch and drinks again. "You know, it's a pleasure to be able to rattle on like this without having resort to my terrible Thai. You were right—we really are just a couple of California boys."

Shen says, "Go to sleep," and hangs up.

Rafferty lowers the phone to his lap, shakes his head to uncramp his neck, and says to Ming Li, "Give me that."

"You don't run *everything*, older brother," Ming Li says. Her voice is as thin as a scratch on glass. "I'm going to pour part of the bottle into another glass and leave it there for Hwa in case Neeni needs it, and I'm taking the bottle with me, into that room down the hall where I can lock the door and drink until I'm finished drinking." She's blinking fast, and there are tears in her eyes. "And I don't want to hear from you about it, and if I'm hungover tomorrow, I want you to baby me without one word about how it's my own fault."

Rafferty says, "Can I get some and drink it with you? I won't take too much."

"Fine." She swipes her arm over her face. "But we're not talking, not about anything, not tonight and maybe not ever. We're going to drink and keep our mouths shut."

Rafferty gets up and brushes her shoulder with his hand, so lightly he's not certain they actually touched. "That sounds great," he says.

35

Köszi

BY TEN-THIRTY THE next morning, Rafferty has seen Vladimir and given him an envelope with fifteen thousand of Murphy's dollars in it, and Vladimir has told him about Janos's death.

"He had wife," Vladimir said.

"I'd like to give her something."

"I will give her," Vladimir said, extending a hand.

"Don't take this wrong, Vladimir," Rafferty said, "but I'd rather hand it to her personally. That way I can tell her how sorry I am."

"Two hours," Vladimir said, pocketing his envelope. "Philadelphia place. Good hamburger, yes?"

So around eleven, when Rafferty returns to the apartment, he finds Hwa and Neeni sitting in the living room wondering about food and the door to Miaow's room still locked. He runs down to Silom and grabs noodles and pork from the best of the street vendors. Once they're eating, he pulls his desk out of the pile of furniture and takes a clean envelope from the drawer, wondering briefly what had happened to the box Ming Li had bought. On the way out, he says to Hwa, "Go look at apartments," and goes down to flag a taxi.

At twelve-thirty on the dot, Vladimir comes into the Philadelphia Hamburger Pub towing a plump little woman of indeterminate age and national origin, although Rafferty guesses it's somewhere in the Balkans. She wears a sensible old-lady dress, navy with tiny white dots, in a style that hasn't been sold in America in decades. She doesn't seem particularly heartbroken, but perhaps, he thinks, her culture finds displays of emotion vulgar.

"Is Mrs. Janos," Vladimir says, sliding into the booth. To her, he says, "Here is real Philadelphia hamburger."

Mrs. Janos says something like "Ach."

"Not too much English," Vladimir said. "They—she and Janos—they spoke Hungarian." He waves theatrically for the waitress.

"I'm very sorry about your husband," Rafferty says to Mrs. Janos. "He was—" He stops, having launched himself on a verbal journey with no destination. What *had* Janos been? "He was good company," he says. "And good at his job."

Mrs. Janos looks at Vladimir, who nods. She says to Rafferty, "*Köszi.*"

Vladimir says, "Is thank you. In Hungarian."

"I guessed that," Rafferty says. The entire situation seems almost ostentatiously bogus. "How long," he says, pronouncing the words slowly and carefully and feeling like someone on his first trip abroad, "were you two together?"

Mrs. Janos shakes her head sharply and says something that's mostly consonants and resentment.

"She shakes head for yes," Vladimir says. "Where she comes from, shake head is yes, nod is no." Mrs. Janos shakes her head again, and Vladimir says, "You see? She agree wery much."

"Well, I am sorry about him. I didn't know him that well." He's talking directly to her, 90 percent certain that he's being swindled, but what's the alternative? Even if it's only 10 percent likely that the woman is who Vladimir said she is, he should do this.

Anyway, it's Murphy's money.

"I know that money can't replace someone you love," he says, taking a very fat envelope from his pocket, "but I hope this . . . um . . . this gesture will make things easier for you."

Mrs. Janos is looking at the envelope. So is Vladimir. Rafferty hands it to her and gets up, saying to Vladimir, "It's thirty thousand dollars." He reaches into his pocket and pulls out a twenty, which he drops on the table. "For the burgers." To Mrs. Janos he says, "Good-bye, and I really am sorry."

She startles him by taking his hand in both of hers and bowing until her cheek is touching the back of his hand and saying, "*Köszi, köszi, köszi.*"

Rafferty looks over at Vladimir, whose big cleft chin is puckering. "Please," Rafferty says, "Please."

And he turns and flees.

BY FOUR O'CLOCK that afternoon, Hwa is out looking for an apartment and Neeni is curled up on the side of the bed Rose sleeps in, drinking a weak whiskey-soda. Ming Li, with four aspirins and a quart of coffee in her system, is running a roller over the wall that ends at the entrance to the kitchen while Poke turns the longest wall a nice uniform shade of Apricot Cream. The short walls—the one between the living room and the bedroom and the one with the sliding glass door in it—are glowing with new color, and even Rafferty has to admit it's nice.

"Warms up the room," he says as paint runs down the underside of his forearm.

With her eyes on the wall she is painting, Ming Li says, "What that man was doing, what he was doing to Treasure."

Rafferty keeps painting. He doesn't think she really wants him to look at her.

"It's sort of like, I mean, what you said about me and—It's a little like, it's kind of like . . ."

"No, it isn't. Nothing like it."

"How? I mean, why do you say—"

"Murphy destroyed Treasure. He turned her into a mirror, someone he could see his reflection in, someone who would be him when he was gone. He didn't love her. Well, maybe he did. Maybe he loved her when he ran into that house, but I don't know, maybe he was chasing himself. Anyway, he's not Frank and you're not Treasure. What Frank was doing was protecting you, in a dangerous place, the best way he knew how. By teaching you what he knew. He did it because he knew he might not always be there to take care of you, and he wanted to give you gifts you could use when he was gone. He did it because he loved you."

Ming Li says, "Oh."

"And he turned out a really amazing young woman."

He hears a long sniff. Then she says, "I shouldn't drink. I get soft when I've drunk too much."

"Frank and I *both* love you," Rafferty says.

She sniffs again and says, "I need some more paint."

"I'll bring it over."

He gets up, can in hand, and there's a knock at the door.

"It's probably not the police," he says, pouring paint into Ming Li's roller pan. He puts the can down and goes to the door.

Andrew has put gel on his hair and spiked it up in twenty directions. He wears a painfully white, painfully new T-shirt with two handprints on it, one in blue and one in pink, and a pair of jeans so stiff they look like he stole them from the mannequin in the store window. He leans back to look up at Rafferty and says, "They're coming. They're coming. Miaow called me to say they're coming." He blinks a couple of times, centers his glasses, and tries it again. "They're coming." As he did all those days ago, he leans to one side to look around Poke, and his face falls, and he says, "Aren't they?"

"Great shirt," Rafferty says.

Andrew's cheeks turn bright red, and he looks at his feet. "The pink hand is Miaow's," he says. "The blue one is mine. We sneaked into the craft room at school to make it."

"Well, I've got something you can put on over it." He steps aside, and as Andrew comes in, he says, "Do you know how to paint trim?"

BY SIX O'CLOCK that evening, Miaow's room looks like the inside of an old bruise, and Andrew has pronounced the color cool. The pigments on the walls are even and flat, and the trim has a certain youthful flash and abandon, nothing Rafferty can't paint over later. He is washing the rollers in the sink when Andrew comes in, back in his two-hand T-shirt, and says, "What time will they be here?"

"About ten tonight."

Andrew's eyes widen and his mouth drops open, and the look he gives Rafferty is rich in betrayed promise.

"Trains," Rafferty says, feeling guilty. "They can't get here ahead of the train. Anyway, that gives me time to put everything back, get it all pretty again."

Dolefully, Andrew says, "I guess."

From the living room come the sounds of Ming Li herding Hwa and Neeni out the door, taking them to a hotel to free up some beds.

Rafferty says, "You'll get to see her tomorrow. Tell you what. I'll keep her out of school tomorrow. You guys can spend the whole day together."

"Mr. Rafferty," Andrew says, "tomorrow is Saturday."

"Why, so it is," Rafferty says. "You lose track of time when you get old. Don't worry, you'll see her tomorrow, and trust me, you have no idea how happy she's going to be. Excuse me for a minute, would you?" And he goes into the living room and forces himself to make the call he least wants to make.

36

Sexual Desire Is Waterproof

THE RAIN IS dense enough to distort the neon across the street like a wet oil painting that's been smeared by the side of someone's hand, but the *soi* outside the Beer Garden is still full of men.

"Sexual desire," Rafferty says, "is waterproof."

Arthit grunts. He has a beer in front of him, untouched, and he hasn't said ten words since he sat down.

"Thank you for coming," Rafferty says. "I think it'll mean more if it's both of us." Arthit doesn't reply, and Rafferty blunders ahead to fill the silence. "Both of us talking to her, I mean. If she even comes."

"I still can't have her back. It won't work."

"I said I could take care of it. I have some money I don't know what to do with."

"Good for you." He downs the first swallow of beer. Rafferty's is mostly gone.

Rafferty says, "What's happening with . . . with you and Anna?"

Three soaked men run by, hooting at one another, and crowd into the bar.

"She told me all about it this morning, before she left. And when she was finished, I wanted her to leave. So what could be happening? Nothing. She was someone else. She wasn't who I—I suppose I was more vulnerable than I should have been, because . . ." He drinks again and puts the bottle down. The muscles at the corners of his jaws bunch. "And I have no idea how I feel about that scene you played two nights ago. I suppose on some level it didn't concern me at all, but you stood in my living room and lied and lied and lied, and you knew what was happening, and you never said a word."

"I couldn't."

"I'm a big boy. Were you afraid of breaking my heart?"

Yes, Rafferty thinks, and says, "No. I was hoping I was wrong. I'm not the one who figured it out. I never would have thought of it. It was one of the spies. And the way they put it, it made sense, and I—"

"And you didn't tell me." The rain rattles the awning above them.

Rafferty feels his friend's gaze, but there's no way he can return it. "I couldn't. Just because they said it, that didn't make it true."

"*And* you needed to get a message to Shen, remember? If you're being honest, I mean, and if you don't mind my saying so, it's about time." Arthit tilts back in his chair, the front legs lifting off the cement. "Anyway, it worked, didn't it? Shen's backed completely away from Murphy's death." He picks up his bottle and watches two girls run by, sheltering together under a piece of plastic sheeting. He puts the bottle back down, untasted. "I'm glad the . . . the *strategy* succeeded," he says. "And I know that what she did almost got you killed and that I'm probably a bad friend for not putting that first. But I can't pretend I like the way you handled it."

Rafferty can think of no reply, so he says, "I'm sorry."

"Yes. Well, I'm sorry, too, but that doesn't fix anything."

A young woman trots by beneath an umbrella, but Rafferty is so distracted he forgets to look at her. Too late, he turns his head to see her retreating back.

"Not her," Arthit says.

"Arthit. What can I do?"

"I'm not sure you can do anything. Maybe we need to leave each other alone for a while. Let the bruises heal. Right now it's like a cold sore. I keep prodding it with my tongue because I can't believe how much it can hurt. Maybe I just need to get used to the idea it's there, and then I'll be able to leave it alone. Maybe even forget it."

"I haven't got anything to say. Anything that would matter."

"I don't know why I'm telling you this, but she did it for her country. The oldest excuse of all, the one they sell us over and over. They told her it was to fight the killings in the south, try to bring some peace down there. They showed her pictures of what was happening, bad enough that she had to ask them to stop. They made it all about children and monks being killed, bombs in Buddhist temples, you know. They said you and I were either one thing or the other, either bad guys or medium guys who were being used by the bad guys, and that she could help, she could save lives, by making friends with me and telling them what was happening. So I asked, 'Did they tell you to sleep with me?' She said no, said that she had no idea she was going to fall in love with me. She said, 'It just happened.' She said, 'All that other stuff is over now, but I still love you.'" He leans forward, and the legs of his chair bang down on the cement. "That's what she said."

"Maybe she does. She told me not to go to the mall because it was too dangerous. She said it twice."

"Of course, all that sailed right past me," Arthit says. "Since I had no idea what the two of you were actually talking about." He shakes his head. "That's enough of that. She also said this morning that she didn't tell Shen about you going—supposedly going—to the mall. She'd decided that he was wrong about you." He stops and drinks. "Wrong about both of us. The only thing she gave him was your information about Murphy. Murphy had already told Shen about the mall."

"Could be," Rafferty says. "They apparently had a terrific fight when Murphy came in."

Arthit says, "This is all miles beyond speculation at this point. And I can't honestly say I give a damn about either Murphy or Shen. What I give a damn about is being lied to by two people I didn't think would lie to me."

Rafferty says, "There she is."

THE STREETLIGHTS SEEM very bright despite the rain, and the world looks jerky, as if things start and stop and start and stop, and she has a feeling that's familiar now, that her feet are a long,

long way down and she's above herself. Above everyone else. Floating.

But *jerky*. Maybe one more hit before she goes into the bar will smooth out the jerkiness. Or maybe she'll just get used to it. Maybe she'll learn to like it.

Even the water flowing past her feet, way down there in the street, moves in little jerks. And so do the men coming toward her. She tells herself, *Smile*, and she feels her face obey. She's not a pretty girl, people say, but they tell her she has a nice smile.

So she smiles.

And she slows to meet them, a bit disorganized, some parts of her body slowing at different speeds from others, and she has to take an extra step, and as she does it, she sees who they are. She sees their faces and their eyes, and she feels the concern and the disapproval and the shock and all the other *strings* that flow from them to her, strings that will wrap around her if she lets them, like the string on a balloon that wants to float free, and a bolt of panic shoots her in the heart, and she turns and runs, splashing through the water to the small streets branching away to her right, away from those men and their expectations and hopes and conditions, and toward the dark, safe place where she can be alone with the pipe.

RAFFERTY'S ELEVATOR SEEMS to take forever to climb the seven floors, and he uses the time to try to shake off the last glimpse of Treasure—although he knows he'll carry it with him forever—the loss of Janos, the sight of Pim wobbling away through the rain toward God-only-knows-what, and the slump of his friend's back as he trudged away toward Sukhumvit to find a cab to take him back to that house, where he'll have to begin, all over again, his life as a man alone. As bad as Poke feels about Arthit, though, it's Treasure who breaks his heart.

When he keys the door and pushes it open, Miaow explodes off the couch with the kind of scream girls her age usually reserve for adolescent pop singers and shoves herself against him so hard that he thinks for a moment she's trying to push him back out the door, but then her arms go around him and his around her, and he looks down at her chopped, red-dyed hair as if it were heaven's meadow and then beyond her to see Rose—impossibly, excessively, ridiculously beautiful—get up from the couch to wait her turn, at Ming Li sitting in an effortless half lotus on the floor, and, regarding him uncertainly from Rafferty's usual seat on the hassock, still in the two-hands T-shirt, Andrew.

Blinking fast, Rafferty bends down and hoists a squealing Miaow off her feet and totes her into the living room, not even feeling her weight, and says, meaning every syllable, "I'm *so happy* we're all here."

THE HAMBURGER ARTHIT picked up because it was the fastest thing he could think of has grown cold and greasy-smelling, and now, as he lifts the latch on the gate, it's also getting wet. It couldn't be as wet as he is, he thinks, but it's certainly too wet to eat. And, come to think of it, who needs to eat?

He's halfway up the concrete walk to the door when he sees her, sitting on the top step with water dripping from the ends of her short, blunt-cut hair, her head down. As he nears, he can see her shoulders stiffen, but she doesn't raise her eyes to his.

He stops in front of her. She still hasn't looked up, and she's in the middle of the step, so he'll have to squeeze past her to get to the door. What does he say to get her attention? *Excuse me?* His sigh seems to come from his center of spiritual gravity, and she dips her head even lower. He looks past her at the house with its dark windows and its familiar, empty rooms, and he throws the hamburger into the hedge and says, "Please. Come in."

THAT NIGHT THE rain upriver eases for a while, and three runoff dams that had been emptied to prevent their bursting are reopened to drain off some of the water rampaging down to the sea, and the level in the river drops. It's not much of a drop, and it's probably only for one night. But it *is* one night.

THE NEXT MORNING, drinking his coffee, Rafferty reads the newspaper story headlined BODY FOUND IN BURNED HOUSE: ARSON SUSPECTED. He reads it again, more slowly, and then puts the paper down and says aloud, to no one, "*One* body?"

Author's Note

The Phoenix Program is historical fact. Those wanting to know more can Google it for a variety of perspectives or, for a more all-encompassing (and somewhat negative) account, can look to Douglas Valentine's scrupulously researched book *The Phoenix Program*. It's also historically accurate that the Pentagon turned to the Phoenix Program as one source when cobbling together recommendations to the president in the days following September 11, 2001.

The bloodshed in the south of Thailand is, I'm sorry to say, ongoing and has claimed more than 5,000 lives to date.

Acknowledgments

This was not an easy book to write and, as usual, I want to thank the people who helped the most: Bronwen Hruska and Juliet Grames at Soho for giving Poke's little family a home, and Juliet for a vigorous edit; my agent, Bob Mecoy, for taking me to Soho in the first place; the staff of The Novel Cafe on Main in Santa Monica for creating such an evocative atmosphere and for keeping the coffee flowing; and all the writers whose brains I've picked over the years.

I use music as an energy source when I write, and for providing the playlist for various components of *The Fear Artist* I want to thank Jason Isbell and the 400, the Drive-By Truckers, Sara Bareilles, Tegan and Sara, Franz Ferdinand, The National, Edward Sharpe and the Magnetic Zeros, Neko Case, Joe Henry, Randy Newman, the late great Townes Van Zandt and Warren Zevon, Arcade Fire, Over the Rhine, Ryan Adams, Conor Oberst, Neil Young, the perpetually energizing Bob Dylan and Emmylou Harris (who have helped with every book), and—on the classical side—Eric Satie and Maurice Ravel.

And thanks to all the folks who have written to suggest music to me. I listen to all of it and buy quite a lot of it. Some of it will be found in the playlists above.

In fact, thanks to all the readers who have written to me at www.timothyhallinan.com, often at the time I most needed encouragement. After a year spent staring at a screen and trying to stage-manage a daydream, it's great to realize at long last that people actually read it.